Two Weeks Till Valentine's

Bodie Raue

Published by Bodie Raue, 2023.

TWO WEEKS TILL VALENTINE'S

First edition. December 15, 2023.

Copyright © 2023 Bodie Raue.

ISBN: 979-8989428311

Written by Bodie Raue.

To my mother who will read this through my own eyes

THE DOCTOR'S VISIT

In a small, chatty town in the Highlands of Scotland, where many still speak of the coming of the Lord Reay and the appetite of Sawney Bean, there lies a forgotten globetrotter, buried beneath a deep blanket of fur, the warmth for which his body can no longer keep. His face so pale, only the shallow shadows of his cheekbones reveal the hint of a man, slowly vanishing into the folds of his pillow. He faces a straw death, told only by the spirit who so desperately poisons his soul. But whilst the spirit awaits his demise, and the locals go on about the weather, this bedridden man fights to be with his beloved in this one final journey of forever hope and happiness.

Tis the final hours of Valentine's Day and sitting by the fireplace with his forehead ablaze is the ailing man's caregiver. He is waiting for a late-night council from a visitor no one in town has ever met. Such is his devotion to have trailed behind his friend for so many years that now he must agree with his request to seek care elsewhere. You see, it is the ailing man's belief that his caregiver's antiquated medicines of tossing vervain and applying dung to his wounds have left nothing but skin lacerations and a horrible smell.

One could delve into all the peculiarities of his caregiver, but for now, the insistence of his friend is to answer the call at the door. Slipping into his long, black gown, the caregiver raises a candle that exposes his bug-like snarl, before he scurries like an insect in secrecy, down the hallways of the manor and away from the lights that might find him. Upon reaching the foyer, he covers his scowl with his long, black hair, then opens the door to the howling, chilly night.

"How do you do? I am Dr. Parlay Cloverly. My wife and I were having a wonderful Valentine's dinner at the Goose and Neck when we received your call."

Without a word of acknowledgment, the caregiver snickers at this rather portly man with thin, yellowing hair, thinking him to be a lost tourist.

"Let's try this again; my name is..."

The caregiver closes the door abruptly and waits for a re-knock before reopening it.

Now wide-eyed with a raised eyebrow, the doctor reiterates his visit: "I was kidding about trying again, but alright. How do you do? I am Doctor Cloverly; may I come in?"

"Yer in," the caregiver replies with a short quip.

"How about far enough that the door can shut out the cold?"

Again, the caregiver remains motionless, still regarding the stranger with much restraint.

"Were you maybe, expecting someone else?"

"I will offer you passageway if you allow me a test. You must turn for me, remove your helm, and surrender your coat."

Obliging, the doctor slowly places a bulky bag on the floor. He then raises his hands, lifts his hat off his head, and hands the caregiver his coat. The caregiver then squints and retreats a few steps back to check on the pockets. "Nice gloves, handkerchief, and hand sanitizer."

The doctor nods his head, "Are we good then?"

"Your bag, if I may."

"This is ridiculous," as the doctor hands him his bag.

"I thought you might complain!" The caregiver's eyes go wide with aggression, then he pulls out a cross from his robe and thrusts it into the doctor's forehead. "Ah-hah, there! You flinched. A sign of one's lack of confidence – and how about this?'" the caregiver spins his body around and slaps the doctor across the face. "You did it again, only there was more horror in your mug!"

"Enough! I'm a grown man!" The doctor yells while pushing his way forward into the room.

"Have a go, will you?!!" grunts the caregiver, who then grabs the doctor by the lapels and drags him to the floor. After rolling on top of doctor, kicking him between the legs, and beating him with his own hat, both finally collapse to the floor. Breathing heavily, the caregiver taps the doctor's leg, "Did you bring your medicines, sir?"

The doctor sticks his arm out and drops the bag to the floor.

"Welcome to the Mills house, Doctor. Glad you could make the journey."

The doctor drapes his coat over his arm and gives the caregiver a curious look. "Millhouse? I came all the way to see a man make flour?"

"No, sir. Mills is the family name. Beauregard Heathan Fox is the inherited keeper of the house now. He awaits your arrival."

"Very good then. Let's be on our way."

The servant lifts up the doctor's bag and kicks up his heels. "I would like to point out that I generally don't make house calls."

"I understand the inconvenience, being it is the final hour of Valentine's, but you are the only Doctor within a midnights journey."

Down the long, musty corridors, they hurry, often redirected by sharp bends and unexpected doorways. The doctor struggles to keep up with the long strides of the caregiver, but he manages to follow the man's breath through the cold corridors. Eventually, the doctor stumbles into a sitting room, where the caregiver bows before a door.

"He waits in the study, good Doctor, the door is not guarded."

"Can you give me some background on Mr. Fox?"

"He's a humorist. He has studied the art of humor and spreads his teachings athwart the world."

"I didn't know one could actually make a living doing that."

"In times like these, it pays quite well."

The door is slightly ajar, and a certain, earthy smell saturates the room's interior. It is dark too, except for the glow from a fireplace, but any hope for further lighting rests on the two windows that remain shuttered and locked. The doctor squeezes his hands together to generate some warmth, noting that the room is only slightly above the temperature outside. It certainly could be made warmer if the hazards about the room were to be used in the fire. There are papers – stacks of them – on the tables and on the floors, even drifting about the air in a slightly felt breeze. Dusty books as well: *Tales of the Misty Thloethum and The Fidi Belurdi* – ancient stories passed down through the Foxes and the Mills for as long as their names can be remembered. Apart from the stale air and the family of book lice, the dead rodent on the breakfast table has the doctor most bothered.

"Hello?!!" the doctor calls to the open door until the caregiver arrives. "What is this place, caregiver? Do I not see a horseshoe hanging above the door? Are these not broken bird shells on the hearth? Am I not gagging before a rat cut in two on a feeding table? Necklaces of shark teeth and baskets of pearls? This hardly seems to be a room prepared for life-saving services."

The caregiver steps over to the windows to ensure the shutters are still locked, "It's not the room that wants healing, Doctor. We have separate services for so." He takes the doctor's bag and sets it on the floor by the fireplace. He then lifts away the table of the untouched soup and divided rat, finally retrieving a chair from the corner and placing it by the bed covered in linen.

"Are you going to explain the dissection of a rat?"

"We prefer sacrificial varmints, Doctor, since Mo Charaid has a fondness for lambs. Are there more questions?"

"The question to what this place is and to why I am in this very room is still a concern of mine?"

"It was Mo Charaid's wish, not mine." The caregiver straightens out the sheets and blankets on the bed. "You need to address that with him."

The doctor scoffs at his remark, "Are we to play more games, court jester? Delay me no more! If an opinion is expected of me, I demand you call 'Mo Charaid' to this very room. My dinner waits for my return, while my wife still holds a seat!"

"You have only but to look, Doctor."

On that very request, the doctor looks about the room before noticing the smiling servant tapping the very spot where a lumpy, tangled mess of sheets appear.

"I see nothing but dirty laundry on this bed."

Again, the caregiver motions for the doctor to take a closer look, and true to his word, the doctor sees a faint outline of a body that could be easily mistaken for rustled sheets. Propped up within the pillows are the ghostly features of a face, so stretched along the bone that every crack and shallow of a skull is made clear. The doctor immediately senses a ruse.

"Is this a sick joke? Displaying a corpse before me in the final hours of Valentine's? Did my wife put you up to this?!" At that very moment the doctor hears a weak cough that causes him to make a startled turn. "Well, his appearance is grave and his heart is weak." The doctor leans closer to the ailing man's face, "Sir, how are you feeling?" The doctor waits for a response, but nothing is said.

"A showl here and a showl there is all he says. Lately, he has not spoken a word. The happy thoughts that supported him through the years, now replaced by a painful remembrance of the past. He speaks very little of it. A blundered attempt to secure one's love thirty years ago."

The doctor looks down at the man's face, "He looks worse than that."

The doctor rolls up the ailing man's sleeve and straps a cuff around his arm, pumping for pressure, "His blood pressure is very low. You spoke to him when?"

"Maybe a week. He spoke about how he was going to be with his lassie in a dream."

"Good God! This man has no pants on!!"

"Aye, and he still says nothing."

The doctor pulls the sheets back to cover him. "Well, it might be important to keep his extremities warm. Has he been taking any medications?"

"Council juice with boneset. I see no reason to prescribe otherwise."

The doctor bows his head with frustration, "Is this how they treat people in these parts?"

"Aye, mallets for cysts, plyers for teeth, leaches for malaise, and a council from Henry."

The doctor laughs, "Henry? The local well-wisher?"

"He scares away the ill dreams; at least so is told. You could ask Henry; he's the varnished skull in goat's bladder beneath the pillow."

"AAAHH!" the doctor falls backwards, surprised by a skull that appears in his lap. "If you believe this is a place to help an ailing man, I suggest you think otherwise! And be it well advised to check the blood flow to his feet, because these are blue!"

The caregiver turns abruptly, not saying a word, retrieving the blankets the doctor let fall to the floor.

The doctor stands and cups his hands over the fire. He leans over a basket brimming with pearls, then snatches a piece of paper drifting before his face. It is a legal document with incoherent words scribbled outside the lines. "The unofficial appearance of thoughts on paper belonging to a man..." turning the paper over with a smirk, "who is yet to reveal a name. How interesting."

The doctor drops the paper into the fire and continues to warm his hands. "Maybe we started off on the wrong foot. Do you have a name, caretaker?"

"Porta Floyd. Aiden Porta Floyd."

"Porta Floyd, you have been in his care for how long?"

The caregiver squeezes the ends of his pointy chin, "Ten and twenty years, I say."

"That's a long commitment. Something to be honorable for."

"It is bit a wee thing to be caregiver. A respectable gesture enacted by an unsigned commitment to offer a life dedicated to the troubles of another. I accept this gladly."

The doctor smiles and turns to warm his backside. "Have you thought about what you would do when your friend is gone?"

"I cannot really ponder over such thoughts while all is well. To dwell on a close friend's inevitable future is like predicting your own. Forgive my curiosity, friend Coverly. Will these inquiries and examinations readily advance Mo Charaid's condition? It's time for his midnight tea and I have prepared the most delightful chocolate truffles."

"Uh-huh," the doctor replies in a solemn tone. "You understand me, Porta Floyd, when I tell you that your friend does not have a long life ahead of him?"

"I understand."

"Then you have made preparations?"

"Of course! You can hear the bell all the way from the Clarewigs of Trough. It's Valentine's, you know. The first you see is the first you get! And each midnight of Valentine's, 'Come-Along-Bessy' arrives at the foreside door, stamping her hoof and swaying her horns. Aye, Mo Charaid should have never fed her those oats."

"Mr. Porta Floyd! He's going to die. Not in a few years, but within the next few hours."

The caregiver slaps his knee and throws up his hands in laughter, "You make me laugh, doctor. So few days ago, he came out of his sleep, happy with a touch of mirth, asking for a taste of haggis. He was making funnies of his weight loss, you see."

"That's the illness and the body bargaining for a last fair well. Look at him – his eyes are glazed, his pulse is weak, and his body temperature is low. His knees and feet are blue, and his hands are covered in liver spots. These are hardly the symptoms of a man at a loss for love. We can only make his last few hours more bearable."

"But I gave him lox droppings! I kept the wraiths out!"

"Hardly a reason to suppose he'd get better. When was the last time he stood?"

"There's no need for him to stood, Doctor! I can hold a mirror! I can comb what wee hair he has! I'll be forth right in saying so, I'm not in agreement with all your cured pebbles, pasty liquids, and metal objects brought to remedy one's health!"

The doctor searches through the contents of his bag, when the servant taps him on the shoulder.

"On the phone, you said you would be of help. Now you claim Mo Charaid would be in the better hands of vultures?! What changed, doctor?! The room not meet your standards?!"

"Know that I have analyzed the situation and have provided my best opinion."

"Oh, an opinion you offer? Fancy so! I'm swithered by your acts of kindness, but you're not a real doctor, are you? You're just a doctor by chance, standing there with all your tools and your opinions. Oh, Mo Charaid, your dying of liver spots and a shortness of breath. What a relief! How about a looly-poop for your troubles!" The caregiver turns away and then turns back,

"You're full of malarkey, man! We ask for a doctor that cures, and instead, we get one that administers opinions!"

"I see no reason for the insult. Do we not practice a touch of urbanity in this household?!"

"A man of etiquette are we too, Doctor?! Maybe you're an expert in the words of love as well!" The caregiver takes a sweep at the floor and grabs up a letter:

> *The air always sweeter, the sky always brighter. The sun never fades when you wake to the morn. But those dark clouds that warn us, with your friends that did scorns us, always they are there when our hearts will be torn.'*

The doctor shakes his head and grimaces, "Are you trying to tell me this man's life is dependent upon a few poorly written love letters?"

The doctor lifts his hand from the mantel, when suddenly the fireplace erupts into several large pops. The caregiver, seeing the doctor's concern, walks over and jabs at a log with a fire poker.

"Don't like that one?" The caregiver swoops up another letter:

> *When the collie calls for goodbye and the lone sheep wants to know why, somehow it's the pony that always has to cry.'*

The caregiver smirks, "Maybe it's not his best, but another..."

"Stop!" the doctor says raising his hand. "Please! I see why your friend should suffer, but I do not see a reason why we should!"

The fireplace, once again, erupts into a series of loud 'crackle-and-pops', prompting the caregiver to beat the log a bit more thoroughly.

"Listen to me; there is nothing I can do about your friend's health. His fight is his own."

The caregiver, all flustered, stammers across the floor and thrusts the windows open to the chilly night. "There, doctor, I am opening the window for you! It's a bit above freezing, but maybe you were expecting the smell of flowers?! There is no love in you, sir!"

"I have a loving wife that is waiting for my return! Unlike, your Mo Charaid, who retreats into the shadows of his mind to hide from tormentors who wish to ruin his love!"

Angry with his response, the caregiver brandishes his fire poker, prompting the doctor to raise his medicine bag in defense, but it is not the caregiver who has come to be the assailant. It is the fireplace, and it is now, coughing out long streams of fiery embers across the room.

Quickly taking cover in the ailing man's bed sheets, the doctor believes he has found a safe refuge, but a hard grip on his shoulder tells him to believe otherwise. This grip is so mind-numbingly tight that the doctor falsely witnesses a delusional, long-haired, praying mantis, beating him with his own hat!

"I told you so, you miserable gommie!"

It is then the cracking sound of fingers that truly explains why his blood flow has been severed from his head. It is not from the angry fireplace or from the deranged caregiver, but from the very five bony fingers attached to the bed-stricken man! Insane with panic and desperate to flee, the doctor can do nothing but listen to the dying man's final words of reclamation.

"Charge into the victors, and be sure to let them know; they have not...YET...WON!"

Mr. Fox falls back into his pillow and closes his eyes.

FEBRUARY 1: OLD ACQUAINTANCES

It is not all bright and clear for what is thought to be a walk in the clouds. Instead, static appears, forming shapes only to be known as visions of his past. It is he who hides beneath a table in preschool, away from a caretaker pretending to be his mother. And will you look at those little shoes? No wonder he keeps falling over. It is his sixth birthday already, and just as suspected, he is avoiding his responsibilities. Of course, in those years, he did not want to accomplish anything more meaningful than a nap. But presently, in his adolescence, he seems quite happy with the few successes he has encountered with much luck. Truly his reason for the rabbit's foot.

All these visions of his past are nothing more than a collage of mishaps, many he thought long forgotten, and too many to even count. Apparently, he had done very little to change his behavior. A life he successfully squandered away with unsophisticated thinking. He now understands what he must do. Even in dreams, one can change what one could never see while awake.

The sound of doors sliding to a melodic swish is followed by a long, drawn-out gasp. Beauregard Heathan Fox steps forward onto the train platform and casts his eyes upon a world he had left thirty years ago. He has returned and feeling young again – twenty-eight years of age, to be exact. He has a rosy complexion and stands upright beneath his shoulders. There is clarity to his eyes too – those very eyes that had become useless to him only weeks recent.

It is hardly the first morning of February. The station is silent and before him is a metropolitan area of one million people. There will be no welcoming him back and he is not expecting one. There is only one person who has any significance to him now. Stunning eyes, a debonair smile, and the gift of words – he has none of these qualities. He never needed them. The woman of his affection does not care about these sorts of attributes. He is sure of that now.

Bo makes his first long steps to the sound of pots and pans clanking in his ears. Instinctively, he reaches around to feel the weight of a little house strapped to his back. In the excitement, he sets the backpack on the pavement and begins rummaging through all the uncouth clothing. The beige shorts – so worn, torn, and frayed at the edges! His wrinkled shirts and his worn-out shoes! And what is this?! His mad-bomber hat! All of it is here from his traveling days!

Bo swings his backpack around his shoulders and struts to the edge of the platform. He holds out his thumb for a cab and waits for his mind to create the noise of squeaking breaks. It should sound a bit mechanical and the air should be heavily consumed with petrol. Oddly, this is not what comes next. Instead, it is a name he hears – or rather, a name he has not heard in quite some time.

"Teuchy!!!"

Bo turns his head down the platform. He narrows his eyes toward a vision of a rather small woman wearing a red pull-over. The white letters on the shirt read: Girls United. She is tan-skinned with thin blond hair tied into a ponytail. Her face is unnaturally red, with the color commonly seen on those plagued with annoyance.

"Can I help you?" seems to be the most civil inquiry, but a civilized response is not what he receives. She beats her head with a closed hand and then spits on the street, not just once, but several times in succession, all ending in a round-house kick. Surely, he cannot be imagining an association with this person. Could this be a chance encounter? Perhaps, but she too has a backpack, much like his own.

Bo has always kept a daily log in his backpack that should shed some light on this untamed person. Here is someone who matches her description. Her name is Mia Pearl; she is in her early thirties and resides in the southwest proper of London. She is extremely feisty and very ornery, often identified with the use of obscene gestures and derogatory verbiage. It is best not to approach her; rather, run if possible!

Bo suddenly feels a shove displace his feet. To his surprise, this cantankerous lady from the southwest proper of London is already upon him. Fiendish, vicious, and smug – her face exactly like this. Being a refined man, Bo offers forgiveness for his possible, ill-stated introduction, and stretches both arms out to embrace her. How amazingly real she feels. So soft and solid – like a sack of potatoes spoiled in places.

"Get off of me, you Pacu Fish, Spit-vomit!" the young lady squawks while pushing Bo to the ground. "What is wrong with you?!"

"I'm sorry, my hen."

"Where were you going? We discussed this you know?"

Scratching his head, "T'wuz yonks. No?"

"Yonks?! We discussed these plans on the train!!"

Bo pauses to search his mind for the right wording. "Aye, so we did."

"Then why the bloody hell were you hailing a cab?!!"

"We are going separate ways?"

"Don't rage me, Bo!! Don't do it!" clutching her fists with raised arms. "I see a dark cloud of foreseeable repercussions coming your way if you choose to continue with this behavior!"

"I'm sorry, my mind is elsewhere."

The lady's eyes turn beady, questioning the sympathy lines on Bo's face, but soon relents. "Forget it, let's go!"

Bo pushes the logbook back into his side pocket and lifts his pack over his right shoulder. He wiggles his hips to get the adjustment correct and then shuffles quickly behind her. He somehow feels attached to this woman, but cannot fully understand why.

"And wipe that smirk off your face; I'm not your hen! You know, I always hear you say you don't hear too well, but to me, you just don't want to listen. I am inclined to believe you are doing this to get even with us. Some kind of wrong you feel we have done to you."

"We? There are more of you?"

"Pardon? Our traveling companion? The one who is picking us up?"

"Oh, sure. What ever happened to what's her name?"

"That does it!!" The small girl grabs Bo's pack straps and swings his body down beneath her, pulling him up slightly above the pavement. "Now listen here, my traveling grocket; you better get your act together or I am..."

Saved by a honk. The horrifying woman lifts her head to see the oncoming car pulling up to the curb. She releases Bo to the pavement while he watches the firestorm quietly dissolve in her eyes.

"Hiya Love!" Mia says, waving her hand to the driver. Then, grabbing Bo by his sleeve, she helps him to his feet and begins swatting the pavement-debris off his backpack. "Here she is. You better not let her see you acting this way."

The mystery lady lowers the window half-way with her eyes peeking above her sunglasses. She is young, light-skinned, with dark eyes. She has a rather unique black hair style, fluffed on the top and braided with red stripes along the sides. Bo removes his cap and brushes a wisp of brown hair that drops onto his forehead, "How are you, Mam."

She looks at him with confused, squinty eyes and smirks, "I am fine, Bo. How are you?"

Bo tries not to look confused, but she seems to recognize him, while at the same time, she seems to be expecting some recognition from him. Bo turns to Mia for some clarification, but she only replies with a playful laugh and smacks him across his arm. "Sorry, Sam. It's been a long day."

"Sam? Samantha! I saw your name in the logbook!"

Samantha smirks, "I am sure he'll come around."

"That invariably remains to be seen. We'll add memory problems to the list."

Bo tosses his backpack into the back seat of the car, then walks around to the passenger side. Sam looks at him slantwise, "Maybe you should let Mia sit in front. You know how she can be."

"Good idea." Bo climbs over the seat next to his backpack, watching Mia's head appear in the doorway.

"What did I miss? Bo still having a skull fart? Did you call ahead, Sam? I want to be sure we have the best room in the city and not the worst night on the pavement. Oh, and we forgot to eat. Thursdays are toast medley with marmite figs."

"Would you like to stop and pick something up?

"It's rather late, isn't it? Thinking Vegan cream cheese would settle just fine. Though avocados and mushrooms might be the new norm, which reminds me: Do they sell crisps here? Probably not. Seems to me too English."

The city lights wink in the distance. It is very late and black spaces, joined with reeling head lamps, are all that appear on the road ahead. Bo rests his arms across his chest, reflecting on his arrival. His love is yet to materialize and it seems that 'out of the ordinary' is to be the 'new normal' with these acquaintances from his past. He is inclined to believe they will be sharing a room, a decision he is not allowed to partake in. Odd how Samantha's name and face are unrecognizable. He isn't aware of any dalliances that may have existed. The logbook may hold more information.

Page thirty-four:

These events, which took place on the thirty-first of January, are a stark reminder of how my behavior can be deemed inappropriate by 'my companions'. It is just after midnight, and we have arrived by rail to the Southern City of Ghosts. Here we have returned to the birthplace of Samantha, who has arranged for us to stay in a posh motel. Posh it is not and it is in the attic where we are staying.

Flip, flip, flip...

With many restraints on my ability to travel freely, I have been given few choices to live otherwise. Under Mia's request, we are traveling to the beach, where she feels she can heal her maniacal convictions with the light of the sun. I have been praying to the various gods for an intervention, but none have accepted my plea.

Bo flips to the page of contents.
"Thievery Problem?!"
"What's that, Bo?"
Lifting his head toward Mia's voice for a brief moment, "Not a thing." Bo reaches into his backpack and finds another logbook, realizing there are many more books to review.

January 1, Saturday:

Happy New Year, Perth Australia: I have been traveling under fits of rage for the past twenty-eight days. Mia's mood can change from not-so good to abominably horrible. It seems a slow speech impediment of mine has developed. I, too, am losing friends as a consequence of our companionship. Smacks are often where full-out disagreements can leave injury to passing strangers. Others whom I may initiate a conversation with are often brutally involved. Farm animals, too, are not off-limits. We are leaving the magistrate where Mia has been charged five-hundred Aussie dollars for striking a bull, scheduled to run in Pamplona. The reason for her action – neither the courts, nor she would elaborate on.

Bo lifts his head, "Yet she still agreed to pay the fine. Interesting."

A shadow cast down on the logbook, interrupting Bo's reading. He continues to flip through the pages but finds very little regarding Samantha. Every page is about Mia, except for a brief encounter with a girl named Keira and an odd bloke by the name of Peetrie. Bo looks out the window to see a large green sign with white letters passing over head. After exiting onto a ramp, they sit idle at a red light. He muses at the information he just read, thinking it must be an exaggeration. He has always had this distorted sense of humor. Apparently, they found a way to make their relationship work.

The dark, purple town with flickering lights looms ahead. Samantha's timing is perfect, with each intersecting road raising a green-eye to their approach. She turns left and then left again, with Mia nodding in agreement.

It is a family motel on the quiet outskirts of the city, and it is the only building lit during this hour of the evening. His memory must be failing him, because this appears to be a very nice motel. Not the one described in the logbook. It is very narrow and lofty; three stories high, and supported by Greek-style pillars. It is fronted by several long, bulky steps that lead up to an oval glass door. There are also two large gargoyles guarding both ends of the entryway.

Mia too, is in awe, craning her neck out of the car window. It reminds her of a vague resemblance to the Age of Romanticism, with the dark gothic molds and the steeply pitched roof in the shape of folded wings.

Samantha pulls the car up close to the curb with Mia's philosophical interpretation on full display.

"Have you ever thought about the hierarchy of evolution? And not by the American ecological or genealogical subcategories, but by the power of the mind and how it is made to create our existential surroundings?"

Sam raises her eyebrows, "Is this another insult?"

"No. Should it be?"

Bo isn't interested; he drags his backpack from the car up to the first step. He then turns toward the city, letting his lungs fill with a cool salty air. Mia sets her backpack down next to Bo and crosses her arms, "I don't much care for the Palladian variations of the Greek revival era. Nor am I fancied by the angelical roof and finials."

Sam approaches lightly from behind, startling both Mia and Bo, "So Mia, what is next in the hierarchy of evolution?"

"There isn't one. We have gone as far as nature is willing to accept us."

Bo takes in another deep breath of salty air and looks up at the gargoyles, "We transcend."

"Transcend?" Sam looks confused.

"Transcend to what?" Mia scoffs, "You mean, like, we become existential ghosts or something? That's ridiculous, isn't it? I mean, you live here, Sam; couldn't that be ridiculous? Ghosts roaming the city, trapped in some impermeable, parallel dimension that allows their communication to be expressed without repercussions?"

"I don't know, Mia. There are a lot of people who support the 'Existence' phenomenon. In fact, our entire city council was elected based on their abilities in Shamanism and how to solve the non-explainable issues stemming from the summer of 1821."

Mia rolls her eyes, "And the llama says?!"

"Don't start this, Mia. You think I'm a nut-pot for suggesting anything that doesn't meet your viewpoint."

"Samantha B. Case, we're talking about an entire country that thought they had a witch problem. I hardly blame you for a collective society that is full squidgy in the head."

"Yeh!! Well, we still have a witch problem!!" Sam stamps the ground and runs back to her car with her hands over her face.

Mia looks at Bo and claps her hands, "So, let's check in!"

They hoist their backpacks onto their shoulders with Mia scampering ahead. She raises her hand to the door and wraps several times with no sound to be returned. Proceeding with a light push, followed by a harder whack, she then finishes off her greeting with a round-house kick. Mia takes a few steps back and drops her backpack.

Bo raises an eyebrow when Mia scratches her foot along the pavement. She kicks up her heels and charges forward at the door, only to find herself falling backwards onto her rear. Bo chuckles to himself as he watches loose chips of paint drift down around her. Mia lays down and rests her face on the cold pavement.

"What is the matter?"

"Transcend? All this time you have nothing important to say, and then you blurt out, transcend?"

"What?"

"It made no sense to say anything like that."

Bo senses it has been a long day of travel for this lady. She is showing her tiredness.

"Give me your wrench!"

"Wrench?"

"The spanner! The one you have been using for work. It's in your backpack, next to your bill roll."

"I don't recall any work involving a spanner."

Mia marches up to Bo, spins him around twice, and begins mining through his backpack. She extracts a wrench deep within the side pocket and shakes it in front of his face. "Add liar to your resume."

Bo watches in disbelief as the little lady sharpens her eyes with her arm cocked back. "You're going to throw a wrench through a window?"

"Why not? It's a marvelous way of getting a response."

Bo sets his backpack down, amazed at such incontinent behavior from this woman. Fortunately, just as she pulls her arm back, someone else's arm appears at the door.

"Sorry for the wait; we are a little low on staff," replies the attendee.

"Our friend informed you of our arrival. Did you not hear from her?"

"Yes, but at this hour of the night, a lot of people who say they have called don't always show up. The night does bring in its own problems that many of us in the city choose to avoid."

Mia aptly conceals the wrench and tosses it back to Bo. She straightens her leggings and brushes the loopy hair strands from her face, then follows the motel attendant into the lobby. "Are you coming, Bo?"

He is dressed in dark and purple, short and stocky, and wears a short ponytail. The motel's assistant manager, likely in his early twenties, quietly takes his place behind the lobby desk. Mia tosses her backpack down and shakes off her coat. She hardly expected the lobby to complement the exterior of the building. She is amazed by the arctic style of the quartz table tops on iron stands. Nice how they are all arranged like chess pieces around the checkered-pattern floor. Also, to be seen in the adjoining lounge, are elaborate murals, tapestries, and Victorian-style paintings. A curator's paradise!

Bo has an interest of his own and it is in the glass-covered pictures hanging on the lobby walls. He is entranced by the characters dressed in old garb, set in a bleak, colorless city. One in particular is that of a pig-tailed child sitting on a cinder block in the middle of a puddle. Bo wanders into Mia, who grabs his arm and starts laughing.

"It was built in the nineteenth century as an infirmary!" spoke the assistant manager.

"Pardon?" Mia responds.

"This motel in particular has a history of a very long and puzzling past. The initial construction began in the 1700s. You can see the progression on the wall behind you. The entryway is where the blocks of ice were carried in from the northern waterways; the adjoining room is where the plant oil and smoke sticks were kept; and the room behind me is where the chapel was once located."

Mia sashays over to the desk, twirling her hair, "Well, how could one not desire a week with all this lustrous decor and dazzling photography. Add to it the windmill fans and arched murals stretched upon the ceiling."

The assistant manager nods his head, "Of course, they didn't actually cure anyone back then. This location was really just a place for experiments."

Mia grimaces, "Lovely."

Bo waves his hand, "What is this wee bonnie on the cinder block about?"

"That picture was drawn in the summer of 1821. She now hangs out at the local cemetery. Not your typical child, most parents will tell you – kind of a pest if you ask me. She likes to follow people around the city, carrying her little basket of arms."

Mia's mouth quivers, "Real arms?"

"That's the story. It's a moneymaker for the city, you see. The tour guides tell the tales better than the lives that lived them." The assistant manager chuckles and lifts his pen. "So will you be staying the week?"

"So, none of it's real?"

"No need to worry, Miss. These very occurrences only become practical to those who are willing to believe it's all true."

"Mia snorts and honks, "So I knew that. You knew that too, didn't you, Bo? What a knee slapper!"

"Now, we have daily rates and we have weekly rates, but if you are staying through Valentines, we promise not to charge you any more than the rate charged by the other inns. It does get very popular down here this time of year. You may wish to book through the holiday. Are you a couple?"

"No, I'm available for evenings."

"Nice, Mia. We would like just one room, separate beds with a kitchenette. It would be a fortnight, and most certainly not past Valentine's Day."

"Then it will be $125 per night. A credit card is fine."

"Pay him, Bo!"

"Okay, about the layout," the assistant manager drops his fingers to a glossy map before them. "As you can see, you are within walking distance of all the historical sites."

Mia immediately turns the map over and pushes it back toward the assistant manager, "Talk to us about the motel."

"Yes, of course, so we have an outdoor pool marked here in blue and an indoor pool marked here in black."

Mia begins bouncing up and down on her toes, "You have a pool! Bo, we have a pool! Lovely, lovely, lovely! And the indoor pool, how do we find that?"

"You will find the elevator at the end of the hallway. On the lower console, it is the button that is marked REHAB."

"Oooh, a lift too."

Bo looks down the long hallway and squints. He has no memory of an elevator in this motel.

"Bo, I knew right away this would be the right place for us! I bet there are a lot of visitors here!"

"Ah, yes, the guests never seem to leave, mam."

"Oh, I knew it! I would like to meet every one of them! Do they like to have fun? I bet they do."

"Well, if I had to describe the residents, I would probably say those on the third-floor seem to be the most active; the second floor I would characterize as antagonistic; and the first floor beyond the elevators seem to have the most in common with denial."

"Oooh, sounds like a great mix of enthusiasts!"

"You will be on the third-floor."

"...with the active residents?!"

"Quite. That being said..." the assistant manager takes a pause and a long, deep breath. "Rooms 331 to the back of the building are occupied by the original habitants; 320 to 330 by those of the seventeenth century; 309 to 319 by those of the eighteenth century; and 300 to 308 are for the modern-day people. If you happen to find yourself on the wrong floor, not to worry; precautions have been taken to ensure your safety with sirens and plasma-filled sprinklers. You will be the lucky tenants of room 300, facing the main street. Always step to your right off the elevator; carry incense at all times; and feel free to use the stairwell if there is a threat of pursuit. Try to enjoy your stay."

Bo feels the tight grasp of Mia's fingers into his forearm that is starting to hurt, "Mia, what's wrong with your face?"

An untrained eye can easily conclude that Mia's motionless shriek, along with a lighter shade of tan, is brought on by an unforeseen horror. The assistant manager, agreeing with this observation, intercedes with a loud chuckle, as does Bo.

"Aha, you're just kidding!" Mia slaps her thigh and shoves Bo off his stance. "Did you see that, Bo? He has humor! Who would have thought?"

The assistant manager rubs his hands and shows a huge grin, "Would you like to know about the many labyrinths below ground?"

Bo shakes Mia's shoulder, whose face has returned to a state of contortion, "No need."

"Here are your keys," smiling at Mia, "I hope to see you soon."

Mia's eyes fall hard on the assistant manager's hands, which are now placed upon her own. Instantly, she feels that connection she has not experienced in quite some time without the aid of reading material. So lovely are his hands – so delicate, so smooth.

Bo taps Mia and takes up his backpack, motioning his way toward the stairs. Mia instead grabs his arm with plans of her own, "We'll take the lift, if that's okay with you."

Mia hurries eagerly toward the elevator with Bo in tow, "Did you hear that?! See me later, will he?"

Bo reaches over her shoulder and pushes the elevator button with a look of concern. He has no remembrance of this place, "Something's wrong. I know I should remember all this, but..."

"What are you on about? I am referring to what the manager said about seeing me later."

Bo looks at her, puzzled.

"It's what he said, Bo!"

The elevator doors open with a glaring light from within. A charnel stench forces Mia beneath her shirt. Blurry-eyed and reaching for the third-floor button, she gags continuously as the lift cranks its way up a shaft. When the final moan and groan come forth, Mia and Bo are coughed out into the hallway with smoke billowing from behind them. Sprawled upon the floor, Mia extends her finger into what appears to be sea plankton, floating about the light of a soda machine.

There is a working exit sign, illuminating the last room at the end of the hallway. Bo follows Mia as she robs him of the key card and presses it quickly into the slot of the door. She barely waits for the green light to come on before reaching for the light switch in the room. She will need to survey the contents of the room if she is going to accept this stay.

Mia likes the two queen-size beds with the small night table. It comes with a lamp and a clock. Who would not appreciate the wide desk with a large entertainment console. It is equipped with a 'telly' and stacks of board games. In addition, there are two large windows with embroidered curtains, one facing the pool yard and the other facing the main street. Now for the necessities: plates, silverware, and cups in the cabinets; a working refrigerator; and – oh, thank you – there is a shower and tub in the bathroom. Annoying that there are no bath towels though.

She was hoping to have a snack prepared for her pillow. In a nice place like this, there should be some tasty morsel to finish on a high note. Still, Mia could not be more satisfied; they have an indoor pool and they are close to all the attractions.

"Good on yer friend, Sammy, right?"

"She's your friend too; don't forget."

Bo tosses his backpack to the furthest bed overlooking the main street. Lying supine with his arms by his side, he reflects. After so many years of being away, he has returned. The tomorrow road will lead him to more familiar sights and reveal more of what he has forgotten. The sun and the moon will now be the clocks for which time is told.

It feels early, and his mind is too excited to keep sleep. It still twitches like the fluttering pages in a picture book, unraveling thoughts wherever his beloved may appear. This time she is out for a stroll in a small city where people are gathering at a market.

A town opens before his eyes with a cerulean blue sky and billowy white clouds. Sounds of horses are heard, thundering upon the stone roads in a galloping stride. There are butchers and bakers; wood shops and iron shops; tubs of fish; crates of meat; and caskets of fruit. There are street vendors calling out goods, and bustling, busy people tossing coins into wooden buckets. All of this appears to be a manifestation attributed to the nineteenth-century pictures on the walls where he is staying. What Bo soon realizes, however, is that he has to be quicker than his surroundings. Nearly tripping over a chicken, Bo hears the yell of '*Gardy loo*' through an open window. It is the very owner of this chicken who warns him of a bucket of water being tossed in his direction. The same owner who pulls him from a rushing carriage. "Mind the grease, ye younker!!" He hears from the carriage driver.

Bo picks himself up off the ground and can't help but notice that his attire consists of a waistcoat and suspenders holding up his trousers. He also has the most outlandish, pointy boots covering his feet. Lifting himself off the ground, he accidentally bumps into a young lady wearing a feathered hat and a wide conical gown. He apologizes for his negligence, and offers her help with her fallen basket of tea leaves, but for this assistance, she wrongfully responds with a puffy mouth and a full-out scream. After hitting him over the head with her umbrella and kicking him to the dirt, Bo is forced to retreat behind some slabs of beef.

He did not see his mistake but somehow knew he had made one. If he must win her favor, he will need to improve upon an introduction. Obviously, she has too much beauty to approach with just an awkward smile, so he will have to offer her a gift – one that is practical in value and not sexually offensive. Bo grabs a non-erotic fruit from a casket and tosses a coin into the bucket.

He eventually finds the young lass confronted by a large seagull that is most interested in a piece of candy attached to her shoe. After squealing at the bird's squawk, she flees away down a narrow alleyway and into an empty house. Bo does his best to follow her, but once spotted climbing over the backyard fence, she is nowhere to be found – that is, except for an abandoned shoe.

Bo climbs the fence and finds a suitable track from her dress through an accidental spill of flour. This leads him to a two-story general store where a saddled horse stands before an open door. With her one missing shoe in hand, he can now greet her properly. It is unfortunate, though, that the mare is eating his gift.

The store appears deserted; only an off-beat clock can be heard ticking against the wall. He soon hears an angelic voice by the millinery rack, and finds the young lady making barnyard shrills at a piglet bonnet. After a flutter of her hand in distaste, she is quickly on her way to the scented powder display. Here, she spends time fingering sachets and lifting lids from decorated jars. She is absolutely adorable when she sneezes a fluffy, white snowstorm over the wildlife exhibit and then swiftly shuffles away toward the hair care department. It is there, with his hand over his mouth, that Bo cannot stop snorting with laughter as she knocks delicate products to the floor with her wide conical gown. She is completely oblivious to the powder all over her face and the crashing sounds all around her.

Undeniably infatuated, Bo is ready to make that brazen attempt with her one missing shoe, delayed only by his *own* awkwardness when he stumbles and decapitates the head of the Antoinette Wig display. This immediately raises the suspicion of an unexpected puppy seen cradled beneath the lady's arm. Predictably so, the little animal just has to let out a yelp once he knocks over the table of haberdasheries. To his fortunes, the young lady is unaware of Bo's disastrous presence, but both their ineptitudes have drawn the attention of the manager, who is now awakening her employee, Sciocco.

After removing the sewing kit from his jacket, Bo quickly follows in the steps of the young lady advancing to the second floor. Naturally, with his fortunes on the side of clumsiness, he falls over a quill at the top of the steps and crushes her one missing shoe.

Realizing his greeting will receive nothing more than another shellacking, Bo finds a pathway to an open window hoping the noise will block out any further calamities. He soon discovers, however, that his surroundings are dedicated to evening wear and debauchery, and although he remains motionless, it is the dog that is most amused by his expression of the lady fondling the gowns. Bo knows he can no longer remain undetected, and his only choice for a distraction is a talent he has used before. The imitation of the wolf will be most suitable. While in preparation, the puppy looks at him with a tilted head, but once his eyes go wide with his fangs exposed, the non-stop yelping easily annoys the young lady into a hurried exit.

Exhausted, Bo lays his head against the wall and lets out a gasp of relief.

"Ello, Diggy!! Fancy seeing you here."

Bo's eyes soon go wide. Standing before him is the shopkeeper, along with her much larger employee holding a sack of potatoes. "Do him, Sciocco!!"

Swallowing down hard, Bo is relieved when Sciocco loses the potatoes he swings from a disintegrating cloth, but it is the approach from the manager that proves to be the deciding blow. Ramming him into his side with a potted plant on wheels, Bo is forced out the second story window and onto the back end of a horse. The same horse he had shared his gift with, only this time, the greeting is not so cordial. The horse's legs deliver Bo into the store's door, causing it to come unhinged and trapping him beneath.

There, he can only listen and squirm while the young lady walks up and over the door and steps awkwardly across the street in her squashed shoe.

FEBRUARY 2: WHO ARE YOU?

"Teuchy! What is with you getting all fruity with that bundle of wood?!"

Bo's eyes widen from beneath a stack of plywood. He looks about to get a better understanding of where he is. The stables and stores have all returned to current city standards with the same modern-day obstacles he has come to expect.

"I'm thinking a carpenter might want their lumber back; what do you think?"

Bo raises his eyes, "It's a fine stack of wood."

"You were making sounds like a horny calf. It sounded disgusting."

Bo pushes the wood aside and lifts himself up with an impish smile, "A calf, you say? Baah!"

"Stop that and behave yourself! You're acting like some – horny herbivore," twirling her hair with her fingers. "I guess I kind of like that."

"Aye, I am, Mia. You're getting me all randy with your talk of varnished wood."

Mia slaps her thigh teasingly and licks the back of her hand. "Well then, you're going to have to catch me first!" Mia lifts off her sandals and sprints ahead down a freshly paved road, her arms circling around the turns. Bo chases after her with his own route – through a backdoor garden, over a low fence, then crashing through a bush before her.

"Alright! Alright! Hold up! You're going to make me pee." Mia bends down on her knees, trying to catch her breath. She then walks to a small cafe with Bo following behind her. He squints at the fancy lettering on the window: "Shmegma's?"

"Shmegegges, and they serve Borscht!"

Bo looks into the window at the empty counters and tables. He then lifts his hand to his ear and smiles. Mia too hears the distant echoing of music: "It's the Charleston!" He begins making his way across the street, shuffling to the beat of the saxophone. Mia follows behind him with her own peculiar dance – stepping to the side, waving a hand, and then kicking her foot out in anger. A move she created while trying to hail a cab in bad weather.

There is a dark, shellacked oak sign teetering on a metal chain that has the scarlet letter 'V', plunged through a beveled heart. The restaurant is a converted household with goat-scented floors, and has the feel of a home dining experience with a rural appeal. No surprise that the patrons are mainly out-of-town tourists who have never been to a city before. Behind the counter are two middle-aged women dressed in overalls. They are busy dropping tap handles and pushing pints to a gaggle of midday tourists. The talk is consuming, but to Mia, it is a collection of obscure ideas originating from back-alley bus tours. Bo and Mia settle upon two timely, vacated stools, and she reaches behind the bar to extract the local paper. "Bo, get a gander at this in *The Spectral City Times*:

> *Little Street Urchin Strikes Again: Sprikkits MacGee, seen here stuffing her finger down her throat, mimics alcohol-induced tourist stumbling down Cordova Street for an evening of vomiting.*

HAH!!" Mia scoffs. "Just what the motel manager had alluded to. The truth always obscured, so others will perceive it as real. Look at this photo; true, I agree the tourists are sauced, but the little girl they speak of? She is just a faded white smudge on a light-reflecting window. Theory of Hierarchy Rule Number Fifty-Eight: When the world starts accepting the 'Conspiracy by Coincidence', we all go back to living in the dark ages."

Bo watches the waitress walk behind the bar, carrying two large platters of scrambled eggs, sausages, and muffins. He lays his top hat on the counter and leans forward to catch the waitress' attention, "Do you serve any Scottish Eggs?"

"Just what you see on the menu, pal!" the lady replies in a raspy voice.

Mia sets the paper down and shoves Bo with her arm, "Stick to the menu, Bo. There is something I've been meaning to ask you and I don't want you to take this personal, but..."

"Yes, Mia?"

"Are you aware that you are dressed like Isambard Kingdom Brunel?"

"The nineteenth-century civil engineer?" Bo looks at his clothing.

"Furthermore, it's not polite to set your top hat on the counter. People don't want to see your head lice crawling around on the counter tops."

Bo tosses his hat out the open window and pauses to look about the patio bar. The talk is light except for the two older women seated beside him. One is very loud with a short cackle and they both wear hats of a great size to complement their fancy dress. The lady nearest to him is weathered, bronzed, and heavily scented. She is chattering on about how society might be better served with abstinence.

"You have been acting very erratically since we've arrived here, Bo."

"The clothing again, Mia?"

"I just wish you would allow me more time to absorb your mentality. Valentine's Day is in two weeks, and I am hoping for a more normalized relationship. One without the dirty talk, cheap food, and boozy one-night stands. I mean, consider who we have become today since our own failed romance."

Bo lightly taps the loquacious lady next to him, "Goamins, my name is Bo Fox?"

The lady grinds her teeth when she turns, "Cairn Barbie from Australia," replying in a southern accent, natural to the area.

"So, what's the crack on the street, Ms. Barbie?"

The lady ignores Bo, and returns to the discussion with her friend.

Bo turns to Mia, "Americans like to gibble-gabble, don't they? What are you going to order, Miss Mia?"

"Huh? What?" riffling through the pages of the newspaper. "I don't know. The Nineteenth Century Special. Why don't you ask the ladies? They seem to be more interesting than me."

"Nonsense, I'm here with you. What else does the daily say?"

"Alright. Here are some fun facts:

St. Augustine could very well be the oldest city in the United States. It was founded in 1565 by a Spanish conquistador, Don Pedro Menendez, whose commission was to block the French expansion into the territory.

Bo taps Ms. Barbie on the shoulder again, removing the hat from her head and tossing it out the window. "I'm asking for your knowledge of the city, Ms. Barbie. What's the crack on the street?"

This time the lady's eyes are burning and her tone comes with agitation, "Excuse me?!"

"The clavers, you know. The clavers!"

Mia lifts her head from the paper, as if warned by some unforeseen trouble that has crept into the room to no fault of her own. From the corner of her eye, she can see Bo has entered into an unsupervised discussion. Knowing that his social engagements are better served in rustic situations, Mia thinks it is best to intervene.

"I'm sorry, Mam. If I might interject, my friend wants to know: 'What is the word on the street?' or 'What is going on around town?'"

The lady places her large-fisted hand with solid forearms on the counter, "And what is your question?"

Mia holds a long pause, while analyzing the disturbance on the lady's face. She is waiting for a different expression that does not come: "I am only trying to smooth over a misunderstanding between two obviously different social classifications."

"Are we having problems at home?"

"Of course not. I didn't say that."

"Of course, you didn't say that," the lady mocks. "Pray tell, you should actually tell us what you are thinking."

Mia bites down hard on her molars and breaks off a metal support holding up the bar. It does not take more than ten seconds for a British lady to sum up a person. She obviously has met her match in evil, and any plan to ease the tension will not work on this woman. To avoid prison time, it is best she retreat. "Righty then, sorry to interrupt your day." Mia grabs Bo by his sleeve, "I wondered if would end this way. Look here in the paper:

There are over nine square miles to this city and more than 14,000 residents, and the population is expected to quadruple in the coming years with the passing of the elderly.

"Everything is about ghosts in this city."

Bo lays his hand on the paper, "What are you doing, Mia?"

"Time to retreat, Bo! Her evil is far beyond what I'm capable of dealing with!"

"I don't understand."

"Bo, you know that backyard presence I have been telling you about? The one that should actually remain in the backyard?"

"Nonsense, Mia. The Scottish language is just as good as any other. Besides, I have the gift for chitter-chatter."

"Lovely. Go right ahead then," Mia squeezes his arm, "but do this for me; speak in English. Don't use terms like crack or clavers. She might have the impression you're asking about drugs."

"True?" Bo turns up his collar and taps the lady on the shoulder. "Pardon, I was not talking about drugs. I've come all this way to meet the lass of my dreams and just asking for a hand."

"You would like a hand, would you?" grunts and smirks the lady.

Mia's eyes close as she bites down on her thumb. Ms. Barbie places one hand on Bo's shoulder, with the other hand open wide.

Bo feels the loss of gravity that once held him to the floor. He is experiencing a supreme lightness from a whirling and swirling perspective, with short voids of darkness followed by glimpses of dodging debris. His internal senses awake him to a more scented part of the city, among rusty buildings and concealed doorways. He steps from a storefront and stumbles into a parked car, quickly taken back by the change in his appearance before a car mirror. His unkempt facial stubble enhanced by gutter dust, along with his attire resembling that found in a landfill, supports this discovery. He hears two noisy people complaining about his existence. It's another voice, and it slowly rises above all others.

"Ebullient! Ebullient!" Shouts the young lady with the wide, hazel eyes and infectious smile. From her office doorway of a tourist agency, the exhilarated, young woman dashes toward a collection of unassuming retail stores across the street. The reason for her joy cannot be more sustainable. A new dress has been raised in the front window of Meeshman's, a woman's resale apparel store, and it has the perfect colors to go with her Muckle-Ma-Geggy, double-chained, Fluvian handbag. One she had purchased there only weeks prior.

Making her way through the many obstacles blocking the road, the young lady apologizes to each vehicle for having to use their horns. She does not wish to put them through this, but her way is urgent if she is to spend her lunch hour wisely.

At the entrance to Argument Ally (the alleyway where store owners and Free Society Explorers argue for territorial rights), Bolivia Meeshman is having an up-in-arms discussion with a police officer regarding the local explorer, Iggy. The same Iggy who often finds frequent comfort in her throwaway boxes. The young lady does not have a liking for Ms. Meeshman, but she sure has dresses. She hopes to try on that very one in the window; wildly assuming that Meeshman's best dresses are available for her to try on. You see, Ms. Meeshman has barred this young lady from ever stepping near one of her pricey dresses, simply because they are unaffordable to her.

Back to the ally, the young lady is comforted to know that the argument will continue for another thirty minutes. This means she will have enough time without interruption to try on the new dress.

Short and cute, with Florida skin, maybe twenty-three or twenty-four years of age with chocolate-cherry-colored hair that is bobbed with bangs on weekdays and curled at the ends on weekends, is Beatrice Gertrude Backlebond. Ever so bouncy, bubbly, and beamish, she always soaks up life with a twist of aspiration and a shout of jubilation.

She rushes through the open door, slightly ajar for lunch-time visitors, and stops to look around. She is thinking her absence has been far too long in the waiting. Meeshman's has everything, you know: Blankets as soft as the skin; hats that can hold the sun; pillows as light as the feathers that fill them.

And the clothing! Oh, does Meeshman's have clothing and all the various styles to move her. Short dresses, long dresses, v necks, and bottle-necks.

Skirts with belts and pants with bells. Back-less, bare-less, and neck-less. There are crop pants and clam-diggers, French knickers and thigh-biggers. Meeshman's has them all, and with all this excitement building inside of her, Beatie just has to...she just wants to...!!

"Ebullient! Ebullient! I want Ebullient!!" Galloping across the floor like a high-prancing pony, she throws herself into the clothing rack, then rolls around in the fallen dresses.

"Beatrice Backlebond! Please!!" After hearing the crash of the display bars, the assistant manager, with two tired legs and buckling knees, hobbles over to Beatie, who is looking up at her.

"Are you an animal or something?!"

"I don't think so."

"You do this every time you come into the store. Last week you dove across the Vicuna display table, and the week before that you were swimming through the Pima cotton bed sheets! Can you not see I am too old for this?!!"

"Yes, Mrs. Bookafleely."

Beatie continues pony-prancing for a bit, but she already has a routine in place. Now retracing her steps to where she left off last week, she counts off her release, "Ready, set, and go!"

Side-stepping and spinning between the stacks of dresses, Beatie rummages through all the displays and touches all the various fabrics adorned on the mannequins. "Yes, I'll have this one, and of course, I'll have that one. Maybe a few in those colors and two in these sizes!" She pauses only for a moment, and always in the same location where she likes to issue a complaint.

"Something is not right here, Mrs. Bookafleely! This one smells like formaldehyde and this one still has a mothball hanging from its sleeve!"

"Then just try another aisle, Beatie!"

Beatie's mouth shifts to one side, "Okay, but I'm looking for the camise with the giraffe emblem! Do you know if someone has already purchased it?" No response. Beatie stops and looks around. The store is supposed to be empty of shoppers, which she prefers, but there is this feeling that other eyes are watching her.

"These are priced differently than the ones over there, Mrs. Bookafleely!" waving her hands to get noticed. Suddenly, her nose tingles before an oncoming sneeze that repeats itself four times.

"What's wrong, Beatie?!"

"I don't know; it's some sort of 'smish-smeesh-shma'!"

"Certain textures of garments do come with certain odors; you do know this."

Beatie smirks; she doesn't really believe this is true. Besides, it isn't really important. It won't be long before she is redirected toward the dress in the front window.

"I'm still looking for a dress for Valentine's Day. It's coming in two weeks, you know."

"Uh-huh."

"What's the dress in the window all about, Mrs. Bookafleely?"

"No, Beatie. Ms. Meeshman has specifically forbidden you from ever looking at her new dresses. You know this!"

"Yes, but I was wondering if – well, maybe – I could just put my arm through the sleeve, just to see if it will fit?"

"I'm sure the dress will fit your arm just fine."

Mrs. Bookafleely is of no help, and Beatie is hopeless without her dress confidant, D.C. Kiebler, a former Meeshman employee. Her dog too, Paco Daublie, an exuberant, face-grooming Bichon Frise with a knack for selecting shoes. They always let her try on dresses, even if she were never to buy one.

Beatie reappears, crossing the floor with her arms filled with clothes. She sets them down on the table before the assistant manager and lets out a tired puff.

"Beatrice, why are you always yelling out, 'Ebullient'?"

"Because I'm happy, Mrs. Bookafleely. I truly am."

"Well, I don't see why. Someday you'll have to grow up and be miserable like the rest of us."

"No way, Mrs. Bookafleely. Genius loci is where I come from." Beatie raises her hands and spreads her fingers far and wide. "Quiet and calm, like the soup before it's stirred and the water before it's flushed. Everyone knows about it."

Beatie turns her head toward the window, still anxious to try on the new dress. Meeshman rules are most troubling. She fears that she will never see the dress again, just like the 'Excalibur' of all dresses: Vivacious. A dress that was once so often on her mind, and then they said it was sold, and it was only on display for one week! Not once was she ever allowed to try it on!

"Where's D.C. Kiebler, Mrs. Bookafleely?"

"Her name is Genevese, not District of Columbia, Beatie."

"But isn't that where she's from?"

"Yes, but that's not her name. How would you like it if people called you – Atlantic Beach Backlebond?"

"I don't know, better than *'Can't-Try-On-A-Dress'*, customer."

Beatie hears something that disturbs her and then turns about. There is a chitter-chatter whisper going on in the back, next to the shoe polish and bus-stop loafers. She sees six salesgirls seated in Meeshman's Rango Kitty padded chairs. They are much younger than Beatie, and their smiles make her uncomfortable, like they are trying to imagine she is funny-looking or displeasing like that.

"Who are they, Mrs. Bookafleely?"

"They are Miss Kiebler's lunch-time replacements. Genevese works afternoons now."

Oooh!!! Beatie's eyes go wide with hate. She had always thought D.C. had taken another position elsewhere. How cruel and cunning Meeshman can be! She did this on purpose, knowing Beatie is available only on lunch hours during this time of the season. After-work hours in the winter just presents too many dangers of her own thinking.

"Beatie? Where are you going?"

Regardless, Beatie is in need of a Valentine's dress. True, she will not break Meeshman rules, fearing a ban from the store for life – or until she actually has money – but she has other options. Beatie has not been to the back of the store in quite some time. Often discouraged for doing so, because this is where retired clothes go to be auctioned off to backpackers.

There isn't a sound, and it is deathly cold at the section's perimeter. Dead or dying moths are seen everywhere, some of the camises look beaten, and there are sundresses suffocating behind a cellophane wrap.

After a few more paces in utter dismay, her heart suddenly comes to a full stop. In fact, she nearly doubles over trying to resume her breathing, because what she sees appalls her! There, surrounded by thick glass in casual inventory, is the 'Excalibur' of all dresses: Vivacious.

She trips and falls, with half her face pressing upon the display and the other half in a full quiver.

She runs her fingers around the containment as if trying to connect with the dress; hoping maybe to find a breach, but neither gives her hope.

"Vivacious, what have they done to you? Imprisoned for what crime? Your beauty?"

Ms. Meeshman has reached a new low. Torturing is not enough for that spinster; she also has to punish her weekly for her naivety and unrefined yearnings. Beatie knows that lamenting will not help her. She cannot free the dress, and nor has it come down in price. She has to let it go so it can be worn on the back of a tourist looking for a better time.

"Miss Backlebond?" Beatie hears speaking in unison. "We overheard you saying you were shopping for a Valentine's dress. Can you please tell us about him?"

"You girls are still in your teens. Are you sure you should be listening to this?"

"Pleeeeease?!!" speak the girls.

Shrugging her shoulders, "Obviously, he's important." Beatie does a quick spin and closes her hands, "He has these scanty rimmed glasses and this very emotionally, styled hair!"

The assistants, all giddy, sit down with crossed legs.

"He knows what he wants, and by all internal temperatures, he clearly wants me! He says to me, in the light of the moon, that I can now be there for you. And with all these kindly words to follow, he grows deeper and deeper inside of me! Then comes a series of soft kisses all over the unclothed portions of my body! That's when he sweeps me off my feet!! And this is when I have to...!"

"Don't be embarrassed, Miss Backlebond. That was a wonderful story of truth and honesty. We'd like to help if we can. Yes. Yes. Yes!! We know about the dress in the window you speak of! Yes, we do! Mrs. Bookafleely has already nodded off by our own making, so we can prepare you without interruption." "Yes, we can!"

Beatie suddenly feels relieved. In the air, there is this sense of empathy that these six assistants will help her with her own dreams, just as D.C. Kiebler would.

They usher her to the front window and pull her into a display. They then swarm about her, shaking and humming as if summoned by the Shakers of Bolton. Even the crowd on the street joins in with cheers of their own, so she replies back to them with a curtsy.

"It's Ebullient. That's what it is. It has never been quite as good as this. Not ever!" Beatie looks at herself in the narrow mirror with a big, open smile. Now she knows she can become all grown up if allowed to, and this is proof of that. "It is perfect. Too perfect and quite expensive, which is just too perfect too."

"Make a wish!" someone squeals. "The dress says, make a wish, Miss Beatie!"

"Yes, I'm sure I can do that. But you have to use a blindfold; it is tradition, you know."

One of the girls grabs a small shirt and ties it around her eyes, slowly turning her about as she makes her wish: "I accept this test; if I am to wear this dress, the man I would have to meet would be?"

Spinning her around and around and leading her toward the front door, "Who is he to be, Miss Beatie?" the six assistants call out.

Beatie smiles beneath the blindfold, "This tradition is most always full proof, leading to marriages almost some of the time. Keep turning me, girls." Beatie's heart swells with anticipation, knowing that she is moments away from a life of exuberance. She repeats her words over and over again. "This man I would have to meet! This man I would have to meet! He's here. He's here. He's here!" Beatie squints her eyes through the fabric. There, she sees a figure taking shape. A bulbous glob, but beautifully bulbous.

"Parker Ken, is that you?" Beatie prepares her lips for the kiss. Her fingers in a full quiver around the edges of the blind fold. She can't do this! Yes, she can! No, she can't! Suddenly, the blindfold is stripped from her eyes, and there he appears!

"Iggy?"

"Get that urinating, box-smelling backpacker out of here!! And Beatie Backlebond, take off that dress!!"

Ms. Meeshman was so mad that even Mrs. Bookafleely fell out of her chair from the turbulence. Beatie is also dismayed to see all the girls striking their fists out at Iggy as he runs.

"We are sorry for that Miss Beatie." The girls apologize in unison.

"No. It's okay. It's a lovely dress, but I can wait. There will be other dresses to come."

Beatie's face fades as Bo withdraws along the shadows of the city walls. He is at a safe distance, sitting back on the heels of his mind now, but he is also awakening to a deeper sense of loneliness, that maybe his dreams will never be realized.

The scene in the city explodes and turns to dust. Through the lingering particles, an arm reaches forward and grabs hold of his shirt collar.

"Everyone, this has happened at other restaurants; there is no need for concern!"

Mia hoists Bo to his feet. He is not feeling any pain, but certainly he is not of sound mind. All the faces before him, with their laughter and finger pointing, are embarrassing, to say the least. Mia grabbing her nose and turning away only adds to this rejection.

"Uggh! Bo, you smell like a used box!"

Bo tries to let out a few words of explanation, but his speech is stammering, "S-s-s..."

"Okay, calm down. You were going to be mistreated, most expected that."

"Urrr...ba...ba...ba..."

"Yes, I know. Come and sit down. Everybody, he'll be alright. He has a speech impediment."

All the eyes are upon him; this is what he feels. Everyone is looking at him and rejecting him. He suddenly feels his face is changing, and his eyes are going crooked. He is developing a stiff upper lip that brings on a weird awakening. What is happening?!! It feels like...like...

"Good show, I say. How I do love a good collie-shangles!" bowing to the crowd and clapping his hands.

Mia picks up Bo's chair and places it down next to the counter, "Lovely, Bo. There is no need to encourage further embarrassment."

"Nonsense, my little chuckaboo. Where are my fixins? I am delightfully famished!!"

"Just sit and be calm for a moment. Ms. Barbie really did lay you out." Mia straightens the collar about his shirt and smiles.

"Ah, yes. I do recall a huffy-puffy, high-falutin laying me flat on my backside."

Mia pulls Bo toward her and whispers, "Bo, what is getting into you? Is this about my comment regarding you speaking proper English?"

The waitress slides the plate over to Bo, "Here you are!"

"Bags o' mystery, my dear!! It's the Nose Bagger Special! Three fried strips of pig, two crunchy muffins with ghee, and a fried rooster? How frightfully mad you are; you have killed the entire backyard!"

With a burst of laughter from the patrons, Mia lowers her face into the newspaper. To her further embarrassment, Bo leaps up onto the stool and champions his hands, "Here, here!!"

Mia watches as the patrons around the bar and those in the adjoining room cheer him along. She rolls up the daily paper and swats him with it, then drags him down to his seat. "Bo, you are making an abstruse scene! You do remember what I said about Valentine's Day? I think it would be honorable if you represented the both of us in a more careful approach, rather than this stuffed wanker before me!!"

"Balderdash, my dear! I'm just having a spit of fun in a gathering wind, can't you see?"

Mia retracts her rage by releasing the tight grasps of her fingers around his collar, "Apparently, these people can't understand an insult, but I can. I'm going to take my time and be polite with you, but I'll be watching."

Bo slides his fork under one of the eggs and carefully places the entire lot into his mouth. He presses his tongue upward until he hears a pop, then listens to another cheer from the crowd. Mia watches the oozing egg yolk run down his chin and grimaces, "I must be in someone else's dream, because this sure isn't one of mine."

The waitress reappears from behind the counter, "Here you go, mam."

Wiping his mouth with a napkin, "What did you get, ole girl?"

Mia leans forward, lifting the dish to her nose, "This is 'The Nineteenth Century Special'?"

Bo leans over, "It appears all in good taste – boiled water and grain." Bo dips his finger into the soup and stirs it around, "Ah, there you see! Your fish is just drowning beneath the vegetables."

Mia grabs Bo's fork and throws it out the window in a fit of rage, "Great! It's over!!" She pushes back angrily on the stool, then storms out of the restaurant – returning moments later, "Come on!"

"Right-O," Bo turns about the bar to address the crowd. "Well! Ta Ta! Chin Chin!"

The sun is bright, and the eyes of the city look down upon the streets with a long remembrance. Bo walks as fast as the crowd will allow him, often having to dodge street obstacles, cross through lawns, and create broken fences. He is in a hurry to see everything and any place he can recall from memory. Many think him mad, and rightfully so; tourists and St. Augustinians find themselves leaping from his path; cars have to veer out of their lane, and horses have to rear up as he climbs over their backs. It has been a long time since his visit, thirty years ago. He is returning to the streets he once knew: the novelty shops, the old-world cafes, all the bed and breakfasts – just as he had left them.

Bo climbs a lamp post and scans the crowd. There is only one precious sight he really wants to see. It is not hard to define her look; the thought of her every day makes it so.

Bo feels a quick pepper-punch into his leg that causes him to flinch, "Why did you leave me?! You embarrassed me back there, and not just me, but the whole city of St. Augustine!! You were an idiot, a wanker, a dobber, and a pile of unflushed, biggy floaters in the morning loo! In your own language of Scotland, you were a grumf!!"

"What? A complainer?"

"Huh? Alright, a gilpie?!"

"A tom boy?"

"A glow'r?"

"Nay, a store."

"What's the word for pig?!"

"Grumfie."

"You are a beastie in the boggin bum hole of a gruesome grumfie!!"

"There you go!"

"And not once, but twice, were you incapable of showing the alternative!"

"Something I said?"

"We are going to start with a change in wear! Put these clothes on. If there is ever going to be any common ground between us, it is going to start with civilized manners." Mia hands Bo each item of clothing hanging over her arm until he is fully dressed.

"I feel much better now!" Bo slips on a pair of boots and kicks the toe points to the ground.

"Chum me about town, will you?"

"I'm easy, but do we have to walk the same circle of roads?"

Bo looks eastward and offers a solution: "How about we take to the foreland?" Pointing across the river. "I believe Samantha is waiting for us."

"What a brilliant idea you have there, but that's a fair walk, isn't it? Me in flip-flops and you in boots?"

"I have a better idea."

Mia watches Bo reach into the bushes and wheel out the most unusual-looking bicycle. It has an enormous front wheel and a very small back wheel, "A Penny Farthing? Don't you think that belongs to someone?"

"It belongs to us for the day. It even comes with a bicycle lock and a helm."

"And you know how to ride this contraption?"

"We'll figure it out. You can sit on the handle bars; I'll pedal the stands."

"What if I fall?"

"That's what the helm is for."

"To keep me from falling?"

Bo pulls his mad cap down over his head while Mia straps the helmet on and climbs onto the handle bars. They ride with Mia's legs stretched over the front wheel, waving away errant walkers that enter the zebra crossings. Bo feels no restraint with his long, quick strides. He is celebrating the relief of his labored breathing and there is no distance that tires him now. After racing over the fourth stone wall and regaining the road with a back pedal spin, Mia finally demands that Bo change his course. The hours of noon are still before them, and Samantha is already waiting.

Squeezed between two neighboring houses is a small, two-story beach home with a second story balcony. It has a grass-less yard with a stained driveway lined with red helicopter pods. Mia has never been to Sam's place before and Bo seems to know where he is. He locks the bike to a tree and turns the letter blocks on the mailbox to an upright position.

"Much better. The Case's will be happy."

Mia swats Bo's arm, "This is Samantha's house! You didn't know Sam's last name is Case? That's lovely. Do you even remember mine?"

Clearing his throat, "Your name? All of it?"

"Knowing that we have spent the last nine months traveling together, sharing our meals, putting up with each other's conversations, even sleeping in the same bed from time to time, one would think the least of your objections would be remembering the other person's name."

"Pearl. Mia Pearl!"

"Just forget it. Let's visit Sam."

Mia trots ahead up the front steps and knocks on the door with her forehead. She steps back and squeezes Bo's hand, "Do you have to wear that silly-looking bomber hat?"

"I don't have to, but I want to."

"Well, be polite this time and stick it in your pants." Watching and waiting, "What are we going to do about Valentine's? I was thinking of clubbing, but I don't know if Sammie is very capable of finding the right place."

"No worries. I have it all planned."

"Pardon?"

There is a humming sound and soon a head pops from the doorway. With a high level of surprise, both Mia and Bo are stunned at Sam's appearance. Her face is a color wheel of process colors made to look like an English garden. Most of the attention, however, is drawn to her dress, or the lack thereof. She wears very tight Lycra shorts that squeeze her waist and thighs, and she complements this with a T-shirt that melts onto her exposed breasts. Even to Sam, she must have looked unrecognizable.

"Anything wrong?" holding out her hand and fluttering her finger nails. "It's peach melba!"

Bo can't help but question his remembrance of Sam. There is still no recollection of a romance with her, as confirmed by the few passages in the logbook. All that is mentioned is that she can become very flighty and even disappear for several days with her belongings left behind.

"Follow me if you want to eat."

They watch Sam scamper barefoot across the floor, leaving behind a light citrus scent in the air. Mia bumps Bo out of a trance, "She could have worn shoes; she has shoes, you know."

The air cooks with the smell of sizzling beef over hot coals. In the middle of the yard, there is a stone patio with a large frying grill. There are also two lichen-covered lawn benches and an audience of untamed, busy lizzies. Not uncommon, even for Scottish gatherings. The anomaly, however, is the geometrically shaped figure a geometrist would marvel at: The square shoulders, a rectangular-shaped neck, circular arms and thighs, and the trapezoid-shaped head are all descriptions one would most likely find in a textbook.

Sam makes a girlish twirl around his circumference and bows, "This is my kinfolk, Justin."

Mia seems aware of Bo's situation and leans into him, "Deal with it, Bo. We will have a little nosh and we will have a little fun; compromise is made, and there is no going around it."

Justin is the first to extend his arm for a handshake, and Bo allows his hand to be buckled and cracked within his grip. Odd how the pain starts in the hand and goes right to the shoulder.

"So, I hear you and Sam have become pretty close over the last six months."

Bo opens and closes his hand to get the blood flowing, "Justin Case, what an interesting name."

Mia can hear the wrong sense of humor coming from Bo, and quickly redirects him toward one of the benches. "Sammy?" Mia wiggling her fingers.

"Why don't you go put on some clothes and look smarty for us all?" Sam provides an awkward smile, then, with a huff and a laugh, she kicks back one leg and prances into the household.

Bo lays back and watches in sympathy, while Mia puts on a performance for Justin's attention. Everything she tosses at him: the eye batting, lip licking, her two-toe ankle rub – all the tricks for the sake of salacity. But like the arrow wavering in the wind, wondering where it will strike, all her questions on how he feels about a date are answered by herself. The arrow falls flat.

Sam returns having ignored Mia's advice. Her body still insufficiently clothed in a loosely tied robe. She serves them drinks and then retreats behind a distant tree in the backyard. Bo does not fully comprehend the purpose of what she is doing, but it starts from one tree, then to another, then to a hammock, and finally into a tool shed. Imagine what goes on in there. Her game soon becomes self-explanatory when she encircles his bench several times, before setting her legs down across his lap.

"Sammie, I'm feeling nauseous. Can you make me a ginger tea?"

Sam returns Mia's stare while her hand is placed inside Bo's mouth. She begins wiggling her fingers back and forth inside his cheeks, but then stops. The pale disturbance on Mia's face, quickly gains sympathy from Sam. She rolls off of Bo's legs, and then she hurries again into the house.

Mia picks up her shoes from the bench and clicks her fingers, "Come, Bo. Let's look at some photos."

Mia switches on the bedroom light in Sam's room and closes the door behind her, "Valentine's is a bloody load of tosh."

"Sorry, Mia."

"Oh, why kid myself. Nothing can persuade a guy like that to be happy with a girl like me."

"Mia, you never told me she had a sibling."

"I never knew myself."

"We have to get out of here. There's no square go with this bloke, and if you haven't noticed, Sam's taken a liking to me. Her brother is under the impression I should think the same."

"What can we do about it? We have to stay and eat. I can't just leave my best friend."

Bo walks back and forth with his hands grasped behind his head, "I'm a dead man. Maybe I should be open with you."

"Are you sure? I'd hate for you to go honest with me now."

"There's another lassy I've not spoke of ... the reason I'm here."

"Oh, great! When did this happen?"

"Thirty years ago."

"That makes no sense, you're twenty-eight. We're not leaving my best friend. She and I have been through too much together. Maybe you should just learn to like Samantha, she's a good girl you know; though shocking to think you would even consider that."

"Don't do that."

"Do what?"

"I love another. More than anything. You don't understand."

Mia lets out a sigh, "No, I don't, but I guess I would like to."

She shows a compassionate expression and smiles, "I know what we'll think."

Mia hears the voice of Sam calling her from the garden and strides over to the window, "We'll be down soon, Sammie!" Mia draws the curtains shut. "Lovely, Bo, give me Sam's car keys."

Bo does not need to hear her plan; he is relieved by her understanding. The Penny Farthing fits in Sam's hatchback just fine. There is an orange glow above the leafless trees as they drive down the other side of the bridge. The end of the day reminds Bo of something to be concerned with. There are shadows that remain at the periphery of his eyes. These are shadows with an everlasting pursuit that leave into question the coming of another tomorrow. These shadows know neither patience nor boundaries.

Beatie scurries down one flight of stairs and knocks on the store window below. It is now 6:30 p.m. to be exact, and already the lights are going dim throughout the city. Wiping the filth from her palm, she raps twice on the window and peers in. She is in haste, and she knows she has gone too far in her quest for a new dress with pleated armpits. Still on the third-floor of an iron-scaffold building, she realizes it might be too late for a safe trip to her car without being – *absorbed*.

It is that hour of the evening when darkness moves in a way no ordinary object can. This darkness can often use noises to conceal its identity. The very reason she does not care to be out this late!

Beatie looks to the street below and reaches into her handbag. It's the flashlight she wants – a mortal enemy of darkness. She bangs the flashlight several times to make it a bit brighter, knowing that she is entering a location a bit more deserted than she would like it to be. There are no car lights she can rely on, and there are no open curtains for people wanting to be seen. She will have to remain on the near side of the road, where the light is the brightest.

Beatie steps upon the sidewalk and looks ahead. It is the street corner that always worries her the most. They look down dimly lit passageways that have more ghastly shapes than any leafless tree over a moonlit cemetery! After forcing a laugh, she rushes into the light of the next block and calmly wipes her brow.

Now for the next challenge. Sir Madam, a Free Society Explorer who wears a woman's burgundy coat with a scarlet hoodie is not supposed to be here. Rumor has it, Sir Madam died just before Valentine's Day in 1899. Beatie tries to discourage Sir Madam from getting too close by using 'shooing' tactics, but the reaction from Sir Madam is so vicious, with smirks and frowns, that Beatie has no choice but flee!

Already over her limit on wits, Beatie crosses the park with a hopeless feeling she may not make it. Her first encounter is with a dark figure, shape-shifting in dance behind a closed curtain! Next, she is confronted with a face on a porch, twisted and engulfed in smoke and flames! Beating her hands repeatedly, she warns them of their participation, but they won't stop! That's when she resorts to combating these contributors with physical confrontation.

She is but half way down the street when she encounters a jogger. Aware of his hesitation, she beats him with a gutter stick. Next is the little yard that is never mowed. While the owner lay sleeping in his hammock, she runs into his backyard and slaps him silly with her glove. Even though he promised to cut the lawn the next day, she still felt it was worth a scolding.

Confused by her own behavior, Beatie removes her shoes and runs, looking back repeatedly to see if anyone might be following her. After a distance is covered, she realizes she has reached Carrera Street. She darts around the corner and stumbles into her car, kneeling before the door until her despair eases.

Beatie sits, listening to the vibrations of the engine for a full five minutes. She is not feeling entirely rescued from the darkness she has to contend with each night. She has yet to admit this, but she really needs someone that can watch over her, someone who likes shopping for women's apparel and pays for it too.

Beatie slips the car into gear. The sky is black without all the little holes in it. Somewhere in the distance – still beyond and not too far away – there is the sun and the start of a new tomorrow. The car lumbers down the street, coughs three times, and then climbs up over the bridge. She is headed home.

FEBRUARY 3: IT IS YOU AGAIN!

Bo stares at the shiny glass clock on the table by his bedside. He carefully watches the small hand hammer its way down on the hash marks for the start of a new day. He is grateful that the morning daylight has returned through the open shutters once again. Mia rolls out of her bed and approaches the window. Bo is already envisioning the sounds of horse hoofs, car horns, and the muffled cries of tourists from the street below. "Aye, it doesn't get old." He is where he wants to be. A place he can call home.

"You wore your clothes to bed?"

"It saves time."

Mia returns to her bed, grinning at the odd-shaped, coiled pipes beneath the window. She throws a pillow at it and ups her arms in anger. The logbook did explain her temperamental behavior.

"What's wrong, Mia?"

"Why do you keep calling me that? First you forget this, and then you stop doing that, and now you're calling me Mia!"

Bo looks at her perplexed, "Isn't it your name?"

"I have been *'Ma'* to you since the early days we met."

Bo's eyes go wide! Amazing how a mind can go through an abrupt awakening simply by the mention of a single word. It's like missing car keys in yesterday's pants, telling him the events of the prior evening.

"Right, I liked calling you that and you liked it too?"

Mia lifts her shoulders and shrugs, "Sort of."

"Some good times we used to have, Mar?"

"Used to? We were together like a shoe stuck in mud."

"I remember the time your hair got caught in a whirly fan? HaHa. And at the beach, when a bumbee stung you on the noggin and you sprouted horns?! Remember?! HaHaHa! How about the water in the cistern that got all over your face, remember Mar?!!" Bo bends over in hysterics. "You came out looking like a Red-lipped batfish!!! AHAHA. Remember?!! Bo falls to the floor, banging his foot against the bed to stop convulsing.

"That never happened," Mia drops her head into her pillow. "You're just making fun of me."

Bo bites his lip, noting he has been speaking too freely, "Aw, ma lass." He crawls onto Mia and gives her a reassuring hug. It was a time of uncensored silliness, when feelings were never thought to be hurt. Uncaring comments for the sake of a laugh. That is all it ever was.

"How about a dance."

Mia lifts her head as if she had just splashed cold water on her face, "I think I see your thinking here! We'll go to one of those dances Sammy is always talking about." Mia stands up and begins twirling about the room with her arms out. "We can be all dressed up like it's a ballroom dance!"

Bo follows her about the room, spinning and tossing an imaginary partner.

"That's not how to ballroom dance, you idiot! You don't make a pizza out of your partner! Let me show you how!"

Mia kicks up her heels and spins around Bo. She reaches for his hands and ducks beneath his arms, "Oh, Bo, do you really think we could have a good time?"

"I'm sure of it, Mar."

Mia plops down on the bed, rubbing her hands together, "Lovely, so be quiet for a moment. If we are planning for tomorrow night and this works for you, because it works for me, I am thinking..." Mia starts a drum roll on her lap, then thrusts out a leg, "we are going shopping!!"

"Oh, no, not that." Bo says sarcastically.

"Well, I'm sorry, but if we are going to a ballroom dance, we should wear the clothing indicative of the time period – the Victorian age."

Mia clicks her fingers twice and points at Bo. "Your idea, and you are paying for it!" Mia leaps upon the bed, bouncing up and down with delight, before doing a backflip onto the floor. "Look here in the daily: Meeshman's Second Hand Clothing."

The streets are crowded, but that does not slow Bo from hopping with one foot on the road and the other along the curb. Mia trails noticeably behind but eventually catches up to Bo standing before an office sign.

Bo knows he has rushed through his life – days, months, and years at a time – inflicted by a stupidity he once embraced. Many of those days had allowed him to pass with a failing grade, leaving him with a knowledge only an adolescent holds on to. He hopes to replace the behavior that has defined him. There are places in the mind that can change that. There are also places in the mind that will not. This is the challenge that lies ahead.

"Happy To Book with You Tours?" Mia leans against Bo. "Kind of spooky, don't you think? And there is this unpleasant smell about the street." Mia wraps her clothes tightly around her body and shivers. "It's cold too; like, the only usable energy around here is you, me, and whatever is creating that stench."

"I made bad mistakes, Mar."

"Pardon?"

"I'm just wondering if I am capable of changing for the better; or is life just a series of faults with a few brakes in between."

Mia clasps her arm around Bo's arm and leans her head onto his shoulder, "I admit life has never been easy for me either. In fact, I find that sometimes the biggest challenges ahead are simply whether or not to leave the household. But you know what I learned over time? As bad as life can get, it can't get much worse with new clothes." Mia takes his hand and smiles. "Meeshman's is across the street."

The room in the back is where the lights are dim, the mothballs are plentiful, and the walls are made thinner with rain erosion. Mia twirls about the racks, putting her hand on all of the trusses, waistcoats, and conical gowns. There are many different costumes to choose from and nearly every shape a body can fit in to. Mia starts with her own pleasures, dragging Bo in tow and insisting he hold the dresses to the length of her body. She pauses to understand why a prom dress would be displayed behind a glass enclosure. "Uggsome!" grabbing Bo's mad-bomber cap from his head, she tosses it toward the display.

"You won't be wearing that tomorrow night. Try this on."

"A bicorn hat?"

"It looked good on Napolean. I think we might find a good uniform to go with that."

Mrs. Bookafleely appears before the room's entrance, rolling about with her knee on a chair.

"Great, you found them. These are our clothes for backpackers and we are offering them for half off."

Mia shuffles her feet while the assistant store manager leads them through the various racks. Soon she retires her aching body to a more solid chair with her milk of magnesia. She quickly disburses her six assistants, who then carry out her orders flawlessly. They are a bit more than what Mia is willing to tolerate, but considering Mrs. Bookafleely is honest about the discounts, Mia believes this is all part of the package deal.

Rapidly, the girls go through the maze of racks, lifting each dress before Mia to measure her for shape. Bo watches from a distance, listening to all the praise Mia has to say about each gown. He also has an eye on some of the girls floating between the empty spaces. Their giggles and animal gestures directed toward Mia are concerning.

Mrs. Bookafleely continues to call for more dresses, but the more they dress Mia, the more they realize a dress is not for her. Still, Mia wants to fit into a Victorian outfit with little figure to go on. This amazes Bo, considering all the poking and prodding she has been contending with.

Drawing in her breath, Bo watches what little waist she has, quickly disappear under the stringing of a corset. Mia is not very tolerant when someone else takes control, and watching the whole incident while they strap her waist, lower her to the ground, and then place their feet on her back for leverage is most disturbing. One cannot help but think that this might be the result of something far more sinister, particularly when the six assistants apply needles to her outfit and a bed of thorns to her head.

There is a squeal from one of the girls; "The dress says make a wish!" The other girls concur.

Mia scoffs, "Really now! It seems over the top-corny, don't you think? And you are requesting I wear a blindfold?"

"It's tradition, you know."

Begrudgingly, Mia goes along with the idea, but Bo wishes she had not. Once blindfolded, they forcibly spin her around and around, crying in unison, 'I accept this test that if I were to wear this dress, the man I would have to meet would be?' Then more spinning and more chanting. As one can see, Mia is having trouble keeping her balance, and it becomes a lot more unpleasant when the girls lead her out the delivery door shouting: "And here she is, 'Miss Lit Bag of Fire Crap'!"

When the delivery door closes behind them, Bo can hear a bit of a contentious discussion. It is followed by the sound of something large being violently thrown against the door. This then culminates into a slam of another type of object that causes part of the ceiling to crack. It is only natural to expect a flock of disturbed girls to take cover beneath the bell-gown dresses. Mia can be very straight forward with her intentions, and violence is rare; however, it did not take long before Mrs. Bookafleely found herself rolling down the delivery ramp to the sounds of honking horns from the street.

While Mia relieves her tension, Bo greets the mirror with a smile and a salute. He can't help but be fond of his appearance. Fastly buttoning up the slots of his waistcoat, then straightening out his white leather breaches, Bo finally shakes each leg for the feel of an old pair of squash-buckled, pointy-toed, black Hessian boots – so worn they fit any size. With a backward stance, he greets the mirror with a wave of his bicorn hat. Amazing how he appears like nobility.

Of course, when forgetting to step to one side for Mia, Bo will always find himself having to stand again. He moves to a chair, listening to all the girls cluster together in a fervor of a disarrayed fear. Their timed wining is cringe-worthy and it is also getting on Mia's nerves.

"Stop that wining or I'll come for you!!" Obeying her sharp words, the wining turns to soft moans.

"I think you made them nervous, Mar. They were helpful, no?"

"The deputation to Mother Ann Lee? Awfully clingy, don't you think?" Mia shakes her arms out and pauses to take in the dress before the mirror.

She runs her hands down the sides of her thighs and applauds the new vision of herself. She does like the nineteenth-century look with all the buttons and strings added to it. "What do you think?"

"Heavin!"

Mia turns slowly to the mirror with a smile that is brief and her thinking that is predictable. What she saw from Bo was anything but a genuine smile, "What is wrong with the dress?"

"Not a'thing."

"Your face. You made that face with the tilt of your mouth and the squint of your eyes. Like you are ashamed to be seen with me."

"You came to that conclusion because something was in my eye?"

"It was like when we were in Perth, and you didn't want to be seen within a block's distance of me."

"Where did this all come from?!"

"I want you to name each time you didn't want to leave me?!!" Mia sat with her hips collapsed upon her feet and her head sagging between her shoulders. The girls in the background still wining. "Best thing you can all do is keep your distance! I mean it!!" Mia slams her hands down, "This stupid dress doesn't even fit!!"

Bo is baffled, as he should be, but his long days behind him have allowed growth and reflection. He leans to one side and then leans back the other way, "I don't know, Mar, what if you try the dress on sideways?"

Mia raises her head and wipes her eyes, "I don't know what sort of kindness you think you are expressing here. That you would rather spend your time making fun of me rather than show support during this traumatic episode in my life! I mean, really, what mother would not think that she made the terrible mistake of raising her son when he offers a stupid suggestion meant to harm the morality of a woman?!!"

Mia stands with her hands on her hips before the mirror and looks over the angles of her body.

"Fascinating! I can try that!"

Mia disappears behind the coat racks, while the shop girls scatter to the furthest point of the store. She reappears shortly with her hands through the bob in her hair, letting it drop free. She tugs on her dress and smooths out the creases.

"Nice, Mar. I like how the bow comes to the front."

"Right? It's like I have this mystery down there. I hope you brought enough money for an outfit Sam can wear."

Mia searches out the six girls dispersed under various garments and orders them to find something for Sam. Setting the clothes on the check-out counter, she nudges Bo. "I'm going to ask Sen, the assistant manager, if he'd like to join us. I think you should ask Sammie if she would like to go too. You are being a bit too sure of yourself if you think that whoever you dream up will just appear as you wish."

Bo reaches into his pocket for some dollar bills and drops them onto the counter. Maybe Mia is right. Times do change, even though his thoughts hope to manufacture a full-proof plan, Beatie might be in a different situation now. After he left her, she may have decided never to go out in public again, and this concerns him. The only reason they met in the first place was because of a horrible experience she encountered at a hotel party. If she fails to appear, there will be no meeting with her at all.

She rises from her bed, but then lies back down. Annoying how the covers are loose again. The cold just seems to seep right through the entanglement of misdirected sheets. She kicks out one leg, sensing both legs should be getting ready to go somewhere else, but she feels so comfortable being nowhere that she shouldn't be anywhere but beneath the sheets. Beatie curls up in a ball and places her head under the pillow. Of course, her thoughts about the morning chores to be completed are a distraction. How can one fall back to sleep knowing that a dirty house attracts bugs?

One arm falls from beneath the blanket, awakening her to another thought. A strange occurrence had taken place only hours earlier. Two nocturnal beings, confabulating in a slurred speech, had stumbled into her room and shook her from her slumber. They confessed to having a very strong stomach for larvae and wanted to digest the insides of her skull. Apparently, she did not take them up on their offer, and instead, drifted off without incident.

Fully conscious now, she realizes her recollection may not have been entirely true. Crepuscular they were, but living dead they were not. They were her two roommates, Nikki and Olivia, and their request for inner skull nourishment couldn't be any further from accurate. However, their intended proposal made even less sense, if you can believe that. They were asking her to attend a party of appealing conviviality, arranged by their parents at a posh hotel on the beach. Just fine, but why would they ask her? She hasn't done anything wrong. I mean, think about it: these girls are the 'Who is Who' and the 'Who Knew Who' of the entire county. They have perfectly oval faces that are smooth and colored to perfection. They have clothing, so lavish, they can't even be worn!

This party will be gaudy and garish. Beatie has but one shade of foundation, one lipstick, and two perfumes. Most of her clothes are borrowed, and her best clothes she only pretends to have! And one can imagine the plate cost – two hundred and fifty dollars!

Beatie rolls over once and then rolls back twice. Rolling over one more time, she tumbles to the floor. See? This is exactly why she likes her bedsheets tight.

Before the mirror, her hair stands in a tangled mess. Most of her make-up is still on yesterday's pillow. She can fix her face, no problem, but changing her unhappiness with a fresh look just doesn't exist.

Beatie sits down at the edge of the bed with her arms filled with linen. It would be a strange acceptance for her if she were to attend. Their lives are way too different from her own. To be like Olivia and Nikki, fraternizing from one place to another would be exhausting, to say the least. Beatie prefers to compare her enjoyment to those less willing to leave the household. Many of her best years have been spent in the comfort of boredom. This is what she likes. In fact, the only reason she can remember what she did on Monday is because the days are no different than what she does between Tuesday through Sunday.

Beatie nestles her head upon the pillow. No way can she attend any party that does not include her happiness. She refuses to give up on a way of life that excludes her stuffed animals and closet full of memories. That settles it; she isn't going anywhere!

A cloud of vapor explodes before Bo's eyes and leaves his face wet. It tingles, like a wet cloth pulled from his skin left cold to dry. He looks about, rubbing his needle-pinned face, fervently trying to return it to normalcy. Somehow, he finds himself lying in a storm drain. The neck of his shirt is stretched beyond his clavicle and there is chanting around him that is particularly annoying.

"She is not interested! She is not interested!"

"What's going on here, Sen? Why are these people protesting, Bo?"

"Well, okay. It seems to be about this sign a protester made. Your friend admitted to knowing the stick figure drawn on the sign as the son of a friend's daughter whose sister once met the sibling of a man who dated his cousin. Your friend admitted that he, himself, was present at the meeting of the Intermittent Fasting Association that the stick figure was also attending. Apparently, your friend asked the insulting question to the stick figure: will there be any Haggis Crisps provided?"

"That's terrible, Bo! Is this true?"

Bo rolls forward and grabs his knees, "Mia, I told this bloke his stick figure reminds me of a bloke I had seen at a Haggis Eating Contest. That's all! A funny!!"

"Well, why would you say something like that? You know humor isn't accepted in this country."

Bo hears the chanting from the crowd getting louder and louder, trying to demoralize him about his chances of meeting with his beloved. These chants seem to be having an effect on his eyes, turning them crooked and shifty, with spinning taking place in his head.

"Come on, Bo. Get up!" Mia reaches down to help Bo to his feet, studying his contorted face and stiff upper lip. "Oh, lovely. It's you again."

"Well, hello, my little scented gerenuk? It's rather rum of you to think I'd be in accordance with these maffickers!" Bo flinches as a head of lettuce crashes upon the side of his head. "Now, see here, you shally-hacks! Is this your excuse for a disappointing education?! Gadzooks!! Why have I been dressed to look like a picaroon, ready to be tossed into a group of sea pigs!!"

Mia sways her shoulders in an awkward acknowledgment, "It's not so bad, Bo."

"No, my dear? And you too, robbed of your nobility and displayed as a Venezuelan Poodle Moth!!"

"Bo, I'm not happy with your tone."

"My dear lady, I hardly think this is about my tone!" Bo picks some squashed lettuce out of his hair and throws it back at the crowd. "Great Scots, I recognize this cad!"

"Now, hold on, Bo, Sen is a good man. He rescued you from these quarrelers! And I would like you to know that he is also invited to the dance, which he has so graciously accepted."

"Boggledash!! Don't sell us a dog, dastardly man; speak your intentions with this woman!"

"Bo!" Mia blushes. "Please, behave yourself!"

"Come on! Kick up those heals, you foul scoundrel, so I may lay claim to your demise!" Bo bounces about with his chin held high, rolling his arms with clenched fists.

Sen quickly takes Mia's arm, "The town ghosts have been known to get into people's heads and stage their own threats!"

"No, Sen. That's not it. He doesn't handle rejection well. I better meet up with you later."

Bo is still bantering with the crowd while Mia pulls him across the street, "Did you see how I handled those ruffians?"

"I know. You'll figure it out. Now! Breath and think positively."

Beatie is warm; her support socks make her feel so; and the extra warmth provided by her decorative sham makes her face tingle with such delight that she just has to purr. She is happy to be in a good mood because she has lots to do this morning. Every morning, she goes about her chores of sweeping the house, cleaning the counters, and scrubbing the toilets. This morning, however, is going to be different.

This morning, Beatie is preparing for a night of convivial hobnobbing at a very fancy establishment called The Gummy Babba. It is run by Famby

Bevin and Millarly Balour, two ladies who are well known to be trendy-way, tony-sharp, and kicky-suave. They know everybody who knows anyone that doesn't wish to be nobody anymore. This is just where Beatie wants to be, because she knows nobody who doesn't know anyone.

It was suggested by her lovely roommates, Olivia and Nikki, who stopped by with a gold leaf offer for her to become the new town, Baby Star. This will certainly insure her an introduction to Parker Ken. He is the 'Beau-ideal' she fantasizes about in all her romance novels. Oh, how she loves Parker Ken with all those winning ways to charm fantasy-thinkers like Beatie. In her dream, 'Swimming with Pool Boys', she imagines him carrying her across the waist-high waters of the Amazon River. There, he would be fighting off the deadly elements of leeches, penis boring candiru, and five-hundred-pound anacondas. This dedication toward self-annihilation is just how she envisions their life together.

Beatie leaps about the room. Of all the invitations she has foregone, accepting this engagement seems to be the most promising! Immediately, she grabs her romance novel and flips to the last page. Her finger now on the yellow highlighted line regarding the book's promise: 'Never ending happiness.' Do you think you can handle that, Beatie?! No longer will you have to rely on reading material to help you realize your dreams. Beatie opens her window and tosses the book at the bird bath. "Now, it will be me who will tell the stories!"

A shiver runs up Bo's spine that shakes his legs and 'un-crooks' his eyes. He no longer feels like he is looking out the back of his head. He sees his surroundings and finds himself back in Meeshman's, sitting on the same hard chair before the mirror. Mia is pulling on her sleeves with no sign of the six assistants. Mrs. Bookafleely is seated at the other end of the room, drinking a tall glass of milk of magnesia.

"How is it possible to have larger hips with a small behind? Can you believe the assistant manager? She told me this dress makes me look like a flounder. True! A bottom, feeding fish!" Mia pauses to look at Bo with a serious eye. "Are you feeling any better?"

"Pardon?"

"Try some Moca. It's free!" Mia tilts her head to the side and draws back her hair, "Help me with this."

Bo pulls up the zipper of her dress and smiles at her in the mirror. Mia walks to the front counter, motioning toward Bo, and once again, he quickly pulls some scrunched-up, loose bills out of his pocket.

"Oh, I should mention, I'm going to ask Sen to join us. We still need a lift."

"What about Sam?"

"Funny as this may sound, Bo, I hardly believe Sam wants to do anything with us now?"

"She didn't press charges."

"Taking a friend's car without permission doesn't always lead to an arrest, but what I foresee are repercussions that will reduce my friendship to a mere acquaintance."

"Can you just tell her we're sorry?"

"Really? What have you learned about women, Bo? Sorry is no longer a respected word today, making all explicit apologies conditional based on four steps: first you have to go through cancellation; then suffering; then pining; and finally, the purchase of a new dress. We're talking forgiveness, maybe – two, three weeks, depending on the price of the outfit!"

"Mar, our Valentine is out there waiting somewhere."

"Hmmm, that's a good point. Let us think. Would you consider sleeping with her?"

"Serious, Mar? A bit immature?"

"I'll check with Sen first."

FEBRUARY 4: IGGIE'S

It is late afternoon already, and Mia has left for the lobby to talk to the assistant manager. She has located Sam, and all is well. She was able to convince her that Bo is at fault for all their troubles and is unfit to think for them anymore.

Mia is quite a mystery. There are many instances that have set off a slew of reminders, and yet somehow, he feels her outbursts are not entirely due to the actions of his own. Somehow, these acts of malevolence were forged, well before the train arrived at the platform. With so much attention to all her regular appearances, it brings to question her importance thirty years ago. Bo reaches into his backpack and fingers through the pages of the logbook.

Mia has an unpleasant disease labeled as Myotonic Narcolepsy Rigoruos Morti.

It is believed to be related to the phenomenon of fainting goats. For five minutes every morning, she falls into a deep slumber and rolls over to her side with her arms and legs straight out.

Bo reaches back in and pulls out the most recent logbook. The club's name is Iggie's, and he will be meeting with his beloved tonight. It's all in these pages. So hard not to look ahead, but over-planning could create a wrong thought. If he misses her, there is a chance he may never see her again. Bo puts the logbook back and retrieves one of the earlier-dated books.

Interesting note here about Mia's toxic situation with children; and here, one of the pages is curled and there is a highlighted section in yellow:

Mia earns her living as a bio-tech property manager for several large cemetery plots around London. Currently on an extended holiday for an unspecified reason.

There is an attached news clipping.
The London Hour: Local Woman on Forced Holiday.

A 30-year-old woman was found guilty of inexcusable practices regarding the recycling and reuse of family plots. It involved the temporary use and release of toxic decaying agents for biogenous, dead-bone decomposition. In a voluntary state of intoxication, Miss Pearl knowingly admitted to stacking corpses and injecting lime and hydrochloric acid, along with other agents, into the individual plots. This investigation began two weeks prior, when Miss Pearl was put on notice for what a former employee revealed as an excessive purchase of lime, for which the defendant had signed for. Lime is used as a means to putrefy the bodies within the ground and to stymie the exploding insect and varmint population, which had become, at the time, an increasing problem in the Kensington area. In her defense from court documents, Miss Pearl admittedly told the judge that the cost of dying had gone up; bodies were not decomposing quickly enough; and therefore, to stay within the budgetary cuts of the city's proposal, drastic measures were imperative for an increasing death population, forecasted for the coming years. Praised for her keen sense of British independence, Miss Pearl is to be placed for further psychiatric evaluation in Freemantle, Australia.

When the stairwell door closes behind her, Mia scurries across the floor and grabs a brochure from the lobby desk. She has a cheerful glow to her face and a plan of engagement that she feels will solidify her Valentine's Day plans. She thinks a compliment on his pictures, particularly the one of himself on a unicycle, should start the conversation in the right direction. The closing remarks will be about the plans for this evening.

She travels across the lobby into the adjoining room, crossing her legs in one of the chairs. She pokes her head up from time to time to see if he might appear. Perhaps he isn't working today. Mia straightens her arms and legs and flings herself forward, toward one of the artworks. It is a life-size portrait, much taller than she, and presents a man dressed in a long, black cape with long, black hair. Everything seems to be dark about this painting, even the stern eyes staring at her as if issuing a foreboding command.

Turning presumably toward the next painting, she is surprised to see, in real appearance, the very dressed man in a long, black cape with long, black hair. The young master of deception quickly calms her nerves by performing a short dance and taking a low bow.

"My presentation is before you, madam. Can you not tell the difference between what is real and what is a creation?" The assistant manager gleams. "The painting is called Porta Floyd. A man who has to compromise his soul for the sake of the imposter. Tell me your thoughts on this curious one."

Mia looks at the painting in an undecided way. She is new to this kind of behavior in Sen and decides maybe it is best to just shrug.

"How about the one next to it? It is the painting called 'The Doctor'. The part played by a buffoon who initiates guessing games with rules fashioned to his own liking. As you can see, I painted him to the likeness of a goat."

Mia nods her head, keeping it simple: "I can see that."

"Come here on the other side of the room." Mia follows while he extends his hand to her without actually touching it. He hurries ahead, before a thick velvet curtain, and grabs hold of a rope.

"Now, let us see the creation of death!"

A bright light from above comes on when he pulls on the rope to part the cloth.

Mia's face is in a motionless gaze until she realizes who she is looking at, "AHA!!" clapping her hands in joy. "It's my roommate!"

"No, this is NOT your roommate! Do not look with a false recognition. Now close your eyes for a clearer mind."

"Okay, I see a tall man with a grave face and an awkward smile. He is wearing a kilt with red patterns and blue stripes. You have also added a touch of blue around his eyes to give him more of a macabre appeal. I see my roommate!"

The painter put his finger on Mia's lips. "This one is called 'Mo Charaid'; and if you had used your eyes from within, you would have seen the truth more clearly. See the lines of his hands that disappear into the fabric of his coat? This is where his heart is suffering. Feel him needing the lint that blocks his blood stream and robs him of his life source."

Mia turns her head away from the painting, rubs her face, and then returns the look with squinty eyes, "Nope. Can't see that."

The assistant manager shakes his head in a pathetic despair and leans heavily against the wall.

Mia attempts to change the subject: "Well, this is all lovey, but the reason for my visit is to ask you about the artwork in the lobby?"

The assistant manager lowers his head, pathetically chuckling, "You prefer my photos in the lobby? You prefer them over the paintings in this room?"

"Is that okay?"

"Well then, shall we take a look at the photos in the lobby? The ones that you say are more preferable." The assistant manager walks with a silly goose step, while Mia follows.

"Here we are before this black-and-white photo of a beach that calls for no imagination. Notice there is no movement. See that you cannot simply plunge into the waves and follow it out to the edge of the frame. Over here, this one called: *The Town*. A simple name for a duotone of nothingness. Thought-provoking only to the most minimalist of minds. There is no perception of depth, nor are there any lines drawing perspectives.

"Finally, this photo of the little girl, floating face down in a cesspool of water, relieving herself from the burning pain she experiences from the black disease. A caption it has: *When there is a demand to reject pity, charity is no more.* Is this what you like? Drowning children escaping discomfort for the sake of a fund raiser?"

Mia lifts her shoulders up and shrugs.

"Even your reaction reflects the boredom you have created within this very room."

"Sen, how about we see something you like? How about that?"

The assistant manager's eyes widen and his fingers flutter, "That would be *The Call of the Lighthouse,* for which we can see in its entirety. It's here in the adjoining room! It is silent for the most part, but its expressiveness can be heard upon the Matanzas River.

"See the rays from the lighthouse upon the tapestry of the black river. Notice the men drifting upon boats toward this spire of hope. Here, the Alteveu waits for their arrival, offering to raise the dead as reparations for the great illness of 1821."

Mia gazes deep into the painting, trying to see the connection between his words and the artwork. "You see all that?" Mia lets out a snort. "Is this why we are fooled by the humanitarian who lives on a secluded island!"

The blank face of the painter does not match the pleased expression Mia is hoping for. She raises her finger toward the painting, "Are those dead animals before the lighthouse?"

"Cats and dogs, and a few cows," he remarks. "Do their appearances seem strange to you? Perhaps you have heard them impatiently shuffling outside your door, wondering if maybe you might let them in?" The assistant manager puts his arm around Mia, tugging her in closer, "Do tell us all what you are thinking, if you would be so kind." He begins raking his fingers through her hair, "It would be scary to know them would it not?"

Mia pulls away from the day manager, clapping her hands together. "I know what's missing! A happy ending. That's what I would like to see!"

"Ah, I see. A happy ending. The sequel to forgiveness. With so many words to describe such a perilous situation, you decide upon – a happy ending?"

"Yes, sir-ee. That's what I'm looking for! And, of course, some bathroom towels. Pretty standard in motels."

"Well, I was hoping my paintings needed no further explanations, but to you ..."

"Sen, please, let's stop this. Your paintings are priceless. They should be locked away from all discerning eyes in the event; one might even wish to take one home. Because they are so – divine."

"Divine, yes! What a wonderful word of expression! You believe that too, don't you? That someone, perhaps anyone, would come to my hall of pleasure, and snatch away these very paintings that you say are so – divine?"

"Well, it happened on Scarlet Street (i)."

"It happened on Scarlet Street? Again, it seems like a pointless assessment of one's body of work, merely to invoke an adjective related to the name of a street. How does one proffer from such a statement?"

"One doesn't. It's a playful reference to a 1940's film about two criminals who take advantage of a painter and sell off his artwork."

His eyes and mouth suddenly go wide in shock. The assistant manager begins collecting his paintings along the wall and then retreats behind his desk. "Good day, madam. I think we have rudely established our commonality for the foreseeable future!" The assistant manager swings around in his cape and disappears into the backroom.

Mia runs up to the desk and slams her hands down, "Sen!! Come back!!! I came to see if you might be interested in...." A door can be heard closing.

It has been a long walk for Mia, and she has been drifting between the sidewalk and the lines down the middle of the road. Her wide-brimmed, leghorn bonnet affixed to her head has proven to be a challenge in the wind. She has learned to adapt by using stiff steps and a jerking motion, but it is the iron fence that provides her with the greatest stability. If not for its placement around the cemetery, Mia would have been dragged off by several stray dogs.

"I cannot understand it; there must be some marrow in the cage of this dress."

"We're almost there, Mar."

Mia stumbles into Sam's car and slams the door. She is disappointed to see Sam in tight shorts and a tank top. "Sammy Love, I bought you this. Bo, could you hold her dress up for her?"

"I'm not dressing like that!"

"Sam, I am dressed to go to the ballroom dance at your school."

"The dance is not until Wednesday. I don't know where we can go dressed like that!"

Mia scrunches her face, "But I'm dressed for now! There must be somewhere to go."

Bo fits himself into the backseat and slams the door, "Iggie's!"

"Iggie's? Sounds like a pus wound."

"It's a club for demented folk." Sam smirks. "You'll get in fine."

"Let's go then! Turn left, turn right, and go straight. Woop - WaHeee!" Mia turns up the music. "Here's where we turn, Sam. No, up there! Quick, get over!"

Sam glances over at Mia with a snarl on her face. "I know where I am going, Mia. There's no need for the play by play."

Sam resumes her driving, but anxiously begins tapping on the steering wheel. "You know, Mia, I think it's something funny that you would just drive away without an explanation. You did a similar thing to me when you and Bo left me in Mount Vernon. You didn't come back! You weren't ever going to come back!" Sam lets out a sniffle.

"It never happened that way, Sam." Mia avoids direct eye contact by preening before the car mirror: "You know how Bo and I can argue at times. We were just unaware that you were not in the car. Same with the second time and any time after that. Besides, you always found your way back."

"But you knowingly took the keys from me and I had to pay someone to find my way back!"

"Well, that's daft, isn't it, Sam? If we wanted to get away from you, we would have taken your wallet as well."

"Yeh. Maybe." Sam's voice suddenly goes nasal, "It was Justin, wasn't it? Why can't you tell me if it was Justin?!"

Mia lifts a brush from her lashes, "Sam, don't you have a better eye lash applicator?"

Mia tries to move a clump from the inner corner of her eye, only making it worse. "Words often fall short of expectations, Sam, and are usually filled with lies later to be revealed. I wasn't willing to risk that with you."

"I don't even know what that means. Are you saying you would have to lie to me?"

Mia drops the brush on her lap, leaving a black smudge on her dress, "You know what's wrong with you, Sam? You live by Sod's Law. Always the doomsday thinking. Oh, we can't go to the beach because the sun will be too close to the earth tomorrow. Oh, I can't go to the zoo because there's a shortage of hygiene washes. Blah. Blah! If anyone just pays a smidgen of attention to whatever you have to say, there would be literally nothing for them to live for."

"Well, maybe it's because I feel like I'm being ignored. Maybe it has to do with whatever I say never meeting your approval! And maybe it is true that you only need me because I do all the driving!"

"So, here you are then. Where's your lip gloss? Thank you."

"Mia, I don't even like clubbing with you. I only go because I feel guilty that you don't have a driver's license."

"Whether you go or not go has little to do with the same matter, Sam. Do you have any baby powder? I have this itch, right... Thank you. It's a fact, Sam – in your company alone, no one could possibly leave the room without feeling more baffled, bored, or, as I might add, dumber than the moment before meeting you. Regardless of any higher education achieved."

"You take that back!"

"And the llama says? Now that looks better. I like how your eyeliner goes on really smoothly. You don't have to apply much pressure. What's that noise?"

Mia looks around at all the honking and hears the sounds of screeching breaks. She closes the mirror and looks over the dashboard to see their car crossing the lane at a Forty-five-degree angle. She shakes Sam's arm, trying to bring attention to her feet, now nestled beneath her rear.

"Sam, are you okay? You look a bit off-color. You might want to look up. There are obstacles... Sam, we're headed for – BUMP! Sam, you're about to hit the – BUMP! BUMP! And now the sign!!!

Bo sits quietly tossing about in the seat with his bicorn hat placed on his lap. Mia's worst behaviors not only appear in the words of the logbook but also in actual observations. The conflict will eventually resolve itself; he knows this. There is a unique bond between the two girls that cannot exist with anyone else. No different than the elements in the universe. Some repel instantly, some bind nicely, and others just explode whenever they come into contact. Blame it on nature.

Bo lays his cheek against the window. His thoughts briefly focused on the specks of light from the passing towns. He knows these lights and where he is headed. She is only a few thoughts away and it excites him. The anticipation of meeting her again also makes him nervous. It has been a while; he knows nothing of her time spent here. His youthfulness always had the opportunity to ingratiate women with sustaining flattery, but does he still have that same virtuosity?

Aye, not to worry. True, they had only met a handful of times, but he knows her better than anyone he has ever spent a lifetime getting to know. There will be no informalities now; no flinching upon an accidental touch, no uncertainties when reaching out for a kiss...

"Bo, what is wrong with you! Weird, wouldn't you agree, Sam? He kissed me, right behind the smelly part of my ear even!"

Bo looks about his surroundings and sees that he is now in a crowded room of gossiping patrons. He is here! This is Iggie's, and the hour chosen when Beatie will arrive. He squints his eyes, thinking he heard the call of his surname, but no one is remotely looking at him. However, there are two men holding pints of beer that cause his heart to skip a beat or two. They are fellow countrymen, two brothers between themselves – Lyndon and Beathen.

"Whar kin aye fin cailleach fer skulldudderie?"

"A Scottish mannie! Foos yer doos!"

"So, whit ye doin' ya dobbers."

"Resting aw day 'n finding energy at nicht. Whaur ye frae?"

"Am frae the Sutherland."

"Ae highlander! We aboots Verness."

Bo lifts his head for a smiling moment when the air suddenly becomes infused with a scented smudge stick. There is also a dwindling smell of a Tattie Drottle that makes him feel at home. Too much so, and this concerns him. Home is four thousand miles away over a great body of water and low-lying lands. This means, someone has entered the room, but not in the room he thinks he is in! A poke comes next and there is a tingle in his arm that wants to ache; and so it does, right up into his shoulder. There is a voice that comes next, "Mr. Fox, are we reaching you?" Followed by conversations he feels no part in.

"Will you not do that, please?!" "Hell, mend ye!"

A feverish warmth comes over him, followed by a shiver that causes him to drip his beer. He falls to one knee and watches Mia travel toward him without actually taking a step. Or maybe it is his side of the room traveling toward her. Regardless, it is making him feel not at all well. She rises a foot above the ground and reaches out for his hand, "This girl I have been speaking with. She is a local, and she seems to be interested in our travels."

Bo is suddenly distracted by the sound of two other voices, voices he cannot see, but he sure can hear. "Don't open the window!" "I don't see how one can!"

He is becoming confused. He sees Mia before him, yet reality may not be what appears. There must be another room nearby. A room he does not create. A room he cannot control.

Hoping to reach a place of normality, Bo stumbles ahead through a line of disintegrating tables. He never hears the thud when his body hits the floor, but he sure feels the pain.

He opens his eyes and finds himself in a dark room. The air moist and pungent, but not from beer or stale cigarettes. Mia is lying on her side, smiling and waving a flashlight, motioning that he should lower his body onto someone that is other than herself. It is her desire that he mold with this body, being that this is the machinery his body has been instructed to become.

The body below him makes little animal noises, interrupted only by short breaths and a drawn-out moan. Confused, he raises his head for further instructions, and sees Mia swinging her flashlight for him to continue. She begins making the same expressions she would make if she were involved in the act. Her face showing that she is really enjoying this.

The machinery continues to swing its balls against the walls while pumping fluids into every crevice and canal of the apparatus. Upon recharging, he does this again and again. All this done with the flashlight barely casting its finishing glow on their bodies.

As soon as it feels good again, he relaxes. Mia returns the look, deliciously tasting her fingers. She welcomes the views, thinking that they would be best served in this kind of environment, possibly enjoying their company more this way.

Bo feels a tug on his lower eyelid and watches a metallic orb roam over his face. There is a familiar voice that awakens his senses. "Do your medicines contain an aphrodisiac, Doctor, or are his bedsheets rising because of the fabric softener I've been using?"

"If you could get some moist towels and fresh air for the room, I'm sure that would make Mr. Fox feel more... indifferent."

Bo's face falls toward the man assuming to be his caregiver's replacement. He watches as he reaches into his jacket for a piece of paper, and then leans over to yell in his ear, "Are you able to hear me, Mr. Fox?! Can you speak, Sir?!"

Why does he have to do that? To no avail will the doctor reach him by yelling. Is it not obvious that his irritable personality exudes a stench of arrogance? And those meddling hands, lifting letters from the floor and analyzing his words, as if clearly, he sees proof of a troubled mind.

> I have left a finger print, the only trace of its kind, for I will no longer be here when you read this. Sometimes the matter is too complex to say in person when there has been that promise of commitment for another tomorrow. Goodbye is not what anyone foresees as a possibility, but now I present to you the contrary. I would wish you thought me a savior for my disappearance, so you could continue on without the uncertainty and despair that I bring to you. It is not the end of all things to hear goodbye; it is just the end of what has come to pass and what we will one day look back upon with a smile. In many ways, this is the best offer to wish for. Promise me you will take care of yourself, and no matter where we end up in life, you will always be the tomorrow that I can never replace. Ours be true, Baueregard Heathan Fox.

Bo wishes to defend himself while the man scoffs and tosses his letter into the fire. The letter is not his fault! One cannot be dependent on words read in haste. Were not his attempts for unity lost to a common enemy? It was her friends who failed to see the admirational side of him, not the thoughts that were revealed on paper! Bo shakes and kicks, hoping to reach this man, but he isn't really moving at all. He is just lying there beneath the cold sheets, soon to be replaced by the cold dirt from the long-handled shovel.

The doctor goes to the window, unlocks the latch, and pulls aside the shutters. He looks out at the scenery of the sweeping, green valley, stretching far into the distant hills. It is hard for him to believe a man is clutching to his life when if he could dissect him right here in this room, he could prove to the world there is a fifty-eight-year-old man with thirty years left inside of him. And yet, he cannot prove why his despair should make him look twice his age. And yet, he cannot prove why this man's despair should make him look twice his age. There is something to this story that needs more answers.

FEBRUARY 5:
SUPERSTITIOUS
CHARMS

He finds himself as a young boy in an untainted meadow, strongly fragrant after a spring rain. The sound of a clanking bell and he turns to a footpath where his going is much easier. The grassy path through the shining blades of dew always leads to a sign that reads: Sango Bay. There in the shallows, where he lies beneath the water, he makes little ripples with his fingers. The world on the other side is coming apart and it knows not why. An object plunges into the water, leaving behind a trail of many bubbles and tears. This object is long, soft, and repulsively fleshy.

"Will you stop hitting me? I'm trying to help!"

Bo flounders around in a tight circle, realizing he is well over his head in deep water. Mia does her best to grab a hold of him, but his undomesticated thrashing challenges her abilities to help his situation. She waits patiently until he sinks below the surface, then she finds a better hold. A hold that surprises them both.

"Oh my, you're naked!" Mia rushes to the shallow end of the pool, watching Bo's body become a smaller distortion of itself. Lunging back, she swims hard along the bottom, searching for a better handle. She drags him by the turn of his ear until he is able to pull himself to the pool's edge.

"I take it; you can't swim. Generally, that is the first thought on someone's mind before they get into a pool."

Bo belches and coughs into his hand, "There's no buoyancy to this water!"

"Pools are like that if you don't know how to swim in them. Never been in the ocean before?"

"In Scotland? It's bluidy seven degrees!"

"Where are your trunks?"

Looking around, Bo points toward the deep end of the pool.

"Lovely. A kilt. Isn't that to be worn on your death bed?"

Bo nods his head and coughs again.

"Are you okay now? As a reminder, bathing trunks are for the common good of all public pools. Respect and remember that."

Bo pulls himself out of the pool and bows to a clapping crowd gathered along the fence. He fetches his kilt with a pool rod and marches over to a lounge chair next to Mia, "Aye, it's a braw day, Mar. I'm amazed we have the pool to ourselves."

Mia is despondent, sitting comfortably with large sunglasses over her eyes and half her face buried in a book. Bo raises himself up and tilts her book upward, "The Illuminator of Foggy Pants?"

Mia yanks the book away from his fingers and rolls onto her stomach, "Sen gave it to me. It's good."

"I'm not going to ask what it's about."

"You shouldn't."

Bo sits back and waits, then begins counting on his fingers: "Two, three, four..."

Mia turns over and closes the book on her finger, "Right! So, the lighthouse by the bay was initially built in the early eighteenth century. It served as a watch tower, you know. One hundred and fifty years later, it was replaced, but what they discovered is that the basement is still active!"

"Ghosts again, Mar?"

"Not the same though. These are the Cadavers of Confident Displeasures. They followed a beacon across the river that a practitioner used to attract lost souls. As they arrived, he provided them refuge in the basement. Unknowingly, the cadavers were misled by the practitioner, who turned out to be some sort of – *Lusus Naturae*. Anyways, he had this very tormentous relationship with nature and used the cadavers to combat the climate – real hardcore stuff."

"You believe all this jaw, Mar?"

"Kind of romantic, don't you think? I don't really believe in ghosts, but I guess I could pretend."

"To think that we have to go through this again."

"Pardon? No, we haven't."

"Mar, this is the same fasherie I've been puckled to reckon with every Valentine's Day, all because you don't take your sanity pills."

"This is nonsense!" Mia nervously laughs, pulling on her hair ends, "I've never been like that, taking any pills or something."

"You became enamored over some derelict captain who had a smarmy reputation as a weather profit."

"This is ridiculous. I never did any of this. You're trying to twist my words. I told you! I don't believe in ghosts; I just think they're cute. Besides..." Mia sets the book down. "While we are on the topic of insanity, what about your crazy entanglement with Sam last night? You specifically said you were not interested in her."

"What?! How do you know this?!"

"I was there orchestrating it! Remember, with the flashlight?"

Bo is having a false interpretation of what took place at the club last night. But what if Mia is correct? Thirty years have passed, and he cannot help but think there could be a change in the situation. He closes his eyes hard, trying to focus on his beloved, but all he can see is Samantha. This is not going to happen! He cannot abandon his thoughts of Beatie. Not after spending so many years thinking about her. There is only one way to get his mind corrected. If he is going to have any wrongful dreams, he will need a charm.

"We're going to Qui Qua's, Mar!"

"Shopping? You don't have to convince me, but it's Monday – late afternoon even."

"Monday? How did we get to Monday already?"

Bo lifts the switch, illuminating a room that once resembled a small, single-family residence. Where there were once walls, there are now long, vertical aisles of produce and assorted jars, the contents of which are unknown without labels. Other former rooms are not so well visited. Such as the former boudoir, where red-stained coverings hang from rusty chains. Even the front room is stocked with oddities that few would expect; and most certainly hard to come by in the twenty-first century. Not just shrunken heads, but full anatomies stripped to the bone and their organs labeled for rituals.

The secret room is the place Bo is most interested in, and he knows who he needs to speak with. It has been alleged that the man who owns this store is in possession of a large collection of spiritual artifacts, many of which were obtained by an explorer's last breath. They are rare and heavily priced, this Bo knows. He also knows that few have ever seen this man and that he cannot be received directly by name. It is a game that must be played, one by establishing trust through another's uniqueness. This game begins with the girl behind the counter.

"I was thinking later, you know, a roast would be nice with some weird toppings. Maybe pees this time, a fizzie, and some tattie's."

Mia has her own agenda, making off down the aisle of soft produce while stuffing items into a hand basket. Bo distances himself from her for the time being. He picks up a newspaper from the display stand with headlines that have nothing to do with the days to come. Its use is a distraction for questions he must ask in secrecy. He rings the bell at the counter and listens for a response.

"Welcome, governor, I am yours," says the yawning, irritably achieved, thirteen-year-old girl sleeping beneath the counter. She is noticeably scented in powders of orange blossoms and dressed in clothing – so worn in places, it almost warrants a hole. If not for the added coverage of a long apron and two long tails of braided hair, she would be accused of prostitution.

Mia steps behind Bo and lays her hand on his arm.

"Get a load of this, Bo! The Florida Gazette on the rack is dated August of 1821. Says here:

Mayor Gabriel W. Perpall announces that St. Augustine has officially been named the capital of Florida, as ratified by the Adams-Onis Treaty. Governor Andrew Jackson issues his first order of business by quarantining all arriving ships. His second order of business is to create a new burial site outside the city limits. This will handle the overflow of new arrivals.

"Isn't that a knee slapper?! This city can't get enough of itself."

"She talks too much." Interrupts the young voice behind the counter.

"Surly little girl. Good luck with this one." Mia turns her head and wanders away.

Bo lifts up the daily and casually looks at the headlines; "Do you have any specials on oddities?"

The girl ignores him as part of the game, and instead, takes a portion of his paper and begins flipping through the pages. He has dealt with these matters before and knows to ask again while forcing a burp.

"Do you have any specials on oddities for bad dreams? BURP!"

Seemingly uninterested, she flips through the remaining pages, then responds. "Flats and sharps are on the wall behind me. To your left, trinkets from the east and goblets from the Nile."

Bo makes a separate suggestion by placing his hand under his armpit, flapping down several times, then kicking his legs out in dance, "I'm looking for something more intrinsic."

The girl then tears out a section, throwing the rest of the paper to the floor. She then leaps up onto the counter and performs a squat dance. "To your right, lilies from East Haiti and roots from down under."

Bo drops his pants and lets out a series of loud yelps. "I'm inquiring about something that the professor himself would offer."

She stops her dance and pauses to look at Bo, soon letting out a violently cough. "Setu!" she says, before falling over the counter and rolling around on the floor. She points toward the back of the store while sticking her fingers down her throat. Bo does not wait for her to finish and instead walks quickly toward the beaded curtain.

Mia slaps Bo's raised hand as she passes him by and continues up to the counter, where the girl is mopping the floor. "How about feminine needs?" Mia says snidely, "You know – for mature women."

"Pass the tar barrels, top shelf above the rain nappers, and you'll find Horse Saliva."

"What use would I have for that?"

"It's for debilitated libidos."

Peering through the curtain, where there are a multitude of objects emitting electricity, Bo senses he might be in the right place.

"And to the likes to you, good sir. I'll be with you in a moment," says the lady in a very cultured voice. She wears a long, silk sari that shimmers with gold flecks, baring one shoulder and barely covering the other. Her facial beauty is concealed behind a wide-brimmed fedora, but it is not her identity that he is here for. This lady is an expert in the aura of human forms and knows exactly their purpose just by looking at them. Bo watches and waits as she addresses a couple in the corner of the room. She already knows what they are interested in and holds it before their faces. She will not be long.

Bo touches several glass creatures of an unknown origin. He is alarmed when he bumps into a large demonic sculpture that he knows to stay clear of. It is said that stroking the horn of this sculpture releases an unseen magic. The same magic that entices one to stroke its horn.

Clapping her hands together, the lady finally calls out, "I am yours now, good sir. I specialize in folklore. Above you is the glass talisman. Is that not something desirable for you to touch?"

Bo smirks; he already knows what he is here for, but he also knows the rules he will still have to play. "I have no use for that, good lady. I'm here for Cornelius Bumpkin."

She ignores his request and looks among the other choices, "Amulets of alchemy, perhaps. Said to be used for matters relating to dark chaos." Bo shakes his head firmly.

"You seem to me an educated man," she takes a deep breath and shakes her hands out as if going into a trance. "Yes, so simple. I see now." Setu extends her hands out to create space. She encircles her arms, then brings a fist into her belly, letting out a loud cough. From her opening hand is a small object, iridescent on its own, even without all the gastric juices.

"Once a common possession of the past, now but a crime to display," she passes it to Bo. "The best I have to offer. One dime, but for you, five pence, nothing less."

"It's disgustingly beautiful!" Mia's voice rings out from the curtain she holds aside.

"Out!" yells Setu, motioning to the counter girl to come forward from the check-out counter. "Miss, you are not allowed in here; you're a ...a...girl!"

"So, you're a girl."

"I am not what you believe I am."

"You're a girl from where I'm standing." Mia steps forward and crowds out the enchanter with her hip, then thrusts forward an open palm, "I found something even better! See? It's a chain with sterling bagpipes! Isn't it lovely?"

"Cute, Mar, but I think I have this handled." Bo steps to the side of Mia and addresses the lady once again. "Charmer, I'm looking for a special kind of charm that does not come at a bargain." Bo hands the charm back to the lady and wipes his hand on his pants.

"Let's go, Bo. She's just a stroppy, diddle-meister!"

"Will you please leave us, Miss Mouth?!" The magician clamps down on Bo's arm and closes her eyes. "You are thinking of poultry."

"Do you sell any hogstones or witch balls?!"

"Teuchy!!!"

"Mia!! We discussed this!! I need a charm that keeps away the bad dreams!"

"What I hold before you – is this not what you want? I'm trying to sell it to you for a special price."

Bo is disappointed; he knows that all these charms are gimmicks.

"Mam, Sorry to take your time, we'll be leaving now." Bo turns to leave when suddenly the enchanter takes him by the arm and leads him aside. She removes her hat, revealing a very beautiful Indian face that briefly turns into that of Beatie.

"I wasn't sure about your intentions or the company you keep," turning halfway toward the counter girl, who has now entered the room with a long stick and a wire loop at the end. "Counter girl, please take Miss 'Whiffit' with you and bar the curtain!"

"Sneeze juice!!" Mia yells at Setu, while the little girl seals the loop around her waist and tows her from the room.

"Nose Bagger!!" Setu responds. "The gas goes right to the brain of that one, doesn't it?" The enchanter then lowers her voice. "There are people that come exclusively at night. Always before the call of the rising rooster. One in particular brought a box without a description placed on it. The professor took the box and placed it in the river beneath the boards. He could not say anything further about it, except that it was a doctor who brought the box. A portly man with thin, yellowing hair and elbows for knees. Kind of arrogant and brash that would inspire the dislikes of his neighbors. This doctor said he found this charm on a letter table belonging to one that faced a certain death. Said he was compelled to take it and was sure to deliver it to the right place. So here it lies. I need you to step aside, please!"

The enchanter stands in the center of the floor rolling up a box on a chain. She kneels down and pulls up the dripping box with ocean water and sea chains hanging from it. She then places it on the floor before Bo and unlatches the lid.

"Anyway, this is it. It doesn't glitter or glow." Setu lifts from the box an ordinary rock with a hole through it. "In fact, it appears quite dull."

"It doesn't sparkle because it doesn't want to be found."

Bo reaches out with his hand and takes the object into his hand. Immediately, he feels something pass through him, like an electrical charge made to invigorate his heart. Rolling it back and forth in both palms, he lifts the object with the hole to his eye. He then watches with delight as the magician dances before him naked.

"Aye, it's a fine stone. How much?"

"It's my only one."

"How much?"

"I cannot guarantee it will work."

"I will advise on risky investments."

Bo walks from the beaded curtain with the amulet dangling from his belt hook. Mia too brings up her basket for the attendant to tally up: potatoes, bread, cheese, and several small bags of rice. She then grabs a handful of match boxes.

"What did you buy, Bo?"

Bo unhooks the charm from his belt and lifts it before her.

"You bought a dodgy rock with a hole through it? I'm not going to ask what it cost."

"It's a hogstone and you shouldn't."

The counter girl collects all the items and places them in a bag, "All on one stick?"

"Yes, all together," Mia secretly bumps Bo and directs his eyes toward the back of the room." Have you noticed all of the outdoor supplies in here? It's like they're going to erect a new city or something. Wood, axes, shovels, tar, and gun powder."

The counter girl tallies the goods and looks up, "Migrants from the north caught some disease down here."

"Pardon?" Mia responds with an annoyed look.

"You said you wanted to know why there are so many supplies."

"I didn't actually ask a question. I made a comment to my friend that it appears they're building something here."

"Seems to me a question is coming."

Bo interrupts, "Mar, please. What disease?"

"Can't say. No one's ever seen it. Doesn't particularly like cannon fire. Doesn't like tar either, so we're thinking that maybe one or the both, work. "The counter girl pushes the bag in their direction and smiles, "Seventy-five cents, please."

"For all this?"

"Don't argue with the girl, Bo; just give it to her."

Bo looks at himself in the bathroom mirror, noticing a few gray hairs and some fine wrinkles. He is not feeling at all ill and his smile reveals a similar feeling; so why the look?

Staring out into the night, he feels a cool breeze through the open window. A half-moon is etched into the dark sky and he realizes another day has come to an end. The remaining days will be shorter, as they always are with life in general. So how many more days of light are needed to see what must come true?

Bo hears the room door close, followed by the voice of Mia. "This place is a mess." She kicks her way through the dirty clothing and lifts her shopping bags onto the kitchen counter, "I can't remember if we ate. How about a cuppa? It's a little late, but we don't have to miss out on our afternoon tea."

Bo sits at the edge of his bed, refocusing his attention on Mia. She is waiting for the water to come to a boil, and her eyes are fixed on nothing in particular. It is as if she is dissecting all the unhappiness in her life. She pours the water from the pan into a cup, then warms her nose in the steam.

"Those two at the store really went facial on me. I felt mugged, you know?"

"It's winter here, Mar. Weather is a way to create a bad mood."

"And yet they were both dressed as if it were summer?"

"All the more reason for them to be upset."

Mia pauses to take another sip and looks about the room, "Nice if we had some bathroom towels."

Bo flattens out on the bed and turns over, casting his eyes about the amulet in his palm.

"Still with the amulet? What an odd being you are."

"As foretold by the Seers of Scotland: 'With the eye through the hole of the hogstone, all dreams can create a new happiness.'"

"If you think that rock will help you avoid mishaps, you need to rethink your philosophy. The people you listen to live at the edge of cliffs."

Bo rolls onto his bed and thrusts his hands beneath the pillow. He is immediately struck with horror to find his logbook missing. It's his only constant source of knowledge. He leaps from the bed and checks the pockets of his backpack. The side zipper is open and the logbook is not in there either!

Mia grunts and gives Bo a sour expression. She then lifts his logbook above her head, "Is this what you are looking for?"

Bo is in shock. She has the logbook. Somehow, she has gained access to his most secretive thoughts he has kept hidden. "Mia, you are not supposed to be looking through my things!"

"Maybe so, but maybe you should explain this!" Mia turns the book towards her and lays a finger on the first line. "Tuesday, the sixth of February at Iggie's. It reads here that you chat it up with a girl named Beatie. I don't recall you ever introducing me to a girl named Beatie!" Flipping the pages ahead, "Yet, you have her in this planner every day of this week! There's more! Saturday, the third of February. You write here that I had a mishap at the beach where I sprout horns. Really! Is there something in the plans I'm missing? And oh, this is daft; I'm involved with a Free Society Explorer and fall in love with their leader? Well, isn't that lovely, Free Society Explorers don't have leaders, Bo. Their whole motivation is to avoid an organized structure!" Mia flips the page and frowns. "We haven't done any of these sorts of things: Alligator Farm, Karaoke, and I get into an argument with a ghost tour guide? Is this the kind of sick fiction you write for your friends back home?!"

Bo yanks the logbook from her hand, "There could be dire consequences for the both of us should anything change!"

"Consequences, yes! Everything about what you wrote is a disaster for me! I develop horns, my head resembles a pumpkin, and I have drug-induced illusions?!"

"It's not all bad."

"What constitutes bad in your world, Bo? When everything is planned for my destruction!!"

Bo slowly raises the hogstone to his eye when Mia slaps it out of his hand, "Don't be pulling any of that alchemy squat on me! I have enough to deal with in this logbook!"

Mia marches to the door with an annoyed look on her face. She places the chain on the door and pushes down on the handle. There is a sweetness of lilies looming in the air and a warm voice.

"I never knew this motel had any rooms," says the voice on the other side of the door. "The hallway could use a bit more lighting."

Bo looks over her shoulder while Mia removes the door chain. He sees the beautiful margins of a guest take shape and immediately feels an electrical shock pulsate through his body. A smile grows large on his bedridden face. It is her! The girl he had so mistakenly left thirty years ago. Never in fifty thousand faces has one mesmerized him quite like hers. It is that precious beauty that a dying man can only pray for in his final moments of life. Bo kisses the amulet and rises to his feet.

The lovely girl addresses Mia with awkward politeness, "Mia, right? I like how you decorated your room."

"Yes, hiya love."

"I brought you something," she says to Bo, reaching down to remove her heels. She takes as many criss-crossing steps as she can, being careful not to touch any of the fallen garments. Halfway there, she finds a clear path in the melee and scurries into a small space before Bo.

She is so mesmerizing, he can hardly afford to blink. How beautiful his thoughts of her have always been. The bright silver colors on the corner of her eyes, and her lips, so soft and curled like a bow.

Beatie's hand rises quickly, striking the side of her head. It causes her to drop a small, laminated card to the floor. Kneeling down, she lifts it straight up into Bo's nose. The sudden pain doesn't even cause him to flinch. Even if she were to blind him, he would still feel all the more satisfied that she be his final vision.

"Your roommate left your identification card with me. I thought it was just me being stupid, but I realized Mia was being stupid too."

Mia rolls her eyes, throws up her hands, and takes several long, heavy steps back to the kitchen.

"How did you know where I was staying?"

"Well, Mia said you were staying in St. Augustine. I have been to each motel in the city, saving this one for last. It's haunted, you know."

"Bo! Why don't you offer her a seat?" Mia sets a chair down on the kitchen floor and pushes it forward.

"No, I better go. It's all about Sundays, you know – things to do." Beatie covers her mouth and giggles. "I have to clean my room and put away my clothes."

Beatie gives Bo a bent wrist and a soft handshake, twisting her mouth in thought: "I don't have any plans for tomorrow. Do you like spicy foods and local beers?"

"About 10:00 a.m.?"

"You read my mind." Beatie lifts her leg in a ballet pose, spins three times, and scurries out the door.

Mia claps her hands together and lifts herself up from the chair, "Well, that was different!"

"You gave her my ID, Mar?"

"Not like you noticed. You were drunk and fruity with Sam."

Bo falls backward on his bed, looking starry-eyed at the ceiling, "Great, it's not over then."

"So, this is the girl I met at the club? So, all the time, Sam and I were waiting for you in Charleston, New York, Boston, and Perth; you were off mouth-mushing with locals."

"But did you see how her feet barely touched the floor, like an angel on training wheels?"

"This is okay with you? Is this how you would like to imagine yourself treating your friends? Encourage me, Bo! You are like a balloon following the path of least resistance, women coming from every direction just to fill your head with hot air, then off you float to the next town, where they blow in your ear again, just enough so your fat head can get you to the next town. Is that you, Bo? Are you that fat-head balloon?"

Bo looking starry-eyed, "Aye a balloon you say? If I only had a charm for that."

"Don't rage me, Bo!! Don't do it!!" Mia raises her clutched fist and shakes it tight. "You're a real wanker! That is the girl in your log book! That is the girl you had planned to meet at the club! That is the girl you were supposed to spend the evening with! This is why she is here, and this is why she'll be stopping by every night for the foreseeable future, until she finally moves in with us and uses up all of your money!!" Mia covers her mouth and turns away with a sniffle, "All along, I have been climbing the crooked steps toward great expectations with you, only to find that those very crooked steps are broken and crumbling and lead to nowhere but a sinkhole! You wasted my life and you can't even see that!" Mia covers her face and lets out a sob.

Bo raises himself up onto his elbows, realizing that he again has been behaving inconsiderately. He holds the hole of the amulet before his eye, tilting it toward the emotionally broken Mia, until her deflated features take on a more joyous transformation.

Mia sits up on the edge of her bed, wiping her face and blowing her nose into the bedsheets. She clears her throat of the raspiness and pauses, "Woo Hoo! Woof! That got pretty corny, didn't it?"

"Aye, it did."

"And the llama says? I've never behaved like that before – crying and all?"

"Not the crying."

Mia grabs the nearest chair and places it next to Bo's bedside. Bo looks at her cautiously, nervous even, wondering what he might have created.

"I think the weather is going to be much warmer in the next few days, don't you agree?"

Bo nods his head slowly, "I believe your right, Mar."

"At Sammie's house? This was the girl you spoke of?"

Bo nods again, holding his words.

Mia's head falls forward onto his shoulder, then her eyes roll up to look into his. "I am hoping – just hoping – you will be honest with me and tell me that this girl here tonight has been a dear companion of yours well before you ever met me or Sam. Am I right?"

"Of course, that is what I could say."

"Lovely." Mia leaps onto her bed. "I'm okay with that. Sam, however, might not be."

FEBRUARY 6: HOW ABOUT A FAIR AND A TALE?

Bo steps onto the sidewalk wearing freshly ironed slacks and a button-down tropical shirt. The bright white leather shoes he once admired on his uncle are a perfect accessory, as are the green gargoyle socks his father once wore. Compliments of his fine memory.

She walks through the smell of flowering bushes by the roadside, as the seedlings from the mimosa trees take flight to decorate her hair. It seems all the floral smells in the city want to gravitate toward her, most notably the various scents in the floral shops that open their doors to her presence. Bo crosses his hands behind his back, and immediately, a few flowers materialize. Beatie elevates her feet and takes them up to her nose, "Yes, I love these!"

The car kicking over makes Beatie smile. She rolls down the window of her beetle-shaped vehicle and immediately releases the child from her restraints. She has absolutely gone mad, bouncing between the sidewalk and the road, swerving around a trolley, and wheeling past a sanitation truck. It is only after the high-speed chase of pooping geese that she finally steers her way back onto the road.

He does remember her better than she knows, and he is enjoying this wildness in her. And why not? His outlook had become dull and bleak, with his own identity lost to consuming friends. But now she has brought him back to the memories and vigor he once experienced in his youth. Memories he was proud of but could never share with self-centered companions.

She circles the roundabout one last time, then falls back into her seat with a hearty laugh. Her face now preparing for the next excitement. Beatie slaps her hands together and stamps her feet on the floor. She is going to need all the boost she can get if she is going to make it into the pillows of the sky. With plenty of 'Ooohs' and 'Aaahs' and a song that includes a lot of squealing, Beatie steers the car in a zigzag motion, hoping to prevent the car from drifting backward. After a few stalls and a reverse thrust, the car does reach the top, and one foot goes out the window, and the other goes on the steering wheel. Beatie even adds a rubber nose and plastic glasses to her face in an exuberant triumph of silliness.

About Beatie, this he knows: flowers in the afternoon and candy in the morning; her favorite restaurants serve Cordyceps; and she likes the general chit-chat about the town. She does not like, however, restaurants with too many varying tones or flowers that grow wild in the cracks of the streets, nor does she care for candy that makes her chew with her mouth open.

They go where the scenery is most gradual, by way of the north road and the west ferry. A bit further it comes to an end and more smiling continues. Visitors, with their packed picnic baskets, garden shoes, and smock-covered bodies, quickly fill the lawn. There is seafood to be served in a variety of cookware to be brought. There are paintings – live and prepared; caricatures of faces gone wild; and drawings of boats that tell the story of a long journey.

The warmth in the air is energizing, and Bo can't help but shake as many hands that are held out to be shaken. Unfortunately, after the tenth person, his mind wanders considerably, and soon he stands before an overdressed lady wearing a large-brimmed hat and tropical earrings. He has met her before, and it has always led him to an unfortunate loss of employment.

"Get the cameras on these two, Graphie!" the lady yells with hurried feet.

"Beatie, we better get a going. I've heard unkind words about nosy people with brightly lit snappy's."

Bo takes Beatie's hand and makes the quick dash across the crowded lawn, hurdling over baskets and pole vaulting over condiment tables. Regrettably, his escape is nowhere in the making. The crowd refuses to part any faster than the camera crew that is willing to follow them.

"Beatie, I'm not very good with these people."

"Just say whatever comes to mind. Have fun with it; it's not like we'll ever see them again."

Bo closes his eyes and turns around.

"Prindy Reeshmen from Ghost City News! Did I hear correctly that you talk funny?"

"Baueregard Heathan Fox, be thy name; near-a-by Durness."

"Get a close shot here, Graphie. Let's figure out how we are going to do this without making it too cheeky. So, is flattering a Floridian woman what brought you here to our Valentine's Day celebration?"

"My best flattery is on Bessie, the neighborhood cow; and Jasper, the chocolate mountain, Scottish fold."

"Scottish fold? Being the little, furry domestic animal?"

"Aye, her trews are black and caramel with white socks, and she has a twitchy tail. The cow just likes the hay."

"And were you able to continue these experiments on women over there?"

"I found alcohol works better."

"So, Mr. Fox, what can you tell our viewers about Scotland?"

"I've been a theorist of non-consensual humor; but before that I was a jobby at a chocolate factory." Bo looks over at Beatie who is gesturing he is doing well.

"Let's continue with this. How do you make your chocolates?"

"The Heilan coo – big furry beast with shaggy, brown hair and oversized, pointy horns. They make all kinds of milk depending on what they get into."

"Graphie, erase that! And your parents?"

"James and Martha Mills, be thy names!"

"Aw, that's nice, I bet you can't wait to see them when you return."

"Ney, the shovel's only for the first time around."

Beatie blurts out a laugh and turns her head away.

The reporter throws up her hands and leans into Bo, "Tighten up on the picture here, Graphie! Young man who works as a theorist at a chocolate factory, poison's cat, and does away with his folks... and that's a wrap."

Beatie claps her hands in joy, "Well, that went surprisingly well; you sure sold them a story."

Beatie's face soon becomes lifeless. She can't blink anymore. She can't look at him either, at least, not without leaving her mouth open. Maybe it has to do with starting to like him, or maybe it's because of his thoughtful kindness, sociability, and politeness. Also, maybe it's his ability to answer questions in a thoughtful manner well before she finishes the sentence. Preparedness is not expected with this species, which is maybe why she likes him. Not sure.

Under a yellowing sky, following the afternoon light into a small market town, it is the smell of a bakery drifting into the street that sets the mood for a fine meal. They hold hands before an eatery that tempts them to savor one of their plates, both semi-aware that tourists are trying to find a way around their unshakeable clasp. Bo's attention is fully on Beatie now, and he doesn't feel the least impolite for his part in agitating his distractors, for there will be no separation from her now. He knows that in the jewelry stores, there is nothing that outvalues her. In the eateries, there is no aroma that can be more pleasing than hers. In actuality, there is no air that he can breathe that would sustain a life without her. She is the eternal source for which he now exists, and anything she wants, she only has to speak the words, wave a hand, or bat an eye, and then he will bring forth anything she desires for as long as she appears.

And of Beatie too, not understanding herself why she has to be so resolute and impolite, even ignoring the peril the two face with the early coming of darkness. Already, a shadow is growing about Bo's feet and is slowly making its way up his leg. It almost makes her laugh when it tries to demonstrate there is no cause for concern, except there is. Darkness is exposing its intentions right there in plain sight. How terribly rude and selfish it is behaving, trying to end a companionship that she has truly longed for since puberty. Purposely testing her patience with what she clearly finds to be encouraging violence! This makes her want to act out; it makes her want to scream; but even more so, it makes her want to... SLAP!!! "I'm so sorry!! Are you okay?"

"What did you do that for?"

"I know. It's not your fault! Did it hurt? Check your teeth." Beatie pulls a compact mirror from her pocket book and holds it to his face. "It's just these issues I have with these malicious images that tend to grow and grow. Like, well, you see, right there on the ground almost."

"You are referring to a shadow?"

"If you follow my finger, see how it's starting up your leg, and now to the other leg. Turn to your side. See how it's growing along the right side of your body, then up the left side. Now it's touching your arm, and now it's touching – AAAHH!! Don't absorb me, Bro!!" .... SLAP!!!

Bo stumbles back and forth, trying to regain his feet.

"I'm so sorry, I did it again! It's not that I like doing it <SLAP>. Well, maybe a little bit. But look, there's more!!"

Bo covers his head while Beatie swings wildly away; finally, taking hold of her hands while leading her out into the open sunlight, "Okay! Okay! So, you're afraid of shadows"

Beatie slips her hand into her purse and pulls out her sunglasses, "And you don't mind?"

Bo looks for an answer in the sky somewhere, then mumbles.

"I know what you are thinking. I have a few character flaws, but I'm almost sure this is the worst of them."

"It's okay, I have flaws too."

"Really?" Beatie can hardly believe what she just heard. In all of her fantasies he is supposed to be perfect, and in no way do her novels suggest there could be any flaws. Could this be flattery? Maybe trying to make her feel extraordinarily special and not so far from different? Beatie then has to look deeply inside his face, just to be sure what he is saying is not normal. True, she hardly knows him, but he does have those thoughtful eyes, and she is pretty certain about his smile too, even though it doesn't bend evenly like it should. What if he's not lying? Or maybe even better, what if he is pretending not to be perfect, just to make her feel exceptional? Could this mean – Uh, Oh? What if this is about a kiss? Bet it is.

<SLAP>

And once a commitment seems to be within reach, she disappears again. Disappointment hardly defines what he is feeling. The slap was most unexpected. An obstacle he did not see coming.

Bo leans back on his elbows, looking out the dark window of the motel. He hears the sound of small chatter going on in the street and leans forward to open the window. A blistering cold is what he feels next, and it leads to an uncomfortable pain that grows between his eyes, "Ow!!!"

"Hey, you from Scotland. It's me!"

"Who is me?!" Bo replies to the dark parking lot below.

"Me! The one who you are planning to see again. Like almost now, even!!"

"What evening is this, '*Me*'?"

"I don't know; I didn't have to work, so I guess it's my Super Sunday!!"

"You always throw stones at folk?"

"If you had left the window closed, we'd probably be drawing a different conclusion!!"

What a bumptious girl. He absolutely loves her. Bo looks over to see Mia snoring in her bed with her arms and legs sticking straight out. Leaning his head out the window, he quietly calls back, "Me? Isn't it scary before sunrise?"

"I ain't afraid of nothing now!!!"

"Shhh." Bo waves his hands, "Okay. Okay. I'll be down." He watches her clap her hands in joy, then closes the window and makes a quick change into Scottish beach wear. Slipping his amulet into his pocket, he is out the door, down the steps, and into the parking lot, where she is once again smiling. Unlike so many times before when he had wished for her. She is so happy and so giddy, and she looks absolutely adorable with her hair tucked beneath a ball of white fur. A bit warmer too, with a long, fluffy white coat and sand-colored Sherpa pants, and yet she neglects to wear proper footwear, preferring to march about in naked feet.

"Ready to go? We'll take the car over to Vilano. It's quieter over there."

Bo reaches into his jacket, pulls out his bomber hat, and plops it down over his ears, "I'm ready."

Brushing the car window with her coat sleeve, Beatie reaches across to unlock her car door. She takes her little Beatle Bug by way of the arching bridge, smiling while it hums along with the popping sounds of the carburetor. The night is bright beyond evening standards and a bit chilly too. The moon over the ocean is as large as it could ever be, illuminating the entire eastern sky while casting a long, blazing strip of light across the dark waters.

She doesn't feel embarrassed at all, leaping like a toad and twirling like a whirligig across the sand. She settles down on a clean towel and seductively taps on the blanket. Bo has a stone hanging from his belt loop, but she does not inquire. It is too early to know about things like that.

She moves between his legs and nestles against his body, looking up at the sky. "The moon should never feel so lonely with everyone looking at it," she says, squeezing Bo's hand and touching her nose to his chin. "Tell me a tale."

"Right now?"

"I thought Scots were good at telling tales."

Bo frowns. He has always been horrible at telling tales and is always being misunderstood when trying to explain their meaning. Thirty years ago, the tale of the pregnant lady and the man who had a wife did not go so well. Hoping maybe she'll forget the request; Bo looks out at the ocean for a long while before speaking.

"How nice if we could stroll to the ends of the earth by way of the lit path before us."

Beatie raises herself up to listen. Her eyes wide with anticipation. "This sounds like a good tale!"

"What? No! I have trouble..."

"In English please!"

"Ah, fankle!" Bo looks out at the oceans before him. He starts off slow, using words that hopefully might not get him into trouble.

"A long time ago, when it was the seals that enlightened the world with the stories of the seas, they spoke of the Selkies (ii), who, for one day a year, could shed their shiny fur to walk upon the land as humans. Now it is well known that if a land-walker beheld the Selkie in human form, they would be so captivated by their beauty that a spell would be cast upon them. Land-walkers, having learned that the Selkie's require their fur to return to the sea, stole them to ensure their captivity. This so happened to one Selkie, who one day was out singing and playing in the grass beneath the waters. Unaware he was out beyond his limit, he was caught by surprise by a storm that sent him crashing into the rocks. By the time the sky had dried, a landwoman further down the beach – much older than he, mind you – found him in the shallows of a grass-laden pool. Weakened and very much without his fur, she gathered up all his tattered, soft hair."

"What was she wearing?"
"What? Maybe gutties and civvies?
"English again!"
"Sure. A wide rimmed floppy hat, laminate coveralls, and boogie boots."
"Ooh, I could never afford one of those. Sounds evil."
"Yes, and she is. Yes, she is!"

"She is very much engrossed with this species of man, and of course, the Selkish man pleads with this woman to fix his fur, but all she can think about is how this man can increase her social status. So, she takes him home."

"Without any clothes?"
"Stark naked, and she bathes him in seawater and shows him the way with her hands." Bo looks down at Beatie to see her face all scrunched up. "What's wrong?"
"I don't very much like Selkies."
"But how? They are cute and cuddly, just like animals that make you say silly, baby things."
"But he's nude!"
"But it was not his fault. He lost his clothes and she took them."
"Yes, but no. I know men like that."
"But you don't understand ..."
Beatie gets up and sits at the other end of the towel. Bo can already see he is returning to the same errors of his past. He can't seem to change what has always been a part of him. This requires a new approach. Bo immediately unlatches the hogstone from his belt and slowly raises it to his eye.
"I don't need a rock!" Beatie suddenly appears before him, slapping his hand away. "Explain!!"
Bo takes a deep breath. "Umm. So, the land-walkers, you see, are not of their right mind. Their world is in favor of the dissatisfaction for others."

"Fooey times infinity!! Don't get political with me. It's the same old story: A naked man meets a naked lady for premarital sex and ends up leaving their backs bent out of shape!"

Bo sees that deep look of concern on her face. The tale is slipping away, and yet the amulet rests at the edge of the blanket. He can still make a roll for it, but... what if he doesn't need it? He is a different man now. He has had that long self-examination that allows him the confidence to speak.

"You know how you see a dress you like, but somebody else buys it, so you can't?"

Beatie's mouth shifts, but she doesn't say a word. She instead shuffles a deck of cards that somehow materializes in her hands.

"The lady turns out to be the Wikkity Witch of Barbie, and she ignores the Selkie's desires to return to the sea. Not only that, she dislikes anyone with secondhand clothing."

Beatie's ears suddenly perk up to resume listening, but continues with her game of solitaire.

"She thinks of him to have little culture by the way he shuffles his feet with his arms out! And that constant affinity for shellfish – she doesn't like that either. Of course, he speaks of leaving, but the Witch of Barbie is not concerned because she has his clothes. She demands he forget his Selkish ways, and so she dresses him in the finest of wear and shows him her way of life at the sex clubs and cigar bars. Then she plans a gathering that night with all her pretend friends to hear the news that she intends to marry the Selkie!"

"But he hardly knows her!"
"True, but there is nothing he can do, because she has her way.

But the Man-Selkie loves another and knows that she doesn't care how he appears before false friends, and every Valentine's Day, he returns to the beach, undresses, and stands staring at the ocean. A wish to go ahead, even without his fur."

Beatie's stares ahead with a look of concern, "But he'll drown."

"True, but at least he would be with her one last time. In the world of adoration, there is only one thought that matters, and that is to be with the one for which we adore."

Bo slides over to Beatie and takes the cards from her hands, looking deeply into her eyes.

"He will never stop looking at her, because it might be the last time he ever sees her, and he will always choose the right words, because they may be the last words he will ever say to her."

Beatie looks up at Bo with gentle eyes, "and all this was said?"
"True."
Beatie turns her head away with wide eyes, "Wow."

"But for whatever reason, what some find in beauty, others find in contempt. The fear of losing the Selkie turned to revenge. Frustrated, the witch decides to attack the Selkie's character by providing a false witness with which he cannot defend. Taking pictures of a real seal in lingerie, she shows them to her false friends, and instantly, they attack him, trip him, and pull his pants down in the middle of the street."

"No, they can't do that!"
"But it does not work, because he is already comfortable without pants."

So, the coming Valentine's Day, the Selkie decides he must return, and once again, on a stormy day, he makes his way to the ocean's edge, where he plays with his bagpipes and sings: '*Grant me a wish that my eyes should be so bright as to see the beauty of my love in this foul, weather night.*' At that very moment, a light glares through the angry clouds, revealing his beloved in the ocean water. That is also when the witch suddenly appears, holding a fire stick to his fur."

Beatie slams her hands down in the sand and puts Bo in a headlock. She then forcibly rubs her knuckles into his scalp, "Not if I have anything to do with it! I'll head-squeeb her!!"

"Ow, my lass, my neck."

"Not until I hear the story gets better!"

Bo waves his hand and spurts out windless words, "Okay, the witch doesn't get her way."

"She doesn't?" Beatie releases Bo and sits with her legs crossed in the sand.

"No, she doesn't." Bo pushes his neck back into place, and then continues to hurry through the tale.

> "Seeing the witch, the She-Selkie in the ocean swims to shore to wrestle back the man's fur, but in the exchange, the witch wrestles away the She-Selkie's fur, thus leaving them with the one fur. The two Selkies then swim away, forever embraced in the one fur, never to return as humans. The End."

"So let me understand this. They both turn back into one seal with two heads, four fins, and two tails?"

"Aye, and they don't care, for they have each other."

"Hmm. And the witch gets to keep the Selkie fur?"

"True."

Beatie races down to the water's edge, having an animated discussion with herself. She soon returns to Bo with her analysis of the story: "So this man likes rare clothing, and this woman thinks his clothes would look better on her, then when he returns to his room, he finds she is wearing his clothes. She refuses to take them off, and in the struggle, he ends up with his shirt and pants, and she ends up with his socks and shoes?"

"I could not have told it any better."

Beatie suddenly leaps into the air and runs around in circles, celebrating the story by howling and pawing at the moon. She then returns to Bo and places her arms on his shoulders. Her gentle, doe-like eyes signal that she is ready for that kiss.

"Just a passing thought," Beatie says. "I would like to see a Selkie one day."

Bo gives a disappointed frown, "Me too."

She backs away up the beach, while a white mist descends upon her image. The mist eventually dissipates, leaving behind the light in his motel room.

"Haste ye back soon, my love."

FEBRUARY 7: DANCE OF THE AUGGIE'S

Bo's eyes widen when he feels a rock digging into his side. He did have the charm at his disposal, but he chose not to use it. Maybe because the hogstone doesn't work that way. It supposed to protect him against bad dreams, not makes the nice dreams better.

He reaches into the feathers of his pillow and pulls out his logbook. His first date with Beatie did not result in a kiss either, so crosses out the line about Beatie being a 'baby wacko'. It was a childish and immature thought at the time anyways.

Bo rolls over to see Mia wearing a night cap with a ball hanging from the tip. Is this his mind playing tricks on him, or is Mia really wearing a flea furry smock and Schnabel shoes? A court jester's attire. She has a harassed look on her face; one she has maintained through the night. It has her pestering the water pipes with a disjointed stick.

"What are you doing, Mar?"

She lifts her head up, looking at him with a sad, defeated look. "Remember 'The Great Baldaldo' on SBS in Australia? It was a three-part series about a man's technique to silence the noises inside his walls. They advertised it for weeks. Anyway, a man used a forked rowan stick and added an enchantment for effects. I was engaged through the entire first few episodes, but then they canceled the series the following week." Mia pushes away the ball from her cap and rubs her tired eyes, "Now I know why."

Bo lifts his bedsheets and sees he is still fully clothed with his boots on. "It's Wednesday, Mia-Mar. Sam's dance is tonight."

Mia looks up with an electrified face, "That's wonderful news!!! We can wear those outfits we bought at that second-hand store!"

"I'd be more than happy to take that shower you've been requesting."

"You would do that for me?" Mia makes a short skip with her feet. "If you are going to have a new smell, then a new hair style might work for me!"

"Great news." buttoning his collar.

"Where are you going?"

"I'm going to ask Beatie where you can get your hair done!"

"Her again? Aren't you relying on her too much already? What about Sam and myself?"

"Can you tell her?" grabbing his cap.

It turns out to be a nice day with the sunlight on everything. These are the perfect thoughts to be having. He is feeling comfortable in the city of old, as if it were native to him. Every turn he finds himself on the same familiar streets with a distinct recollection of the people he once knew. The pipe smokers on the balconies, the ladies chattering in the tea shops, and on the park benches, the old timers are clapping and chirping to children stomping about the lawn. These curious details he remembers.

He holds his head high and swings his arms until flowers appear, then he sniffs the flowers to ensure they are fresh.

Her work outfit is a light blue emblem jacket, and her hair is rolled beneath a white baker boy hat. She wears chain-ball earrings of her own choice, but the knee-high, white go-go boots, along with the short, green skirt, are all part of the required dress for Wednesdays. Bo looks in the window and sees Beatie suddenly straightening up with a flushed look on her face. There is a formally dressed man behind her, trying to release his fingers from the entanglement in her hair.

Beatie advances toward the door, opening it slightly, "It's the gal-sneaker from Scotland. Are you stalking me? Not that I mind."

"I wanted to see that you actually have a job and get a keek at the fellow that would hire you."

"And that's all well and good, but I'm more interested in the salesperson who sold you that hat."

Bo smiles and stuffs his hat into his jacket, then hands her the flowers. It brightens her face to see him again, and even more so when he comes with a gift. The owner of the establishment with the creepy fingers is not so thrilled and inquires immediately.

"Beatie, who is this inquisitor?"

"Our first customer, Mr. Happiness! I am following your instructions to be more aggressive." She releases Bo from a hug and winks at him.

"Keep up the good work then," the owner returns to the back office and Bo quickly makes his proposal.

"I want to see if another date is in order."

The manager reappears at his door with a look of concern, "Beatie, is there some holdup?"

"Uggh! No, Mr. Happiness!"

Bo looks at her quizzically, "Mr. Happiness?"

"It's just his name; it doesn't mean it's true."

"Beatie?"

"I am offering a tour to this traveler who is in town for..." she pauses and turns to Bo.

"As long as it takes to win your heart."

Beatie covers her mouth to hold back a laugh, then quickly composes herself, "Through Valentine's Day, Mr. Happiness. I am showing which sites are best." Beatie reaches into her drawer for a map and directs her attention toward Bo. "Now, this is where we are and this is where you are going..." Beatie waits for the door to close, then sits on her knees behind the desk.

"I'm so glad you stopped by. I'm not sure how you plan your meals in Scotland, but here in America, we have what we call dinner. I was wondering if you would like to go to one of my favorite restaurants in the city. It's Indian food from India, but they make it here."

Bo raises his hand, and she replies, "Yes?"

"What about a dance?"

"Yes, of course!" clapping her hands in joy. "The Dance of the Auggies held outside the cemetery! It has become really popular with the recently deceased."

"No, I was thinking a classical dance at a friend's workplace this evening."

Beatie pulls Bo's hat out of his pocket and throws it to the floor, then leaps around it in circles, "Does it require dancing around a hat?"

Mr. Happiness now watching them with the glasses on the tip of his nose.

"Shhhh, look what you made me do!" Reaching out to Bo, she pulls him beneath her desk and rolls onto her back. "Sounds super, but I don't know how I can get there with my car having trouble."

"No worries. Meet at the corner of Boulevard and First; half pass six?"

Beatie looks down at the phone ringing, "Can you answer that, Mr. Happiness, please?"

Beatie's boss can be seen squeezing his hands into a fist before shutting the door to his office.

"I have to ask a favor. Do you know where my roommate can find a barber?"

"Of course," Beatie reaches up to the desk and grabs a pen and paper. "I use Parfie Der Barbeeb on Make Street. It is south of the city, on the other side of the park. He refers to himself as some kind of a hair goddess."

He prances about the room, flapping his arms and lifting off on a pair of thick-healed Venetian clogs. The barber, with very dark skin, a black vest, and a manicured pompadour, is quite occupied with shaping the golden spirals of Mrs. Giggletree's hair. He leaps behind another chair to lift the curls off Mrs. Picklemeyer's ears, then onto bleaching the brows of Ms. Figglechoker.

Mia anxiously claws her fingers around the window where adverts are blocking her view. She is trying to get a better idea of the atmosphere inside.

"This is it?" pulling back from the window. "I was expecting a queue, Sam."

"Mia, this is the only Beautiful Barber Shop in the area, and it is here on Lake Street. I don't know of any Make Street in St. Augustine. There are three people in there, and they look rather old. I mean, casket-ready old. Are you sure you want to get your hair done here?"

Mia taps her fingers on the window, "What do to? I know what we'll think. We'll walk in, pretend to be one of their grandchildren, and if I like the place, I'll stay and get a haircut. If not, we'll walk out when one of them is ready to leave."

"That's ridiculous! If you don't like the place, let's just leave."

"I don't want to offend anyone, Sam. Just play along."

Noisy is the silent word that enters both of their minds when they enter the shop. Though there are only the three elderly faces and a barber, the air is plenty chatty with senseless talk about health issues.

"Hi, Grandma!" Mia calls out before taking a seat by the door.

The three ladies reach for their spectacles to get a better look at the two girls before returning to their chatter.

Mia looks about the room, noticing five flowerpots on display with numbers on them. She is fascinated to know that these are hairstyles meant to mimic a botanical garden. When the barber spins Mrs. Giggletree around in 'Flower Pot Number Four', Mia cannot help but feel overwhelmed by the blooming Azalea's and a path of fertilizer forged in the middle of her scalp. She can actually feel the Miracle Growth stimulating the roots on her own scalp.

Sam is aghast, "Mia, what kind of license would allow someone to dig up a section of a yard and place it on top of someone's head? We better go."

"Sam, just calm down. I truly believe this barber of earthal structures can finally bring forth the naturalistic look I've been yearning for!"

When the humidifier shuts off, the elderly retreat into the dark corners of the room, to which the barber replies, "They are off to let their hair take root, Madam. This chair is for you."

The barber unlocks his desk drawer and pulls out a wire brush, signaling Mia to sit down. Mia floats across the floor and climbs into the chair, sliding back and forth for a little extra comfort. Feeling so giddy, she lifts off with her feet and revolves around and around until the chair sticks.

"Mr. Der Barbeeb, I am here to have my true identity revealed. I have been thinking it should be representative of rigor and growth. I am thinking earthy and mountainous. I want a Honey-Bee hair-do!"

"The barber chuckles, "You mean a beehive."

"Yeh, that's it!"

The barber tilts her head sideways and grabs a few strands of hair, "Well, there is not enough hair here for a full hive," tweaking her ring-less earlobe, "and the condition of your hair and the small size of your head will not lend themselves to extensions."

The barber steps back for a moment, "However, I do have an idea. If I can raise the sides, pluck a little from the neck, and bind it with some split ends on the forehead...," he rubs his chin and lightly pushes down on the top of her head, "...I can create a 'pancrustacean hexapod lair!' See here, by invigorating your roots, and then....," the barber sings out, "...mold them into a crescendo while solidifying it with reinforced fencing - magnifichismo!"

"I like the sound of that! It's like some sort of vision! What do you think, Sam?!"

Sam's mind is elsewhere, but she looks up from a magazine and squints her eyes, "Mia, I don't think this is the right time for a 'new look'. Get something that is more current with the town vibe. Like the sporty bob you see at all the fancy parties today."

"Well, La-Di-Di- Da, Sam," Mia says, turning her hand over and over again. "Even at a fancy party, one does not have to look the same to be treated differently. Most would want to be treated even better than different, than the way they were when they first looked the same. I'm speaking of a difference that far extends the uniqueness of one's inner separation. Even beyond the boundaries in which we find ourselves with similar abnormalities. We should be determined by our expression of originality and not by our quest to be comparable to what some truly believe are our differences.

"Ouch!!" Mia winches as the barber removes his entangled fingers from her hair.

"Now I'll go ahead and prep this, Miss Mia." The barber marks her hair with a thick blue marker, pulling bobby pins from his closed mouth and placing them in various areas around her head. The unexpected pain is a bit concerning, but Mia listens to every word the barber has to say and is still quids in when he reaches for a garden tool in the storage cabinet.

The barber stands with a wide smile, "Now you see the beginnings of perfection! Build it and the termites will come."

"Termites?" Mia looks up into the mirror. "I thought we were talking about bees."

"You want something earthy and mountainous, am I right?"

"Yes, but I don't want just a pile of dirt dropped on my head. I'm really thinking about a fairy tale setting here. Something indicative and animate to your own country."

The barber murmurs to himself, followed by a grin, "I'll return."

Mia looks over at Sam, seated comfortably in the chair and reading a magazine. She now can confront Sam about her insipid infatuation for Bo. On the level to which Mia can insult someone, there are generally no boundaries. This will be difficult for Sam. She will be testing their relationship, which has continued for five years now.

Mia unhooks the start of some fencing around the side of her head and swings her legs over the arm of the chair. "There is something different about Bo, have you not noticed?"

Sam looks up and tosses the magazine into an empty chair, "I thought it was just me!"

"I am constantly having to remind him of how often his absences are affecting our group. I was really hoping my mention of it would lead to a correction, but it hasn't. He can be absent-minded, and I do understand that, but to exert this kind of rejection on a daily basis seems intolerable at best."

"It was Bo's decision to send us here, wasn't it, Mia?"

"Is this not who he is?"

"He seems so immature sometimes. He didn't even look at me at the barbeque."

"Clearly another attempt to make us feel unwanted."

"He's just not possible!"

"He's not even conceivable, Sam. I really do think you should find someone else."

"What? What are you talking about?"

The barber re-enters the room pushing a cart lined with operating utensils and clean cutlery.

"La-di-di-da," the barber sings as he swings Mia's chair back around to the mirror.

Mia watches carefully as the barber straps her arms and legs to the chair, "Mr. Parfie Der Barbeeb, what opinion do you have about men?"

"Men? What sort of opinion do you need?"

"Well, I'm thinking of a man in confidence who will be known as *Botanio*."

"Ah, so talk to us about *Botanio*. Bad, bad Botanio."

Mia joyfully looks over at Sam now glowering at her, "Lovely! Well, he would be a man of...oh, about twenty-eight years in age; born in February; fifth day of the week – early morning, of course."

Sam stamps her foot and tosses the magazine to the chair, "Mia! Twenty-eight years of age? Pisces? Friday morning at 7:00 a.m.? I know who you are talking about!"

Mia rolls her eyes, "Simply a coincidence, Sam! So, Mr. Barbeeb, he's totally comfortable in backpack wear, prefers to travel with women, and he has this really cute Scottish accent! And yes, he would be the man that would ease my pain, comfort my worries, and dress my needs."

Sam picks up the magazine and throws it across the floor, drawing the attention of the barber.

"Madam Sam, could you come here, please. Thank you. Now lean down on Miss Mia's shoulders, if you wouldn't mind."

"I would be happy to!" Sam grins at Mia and steps up behind the chair. She steps back for a moment, confused at the belts latched to Mia's ankles and wrists.

Mia looks up at the Barber, "True or false? Suppose there is this woman, as quiet as she is, who comes calling for a man that she thinks she can fall in love with, yet fails to see the negative reactions he displays."

"The wrong answer to the right question is always untrue, Madam." The barber leans down behind the chair and pulls on a cord that starts a low engine. "Please step back a little, Miss Sam."

"Woo-hoo!" Mia sits up in her seat. "It just got really warm in here. Isn't it warm in here, Sam?"

Sam's is busy snatching at Mia's hair rising in the air before her face.

"Don't be alarmed, Miss Mia, I'm just setting the ends with a touch of nostalgia."

Mia relaxes for a moment, resting her feet on the foot-bar and feeling the cozy warmth of the barber's fingers against her neck.

"Just what I was thinking, Mr. Darbeeb. I myself have had that bitter taste of false love and that swallowing truth of deception. Both have always left me with that bitter taste of conclusion."

"Stop it, Mia! There's no need for your gruesome choice of a soliloquy! You always speak from this moral high ground! So clear are your own perceptions of people that you end up disclosing why you hate everyone in the first place!"

"That's not true, Sam! You act like I'm writing a screenplay for some noir film."

"I know who you are talking about, Mia! It concerns Bo and me: admit it!!"

The barber leans forward on his toes, forcing Mia to sink down into the seat, "Steady now, Miss Mia."

"Ouch!" Mia's teeth clench.

"See Madam Sam, you pull as far as you can go, just before the root actually pops."

"Ouch!" Mia raises her hand for the barber to halt so she can resume breathing.

The barber wraps a wet towel around Mia's head and requests that Sam step forward. He pushes the chair onto a platform with four circular locks in the floor, then slowly, they descend down into a small, enclosed electrical pit.

"I'm not talking about either of you, Sam. I'm your friend! Friends don't turn on one another, am I right?"

The barber lightly touches Sam's arm, "Push in those rubber blocks beneath the chair, will you? And hand me those wires."

Sam raises an eye brow while lifting her nose to the air, "I smell something burning."

"Put your hands back on the shoulders, contemptuous one. You will both need to be silent during this next phase."

Sam looks down at Mia, who has a disturbed expression on her face.

The barber pulls up a tray and lowers his forehead onto Mia's forehead, then reassures her in a soft voice, "Take a deep breath, little one; we're almost there. I'm going to need you to bite down on this." He places a wooden spoon in her mouth and smiles. "Comfortable?"

Mia reaches around behind the chair, her hands holding hard on to the back of Sam's legs. Her heels are raised with her head tucked down into her chest. The barber then touches his right hand to his forehead, then his chest, then to both shoulders, and looks at Sam, "I am assuming she's Catholic?"

"We'll find out."

Mia clenches her teeth and nods her head. She has agreed to this and knows this is about her hair and not about the pain that is soon to come. There is a very loud, but short, pop as the barber pushes a six-pronged, electrically charged, wire brush through her scalp. Sam looks down at Mia. Her face is bloated and very red. Her eyes are crossed with her lips pursed around the stick. She looks as if her tongue is about to explode through her flapping cheeks.

The barber twists and yanks with sparks flying wildly in every direction, and then suddenly – it comes to an end.

Mia drops the wooden spoon from her mouth and lets out a series of short breaths. Her hands slowly release the grip on the armrests as the barber releases the latches from her arms and ankles.

The chair returns to the shop and Mia sits erect, "Wow! I need a change of clothes after that."

"It always takes a lot out of me too, Miss Mia, which is why I only do one of these a year."

"It felt like I was giving birth."

"And so you were, my dear, with the tool thrusts of my creation."

Sam taps Mia on the shoulder, "That was something, Mia; your face went from completely white to deathly blue. You even blacked out for a moment!"

"She'll be pretty sore and tired for a while. Some bloating and redness will be expected, but most of the swelling should remain outside the tongue."

Without much delay, the barber unwraps the towel from Mia's head and feels along the top and sides.

"No! No! Wait!!" Mia does not want to see her hair right away. Remember, this is how she wants to present herself to the public and to all those who wish to know her true identity.

"Oooh, look at me; I'm all aquiver!" Mia turns slowly toward the mirror. "Okay. I'm ready. No wait! Just wait!! Please!! Before I look, I want a preview from my best friend in the whole world – Samantha Beufort Case."

Sam smiles. A testament spoken of their unity that still remains unbroken to this day. Rocky at best, but smoother rocks can always be found when stepping into an adjoining stream. At least this is how Sam has always understood this.

The barber lifts the two corners of the towel for Sam to view, and with a quick glance, she nervously laughs. "Wow! Mr. Darbeeb. I'd say you've put one in the encyclopedia with this one. And your commitment to animation – again, 'wow!'"

The barber places the towel back down.

"Sam! Don't pussy-foot with me like you always do! Describe what you really see in a few choice words!"

The barber lifts the towel again, and Sam pauses. She steps sideways and backwards, trying to find the exact words to describe her best friend's defining look: "Well, you kind of look like..." Sam makes a faint gesture of uncertainty with her hand.

"Sam!!"

"A North-Going Zax (iii)!"

"Dr. Seuss?"

The barber takes hold of her chair and spins her around several times before letting her come to a complete stop. He then snaps the towel from her head before the street window.

Mia looks carefully at all the street walkers, who at first appear confused, but then become alarmed when their children break off into a panic. Mia cannot help but feel uncomfortable at that moment. Her permanent childhood thoughts of humiliation are suddenly materializing before her eyes.

The fanatical barber then swings the chair around, lays his foot on the break, so Mia can view herself before the mirror, "What happened to beehives and termites?"

"Compromise made me go around it." The smiling barber puts a pair of layered work gloves on and then cups his hands around the sides of her head. "It's the Pompadour Zax. Will that be traveler's checks or food stamps?"

Doctor Cloverly looks down in amazement at the biggest smile he has ever seen on a man's face. A man who has no apparent reason for having one.

"Come, look at this! What could he possibly be smiling about?"

"Possibly a problem?"

"No, laughter is the best medicine. Even a smile can turn away the relentless pursuit of aging."

Though it may not appear obvious, Bo is on his back splitting a belly full of laughter. The caregiver seems to be rejoicing as well, shifting from toe to toe and moving about with a light air beneath his feet. He retrieves a wooden tray filled with cakes and sets it down on the mantle.

"This is very good! I particularly like the spices."

"Anything to help with the healing of Mo Charaid. He is doing better now?"

"He should be smiling for a while. I gave him a shot to increase his cognitive activity. The mind does play a big factor in treating ailments."

The doctor rises from his seat and stretches his arms. He begins breaking sticks over his knee by the fireplace and looks down at the broken shells arranged around the hearth.

"It is still difficult for me to understand the joyous man in the photos about the room to this same man clutching to his life. Caregiver, these eggshells about the hearth – he's not a superstitious man, is he?"

"Witches, sloughs, and wraiths – all need a stopping, you know."

"So, all these collections of oddities are somehow tied to the recovery of this man?"

"I cannot account for all of Scotland, or the whole world for that matter, but in the Sutherland we take dying very seriously."

"That makes no sense to a sensible man." The doctor walks over to the table of papers and finds a damp, bloated logbook. It is held closed by a stone with a hole through it. He flips through the pages and notices the contents are chronologically written up to the fourteenth of February. The very page where there is no entry at all.

"How old would you say he is?"

"I'm not sure. Maybe late fifties."

"This young pictures of him with the young lady?"

"He has me clean that one three times a day. I thought him mad; always staring at it in the morning and before bed."

The doctor approaches the plate on the mantle, lifting several of the deserts and smelling the fruit. He takes one into his mouth, "The drawings, the letters, and the sorrow in his words. This letter written thirty years ago:

I have left a finger print, the only trace of its kind, for I will no longer be here when you read this.

"The letter he was supposed to have left on the windshield of her car."

"And this one, written only a week ago:

These words written beyond the confines of the lines are the very words for which my hand has had trouble accepting. I beg forgiveness for the thousands of miles that I have fled, only to find myself even more discontent. I have but one mind, and with that mind, I am capable of an infinite amount of love, and yet it is also capable of the worst pain that I have ever known. It is with this blessing of pain, however, that I see our future more clearly now with my eyes closed than when they were ever open. I just pray that when I do see you again, it will be as the man I wish I could have been and the woman you were always meant to be. My love to be with you soon. Baueregard Heathan Fox.

The doctor sets the letter down and picks up the logbook, "And this logbook, a discourse of his failures that took place on his travels?"

"I often thought what they were about, but I dare not ask. I have learned much from my friend, but there are thoughts he will not share."

"It might help to know the cause of his condition."

Mia steps from the door of the barbershop to a stirring group of tourists. She ignores their smiling faces as she makes her way to the nearest parked car. Eying the mirror, she brushes her hair from every angle in utter dismay.

"Just look at me, Sam. It's not even soft, and look at this! I even cut my finger!" Mia stamps her foot and shakes her head. "I'm supposed to be dining with royalty in this hair, not using it to clean pots and pans!" Mia covers her face, "I'm not a grumpy old Zax, am I, Sam? You know me best. Is this how people think of me?!"

Sam lays a soft hand on Mia's shoulder, "Truthfully, it's not so bad. Look around you! See all the joy you bring to these people's faces. They didn't come to St. Augustine to wallow in their depressing, oppressed spirits; they came here for an experience that only a Mia Pearl could give them. People of all ages, young and old, will remember this trip as an inspiration to step outside and enjoy life, no matter how they appear"

"You think so? It's really not something I would do back home."

"Mia, you are thinking about this image in a bad light. See it this way: The North-Going Zax is a passionate yet stubborn euphemism, demonstrating one's life struggle to get from point A to point B."

"Yes, I can see that, getting from point A to point B. That has always been a challenge for me, hasn't it, Sammy? Thank you. I'm sorry about the rough comments I made in the barbershop."

"That's alright, Mia. All your comments are mixed up in my head anyways, so forget it."

"Still, it's quite habitual of you when reaching out for the illusion you can't seem to let go of."

"That doesn't soften anything."

"I think this fondness towards Bo is a bit of a fantasy-farce, don't you think?"

"I can't believe this is you! Is this intentional, Mia? Are you making fun of me?"

"I'm just being honest, Sam. Admit it, you're not well." Mia grips her hands together. "So, I was thinking, do you mind if Bo and I go to the dance alone? We'll call you to let you know how everything is going."

"No! Absolutely not! It's my dance! You can't even get into the auditorium without me!"

"That won't be hard. I'm thinking if I dress like you, walk around with that boring demeanor of yours, and greet people like, 'Hi, I'm Samantha B. Case, I want to be your friend for life.'"

"I cannot believe this in you, Mia! This is what a normal person would say behind someone's back, but not you! You've always been inconsiderate, spewing out your evilness in everyone's face!"

"Well, you know me."

"No, I don't. And if I had known you were still infatuated with Bo, I would have never invited either of you. Bo, I would have never invited either of you. You said yourself, you and Bo are just friends, and that your time in 'Aus' was just a trial affair!"

"Oh, spare me the story, Sam. It's not me trying to find myself. I mean, really. Maybe if you practiced a little emotional prudence."

"No! It's not right that you should say those things! That does it! I am never talking to you again!" "And the llama says? Wait! No! Sam, where are you going? Don't crawl under... Lovely, a delivery truck. What are you doing under there?"

"I never ever thought you would ever say those things to me! Never thought it was possible!!"

Samantha won't look at Mia, nor will she listen to any of her apologies. She has even moved further behind the exhaust assembly, making it more difficult to reach her without injury. Mia paces around the truck for a little while, does some window shopping, and goes to the park to lie in the sun but eventually returns to Sam, still beneath the delivery truck.

"Hiya, love, may I sit here? I had time to think about this whole Bo thing." Mia takes a deep breath. "Do you see what he is doing to us, Sammy?! It isn't my fault! It was never my fault! It's 'friggin' Bo!" Mia slaps her hand on the truck's undercarriage. "Why is it he that always gets to deceive us? And why are you siding with him rather than with your best friend of five years?!"

Sam bites down on her lower lip and tosses a stone at the front tire. "Then you were not making fun of me at the barber shop?"

Mia picks up a gutter stick and scratches an itch between the barbs in her hair. "No, I was. Then again, I wasn't. It's the hair, Sam!! Remember what you told me about changing one's hair style, and how it can shape the personality that person?! Well, you were right. I should have listened to you."

"So, it is the barber's fault?"

"No, I'm not saying that either. What I am saying is – if you are going to count on anyone to be there for you, you may as well rely on someone you know rather than someone who is using you."

"Mia, I guess what I really want to hear from you is that there is nothing between you and Bo. That you and he are not an item."

Mia puts a dopey look on her face, stiffening her body like a mechanical doll, "Hello, I'm being Sam. I'm falling for a Mia prank."

Sam's eyes light up, "Really, Mia?! Ha! I can't believe I fell for it!" Sam gives Mia a hug.

"You see, Sammy. It's just your usual way of going about listening to things that don't really exist, am I right?"

"You are right. You were probably just confused, like when you met Bo in 'Aus' for the first time. Remember, you thought it was he who liked you? What a crock that turned out to be. He even ended up with that girl, Keira. You must have felt like a big fool! Who would ever think you would go through that again?"

"These old feelings?"

Sam swings her arms around Mia, "Mia, forgive me for doubting you; you will always be my trusted friend."

Tuesdays can be a blue day for '*The Happy to Book with You*' tour shop, but after Bo's visit, Tuesdays are no longer the snooze day, but the choose day if you want a new day with results. By late afternoon, Beatie had booked nineteen tours, scheduled fourteen flights, and sold thirty-two history booklets, and if Mr. Happiness had had his way, Beatie would still be there for a moonlight rally. But as soon as Mr. Happiness put the wheels on the music box for the rally song, Beatie was already cold-earth-slapping-it, arm-lift-flapping-it; running with barefoot credentials across a permeable paved road.

Beatie has faced too long a commitment to loneliness, and she has really grown tired of sleeping in her room with old memories. For the first time in her life, she feels a new birth coming and it starts with this dance. This is truly her first public date, and it comes with a dance she so desperately wants to be a part of. Never has she ever been asked to attend a ballroom dance before, and then possibly fall in love afterward? Who would have thought that possible?

In the crowded delivery room, occupied by dresses wrapped in low-density polyethylene, Beatie's spirits rise when she hears the chatter from the six young assistants with the one and only D.C. Kiebler! It is regarding the modeling of her new outfit. It is clearly known that ballroom dresses from the nineteenth century are not considered a stock item. This means substitutions and alterations will have to be made; it also means there will be no open-arms greetings from Miss Kiebler. Not that smiles are likely for 'The Kiebs' anyways; this is just part of her process to get Beatie ready on time.

After leaping into the dresses, Beatie props herself up from the display bars. She watches D.C. orchestrate the six assistants around, using a three-foot ruler and chasing them between the aisles, even putting their activities in song so she can locate them should they try to slip out the back door.

She puts on a nice dress that comes with plenty of touch and care. It is a sleeveless tulle gown or an off-shoulder jacquard. Perhaps one of the other or a combination of both. The explanation from D.C. is unsure. Beatie really doesn't care. She hurries before the mirror with all her cuddles and curtsies, lifting her skirt tails and remembering to smile. This is how it is done you know.

D.C. and the girls stand back, allowing Beatie time to think about the look – and she does. She gives it one of those hard-twisted, pressed-finger, head-tilting "Wa'ja Tink?" looks. She likes it. She really does, and it smells perfectly nice too – friendly and clean without all the mothballs. Beatie bites down on her fingers. She knows from her ballet lessons that timing is important and mistakes are not expected. A wrong step could ruin the entire evening and a chance at happiness.

The girls quickly follow behind her, tossing handfuls of rice onto her back. It is a bit dramatic, but it pleases the girls. And true to her word, Beatie is feeling not too far from sumptuous right now.

"Say the chant, Miss Beatie!"

"No! No!" batting her arms like a child. "It's too late for that. I have already found someone."

"Ohhhh, pleeeeeaaaase !!" the girls moan in unison.

"Okay." Beatie closes her eyes, and with her hands together, she repeats the words, "I accept this test if I am to wear this dress, the man of my dreams I would have to meet...?" Beatie is suddenly surprised to feel a yank on her skirt tails and a growl about her feet. She reaches down and extracts the little Daublie. "Paco Daublie!!" The little dog licking her with a friendly flurry of face kisses. "Are you here to tell me about my 'enthuzie' new shoes?"

The little dog squirms and leaps from her arms, then skirts between the six girls and hurries into the dark. Everyone urgently chases after him for the very reason that if Ms. Meeshman ever found signs of an animal in her store, she would surely set traps.

On the lower shelf, below the rain glitter and next to the garden slippers, they find the little dog. He is lying on his back with his belly exposed and scratching at the air.

Beatie claps her hands in joy, "You found them, Sir Dauber!" She scrunches down, lifts up the box, and pulls off the lid. "Mauve, satin, dance shoes with rhinestones. Only $25.95!"

The girl's gasp and Beatie responds, "I know I shouldn't hide things, but someone is sure to buy them if I didn't."

After putting them on with a playful laugh and twice the curtsy, Beatie is ecstatic. What a difference a dress can make with the right pair of shoes. Everything is so grand now; thinking, how could it get any better?

Paco Daublie suddenly goes non-compos, screaming toward the back of the store, spinning around to see the girls are still following. Under a distant light that can never go dim, there is a sparkling shine in casual inventory. Beatie's heartbeat takes a quick step upward and a few steps sideways. It is Vivacious.

Bo's mind is fluttering on high alert. He finds himself seated in the middle of his motel room with Mia and Sam exchanging unpleasantries.

"Smell-bottom!!"

"Hip-less tart!!!"

"Bo, we thought we would have a dance-off to see who you would prefer to dance with tonight."

Sam goes into the bathroom, while Mia disappears into an open closet. Within minutes, both stumble into the room: Mia, like a newly born giraffe on tall heels, and Sam, like an e-collared house pet wearing a bell-shaped gown. Mia's dress has a few more bare spots on it, but what really stands out is her hair. It is like that of a Russ Troll Doll, an article the farmers would plant on their land to bring the crops good luck. Mia snaps her fingers and bobs her head up and down while Sam sachets toward Bo, blowing him kisses. Mia, not to be out-bested, shakes a maraca and stutter-steps across the floor.

"What do you think now?" Mia pursing her lips with a pout.

Sam edges Mia out with her shoulder and starts to twirl, "Good one, squeeze butt."

Mia quickly steps in the way, forcing Sam onto the bed, "Foul Tasting; Larvae Breathing; Mother of all Varmints!!"

Suddenly, both are slapping at each other's hands until they tire.

"Mia, your hair!" Bo interrupts.

"You 'likey'?" Waiting for a timely response that does not come. "I'm not sure about it either. It's not soft and bouncy like I had always imagined it could be."

"No, it's definitely you."

"What do you mean? Like a grumpy old stinker or a passionate but determined life-changer?"

"Definitely the latter." Bo slaps his top hat down on his head, then slides his amulet into his coat pocket.

Mia rushes past Bo and reaches around to give him a kiss. She then pumps her arms up and down in front of Sam, "Show me up!"

Darkness has filled the voids in the sky and the air is a tad frosty. Beatie hugs herself with her warm mittens and steps from the backdoor of Meeshman's. She can't help but repeat to herself how wonderful everything is for her right now. She is wearing Vivacious without any regrets. Stealing has never entered her mind before, but there are certainly things worth taking. Paco Daublie even said so, and he is more of a shoe specialist.

Beatie is now more convinced than ever that the dance is the right move for her. While such opportunities have come to her in the past, she has always quickly rejected them This time is different; his visits strengthen her belief that she is ready for a relationship, even against her father's wishes that she wait until the age of sixty. Consider, for a moment, the odd feelings she has for this man. Feelings that she can walk and talk in a new way, feelings that it doesn't matter what people think of her, and feelings like how it makes her act jiggy and shiggy with a stanky legg yelp. She may not understand the full promise of these feelings, but for now, she notices that even darkness has to retreat incontestably.

Beatie hurries to the meeting place where she is to be received, noticing a surge from the wind that blows her soft curls into deterioration. It is followed by another strong gust that assaults her dress and makes her feel violated. Naturally, she shuffles sideways, like she is supposed to do when the wind exceeds its temperament, but never has she had to do this before!

She leans into a lamp post, the only one to deliver a warm light. Her dress tails already flipping over her head while she fights back a squall threatening to take her bonnet. She knows these streets; nothing out of the ordinary about them, so why should there be so much bad weather?! The instructions are few: meet at the corner of Boulevard and First at half past six. This is what her watch says too! She is here! She isn't anywhere else!! "My, gosh! Can it get any darker?!!"

Beatie's nerves are already shaken by the flickering lights, and don't think for a minute that the branch movements haven't gone unnoticed either. They no longer stand still like they are supposed to, and they are creating a shadow that is making a pressing move on Vivacious, even briefly consuming her sleeve!! Now it is etched into the fabric of her dress, and there is no man-made spray-and-wash that can remove this!!

No longer does Beatie feel safe and secure. Even worse is that there are more shadows arriving, and they are so much taller and so much larger that they are making her feel like shadow prey!!

Behind her is a building flanked by a mountain of scraggly bushes. She rushes in and finds a wall to crouch against, immediately dismayed to have her back soaking up squished frog juice. She curls into a ball with her hands on her heels, trying to think up a chanty to calm her nerves. "Genius loci. Quiet and Calm. I'm starting to feel better. Ohm, Calm, Ohm." She continues to repeat her mantra until two lights, closely set together, finally make their approach. A smile is already on the way! Her legs can spring forward and she can begin to wave and shout!

"Demented Wombat!!"

"Worm-Infested Witchety Grub!!"

Bo is feeling the pain in his hand from clutching the amulet too long. For whatever reason, his magic hogstone won't quiet his two friends' quarrel.

"Will you look at that, Sammy? There's some crazy girl standing out in this cold and windy night, and she's wearing a prom dress – in February, mind you!" Mia hangs over the dashboard and follows the girl with her finger.

"There's Beatie! Slow down!!"

"That girl? I thought you were kidding about someone else coming!" Mia quickly rolls down the window. "Hey! Shez-Malarney!!"

Sam watches Mia roll the window back up, "What does that mean?"

"I don't know; she waved, didn't she?"

Sam watches the girl in the rearview mirror throwing a tantrum, "Who is she, Mia?"

"Who does she need to be? We're going to a dance, aren't we?"

Sam continues to look through the mirror, "It sure is cold out there, and can it get any darker?"

Bo leans forward and pushes on the chair. "Sam, I know you will do the right thing and turn around."

Mia throws up her hands, "Oh! Go ahead, Sam, but take your time! I don't want to get into any accidents out here."

Sam swerves through a roundabout with Mia drumming her hands on the dashboard, "I bet she's pissed. You think she's the 'pissy' type, Sammie? I bet she is. Turn on your high beams, so I can get a proper look."

Mia presses forward to take a closer look. She doesn't care at all for the girl's dress, as previously stated. She also has little taste in shoes, and her bonnet is childish, but what does not make sense to her is that high-stepping, mid-frolic, astro-wheeling approach toward them when she should otherwise be mad.

"What is this, Sam? How can this be? This girl comes without acceptance; she comes without respect; she comes without sorrow, pity, or regret. Maybe happiness does not come from one's intellectual capacity. Maybe, just maybe...(iv)"

"Mia!" Sam slaps Mia's arm. "Your hair is talking!"

"Sorry."

Bo opens the backdoor, and Beatie rushes in beside him, slamming the door behind her. She bounces up and down on the seat, rubbing her hands all over her body.

"Breathe. Breathe. Shwarm. Shwarm."

"Aye, you look fine, Beatie."

Beatie lifts up her legs and points her toes, "And the shoes too?"

Mia hearing about the shoes, swings her shoulder over the seat, "Seriously, Bo, what do you know about a used 1960s pink chiffon prom dress with Latin mauve shoes marked down to $25.95?"

Beatie places her hands on her hips in a huff, "It is not a prom dress! Most certainly not! It's-a, it's-a ... it's a Vivian!! From Vivinia. It's this new country everyone is talking about. I've been there, so it's real. The shoes too, are not from there, sort of."

"Uh-huh." Mia looks at her carefully, taking a full British ten seconds to form an opinion about her. Of course, there is no way she can pretend to like her. Her attempt to raise her social status with clothes and makeup is a fool's wish. The facial expressions and all that pouty playfulness are a clear facade. That scent too, like squished pond amphibian, as if she spends her time waiting behind bushes. But most of all is that Chicarion smirk. Well, alright, it is kind of adorable and very isolated too. It requires that rare neck-lip-to-chin facial ratio found on most baby faces.

Mia sends a glare of rejection toward Bo, but she knows it doesn't matter. His expression is already showing she is going to be a part of the group now.

"Sorry, my manners. Sam, this is Beatie. Beatie, this is Sam. And you met Mia?"

Mia frowns at Bo and mimics the voice of a grouchy old lady. "And you met, Mia."

Beatie immediately takes a double look at Mia's hair, "Mia? Is that you?"

"So what!" Mia snidely replies, "Your barber on Lake Street designed it."

Beatie snickers, "My friend Parfie Der Barbeeb is located on Make Street. The Barber on Lake Street is a revolutionary-reenactment specialist. He designs, destroys, and deposes warrior mannequins." Beatie places her hand on Bo's leg. "It's really quite interesting how he makes a whole day of it. He even gathers a handful of seniors from the nursing home for casualty effects."

Mia looks at Sam with burning eyes.

Beatie lifts her bonnet off her head and swings her hair around, "If you would like to see a real Parfie Der Barbeeb hairstyle, see this!" Immediately, her soft curls bounce six times, then sparkle twice. Both Sam and Bo gasp while Mia just shrugs.

Beatie stops for a moment and looks up at the driver's face in the rearview mirror. She has been looking at her repeatedly the entire time. Both searching for more visual information.

The air smells of licorice and baby powder. The sound of little children munching on doodle snacks and sipping color-coated bottles of water resonates loudly, like ants invading the sound system. It is a light-filled gymnasium with variations of brown in the parquet floors. The pastiche ceiling is decorated with winged babies playing instruments on puffy white clouds.

Sam is the first to glide across the floor, tilting from side to side in her lanolin cage gown. Bo and Beatie soon follow arm-in-arm in a quick gallop behind her. Bo is comfortable with the setting, having prepared this in his mind. He knew Beatie would be nervous and felt these surroundings would ease her tension.

Mia enters the gymnasium, still wobbling in the heels that Sam lent her. She is having even more trouble maneuvering around gum balls, broken bags of corn chips, and leaking cartons of soy milk. She is further annoyed when a little girl approaches with a soiled napkin, followed by a little boy crawling along the floor to grab her heel. Children give Mia the willies every time she sees one. Their little minds are not adjusted to an adult's well-being. They don't believe in rules, regulations, or any etiquette that applies to them.

"Give me back my brain!" shouts the little boy.

"Only if I can show you how to use it!" shouts the little girl.

Their attendance raises a suspicion within Mia, so she hurries to catch up to Bo. "Who invited these unruly children?"

Mia looks at Bo shuffling his feet and pumping his arms up and down, "Choo, Choo! All aboard!"

"Stop that! That's a children's dance?!"

"Where do ye think we are, Mar?"

Mia lifts her head to hear the melody of Wee Willy Winky playing on the loud speaker. She stares in disbelief when a horde of children leap down from the bleachers and dance around in their own peculiar way. She further notes that the atypical male is not present among them. In fact, every single body on the dance floor is so androgynous that none possesses a sexual identity of their own.

"May I be the Aeneid of Virgil? This is a dance for grade-school children? Sam, were you aware of this?"

"Of course, I substitute teach most of these children. Aren't they cute?"

"They are all lean-limbed, burnished-faced, sticks in shoes!!"

"Mia, let's not start this again."

"This again?! Hello, Sam! I am looking for young love tonight! An evening dedicated to mush-mouthing and cuddle-crushing! These boys are too young to know what their 'dinkies' are for!"

"Keep your voice down, Mia! I am relieved to say these children have no idea what you are talking about."

"Let me rephrase it then: Their Spitting Johnsons!! Their Wobbly Do-Peckers!! And for the elderly? Their Shranky Wanky Do Littles!!"

"Mia!! These are my friends around here!"

"Sam, Valentine's is a week away, and I should be finding my perfect match right now. Remember what I told the barber? I'm going to a big dance tonight to meet my first love; to be loved; and to make love for the first time."

"You've never made love, Mia?"

"Not for dramatics."

"Mia, come talk to my friends. Most of these people on the bleachers are parents, but of course," Sam claps her hands, "there are some single ones too!"

"Yeh, like which ones?" Mia asks doubtfully.

"Like, well, I don't know. Look up there! There's Peetrie! He plays in a band. He is intensely interesting, highly unique, and might I add, he is looking to settle down with that one unsuspecting foreigner."

"What's wrong with him?"

"Nothing's wrong with him," Sam waves her hand in the gentleman's direction. "Over here, Peetrie!! Woo-hoo!"

A man with a yellow tie and angled shoes, lifts the brim of his hat and in three quick motions, places his hands beneath his rear, raises them to his face, and coughs.

"Lovely, was that some sort of a signal?"

"I'm sorry, Mia."

"Not at all. At least he's sure of himself."

"Don't worry, there will be a new crowd when the ballroom music comes on. We'll blend in for now. Where is Bo? Have you seen him?"

Beatie touches Bo's shoulder and leans into his ear, "There's a little girl over there that wants you to say hello."

Bo looks over to see a little girl on the far side of the bleachers, sitting alone on her best behavior. She wears a long white gown with canvas slippers and sports a very unique hairstyle. It is tall, wide in range, and in the shape of angel wings.

"Come you will; sit here by Sprikkits. You are just in time for my Staten Island Tea Party."

Bo takes notice of a basket of five arms next to her, before removing his bicorn hat. She hands him a small cup and pretends to add hot water. He looks down to see a shiny black substance on the bottom of her shoes. "There is tar on your gutties?"

"I've been playing with insects. Haha!!" clapping her hands in joy. "Yes, sir, indeed. My name is Sprikkets! Sprikkets MacGee. I'm just fine, thank you, friendly."

Bo raises his tea cup and takes a pretend sip. "Hmm. The cup is very tangy." He then watches the little girl's face transform into an elderly woman, even adding a smoker's cough to it.

"Bettah yuz don' wash it first." she touches her hair and bends her lower lip into a frown.

Bo chuckles while she pauses to take several long sips.

"Retired to Flowida. They all bake in buttah down there. Some wanna kiss me with their bumpy gums, so I saz to them, 'Donna even think about it. Wanna fix your teeth? Mouth a scallion bagel with walnuts!' Am I wrong, Boobalah? Jack and Jill went up the hill and fell all the way to the bottom."

The little girl sets down her cup and collects the silverware, "That's enough tea." She tucks the dishes away beneath her basket and smooths out the creases in her dress. She then shuts her eyes and shakes her head.

"Are you alright?"

"I'm not very well," admits the little girl.

"You're not?"

"Everyone knows that Darby Futon's play is unfair."

"Darby Futon?"

The little girl motions her hand across the floor, "Over there by Temper Peggy."

Away from the crowd are two children playing a game that requires them to avoid a pretend object from hitting them. Their character in question, but their clothing is definitely worth a discussion. The boy wears a burlap bag tied at the waist, and the girl wears a dirty cotton dress that shows a hint of white. Their hair, too, is uneven with an undefined direction, as if maybe they have been scratching it all day.

Bo changes his smiling face into a compassionate look, "Wanna tell me about it?"

"Darby says my dress belongs to a sick spirit in need of a burial."

"I'm sure he didn't mean it."

"I don't see how he could mean it any other way."

"He's only a child."

"Well, he can't be a child forever. His comments were mean and stupid, and he's taking up some very important space in our world!" Sprikkits frowns and squeezes her fingers into a tight fist.

"Darby won't change what Darby always does."

Bo lifts his head with a smile, "And it's hard to understand what Darby really loves."

The little girl chuckles, "What's wrong with you?"

"It's from *The Tales of the Misty Thloethem.*"

"You are very unusual, but I think for the most part, I do like unusual things."

Bo mimics receiving a flurry of face punches, provoking a laugh from the little girl.

"You're absolutely delightful!! How happy I am to meet with you!" The little girl looks up to see Mia on the other side of the room. "There are many distractions from those that pretend to know you."

"I don't understand?"

"The one you invited, Mia? She's a distraction." Sprikkit's adds gloomily.

"I know, but it seems she has some part in all of this."

Sprikkits shakes a paper cup with the clear sound of chinks from within. Bo drops a shiny penny into her cup and she smiles, "seems she's not worth it if you ask me."

"I remember you! You were the wee girl on the street corner selling history thirty years ago. Mia was not very happy with you?"

"Ha! You don't know me, but you will," Sprikkits standing abruptly. "Gadzooks! It's time!"

Bo's skin tingles with a change to a lower air temperature in the room. A great darkness grows along the edges of the gymnasium, and he watches as all the children scurry toward the exits. Sprikkits tugs on Bo's sleeve and stretches her arms out. "I better go. The next dance is for those much older than you or even me."

Bo reaches up and lifts her down to the floor.

"Do you think, maybe, when the time comes, you could accompany me home?"

"Yes, Sprikkets. I'd be glad to."

Darkness forms on the outer edges of his eyes, closing in around his irises to form a narrow tunnel before him. Many smells suddenly fill his nose, most notably those of orange blossoms. It isn't long after that when he sees professional dancers leap in from the dark edges and begin moving around the floor like chess pieces.

Beatie's voice cracks with a brief whimper as she grips her hands tightly, wondering whether or not she has done the right thing by getting involved with a pregnant, compulsive, foreign advisor. New people have arrived, and the women with their corkscrew-style hair are racing about the floor dressed in long, conical-shaped gowns. Meeshman's doesn't carry garb like this and she is pretty sure there is no store that would. Could they be from Georgia? A further surprise appears when the men jump in to join them. They too are dressed oddly with coat tails, trusses, and hoses. Their hair is meticulously combed, exposing long, trimmed sideburns and pointy beards. Beatie waves her hands before her eyes to make sure what she is seeing is real. She then closes them tightly and reopens them again, and they are still there. Only now the men are high-stepping and the women are twirling beneath their arms. Does this clothing somehow bring out this dance in them? So many questions to ask these Georgian people.

Even Bo, who is also startled by this strange imagery, knows too well that this will confuse Beatie. He quickly looks about the lighted circle and sees her where he least expects her, seated with her legs crossed in the center of the floor. The dancers are circling around her, and he has to wonder how he might reach her. Suddenly, to his good fortune, the dancers fall to the floor in an abrupt finale. Bo dawdles his way over to Beatie, who stands and jumps into his arms, "It's scarily salubrious!"

"I can go along with that."

Beatie draws in her breath for composure, "Put me down. I know something about dances. I take ballet lessons."

Bo can see how this dance is already the happening thing for her to see. She already wants to push her boundaries and hoof it with these professionals, so she piles up her hair on top of her head and steps out of her heels. It takes very little courage to get her feet started, and once she does, she is spinning like the rest of them with confidence.

When Bo catches up to her, the two exchange hands at the shoulder and waist and then set off on their first march without knowing a step. There are moments when they fail to keep up, but Beatie seems happy with her improvisational techniques, and soon, they are kicking up their feet right behind the heels of their fast-paced guides. This naturally catches the attention of the attendees, who are fascinated to see Beatie and Bo threading through the dancers with such unabated spirit.

Beatie, feeling this is the right moment for a finale, lets out a loud guffaw and begins bouncing off the dancers until she ends up on her back, twirling about the floor.

Bo bows before a line of spectators stepping into the light. There is a big ovation from the bleachers too, particularly toward Beatie, who is walking around in circles, pumping her fists. She is so happy to hear them calling her name. Never has she ever received such praise like this before, not even from her stuffed animals.

It is Samantha on the bleachers, surrounded by a group of her cohorts, who notices something is wrong with her lover-to-be. It is regarding that cute, beamish girl scurrying around the floor like she is happy to be alive. This has her concerned. All had been going well, as it should have; she had been proper, supportive, loyal, and obliging; now she is in a position to be defensive again. Her friends seem concerned too, because she has been irritably ignoring them and often stepping away to be with that rude girl in a sideways dress.

"Mia, what did you do?"

"Nothing! Let's get something to eat. I have not swallowed a morsel since we arrived here." Mia leaps down to the seat below and begins sifting through a left-behind lunch bag. She pulls out a partially peeled banana and looks it over for teeth marks. After sniffing the rotten spots, she shoves the whole bent stick in her mouth.

Sam's face, a flush of temper-red, taps Mia on the shoulder, then points across the floor. Mia follows her finger and swallows.

"Aw, the courtship of the Hooded Grebe. What do you expect, Sam? It's a dance."

"But how could he have the same feelings for someone else?"

Mia takes a double-look and squints her eyes, realizing the couple is Bo and *'that'* girl. "Oh, Teuchy." She pops the lunch bag and rolls her eyes. She does not want to deal with this again.

"What sort of kindness is he expressing here, Mia? There must be some answer to this?"

Mia puts her forefinger in her mouth and cleans the banana from her gums. "Like what?"

"Like my dress for one! He prefers a lady in a prom dress with loose buttons and frills!"

Mia walks away from Sam and scours for more food in another forgotten bag She had tried to convince Sam before that they are not an item. Another attempt to smooth things over, most likely, would fracture their already-tested relationship. Mia hears the thundering thump of Sam's feet and again, a tap on her shoulder.

"Well, Mia?!!"

"Sam, I don't know if it's the outfit. I mean, look at her; she is certainly pretty enough to win a man's favor."

"You knew this about him, didn't you!"

"Are these peanut butter crisps any good?"

Sam squeezes her hands together, "Oooh, it is true; you do want him for yourself!!"

"Okay, I was thinking the issue was about the *'other'* girl, but now I see your problem is more about me again. You know how your brain ..." Mia quickly stops before reeling off a line meant to insult her. She promised she would not take the intentionally cruel and cynical approach, so instead, she fills the bag with air and pops it. "Please, Sam, we're best friends. It's not me who likes him; it's the pretty girl with the Florida skin and silky hair. These very things you will never have. In fact, if you put the two of us mushed together, we still come up with peaches and cream, not hot mocha with caramel."

Sam sits on the bench, "So, you're sure you're not an item?"

"I'm sure. We're both sure. He's the troubled one, Sam, not me. It is he who is the Zax; unwilling to change his tracks while forcing us to go around him."

Sam leans her head back and takes a deep breath, "Maybe so, but what about her?"

"And what about her?"

"Do you think she'll come on to him sexually?"

Mia tosses the bag of chips and rubs her hands of the crumbs, "Many believe she will."

"But he is our friend! How is it possible that he could do this?!"

"Coming and going. Coming and going." Mia turns her hand over and over again. "Constantly staying in touch with the insides of his mouth. It can be like that with new love."

"Oh, no! Marriage and babies too?!"

"Too early to know about those sorts of things, but most likely a lot of fornication."

"And you are okay with that?! How are you okay with that?!!"

"Does it really matter? Hello! Love Enforcement Agency Bulletin Number One! He gets hooked easy, Sam. We know this behavior in him. He's wishy-washy and undecided. He's intolerable at best." Mia pops another bag and watches Sam's mouth go ajar.

"Oh, seriously, Sam. Jacobis of Boston, Bon Bon of New Jersey, and Trinity of Rehoboth. And who can forget Keira of Perth? An incursion that nearly killed us both. I think you need to have your medulla oblongata checked out; you're missing a lot of connections."

"I can't believe this in you!"

"And the llama says?" Mia picks up another bag, disappointed in the lack of food left behind. Wednesdays are Cornish pasties with pudding cake rolls. Maybe include peas and hash browns. Oh, how she wishes she were home right now. "You sure you're not hungry, Sam? Sam? Oh, not again?"

Bo and Beatie clap and bow to each other. She slips her hand underneath his arm and they dart back to the fringe of the lighted circle. She is having a great time, and Bo can see that. She even says to herself that this is everything she wants it to be.

She leans her head against Bo's shoulder just before the lights go down. There is a great chatter, and those in the bleachers hurry toward the exits. Something seems wrong. Beatie twists her mouth in thought. Another dance is coming and she can feel it, but his time she wants to be the first on the floor. She playfully beckons Bo forward by circling her arms.

Mia steps in front of Bo with her hand out, "We can't blend here anymore, Bo. You better follow me if you want to be assured a seat for meat and veggies."

"Mia, I'll have some grub later."

Mia grabs Bo's arm forcefully, "Bo, how long have you been imagining you're someone else? You have friends already. Those people out there are not your friends! Now let's go."

"I'm here with Beatie, Mia. Sam and you should find a partner and join us."

Mia looks over Bo's shoulder to see Sam exiting the building. "That's sweet, Bo. However, this is a choice made by peers, and that means you are outnumbered!"

"Nonsense, Mia. I do have a choice. I'm here with Beatie. If there's a problem, consult the llama."

"Lovely, you wanna know what the llama thinks?"

Bo feels the solid punch to his lower section, followed by the feeling of his legs going weak. It has never gone this far with Mia. He had always acquiesced to her demands, and now he knows what would have happened if he hadn't.

Mia waves her fist at him, "It seems to tickle you to no end that while this local doxie parades about you, Sam and I are looking to schedule our Valentine's watching the David Attenborough Mating Special again!"

Bo slowly rises to his feet with a belch. "Mia, have a chat with Sam. She deserves that from you." Bo staggers off with Mia's face ablaze.

"Don't take that attitude with me, Baueregard Heathen Fox!! I am already over this. You do as I say, or I'll never, ever, forever make you forget it!!" Mia stares for a while, watching Bo lift Beatie up with a happy smile on their faces. She turns toward the exit door, where Sam should be waiting, but once there, she is met with a very strong tug, sending her forward into the parking lot grass. "It's you! The little girl who thinks she knows everything!" The door shuts.

The light in the center of the floor flickers on and off. The music begins with a very soft bolero beat, followed by a mingling of voices calling for more instruments. Beatie slides in front of Bo, looking at him with a large smile. "One more for the floor?" She gently drops her hand for Bo to take. There is a cold, damp breeze pushing into Bo's face that forces him to take a cautious step backward. He is having second thoughts. There have been many smells that have filled his nose, but none like the one before him. It is very earthy and unnatural.

Beatie does not travel far either, quickly backing up when she is almost seized by thick tentacles spreading through the light. It is like dark ink slithering in the water, reaching forward her to squeeze out her internal bodily functions. She steps back into Bo, "This is no customary waltz." She spins around to look at him. "Maybe we shouldn't."

There is a loud crack, like a whip, that sparks the air. The tentacles, having formed a long, intricate web, slowly pull back their taut strings, and when the last string snaps, then comes a new set of people with a new set of rules. These new entertainers come dressed in large black robes with oversized hoods. They raise their long, blue fingers with crusty, cracked nails, and throw back their hoods to reveal the most ghastly, blue-colored faces that even the dead would be scared of.

Beatie squeezes her hands together and turns them inside out, then into a knot. It appears the floor is now attended by a gloom of overcast participants. "I can do this!" she says to Bo. She is not awestruck – no, not at all. It is a bit frightening, true, and she wishes them well in their attempt to be spooky, but she'll have none of that tonight. She is here to dance.

The music abruptly halts as the women separate from the men and move into a new position. Their eyes are fixed on their partners, and it is the women who are the first to act out. They begin with the fluttering of their hands and then the curling of their fingers, as if beckoning their partners into a trap. In accordance with their wishes, the male partners remove their capes and take a slow bow.

Bo folds up his sleeves, while Beatie races ahead to join the women. The music starts with a slow plucking of a lute, adding a slow drum beat. Bo joins the men and follows their lead by arching his back and kicking out his right foot. They then draw horns with their fingers and begin scoffing at the floor. A cornet blows along with krummhorns and sackbuts, a cue for the ladies to quickly toss their robes aside and shimmy their shoulders. The men respond with a high-stepping charge into the ladies, who mockingly slide aside and slap them on their backside.

Beatie soon finds herself following the ladies, rushing away from the embarrassed men, who follow right behind them as the violins strum faster and faster. They plunge and rear, and 'Bob and Ney' as a horse would. Beatie does the best she can to escape, but she cannot seem to shake the one intimidating hoofer that is nipping at her heels. She stumbles and falls, and when she turns to confront the pursuer, what she sees next makes her hold her breath. It is the head of a horse with the eyes of a flaming demon.

Beatie dashes directly across the gymnasium, and does what comes naturally, she leaps onto the back of Bo, wrapping her arms around his neck, and dragging him to the floor.

"You're not having fun?"

"No!" Beatie replies with a defiant gesture. She seizes Bo's hat from his head and tosses it to the air.

"My hat!" Bo sits up and watches his hat disappear into the dark corner of the room. Disappointed, he frowns, then looks over her shoulder in fright. The dancers are standing around them and the music has stopped.

"I think they're coming for us, Beatie."

"No!!" she says in a demanding tone.

Bo's eyes grow wider as the ghouls edge closer. "They are coming, Beatie'!!"

Bo closes his eyes; he knows exactly what is coming next. These gloomy attendees will soon be crushing them under their large mass and leaving their bodies broken and bleeding. Beatie sees her own version of what is to come. They will be digesting and draining them of all their bodily organ-stuffings, and using their bones for a Beauregard yam broth. All of this is just moments away! Beatie and Bo embrace, clasping their arms tightly around each other. The torment of waiting is almost over.

Beatie screams, holding one hand out while trying to shield her eyes with the other. She is witnessing the horror from every horror movie she has ever seen. Lights are flashing, and gruesome skeletal heads are popping! There are floating torsos and insects flying from within the fragments of their eye sockets! Their knobby fingers and dirty nails are latching onto Beatie's arms, trying to bleed her of her soul! Bo does his best to cover her from their wretchedness, slapping at their fingers and kicking at their torsos, but there are just too many of them! As he watches Beatie being torn apart, she stretches out with what arm length she has left, then deathly whispers, "Happy Valentine's Day."

There is a great puff of dust and a rising cloud that leaves them covered in ash. The lights go out, and at that very instance when Beatie feels her body is whole again, she quickly fumbles for her phone. She finds her flashlight, then aims it toward the ceiling, watching with fascination as the roof breaks into many small pieces. Bo rises beside her and they both watch as the winged children of the decorative pastiche flutter away into the night sky.

"That was 'zooty'!!" Beatie jumps up and down and runs in circles around Bo. Hard to believe that her response to this madness would be joyous screams. Can one not see how preciously beautiful she is?

She leaps into Bo's arms and gives him a long kiss on the lips. When she lets go, her eyes are a warm swirl of emotions. The emptiness within her is suddenly filled with exuberance. Bo smiles and watches as the margins of his body, and that of Beatie's, begin to fade. The wish he had made has come true.

Mia appears beneath the bright light in the stairwell, looking up at the long, steep climb she has to make in Sam's heels. She draws up her gown and carefully sets her heel down on the approaching step. She knows very well the danger she faces if her foot were to slip. Does it matter? Is this not a justifiable punishment for her treatment toward her best friend, as long as it only results in a light ache or a temporary mark?

It really does suffer Mia to have said so many horrible things to Sam. All at the urgency from Bo. A request she should have readily denied. When she reaches the top of the stairs unscathed, she breathes a sigh of relief. She enters her room and shuts the door, rubbing her tired eyes. The windows are shut and the curtains are drawn. The room is dark except for a low-grade night light casting a glow on the floor. In the bathroom, she turns on the faucet and splashes her face, careful not to touch her hair. She searches for the tweezers to remove one of the split-ends that had broken off under her finger nail. There are no towels in the bathroom and her hands are still wet.

Mia wraps her coat around her shoulders and swings the door behind her with a loud slam. She has had enough of the manager's false promises. It is time to seek out a guest who is said to be – most active. Maybe she might meet someone interesting; would that not be a treat?

The hallway beyond the elevator has a different look to it. There is no perception of depth, just a solid black square. Lifting her flashlight and aiming at the strange phenomena, she is fascinated by how the light just forms a ring in the open space. She grabs hold of the wooden guard rail and continues on until she reaches the concession machine. No longer holding onto the railing, she stumbles forward and bangs her head onto a wobbling piece of space.

"A Melamine Board? This is ridiculous!" Mia tries to focus her eyes. The collision is bringing about a glaring light that blinds her. It is also having a disturbing effect on her hearing with a deep voice that echoes in her ears.

"Does my appearance seem strange to you, my child?"

Mia looks up with the feeling of euphoria. To have in her honor the immense privilege to be the one person that the almighty would speak to is beyond her satisfaction and completion to an otherwise worthless life. And then for whatever reason, this voice just wants to talk on and on without interruption, about nothing of importance. Who cares about the libidinous children in the back alleys, or the scatological humor from the sisters at her orphanage? Even while banging her forehead continuously on the melamine board creating a contusion, the voice still carries on!

"And what have you done to your hair?" Mia looks up, drawn to a wavering finger reaching out to touch her hair. "Ooh, ouch. It stings."

Mia scoots back against the wall, "Please don't touch the Zax."

The voice chuckles, "I see. Arrr! Growl!"

"You're not a deity or a head concussion illusionist!" The elevator doors close with Mia's flashlight shining upon a human face. "You're an assistant motel manager!"

The assistant manager helps Mia to her feet and directs her toward her room, "What brings you down this way so late in the evening?"

"I am looking for some towels, remember? I've been out of them since taking up the room."

"Miss Pearl, there are no towels beyond the elevators that you can rely on. It is late. Would you not appreciate it if someone floated down to your private happiness and asked for clean towels? So, how about if we bring you fresh towels at the first sign of light?"

"Sure, I guess so, and the radiator too? It's still making a lot of noises."

Sen turns abruptly and tightens his fists, "Butter Corn!"

"Butter Corn? Did you whisper something?"

Sen places his hands on his tool belt, "We will take care of the pipes as well."

"Oh, come now, Sen. What's behind the board blocking the hallway?"

"Miss Pearl! Please part with your nosy curiosity and leave the others to be. I'm sure you would prefer if they extended you the same courtesy."

Mia shoots a quick look down the hallway after a large door slams, followed by a long, drawn-out moan. Sen takes the door key from her hand and slides it into the door slot, "Good night, Miss Pearl."

Mia takes the key from him, "I still don't understand the secrecy."

"If your curiosity is still on high alert, then maybe accept this ...finish that city tour with me! You'll get a great perspective from a true local."

"Tonight? Now? I don't know, Day Manager. Not to be rude, but don't you think you are a bit strange?"

"The guy you are rooming with isn't strange?"

"True, but he comes with the strange I know. Thank you for the offer. First thing in the morning? Not kidding. The towels?"

The assistant manager shoots off his finger with the click of his mouth. "Right on it."

Mia closes the door and puts the chain lock on, listening to his heavy steps trample down the stairwell. She snickers and remembers from past experiences, how men used to flirt with her in unsustainable ways.

Mia stumbles out of her heels and departs from her dress. She pulls the drapes aside and opens the window to the dancing lights on the streets below. She smirks and chuckles when she sees Bo relegated to his uncontrollable cravings upon a tree. An innocent red oak, mind you, and really going at the woody tissue too.

She pauses for a moment. Something about his anatomy is all wrong. His hands are in his back pockets, he has two sets of misdirected feet, and his clothing is a mix of nineteenth-century garb and a pink-chiffon prom dress. Mia grovels and throws up her hands, "It's *'that'* girl again!"

Mia sticks her head out the window, ready to confront them both, but there is something unusual about his abnormality. Mia pulls the blinds to a slight close, utterly baffled by what she sees. The behaviors from *'that'* girl are unquestionably insane: skipping from side to side and twirling about in a nonsensical manner. Why doesn't she just run away while she has the chance? Stranger still is when Bo touches her cheek and she doesn't flinch. In fact, all indications show that she is obliging. Even her facial expression shows what she is doing is no accident!

Mia weakens her grip on the cord and crosses the room with heavy steps. She has never treated Bo with this kind of affection before. Never encouraged that he should even try. Truthfully said, if Bo had ever tried anything like that on her she would have slapped him silly. And yet, this girl makes no such gestures of the kind.

Mia sits down on the bed disappointed and overcome with the look of shame. She is feeling suddenly miserable about her treatment toward her two best friends. Two bad happenings in the same night. Mia can no longer ignore her true desires. She must focus on what really matters.

FEBRUARY 8:
BARSTOOL
CONCLUSIONS

When the vision of Beatie leaves him, Bo is once again left pondering why his dreams of her keep falling apart. It can only be about Beatie now. There should be no other thoughts.

"It's nice outside, but I can't tell if there is a cold breeze. Can you unlock the window?"

Bo turns his head in surprise. Mia is oiling up her legs, dressed in her backless, neckless, gold-metallic string bikini. It is the one she wore when they first met in Melbourne. Not surprising, she is trying to relay her thoughts to him by batting her eyelashes. Stretching out each leg, all shiny and smooth, Bo watches while she walks seductively about the room. Her glistening legs angled in the light to attract attention. He has seen this behavior in Mia before when she wants something.

"Guess what I have for you?" Mia steps on a chair to reach the top of the entertainment center. She carefully arches her toes to reach a box wrapped in newspaper. She then prances over to Bo and slides in next to him.

"What's this, Mar?" Bo pulls the wrapping paper apart. He looks with curiosity at the picture on the box of two brightly colored, inflated sacks strapped to a child's arms.

"What are these?"

"Mum Boats."

"Mum Boats?"

"It says so right on the box. You blow them up and put them around your arms when you go in the water."

"What for?"

"So, you won't drown. They're neon red should they ever deflate. See, it says here: Good for viewing up to forty meters in fresh water, thirty meters in salt water, and ten meters in a black pool." Mia watches closely as a quizzical expression appears on Bo's face.

"So nice, but I'd rather..."

"You would rather drown?"

"I would rather not go in the pool if drowning were the only option," Bo pauses to see the disturbed look on Mia's face, "...but since we are on holiday and spending more time in the pool, I'm happy."

Mia reaches around Bo and gives him a kiss on the cheek. "It's great we are together again. I feel better knowing that you plan to hang around more." Mia retrieves a comb from her backpack. "And that other girl, the 'Concubine of Displeasures'. It's peculiar how you used to like her. She had that uncomfortable, blaze attitude about her. It was rather bad of her age to act that way, don't you think? Well, anyway, it's for the best. I'm glad you called an end to it."

Mia brushes her hair and looks toward the window, "The weather is quite warm for February, don't you think?"

Bo puts his feet down on the floor, cringing at what he is going to say next, "Aye, it's a braw day." Leaning forward out of the bed and fumbling into his clothes, he stuffs the amulet into his pocket. "Anyways, I have to see the 'Concubine of Displeasures' now."

"Poppycock!! It quiets me to no shame that you would rather spend time with that shiny, underdressed hussy than with shiny me and 'Simple Sam'. That girl seems to have some special rights over us that I am not agreeing to!" Mia throws down her brush. "I saw you out there in the parking lot, mushing your faces together!"

Bo gives Mia a surprised look.

"If you thought you were going to give us a blind eye to all of this, it isn't working!"

"Mar, I never ...

"Oh, like you didn't know! I could never see why you would choose to be so secretive about this affair, but I can see why you ought to try. You want to get rid of Sam and me, and this is how you are going to do it!" Mia crosses her legs and sits heavily down on the floor, sniveling.

Bo is in a hurry. He reaches into his pocket for the amulet and raises it to his eye. Mia is soon tugging on her nose and wiping her eyes dry. "Well, lovely. Go do what you have to do; just don't catch a disease."

"I knew you would understand, Mar."

When Bo steps from the elevator, there is the penny farthing. He has made frequent use of the bike so far, taking him to where all his memories still remain, but now the pleasure of seeing her again is most on his mind. The remembrance of last night seemed most treasurable, having never experienced anything like that in his real life before.

And what a wonderful day it is so far. There is little traffic and few tourists, so he can go wild into the street. Riding a penny farthing at a forty-five-degree angle is quite amazing to see, but performing a 'tail whip' with a somersault was really what the residents were clapping about.

He turns the corner at King George Street and pedals faster and faster until he feels the burn in his thighs. In several long strides, he coasts along the cobblestones toward her workplace. Mr. Happiness opens the front door and watches Bo travel past him into the back office. He waits for all the broken items to come to a silence before addressing the matter.

"I wish to point out that the Renaissance Festival is not until late November." Snickering at his nineteenth century attire.

Bo looks down at the empty, tidy desk where he expects Beatie to be, then looks around to see where she is not.

"Do you know how much damage you cost me? Do you not speak?"

Bo glances under her desk, still thinking she might be present, but soon gives up, "I'm here to see Beatie, good sir."

"I sent her home."

"Home? What for?"

"'What for? I'll tell you – what for!" Snidely replies the manager. "My 'Baby Star', as I used to refer to her, started the morning by booking two seats on the space station for an Irish couple. They were asking for a better view of the lighthouse. Somehow, Beatie had obtained outfits and security passes. The greater part of my morning has been tied up with NASA about how to get them back."

Bo fingers the edges of his hat, "Unusual I admit, but the Irish can be a bit wily."

"And the Canadian family interested in a trip down the Matanzas. She insisted that the tires on the scooters were meant to keep them afloat. Hats off to the lobster fisherman who hauled them in."

Bo bites on the rim of his hat, "Have you thought of offering life preservers with the tour?"

Mr. Happiness leans on the table and gives Bo a stern look, "She booked a car rental for two nine-year-old's, including free tickets to a wine tasting. The insurance agency told me that the least of the offenses would be for the underage intoxication without a license. However, leaving the scene after running over a government official is apparently prohibited by federal law."

The manager shakes his head from side to side. "I sat with Beatrice for a full hour in my office, just trying to understand why she would do this to me. She just stared and repeated, *Ebullient*," as if she were in some sort of a 'La La Land'." The manager takes a seat at her desk and slowly slumps down, "In all my born days of building this business, never once did I believe I could lose it all in one. Who would possibly book a tour with me now?"

Bo squeezes his hands and presses his lips together, "Have you considered advertisements in Europe?"

"Out I say!!" The manager suddenly stops with his finger pointing. "Wait a moment. I know you!"

Bo stumbles out the door, leaping onto his wobbling bike. The store owner nearly closes in on him with a potted plant, but it was the timely delivery truck that allowed Bo to escape without incident.

Bo's long limbs continue to pump hard on the pedals. He flies around all the connecting streets, hoping to avoid anything that might be chasing him. The start of the day seemed joyful, but now his precious time is being disrupted by the same failures from his past. He has the stone – true – a real game changer; however, a charm is only a deceptive practice that corrects a single mistake. It is not for a lifetime of problems. He will need a drastic change in his thinking.

Bo turns up the roadway, slowly toiling up the bridge. He will be riding the bike well beyond city limits this time, and to a place he knows he can receive personal assistance.

There is a little watering establishment beneath the endless rays of the sun in the outback of the city. It is sequestered on an isle of sand, surrounded by the shallow depths of a watery image. The area resembles no other place in and around St. Augustine. It is treeless, sand barren, and its inhabitants are wee-winged beasties that seek whatever moisture nature can deliver.

You will find few features in this establishment that one would likely pursue. The odor of cigarettes is hardly complementary to the food that is hard to digest. The Rumple-de-thump left-overs from the stew are overly gritty; the ingredients of the periwinkle and stargazy pie are collected from the mirage outside; and rumor that there is human, not animal, fat in the pork scratchings is apparent from the anatomy drawings on the kitchen walls.

Not to sound too disparaging, you will find your Bangers and your Mash, your Biscuit Tatties, your Fish Pies, and your Hash. And if you come by any other evening, or if you come in the morn, peas on Sundays, baked beans on Fridays, and all the other days come with corn.

Be it known that this visit is never about the gimmicky menu items, nor about the pubbery furnishings previewed in the Ghost City News. There are solutions to the acts of idiocy within these very walls, and there is no better person to have their futures sired than from the man called Connor MacSheen.

He is a trim man, a baby-faced man with eyes of blue and a face with a florid hue. His hair, once a fiery flame, is now held together with the magic of glue. He has the knees of a goat but the heart of a lamb; Shralea, Creagh, Ballinasloe, co Galway – this is the home address of this Irishman.

Bo stands before the empty room and adjusts his eyes to the darkness inside. He looks to every corner of the establishment to find the place empty and is relieved because this means his time is his own, and that time will be spent with the man placing glasses on a rack behind the bar. Bo wastes little time approaching the counter. He props himself on a stool and unfolds the morning paper.

"I'm here for a swally, Connor."

The barkeep, with his bow tie, button-down shirt, and rolled-up sleeves, turns about and grabs his green vest. "What be your pleasure?"

"How about a heavy." Bo reaches into his front pocket and slams a twenty-dollar bill down on the bar, still keeping the printed paper clutched in his fingers.

The barkeep kicks the barrel below, turns the pour on the nozzle, and fills the pint to a drooling rim. He then engraves a shamrock into the froth and sets the drink down on the bar. Bo watches carefully as the hoarfrost forms along the sides of the glass.

"Should we start a tab?" asks the barkeep.

Bo runs his tongue through the froth and lifts the glass, taking a critical glance toward Connor, "When did it' come off the boat?"

"Three weeks ago."

"Are you offering it for free?"

"Want something else?"

"You put on a wee bit of weight around the belly, have you not, Connor?"

"Gravity over time has a way of settling above the belt, does it not? Would you prefer I stand on my arms so I have broader shoulders?"

"Enough, Connor MacSheen! You know why I am here. Granting utterances from the wise whilst the money pays for the beer. Being an Irish barkeep, I believe that be your calling."

"Aye, it is."

"My name is Bo Fox, and I am a highlander and I have come for advice."

"Not by that name, you aren't."

"What?"

The barkeep grabs Bo's arm and pulls him forward as if prejudiced ears had just entered the room, "This may be a bit sensitive to you, Highlander, but the Fox clan is not associated with the Mackays. The Foxes are found on the lower Isle of Ire. Their colors are red on white, but it just so happens that Fox is a common English surname too, and they found their way north to the mucky, little land of wet peat. So, the choice be yours."

Bo stumbles back, clearing his airways of beer, "You are saying I could be English?"

"I'm saying your descendants 'were' once English, and you became Scottish in a roundabout, kind of way."

Bo wipes his chin with his hand, "This be your knowledge of me, Connor MacSheen?!"

"Hmmf! Parleys are my specialty, but I sense this is about – a lady?"

"Aye, you already read deep into my soul and it burns."

"Be out with it, English-Irish-Highlander."

"I tell this story only in secrecy."

"Be out with it, man!!"

"So, there are these reoccurring dreams I have had for quite some time now, where they start out fine with wee furry animals and throwing rocks at the Clan Campbell, but for the past several years, my mind has taken issue with a bonnie I met many years ago. Now it has taken an ill path and has clutched onto my spirit and it's drowning my soul!"

Bo looks down into his empty glass. "You have run empty of this stuff, have you?"

"Taking a holiday of strength?"

"Just making sure your age hasn't slowed your pouring."

Bo runs his hand along the bar, "She was not like the others. A mind of innocence and hope. Every day, like the day before it, there were no worries about what could change. Not by a wrong word of my own this time, but by outside influences. It was two weeks till Valentine's, and their eyes were upon us; evil acquaintances were now becoming her friends. Maybe her own happiness is what they despised, not having one of their own." Bo tilts his glass from side to side and smirks. "They played around with the poisons to see which would work best. Consuming her with fiction and phony claims. 'Your relationship is only a seasonal occurrence,' they told her. I thought there would be a discussion about it, but I was wrong. She was silent the entire time. Thus, it led her to this world of conclusion that there are better opportunities out there but not the one confronting her. She wanted this as much as her friends did, so I gave her this note."

Bo pulls a note from within his pocket, "I was not sure I was forthright about my intentions."

The barkeep pulls out his spectacles and sets it down on the tip of his nose.

'I felt necessary that we should not meet again, and this letter being the final words to that promise.'

The barkeep hands him back the letter, "No, I would say you properly stated your purpose."

Bo takes four loud gulps and places the glass on the counter, making a gentle wave of his hand for a further refill. "I was not happy with myself. I was a bit surly, so what! Her friends were stinky, indigestible, fur balls that I should have...!" Bo looks up at Connor and smiles. "So, I'm here before you, at this very moment, where one would ask, Connor, is my hope for this good woman lost?"

"Ahh, you are dealing with a young man's mistake that grows with him for the rest of his life. Not being a married man, I offer you advice from only what I hear."

"I understand."

"First, your attention must be focused on her, not on her friends. You should be listening to her more closely. Her true thoughts are often hidden in the words that she speaks. It is a defense mechanism that she is not comfortable enough to use the words she wants to reveal."

The barkeep takes Bo's head in his hands, "Understand, man, you are at a grave disadvantage! Her 'so-called friends' have already seized her thoughts. She still wants your acceptance more than their point of view, but remember that her suggestions must be more important to you too, now more than ever. You might try agreeing with her all the time at this juncture, even if you do find folly in her words. You must realize that seeking her comfort means her opinions work better for her, and not yours to you."

The barkeep takes Bo's empty glass away and wipes the counter of the condensation. "There is a pay phone by the loo that operates under a wish. Her number is already installed in its mechanism; all you have to do is pick up the receiver."

On cold-covered bed sheets, Beatie rolls one way, then back the other. She is trying to create a warm setting for her legs, but the bedsheets are loose again. A draft has found its way through the openings and it makes her want to cuss.

She has to get out of bed, though; the morning is waiting for her. Tilting her head sideways, she immediately falls to the floor, and then she makes her way over to the vanity, only to laugh at what she sees.

Her face is completely unrecognizable, distorted by the partially removed makeup left on her pillow. Assuming that the pillow might have something to do with her hair in disarray, it may also know something about her missing earring. Normally, she would be distraught by such calamities, but this time she just sticks out her tongue in defiance.

The events of last night are still with her. She is still trying to soak up every Scottish word she heard, hoping to understand their meaning in a less complicated way. Some words she felt were about passion and pining, and other words about motorcycles going off ocean cliffs. The latter will need professional counseling, but the foremost words seem to be preventing her from blinking. Truth to be told, his words are not the only thought making her feel 'Lilly-Willie'. It was kissing him that convinced her she could belong to the exclusive club called 'Love'. And it comes with a password – a choice between two simple words. "Will you be my Valentine?" She asks, hoping for the correct response. 'YES', he answers, and she smiles. Just to be sure he is not guessing she repeats the question. "Will you be my Valentine?" She asks, and then he says, 'YES'! He did! You read it!! Never before has she ever heard anyone guess the password twice! It feels like... it feels like...FLYING!!

Beatie stands on the tips of her toes and pushes her chest outward, then she reverses her arms. She lowers her head and races forward into the hallway, gracefully coasting across the floor with a slight tilt. She picks up her missing earring, and then, with very short steps around the kitchen table, she flaps her arms five times to stop before the stove.

Her two roommates are seated with a glass of wine, peering above their fashion magazines. They are not used to seeing their housemate break six eggs into a waste basket, and then proceed to scatter the shells into a frying pan.

After Beatie playfully winks at their snickers, she follows up with four squirts of soap into the skillet. When it sets off the fire alarm, it is finally Olivia to issue the first response, "Is there something bothering you, roomie?" she chuckles.

"Everything is fine and dandy over here, captain and co-captain."

"Rough night?" inquires Nikki.

"Quite the opposite, my good aeronauts; it was simply – how should I say – ineffable."

Beatie walks out of the kitchen with the smoking frying pan, suddenly aware of her forgetfulness.

"What am I doing? Silly-self. Y'all need dishes!" Setting the sizzling pan down on top of the lamp shade, Beatie returns to the kitchen for plates. She closes the open door of an empty bird cage and spins several times before making an abrupt stop. Her mobile phone just vibrated off the living room table and it now flops about the floor.

"Oh, my goodness, it's time to wake up!"

Beatie turns to her roommates, "Miss Pringle and Miss Mufflebun are in the oven. Would you please check on them when they are ready?"

Watching her fly back to her bedroom and hearing the door shut, Nikki raises the receiver to her ear, "Hello? No, she can't come to the phone right now; she is a bit occupied. Yes, we are quite sure. Can you leave a message?"

Beatie sits at her vanity and stares for a while. She takes out the cold cream and spreads it over her face, leaving a twisted mess. The little child has gotten out of the playpen again. She wipes herself down with a cotton sock, then begins fanning herself with a hairpin. Something is wrong, but she cannot tell what it is without rational thinking. She measures the warmth of her forehead with an emery board and then tries to determine its temperature with her tongue. For some reason, this only hurts her.

Her mother's erudition says it is a different kind of illness and it will pass, but when Beatie tests this theory by holding a sharp pin to her eye – without a blink – followed by moving a pin beneath her fingernail – without a flinch – she is sure this ailment is not going to pass. She is also sure that this sickness cannot be cured with pills, bags of ice, or bed rest.

Beatie stares long into the mirror. She knows what she has, and she cannot believe this is happening to her. She has spent her entire life trying to avoid just this very ailment, and now she has it. The Amoebiatic Fever:

When all complex synapses of the nervous system are reconstructed into a single-cell organism. The symptoms may or may not include:

 *Taking a shower after getting dressed;
 *Driving down the highway in a parked car;
 Or
 *Riding an escalator clearly marked as stairs.

The symptoms could worsen if the illness were to go unchecked, and she would require round-the-clock care. In a pure state of amoebafication, she would no longer be able to eat, sleep, or ex-foliate inside or out! Her insurance does not cover this; she has already checked!

Beatie walks from her vanity and lies down on the bed. She hears a loud squawk and turns her head with her eyes crossed. She then bursts into tears. "Miss Mufflebun, you got out! This means I forgot to turn on the oven!"

Bo sets the receiver down, "Connor, she would not take my call?"

"Highlander, you must try again, and when you do reach her, remember what I said – listen and engage. What does she enjoy more than anything?"

"This works?"

"It will if she cares."

Bo lifts up the receiver and hears a soft voice on the other end of the phone: "Hello?"

"Beatie? It's me, Bo!"

<Click>

Bo turns to the barkeep, "That's the second time, you know!"

"Try something more thought-provoking. You must energize her! You are there with her in the countryside! Only the two of you! Now call!"

Bo sets the receiver down and picks the phone up, clearing his throat: *"The hills are alive with the sound of music...(v)"*

There is a faint, hesitant voice on the other end: *"With songs they have sung for a thousand years."*

Bo looks at the barkeep for confirmation, *"You spoke to me one day about a taste of dinner."*

Listening to the soft tone reply: *"And I wondered if Scotland might do the same."*

"Beatie!! It's me, Bo!!"

<Click>

"This is ridiculous, Connor!"

"You must remind her of the words she has told you that bring joy to her life." The barkeep comes from around the counter. "She needs constant reassurance that you'll be there for her, even in the worst of times. Sing a song about how you cherish her faults and all her disgusting habits to follow."

Bo lifts up the receiver and hears a lot of static, but it disappears when Beatie starts to speak: *"Are you going to Chuck Scarborough's Fair? (vi)"*

Bo looks at Connor who is rolling his hand to continue with the melody: *"No, I'm not, but I'm already there."*

The voice pauses before a response: *"Remember me before I shave my armpit hairs."*

"You will always be a bonnie of mine."

"Really?"

"Beatie, it's me!"

"It's me too!!"

Bo turns to Connor and raises his thumb. The barkeep then hurries back to his place behind the bar.

"Of course, I didn't think it was your fault, phones are like that when they hang up. I agree. No, I've never heard of ameobafication. Excuse me? I do remember you asking me if Scottish folk celebrate dinner. Well, no because it doesn't get dark until around ten in the evening, so we just have two lunches. I agree, it's silly. I would like to try something new. Parageusia's? Sounds great. Pardon? I didn't hear you, the phone connection was off. Of course, I'll be going. What? No, I won't be sleeping with Mia beforehand. No, I have never seen her with a chastity belt. I don't know what riding a hobby horse does. Parageusia's it is. East Hurl and Puke by the ten-foot-tall wax-work called Chappaqua. Yes, I'll be there. Half past six."

Bo set the receiver down, "I have another date!"

"Congratulations, my man!"

"I thank you for the advice, Connor. If only I knew there were magical words to describe all the things I could have said."

The bartender chuckles, "A will toward your ways and a will toward your words that they won't be taken out of a will toward your faults!"

Bo takes a seat at the bar and raises his empty glass, "Here's to us!"

Bo enters the restaurant and looks about. It is very busy and certainly not large enough to allow for more tables. Odd that he has no recollection of this place or why this location would even exist. Beatie selected it, so it must be happy.

He has arrived a little early and Beatie has yet to appear. The small table in the center on the slow turning pedestal appears too nice to overlook. Without hesitation, Bo reaches out to the young captain and signals to him that this is the very table he wishes to occupy.

"I doubt it, sir, being that there is a line ahead of you and the seat you so gracefully selected is still currently occupied. Without reservations, the maitre'd will have to seat you at the earliest convenience."

Bo stands before the maitre'd straightening the collar about his neck. She is giving off the impression she does not want to be bothered, and decidedly, sends Bo into a quiet submission by the coat racks. Cupping his hands behind his head, he stares aimlessly at the ceiling. It is beyond half past six, but where else is he to go?

"Pardon, I am waiting for Beatie Backlebond, do you know her?"

"Miss Backlebond? Beatie Backlebond? Aw, that's sweet. You're not aware of her dating habits, are you?"

"I most certainly think so. She likes the general chit chat, and the type of food on her plate that she can play with. She doesn't like to be overpowered by strong wards and eloquent good looks. She feels more secure with a man's vulnerability and careful approach, than the decisiveness meant to control her. She also likes..."

"I do not doubt your abundant description of Miss Backlebond when she is properly seated. It's rather, if she is ever seated at all."

"Pardon?"

"There is a six percent chance she will come through that door tonight, a seven percent chance she will make it out of her car, and if we are being totally honest with ourselves, I would say a clear zero percent chance she ever leaves her home."

"There have been other dates?"

"Quite a few; she even met one here half her age."

"This is ridiculous; I should know the lassie of my own dreams!" Bo scoffs, takes his seat by the coat closet, and waits. And waits. And waits. There is a cold draft by the door that blows a chill into his clothes, sending his hands deep into his pockets. While playing with the lint within the stitches, his amulet falls to the floor. "It can correct a simple mistake, and this is certainly a simple mistake."

The air suddenly smells of sweet florals from a light breeze that blows his way.

"Excuse me, Mr. Fox?" Bo lowers his amulet from his eye with a coy smile. "We reached out to Miss Backlebond, and suspiciously so, she would not answer her phone. However, we have the luxury of a 'Bobo'. He's a courier of sorts, specializing in mail-order, lady drifters."

Bo looks at her, confused.

"Miss Backlebond is already here, sir. She's a bit of a flight risk, so we have prepared the normal seating arrangements."

Bo looks toward the front door, listening to the sounds of scratching with childish cries of, 'No!!' How amazing she looks, partially hidden behind an assembly of fronds. So beautifully dressed in a delicate shade of blue with white fringes about her sleeves. She wears makeup too, a painted expression of liveliness and joy. Her eye liner, as sleek as a well, placed hair across her face.

Despite all this beauty, she still has a disturbed look. It may have something to do with the large man holding her over his shoulder. Of course, when he reluctantly sets her down at the request of the maitre'd, he is not surprised by her attempt to escape through the carry-out window. It is quite humorous, in fact, to see her waving to him while nestled under Bobo's arm. As if everything is normal.

It is a gable-style rooftop, overlooking the city limits with a view of the other side of the bay. This apparently is the restaurant's recommended seating for Beatie and all her dates. Though it may not sound appealing, it is pleasantly outdoorsy and warm. Even the harbor boats add a touch of appeal, creaking to the splashing waves along the banks. Bo places his feet firmly on the slopes of the roof and holds tight to the table to keep it from teetering. Beatie has already settled down, maintaining a perfect balance with her bare toes pointing out over the ridge.

"Nice view, isn't it, Beatie?"

Beatie smirks and tosses a pee down the roof's slope, "I've gotten used to it."

Bo has already taken the liberty to surprise her by ordering an appetizer, the Terradaffy Squeege.

"Because I know how much you like soups." Waiting for a smile that does not come, she fixes her eyes instead on a pea drifting between the carrots and the corn.

The waitress appears on a ladder through an opening, where the chimney once appeared. By pulling on the anchor straps, the waitress is able to lock the table into place. She then turns over their empty water glasses and fills them with a sparkling drink, "Miss Backlebond, how do you like your basted Meeley Worms," Beatie's response is a disinterested flick of her finger, still angry at the restaurant staff for their issuance of Bobo to her home.

When the waitress leaves, Bo seizes the chance to employ one of Connor's tactical ploys. A thought-provoking wangle taken from the words she spoke regarding her employer.

"There are many thieves among the streets, but none like the manager of Ghost City. The gal-sneaker who chases after the hearts of young lassies by visiting the local tourist shops."

Bo watches carefully for a change in her expression, but only sees a smirk.

"He inappropriately places his fingers on everything, but it's his words that concerns them the most: 'Come to my office where the clothes are worn less frequent', he says."

Beatie fights back a smile and finally relents, "He's really not that bad."

"He chased me with a potted plant. Hardly a fellow interested in the preservation of horticulture."

Beatie smiles and continues to stir her soup.

"May I have a pea?"

"You should know, you're not supposed to eat the food here. It's just a conversation piece to help couples get over their first-time jitters. See this fortified plastic spoon? They're for flipping veggies."

Beatie loads a pea onto her spoon, bends it back, and releases it at Bo.

"Hey!!" Bo retrieves the pea from his mouth, "It's awful!"

"I told you."

They return to silence, while Beatie makes whistling noises and flings garden selections from her spoon into the roof's gutter.

"What are you whistling?"

Beatie looks about oblivious to his question.

""It sounded like a supernatural crime jingle from the seventies."

She claps her hands on her face, "Yes – oh my! You are so right! How did you know that?"

"I put the show on for Mia while she sleeps. When she wakes, it would be to the images of this horror show. It's immature, but you have to understand our relationship."

"No, I get it. I do the same thing to my mum!"

Beatie looks over the edge to hear a man crying out from the street below, requesting that she stop tossing food. Beatie laughs and fires off another pea, quickly stirring up her soup for another one.

"Less queer are those days when one can just walk freely on the city streets without any intrusion." Beatie finds a miniature carrot and sends it sailing down the chimney, then sets her spoon down. "I'm referring to this book I am reading, 'The Illuminator of Foggy Pants'."

"Mia talks a lot about ghosts."

"Well, you've probably heard the story about Meanburn Furvery, the city's former tax collector? He had been resting on his backbone for several hundred years, then suddenly, he decides to leave his resting place to pester the residents for the back taxes their ancestors failed to pay. He even goes to their homes to yell at them. As you know, words from ghosts are generally unrecognizable to living ears. So instead, he goes on these rampages: water contamination, power outages, fire break-outs. He even forces a trolley off its path!"

"Just natural occurrences, no?"

"I don't think so. Anyway, an intercession was required by digging up the city's mayor at the time. He had issues of his own, of course. It worked for a while until the city's monetary supply fell short, so they had to tax the suburbs for the losses." Beatie fires another pee into the chimney hole in a self-congratulatory fashion.

"I guess trying to regain a normality with the preceding world presents many challenges. The whole city is spooky, kooky, and hooky, and it's all in this book. Everybody knows about it!"

With a giggle and a lot of laughs, the evening goes predictably well. He listens carefully to all her words, even reminding her teasingly when she is side-tracked and has to be reminded where she left off. When Bo slides his hands across the table beneath her fingers, this is when he clearly feels the little organ in her chest quicken. He softens his voice to a slight whisper and watches as she bites down on her hand.

"I read there is a place we can go called Talbot?"

"I really enjoyed my time with you, Mr. Bo Fox. Goodbye!"

And just like that, it is over. Down the ladder she slides, and even takes it with her, strapping it to her car and speeding off down the back roads.

It is not true that dreams are left unfinished; this one still comes with the most promising ending.

FEBRUARY 9: WHAT IS
IN IT FOR TALBOT?

She starts her mornings early, filling a cart with elliptical coins, incense sticks, and pictures of deceased relatives. There are over one hundred rooms she must see, and more than a thousand meters of dark hallways she must walk. She has to see them all. She has to know what is taking place in her motel. It is not a choice but a requirement if she is to keep sanity within its walls. Things can get out of hand very quickly, particularly when the sun reaches the edge of the horizon and these *'things'* are left alone.

The elevator rises quickly to the third floor, and the owner of the motel steps into the hallway. She stands with a motionless gaze toward Rooms 309 to 331 when the elevator comes to a close. The hallway ahead does not open for any light. So, brave it before her, while uncertainty is always there; knowing that it helps not to ask – who, what, why, when, and where.

The room glows with the early morning daylight, and once again, Bo awakens to the finer things in life. He could never believe there would be another day of light unless the night time preceding it would relent. He lays with his hands behind his head, soon enchanted by the same clinking sounds from the water pipes that torment Mia.

She lifts her oiled legs and stretches them across the floor, dressed in her backless, neckless, gold-metallic string bikini. He has already seen this before, but senses he has to go through this again.

"So, how do you feel the world will come out today?" Mia trots along the floor to the window, where she quickly pulls on the string of the blinds. "The window is stuck." She presses her face against the glass and flickers her eyelids, "Ooh, that is cold." She turns her head toward Bo with an inquisitive look, "I made the most dumbfounded discovery about this motel. It was actually a psychiatric hospital two hundred years ago."

Mia springs on top of Bo and waits for the bed springs to settle. She then lowers her face so close to his that their noses press together and their eyes cross.

"Mar? You're a wee close." Bo puts his forefinger on the side of her nose and tilts her head to one side. She then yanks the pillow from beneath his head and throws it across the room, lowering her face with only an inch to spare. "Better now?"

"What's this about?"

"Why don't we see the other residents?"

"I kind of like it this way."

"Don't you ever wonder why the pipes rattle and the doors slam at night?"

"Natural sounds, that's all they are."

"Seems to confirm what the manager has been pointing out all along. Ghosts do exist."

"All the while their presence concealed behind closed doors?"

"Ghost fingers do not open doors, Bo."

"Yet, they're able to slam them?"

Mia pauses to analyze some gray hairs on Bo's sideburns but says nothing. She paddles on his chest with her open palms, "I need more information! You're the magician with the charm!"

"Okay. Okay. You numpty, gibble-gabber!" Bo reaches under his pillow and opens up his logbook.

"Friday, the ninth of February – already?"

"Seems so." Mia shrugs.

"From what I am to remember, there's word of an unbalanced granny that walks these very hallways. She knows something about this place."

"Where can I find her?"

"One just has to listen."

Three knocks appear on their door that startles Mia, "Don't just dawdle; you started it!"

Bo rolls out of bed, trots to the door, and opens it. Debuting with an older face, mischievously drawn in brown markers, is the owner of the motel.

She is possibly two or three centuries old, preserved in some gold covering from head to foot. There are sticks intertwined in a ball on top of her head, and her eyes are so beady, one would question whether they are really eyes at all. "You must be..." Bo feels a tied bundle stuffed into his stomach and buckles down to his knees.

"Silence please! I am who I am, and you are who you are!"

Bo choking, looks up at her with recollection, "I've seen you before."

"I am Norba Hebe! That is what I do. What you do?"

"I do very well, thank you, mam."

"Then maybe I do this to you!" The owner stuffs three fingers into Bo's mouth and extends a finger into his nostril. Wiggling her fingers inside his cheeks, she rolls her eyes and chants in a haunting voice, "See Street Thomas play unfairly with Yard Mary. Watch Store Cindy paint happily with House Wendy. Acts of malevolence and benevolence creating disease and life. Good will only return when evil has run its course."

Bo hears the door of the stairwell close and quietly shuts the door, "Mar, your towels are here."

Mia stands before the full-size mirror, admiring herself with her legs in a pose and her hands running up and down her thighs, "Oh, what am I to do when all those judging eyes take a gander at me?" Mia turns abruptly and snaps at him, "Are you going to put your trunks on? The plan is a day at the pool, shopping, then dining, like always."

Bo looks out the window, where a black cloud covers half the sky, "Change of weather, Mar. It's going to rain."

Mia hurries to the window and is disheartened by what she sees, "Aw, it's gonna be a real pea-souper! Change of plans, we will have some breaky and then to the indoor pool."

"I'm not hungry, Mar."

"You haven't eaten anything since we arrived. Chipped beef and a cold fizzie? Does that not sound like a meal you would want to eat every day?"

Bo rolls up his sleeves and slips into some flops, "I have other plans, sorry."

Mia stamps her foot and throws a barrette at him, "Fine Bo! Why don't we just go ahead and play Tree-Dog?! I'll be the tree, and you go ahead and squirt all over me!!"

"It's not like that, Mar."

"No?! I'm looking all dishy, and you would rather play with infants. She's a baby, Bo! With baby hands and baby shoes!"

Bo reaches into his pocket for his amulet, "But she's my babbie."

Mia grabs the charm and races back to the window as he watches in horror while she encircles her arm as if ready to toss the stone to the street. "I can see a lot of problems for me with this rock," tossing the rock from hand to hand before letting it drop to the floor, much to the relief of Bo. "You've really changed, Bo; you would never have abandoned me and Sam like this before."

Mia turns away to avoid being seen with a flow of emotions. "I'll just go into the bathroom and put on more oil, and you can't watch!!" Mia disappears into the bathroom and shuts the door.

It is still morning, and the schedule for lunch is hours away. Dropping some matches into her smock-pocket, Mia slips into her flops. She grabs her bowling bag and tosses a bathroom towel over her shoulder. Within a short moment, she is standing before the elevator and looking down at the motel map. Somewhere on these lower floors, there is an indoor pool waiting for her, and this is how she is going to celebrate her independence.

Mia pushes on the elevator button and looks into her beach bag. She rummages through the contents: Sunglasses – check; a neck float – check; book – check; a flashlight – check; a bag of doodle snaps – great; and her court-issued, crazy pills – of course. Again, she pushes rapidly on the button, alternating it with a grab of a doodle snack. She responds to a chill that runs up her spine and notices that the hall is much darker than it was before.

When the carriage finally arrives, she rushes into the elevator with an odd feeling that something else is approaching. The doors could not have closed any sooner, leaving her wondering what may have been trying to get in. She presses the REHAB button and rests her back against the wall. There is a faint scent in the box that is very familiar to her nose. It has that lime with formaldehyde smell that she is forbidden from possessing.

The floor light blinks and the doors noisily strain to open. Mia winces repeatedly when the air in the hall replaces that in the elevator. She turns away, trying to hold onto the contents within her stomach. It is that old decade smell of cadaverine, putrescine, and skatole that she could never get used to. It's already saturating her nostrils and leaving her eyes in tears.

Mia throws back her shoulders and resets her nose. A trick she learned from her many years of dealing with the dead. It is certainly not the worst smell she has ever consumed. This will not deter her. This is about her independence and not about smells from her past. Mia holds the door, peering cautiously out, with one foot serving as a brake and the other as an introduction to curiosity. What she sees is a long black corridor, stretching both ways.

"Hello?!" Mia sets aside her doodle snacks, hoping to shine a better light on her path. She reaches inside her bag and finds sun-tan oil, a change of shorts, and Saturday's newspaper. More items than she started out with. How does this happen?! Why is the flashlight missing?! She is sure she checked that item off!

The bag slips from her shoulder and the contents spill out into the hallway. Quickly moving forward to collect the items, she realizes her mistake. The elevator is making that cranking noise back up the shaft. Mia rolls her eyes in disbelief, wrapping the towel around her shoulders and reaching around in her bag for the newspaper. She fingers through her pockets and finds a matchbox. Striking down on the rough surface, she then holds the torched newspaper to the air.

On the floor before her, there are chunks of foundation, a dislodged generator hanging from the wall, and everywhere, there are dark pools of liquid that smell of machine lubricant. She extends the burning newspaper higher into the darkness and is relieved to see a glare at the end of the corridor. This means the prospect of a nice swim is still on the agenda. It is not a long walk, just one she has to make beneath the entanglement of hanging wires. Lingering back and forth from wall to wall, Mia is happy to finally make it to the last barrier – a metal frame door. It is heavy and plenty broken, but Mia did come with determination. She places both hands on the door frame, and with one mean facial expression, the door comes off its hinges rather easily.

It is a very natural setting, with creeping vines and black locust trees reinforcing the ceiling. There is a large skylight with layers of green lichens that provide a hazy warmth to the room. Noteworthy too is the spicy scent from the tall weeds blooming from the fissures in the floor. But what has Mia most excited is the pool. It is as black as the insides of a tar barrel, with flowering pods in a gentle spin about its surface. It reminds her of the summers spent floating in the clay pits of Cornwall.

Mia does a quick spin and clasps her hands together. Maybe she can get in a few laps before delving into her book. She prances upon the green mold along the pool's edge and quickly finds a bucket to release into the center of the pool. "Bung yer up!" she yells, and waits for the sinking effects of the bubbling bucket. She swings her arms together and bounces on her toes in excitement. "Bubbles! Bubbles! Bubbles!"

There is an electrical box on the opposite end of the pool that sparks her curiosity. She rushes over to press it, and instantaneously, bubbles rise to the surface. Mia does a quick dance to the staircase and then places both feet in the water. How fun it is to watch the little eddies form circles around her ankles.

Enough already! Mia is ready to drift in the Adam's ale, among the pods in a gentle spin, sink down into its indeterminable depths, and then blow bubbles until her face turns purple!

"What is this?" Mia reaches down to retrieve a substance gathering around her ankles. It appears to be strands of hair attached to a band aid. There is something else that is rising to the surface and it looks to be some sort of surgical tourniquet. Mia leans out to retrieve the apparatus, unaware that the condition of the railing is fragile. She plunges beneath the water and grabs onto a drifting swamp root to lift herself back out. Shivering on the tile floor, she stares with disgust at a rusty grease spewing from where the rail used to be. It bothers her that it is creating a morphing shadow that is darker than the pool itself.

Mia is having second thoughts about that swim. She wraps herself in the towel and stuffs the paper into her bag, pausing only to allow a three-headed, two-legged, yellow snake wriggle past her into the pool. Mia is repulsed by the lack of cleanliness in this hotel. She most certainly will be issuing a complaint to management. The only delay might depend on whether she escalates another incident to an even higher authority! Three-headed, two-legged, yellow snakes should not be rising to the surface, dressed in a green hospital gown, and waving a sleeve at her!

Mia quickly retrieves a pool net, hoping to collect more evidence, when she is shockingly detained by some large-headed, six-footed, flowering weed that drops down from an air vent.

"Get out!" It spews.

"Bloody hell! Are there no lifeguards to control this madness?!"

Mia begrudgingly chops the head off the weed and tosses the net into the pool with a chuckle. Just the usual day at the office, really. That is, until the pool water collapses several hundred fathoms below the surface, and then the water rushes back up with a chainsaw roaring from its depths. Mia now realizes what her mind would not let her see before: that this pool is alive and breathing!!

Slipping and sliding, she somehow manages to make it through the angled space above the door. She then races down the obstacle-strewn hallway, only to find herself tripping over a collection of nauseating black bags that reek of body waste. She quickly searches for some relief in her bag with her mind in a whirl to what could possibly be real anymore. None of these obstacles were here before: the waste bags and the red-stained water! And why are her pills missing?!!

Emotionally exhausted, Mia remains silent, draining herself over a large mesh drain covering set below a high, placed window light. She wipes a few cold tears from her cheeks and frowns. A change of thinking is necessary, and that starts with resetting the flame on her newspaper. She then fastens her bag around her neck and smiles. There is hope! A dim light peeks around a bend in the hallway. It is not a long walk; it would be even quicker if she picked up her pace.

"Move it, Pearl!" Mia runs wildly toward the light. Her arms pumping up and down, and her flip-flops clapping across the floor! Closer and closer! Run, feet, run!!

Mia eases up, breathing from fear and exhaustion. She makes it, though. There are ceiling lights, lit every thirty feet. There are also double doors not far beyond that. In the opposite direction she sees a long ramp descending into darkness – go with the lights and the double doors.

Down the hallway, Mia notices that there are rooms along the way, with a light source of their own. She pauses before the first room to see if she can find help. It is not very deep and it is oblong in shape. It reminds her of a display case in a museum, occupied with wooden beds and linen stuffed with hay. The next room appears to be a supply room. There is a rickety table with clear plastic tubs of green water. The next room is not very calming either; it is a preparatory room of sorts with warped tables and restraints. "Breathe and laugh; breathe and laugh. My name is Mia Pearl; I live in the zoo. My name is Mia Pearl; most everyone knew."

Another preparatory room of iodine bottles and extracting tools. Next room!

"My name is Mia Pearl; it is the place where I grew."

Wax strips, tourniquet kits, limb chips, and worm pits. Next room!

"My name is Mia Pearl; I had nothing to do."

Chest claws and Utica cribs. Skull saws and blood-spurting bibs! Next room!!

"My name is Mia Pearl; what can I do?!"

Night wear and day wear, everywhere a broken chair, chair!!

Every room she passes and everything she sees are destroying her spirit, and if it could get any worse, it would have something to do with the ceiling lights going out! "Bloody hell! Run, feet, run!!"

Mia dashes ahead without looking into another room, finally reaching the double doors as the lights expire. A cold blast of musty air follows, sending her tumbling backward into the unlit hallway.

All alone in the dark, with only the red emergency lights flashing, something begins to caress her neck. Though it feels warm and soothing, it is far out of the ordinary to think it is reassuring. A surge of frightened electrodes runs through her torso, forcing her up to her feet as the lights come back on!

Standing before her is a creature, so hideous, only in a subterranean culture could anything like this evolve. It has a large tentacle protruding from its untamed head. It also has two large, bulbous eyes capable of locating the most tastiest portions of her body. The creature shakes and bellows in hunger, "It-shma, It-shma, It-shma," it cries out, before setting forth its rubber hands onto her face!

It has never been in Mia's nature to surrender herself to an oversized insect, and now isn't any different. She takes the remaining portions of the newspaper and quickly turns on the beast, pounding, and slashing, and tearing away at its protruding lump. Off comes the creature's swallowing organ, along with spews of great moisture. The creature cries, "It-shma! It-shma! It's me! It's me!" How horrible it screams, trying to parlay with Mia in her own native tongue. She continues to beat it with the last remaining pages of the daily, and then she gives it one final kick to its groin. In triumph, she watches as the two-legged, bulbous creature sinks to the floor in agony. "It's me, it's me! It's Sen, it's Sen!" repeats the weakening voice. The creature isn't kidding; it is Sen!

"Sen?!" Mia bursts into hysterics and kicks him again and again, aiming for the same region that brought him to the floor. "What is wrong with you?! Bloody hell, sneaking up on me like that! And why the #%@#! Are you wearing that rubber hazmat suit?!!"

"I was looking for you." Replies Sen, in-and-out of consciousness.

"Maybe I did not phrase that question accurately. Why were you trying to scare the bedazzle juice out of me?!" Mia, impatient for a response, is ready to kick him again when Sen finally interrupts. "I wasn't trying to scare you. You were on the display monitor behind the lobby desk." Sen unbuckles his pants, relieving some of the pain. "I put on the first outfit that came naturally. I would have come earlier, but it's hard to find people willing to work these days with all this government assistance."

"Did I hurt you?"

The manager rolls over onto his side, "A bit. I find wearing a protective cup reduces hospital visits."

When Sen recovers, Mia helps him remove the remaining strips of his suit. "Sen, what kind of place is this? Is this one of those experimental laboratories, like in the book you gave me?"

"Miss Pearl," the manager having regained much of his hearing and vision, "All we have here is a little motel that has a troubling past. Your curiosity about the unknown should not be used to extract anyone's bodily fluid gestation. I don't know why you even came down here."

"You mentioned an indoor pool, remember? You advertised specifically that you have two pools! One inside and one outside!"

"I never advertised an indoor pool!"

"Yes, you did. It's on the map for the guests!"

"It's not an advertisement if I did not remotely suggest or, in any way try to influence, anybody to swim in that pool. Seriously, just to get from the elevator to the pool alone, should have set off all sorts of alarms. Have you not been to the pool?! In what sensible world would anyone conclude that the pool would be worth swimming in?!"

"I admit, it is a little dirty."

"A little dirty?! It hasn't been operational for over two centuries!!"

"No need to yell."

"The only one who might ever consider using it would be Butter Corn, but even he ..."

"Butter Corn? That name again. Creatures from the dark abyss! Like in the book you gave me!"

"Butter Corn is my three-headed, two-legged, yellow python. We let him loose down here to exterminate varmints."

"How do you explain the lights going off? The Cadavers of Confident Displeasures would do something like that!"

"The lights are on a timer! We are required by the Safety Act to provide lighting to all access areas, even if we don't use them!" Sen lowers his voice. "We get a tax break if we can keep the usage below that of a larger hotel."

"Ahah! The screaming! I heard that too!!"

"The building is two centuries old; it's going to have some settling."

Mia gathers up her items and places them in the bag, but before she can scoop up the doodle snacks, Sen catches her by the arm, "Listen, Mia, you have to forget what you saw down here and tell no one."

"Oh, so we are on a first-name basis now? Well, don't worry, I'm not here to screw up anyone's taxes."

"It's all around here. The motel. The streets. The Graveyards. They call it the phantom air."

"The phantom air? They?"

Mia watches as the corners of Sen's mouth begin to rise, "Ah! You fooled me again!"

"I know a little humor. Come, Mia. I know a safe way out through the boiler room."

Mia tugs away from his hand, "What did you just say?"

"I said, I know a way out of here."

Mia stares deeply into his eyes and over his shoulder, then down the ramp to the other end of the hallway. "That is not what you said, and not in one movie has anyone ever said – you can get out safely through the boiler room." Mia slowly steps pass Sen.

"Mia, what are you thinking? Miss Pearl!"

With wild steps in a zig-zag motion, Mia bolts ahead without looking back.

"Mia Pearl!! Are you crazy?!! That's the way to..." Sen frowns as Mia makes her way down the ramp and sighs. "The Morgue."

Bo steps off the bus and pulls out a map that he once carried thirty years ago. It is a bit faded and the words are difficult to read, but the layout is understandable. The sun so far has proven to be a great working clock for his mind. It appears to be the middle of the day with much time left on the horizon. Her home is just around the block and he carries a stuffed tortoise-bear under his arm. He gave it to her once before and thought he would give it to her again, since it had received a great response thirty years ago. He stops at the corner. Memories returning with great clarity. It is the house beneath the shining sun with a rainbow casting its colors onto the walkway. Bo closes his eyes. She is almost ready.

She runs barefoot behind a mop, swatting the counters with a dust cloth and tossing a few coasters to the tables. Despite her many fribble-freezes (a word she uses when wasting time thinking about pretend affairs), Beatie certainly has not forgotten how to give a house a fine cleaning, nor has she forgotten how to have fun with it – step forward, step back, twirl and clap. With long, traveling steps down the hallway, Beatie sidesteps into her room and gently drops her hand to an overly ruckus crowd of stuffed animals.

She sits before the mirror, resting her chin on her hand, heaving a great sigh of pleasure. It is about last night, and true to her thinking, it was fabulously delicious. She was finally able to share her thoughts with someone so free of all that vulgarity. She just isn't comfortable with all those sexual descriptions of one's anatomy on a first date. Bo seems much more sure of himself. It's like she is dating someone who is fifty-eight.

So, another date is planned, and there are many places she knows about, but Talbot is probably the best spot for a quiet, people-free atmosphere. The question is about what to wear. She has been struggling with this all morning because, frankly, she does not know what a fourth date entails. She is certain she will be leaving her hand on his leg by the end of the evening, and therefore, the selection has to be important.

She turns over her beach basket, looking for the right combination of Talbot Beach wear. How about this cottage cabana or full-coverage maxi dress? Maybe the Plume de la sweater with the high-water, sissy pants. Then, of course, there is the neckless, stringless, crotchless, gold-metallic bikini that pulls away when...

"What?!! Where did this come from?!" Beatie didn't even know anything like this existed. She kicks the basket away and immediately reaches for the hand sanitizer. She then takes a deep breath and turns to her animals in recital:

"Talbot is not a place for smocks and flops or G-string tops.

Talbot is a place for dresses and sandals, soft music with candles.

Talbot is not a place to dance to a song in a camel-toe thong.

Talbot is a place where you can throttle with a bottle until you walk with a – AHH!!! What is wrong with you, woman!" Beatie slams her head on the floor repeatedly. "Stop it! Stop it! Stop it!! You wanton, thigh warming, breast feeling, bunny bumper!! AHHH!!!"

Somehow, she is developing a potty mouth to go along with her thinking, which, to say the least, is both very unbecoming. Beatie is about to kick her bedpost, knowing that pain had worked well to counter a fever; but with this new disease, what if she actually likes it?!

"Genius Loci. Ohm. Ohm. Ohm. Loci Genius, Ohm Diddy Ohm. Better now."

Beatie storms into the closet and switches on the light, poking her fingers through all the plastic coverings. Such a hard decision, so much to choose from. Okay, there is the floom dress, which has great mobility but doesn't stay on very long, and of course, there is the Bejewelled Go-Go dress that has a surprise at every angle. "Think, mad woman! Think! This is Talbot!!"

"Okay, okay." She is most inclined to go with her conservative demeanor: something polite and something calm; flowering beavers with penis-shaped palms! "AHHHH!!!" Beatie races out of her closet, feeling her boobs and fighting back her hands from going any lower, "Nooo!!!"

She finally gains control of her thoughts and locks her hands to the vanity! "I'm absolutely appalled by this behavior in you!!" Beatie is truly taken aback by this behavior. Is this yet another disease to contend with? That does it! She needs a mind-cleansing, soul-searching, detox-completion.

The shower was cold, and whatever was in the aerosol can, really worked wonders on creating the pain in her eyes. Now she can revisit her choice of clothing. With a reversal in thinking, the dress she settles upon is a light blue sundress, along with a comfortable pair of tall-wedged sandals for kissing height. She looks deep into her mirror and knows change is coming. This makes her nervous, but she also understands that change is necessary for her happiness.

Beatie sets a bowl of passion fruit on the 'yearning' table. She pulls the curtain slightly aside and watches anxiously. How easily she could be infected by his devotion if every day he brings her a gift, sits faithfully listening to all her squabbles, and learns to protect himself from her physical outbursts. She opens the door to see the leather top hat making its way up the lawn. Closing the door, she sits at the table, trying to keep her composure. The sound of his feet coming up the steps just can't seem to come quick enough. When she opens the door with her arms and legs all around him, who would not expect the spinning to lead them over the porch rail? Landing in the hedges, they immediately speak the words that would never make it into the annals of literature: "It's you!"

"I didn't know if telepathy worked on Scottish people, but I'm glad you got my message. I see you brought a gift?" She rolls off the hedge and bounces up and down. "Mr. Silly, you didn't." Beatie's eyes open very wide but then immediately become very narrow. "Arm floats?"

"Arm fleits?" Bo reaches into his jacket and even under his hat. "What happened to the turtle-bear?" He shrugs his shoulders and gives her the box, "Aye, arm fleits."

It does not matter; the expression on her face tells him everything. She is truly happy and excited to be receiving a non-practical gift; at least for now.

"I like your hoos!" removing his hat and stepping through the door.

"Yes – this is my 'hoos', except I'm renting it. You've seen the porch and the door; well inside is the living room. My bedroom is down the hall to the left, across from Nikki's room.

"Aye, Nikki."

"And the hallway straight ahead, past the kitchen, leads to Olivia's room."

"Aye, I remember Olivia," Bo puts his hand on an empty bird cage. "You have a bird cage!"

"I have two birds," Beatie clears her throat, "but for their safety, I've decided to let them roam free. Should we go to Talbot? I packed some chicken and potato salad, along with some deviled eggs."

"I like devil eggs, wrapped in a breaded sausage and fried to a crunch."

"Not that elaborate. Just a hard-boiled egg cut in half with yolk and mayonnaise, mustard, pickle juice, and hot peppers. The basket is on the counter."

They ride in the hum of her little car, puttering ahead with small puffs of smoke extending from the tail pipe. They reach an overpass with a circular ramp that requires a little extra throttle to make it to the top. Beatie calls to Bo in urgency to put his arm out the window and start flapping. Sounds crazy, but in unison, they make it over, even tilting their arms like a soaring eagle on the back side. While the little car soars down the ramp, Bo begins a conversation about himself thirty years ago. She seems to listen with an incurable smile, even helping him with the details when he becomes stuck.

Talbot is just as he imagined, maybe a bit too much like Scotland. He added some sego plants and white sand from memory, but still kept some bleating sheep in the background for home appeal. Bo strolls to the other side of the car and opens the door for Beatie. She looks around with curiosity, "Do you hear sheep?"

He lifts his ear to hear the murmuring sound of thunder. It alerts him to the coming of the Scottish Stoorworm, a magnificent water beast known to engulf beaches. Oh, how he remembers in fiery detail, thirty years ago, when he drifted off in her car, leaving her to confront the weather beast on her own. Fair to say she was quite disappointed.

Beatie senses the storm coming as well, but reaches for the food basket anyway. "I think this will work out just fine. Could you grab the music player?" She says nothing further about the rumbles, and instead, flings a towel over her shoulder. Bo follows Beatie down a crooked path through a sparse collection of coniferous trees. He is mesmerized by her dress flickering in a strong breeze. Her hair too, like waves in a spring meadow under a pressing wind.

Beatie flips off her flops and races ahead upon the white sand, quickly finding the perfect place to spread her towel. She sets the picnic basket down and waits for Bo to sit next to her. He has never been to Talbot and is fascinated by what his mind is creating. The water remains dark and flat, but the sky above has its own idea of how it should appear. Colors that undulate in orange and yellow, splashing against a backdrop of azul.

Beatie leans against Bo and takes his hand for reassurance, "I was very happy you were at the restaurant when I arrived. There was a lot to think about: the Fair of the Crustaceans, the Selkie on holiday, and the dance when I liked you and you liked me. The feeling seemed so mutual, which I guess made me uncomfortable. I get so nervous when I feel uncomfortable, so much so I have to turn away without drooling. It's like guberstagnation, you know?"

Bo still looking at the sky, shakes his head in confusion.

"Oh, my mistake; you're from Scotland. Very well, it's like being all choked up inside, but you're too dry to have any tears or blow your nose. It's like having dry heaves in your sinuses and beach sand in your eye sockets. Present tense: Guberstag. Past tense: Guberstagged."

Beatie lays her head on his shoulder and looks at what Bo can't take his eyes off of, "Would it not be nice if we could just stay here forever, and never grow old, and live like Selkies?"

"*Ode on a Grecian Urn: For youth beneath the tree, thou canst not leave.* (vii)"

"I like that. How do you say that in English?"

"I gather it's untranslatable. John Keats, he wrote poems like so."

"I would like to read the English version one day."

Bo watches a dark cloud float across the ocean, now trolling a shadow up the beach. He reaches up to catch Beatie's flying hand and looks to see her smiling embarrassingly.

They are really not too different from one another, welcoming each other's faults when no one else will. And as much as she welcomes his peculiarities, he welcomes all of hers too. Together, their infectious laughs, silly words, and unrefined conversations show the world a charming innocence that can bring smiles to the most cynical of minds.

She lifts the music player onto the towel and presses the button to hear a melody. Beatie takes his hand and leads him to the center of the beach. There, she spins once and grabs his arm twice. The sand acts a lot differently than a hardwood floor, and it causes her to stumble, but with his hand steady on the small of her back, she is confident to try again.

They slowly shuffle through the smooth grains of sand, soon lifting their heads to see a celestial beam of light fall upon them. Everywhere she steps it is sunny and clear, and if she can create a sunny, blue sky during the dreariest of days, there would never be a dark day to think about.

He twirls her around and brings her back, releasing her into another spin. How so real this all is, and how so beautiful to be feeling these thoughts of her. He cannot help but wonder if this happiness could ever really exist outside of a dream.

He inhales a lungful of cool and damp air, then turns an eye to the first street light to come on. Turning back to look over her shoulder, he can see the blue ocean darkening from the advance of the smudge in the sky. Within moments, a gust of wind blows strong along the branch tops, and the air becomes niveous with pine needles.

"Is it here yet?" she says softly.

"Aye, black as the earl of hell's waistcoat, it is."

She shivers and squeezes Bo's hands, requesting that he provide a little shelter from the gusting winds. Already, small rain droplets are cascading down the gentle slopes of her face, and her eyelashes are doing their best to sweep away each glob, but it is his fingers through her hair that allow her to keep her eyes on him. This is when he notices her face is no longer as happy as his, and he can see through her eyes the connection of doubt she keeps in her heart. It is supposed to be in the forefront of her mind as a daily reminder, but she often forgets to check. Not this time.

"I don't want you to become a Merman!" She forcibly frees herself from his extended arms and rushes off the beach.

"Beatie, where are you going?" Bo grabs the picnic basket and follows her through the rain. The water is already expanding beyond the edges of the street, forcing him to retreat to higher ground. He can only listen carefully to a gentle voice and splashing in the water, but it is not what he thinks – for it sounds like joy!

Beyond the glare of the street lamps at their full strength, Beatie finally comes into view. Her actions are most absurd, playfully lifting her legs and dropping each one down into a deepening puddle, but the storm does not bother her; in fact, she seems to welcome it for reasons only she understands. As the puddle diminishes in size, the sky reacts by becoming brighter and clearer. She may not know how to convey the feelings she has for him, but somehow the answer resides in this dance.

The rumbling storm echoes far away and past the city. She kicks through all the remaining puddles, as if she has something to do with the storm's retreat. She then circles around Bo, stopping before him with a gentle swipe of her finger down his nose. He can see she has made a thorough inquiry from within.

"Why do you stay here, instead of Scotland, I mean? You are so there, you know?"

"It's your roommates, isn't it?"

"But their talk makes me doubt you!"

"I'm not going anywhere Beatie. This is now home. There's nowhere I can go. There *talk* is just so. It's *talk*."

Beatie's mouth twists to one side. His explanation does not sound well thought out, at least, not enough to defend against her roommate's claims. It is disheartening to hear a man with the inability to speak his true words. A man who would so cowardly move on because his words were not meant to be dear.

Beatie watches as Bo unhooks a rock from his belt buckle. He then places the hole over his right eye. It looks creepy at first – the white orb of his eye stuffed in a hole – but in reality, it is quite peaceful. As he lowers the rock, she then tries to find any hint of deception in his grinning expression, but surprisingly, it's not there anymore. Her peers have been wrong about him.

"I don't know why, but I believe you," Beatie's toes rise up. "I accept what is true; if I said what I knew, the man I would have to meet would have to be ...you?" She hands Bo her car keys.

Bo reaches down to remove his boots, grimacing at a trail of dirty water forming pools around his chair. He is dressed only in a towel, with the rest of his clothing hanging on a wire. Beatie un-bunches her hair while waiting for the water to boil. She leans her head over the pot and lets the warm steam moisturize her face. She pours the water into two cups of powdered chocolate and carefully, tiptoes across the floor. She extends her arm toward Bo, opening her palm with a handful of sandwich meat, "Try this; I made it myself."

Beatie has never prepared a meal for anyone besides her parents. This time, she is showing her nervousness. She forgot to wrap the meat in bread, but at least, she concentrated long enough to spread mayonnaise over it.

"Did you make cocoa?"

"I did, but not from a heilan coo."

Bo takes the slivers from her hand and, instinctively, sniffs the meat. It has a slight discoloration, but that's not why he is not eating. He's no longer hungry.

Beatie folds her hands in her lap and watches him take a nibble with a sigh, "Don't you like food?"

"No, my lass. For some reason, I have not been eating."

"I am nervous too, not knowing what to expect. I've never been with anyone long enough to make them a sandwich." She places her cool fingers on his cheek, allowing the intimacy to run between them.

Bo is standing outside her bedroom door in the faint light of the hallway. She lifts up on her toes and presses her nose against his, giving him a quick recognition of foreplay. She closes the door behind her, leaving him alone with his thoughts. Bo tightens the towel about his waist and leans his head against the wall. Several incidents just like this ended with unfortunate laughter. Nothing to suggest this would happen again, but his buffoonery has always preceded his rational thinking. He tries hard to reshape his mind, focusing on his need to be confident.

"There she will be on the other side of the door, wearing what could be something loose, something French, and something very pleasing. Yes, this is working!" The excitement is already building. He now feels like a man and it grows. Bo turns the knob – foot first, arm next, head last.

She wears a smock – an oversized shirt too small for her father. Not that it matters; he isn't here for her undergarments anyways. She is lying on the bed, propped up on her elbows, with her toes pointing straight out. There is a mischievous look on her face while she wiggles her fingers and beckons him forward. He has no problem engaging in this sort of foreplay; it's just that he can't seem to let go of the same accidental facial expression that replaces his maturity.

Beatie covers her mouth with an uncontrollable giggle, "Did you just make a face at me?"

Bo blushes an embarrassing red but quickly turns a flustered look into a stance of confidence, "I'm just playing aboot."

Beatie grins, "Oh, I see. You want to play *aboot*, do you? Well then... *I better show you what you should be playing aboot with!*" She quickly disappears beneath the sheets, then moments later, pops up from the furthest corner of the bed. "Aren't you going to hunt for me?"

"As many times as you like, ma love." Beatie drops her jaw when Bo's towel hits the floor with just his skivvies on. Then, in several short steps, he dives onto the mattress and all goes wild! The springs fall to the floor, the stuffed animals fly through the air, and her screams cause the windows to vibrate. Bo playfully growls and Beatie scurries with little yelps to the opposite end of the bed. This, however, proves to be her mistake. Bo then grabs the ends of the sheets and rolls toward Beate where she lies trapped. Knowing her peril, she can do nothing but bite down on her lower lip.

"Before we do this, I want you to show me your 'thing' first."

"Pardon?"

"Your lagoon creature from the black hole. I have to see it again."

Bo reluctantly agrees. He curls his lower lip outward and opens his mouth with wide eyes, "I'm going to eat you, Beatie!"

Beatie is in so much delight that she rolls back and forth, miss-clapping with her hands. "It's the creature from the black lagoon (viii)!!!" She roars in laughter. Beatie then rolls and wraps herself around his body, rubbing him with every part of her forearm. After three nose bumps and a neck lick, she sinks down into the bed, exhausted.

"That felt good! I hope you wore protection."

And that's just how things went for Bo.

She looks at him oddly, "Do you think I'm weird?"

"I would say you are out of your face."

"No, but normally."

"Normally? Depends on what other weird things I can compare you to."

"You're funny. Guess what? I have a day planned for you with my father. You're going hunting!!"

Bo slaps his hands on his chest. "I went hunting with me own father, and it didn't go so well."

"It'll be fine, and afterward, I am having a barbecue that you are invited to." Beatie gives Bo a kiss and lays her head on his chest. "I'll always remember this evening; I hope you will too."

"Aye, I most certainly will."

FEBRUARY 10: SORTING OUT FASHERIES

He sits upon the penny-farthing before a heavy iron door, surrounded by a grass-covered mound. A rather tall, thin man, dressed in a petticoat and a cotton pinafore, approaches with a cold pot.

"Six pence, governor!" the gatekeeper requests.

Bo shrugs his shoulders and places a handsome some of coins into the keeper's palm, who then graciously bows and dips his hat. "Worthy to you, good sir."

Bo looks at him rather perplexed. His dreams have presented a lot of questions; so boldly so, he wonders if any answers have been provided at all. At times, a displaced wanderer, and at other times, a dashing young nobleman. For now, he is to be the nobleman, and his direction with this cold pot of colored ice is to be determined.

Bo wipes his sweaty brow with the cravat about his neck. He looks above and sees a pale blue sky, but below there is a town covered in a veil of dusky red. A deafening sound of cannon fire can be heard, followed by drifts of smoke about the buildings. It must be a celebration, perhaps the reason for purchasing the pot.

He looks ahead to see an errant path through an open field. It is not a direct path into the city, but he will make use of it as long as he needs. Bo gathers his wits for a charge, and standing tall, he launches forward onto the trail. The bike screeches and flies through the air, but it is his coattails flying behind his back that give him the appearance of riding a scared horse. Though he has a handle on the pot of ice between his legs, the bumps and bruises to his buttocks are becoming too intolerable. He crosses through a short field, crashing through a tight line of coniferous trees, but when he strikes a quarantine sign, the bike naturally pitches forward and sends him down into a watery ravine. It has an unpleasant smell – a mixture of dead fish and salt water – but it does provide relief from the heat. Bo pulls himself out by the leg of a cow carcass, and with his hands on the seat of his bike, he pushes his way up the muddy bank.

The road ahead and the city beyond are where his journey continues, and below the arches of the entryway is where it starts. He is expecting to hear the roaring sounds and the good-humored calls from a celebration, but such is not the case. Instead, there is only the sound of crackling wood and soft moans from behind the establishments.

Bo pushes ever so lightly on the pedals, coasting with his nose to the air. Something is making his eyes tear and it bitters his taste. He avoids a cart rattling down a causeway into a side alley, and while sliding sideways, he runs through a puddle that produces a curtain of bugs. It is while cleaning his face of the muck that he is shocked to see linen burning and blowing in the form of ash. It may be for a good reason that people should hold handkerchiefs before their faces, but not reasonable enough that they should be dressed only in oversize coats. He is disheartened to realize that these are the same shoppers in an earlier dream. At that time, the men wore waistcoats with high, stiff collars. The ladies had fancy caged dresses and twirled colorful umbrellas. They all had money to spend and goods to sell. These people have little of any of that, with plenty of thieves among them. A well-dressed man, such as himself, carrying a tub of a tasty profit would surely be asking for trouble.

"Good day to you, your most obedient and humble servant," yells a voice. And there he is, tall with broad shoulders and a narrow chest. This is common for a young man who has not quite grown into his body. He carries with him an empty baldrick around his waist, a sign he is trying to reach manhood. It is the brick in his hand, however, that makes him feel like he has obtained adult status.

"What a fine day it is." Bo replies, pedaling his wheels a tad faster.

"Bit of a fleshy body you have there, my lordship. To be so well fed in these parts."

Bo ignores his remark and tries to conceal the bucket between his legs. Obviously, a treat the boy cannot afford.

The youngster catches up to Bo, walking at a brisk pace alongside his bike, "Bend a buck for me, will ya, so I don't have to hurt you."

There suddenly comes a sharp, disruptive voice from the shadows of an alleyway, "Be off with you, Mister Pennywacker!! No sneeze-lurkin here needed!"

Bo turns his head to see a middle-aged woman, simply dressed and concealing very little skin with what little clothing she has. She is slightly bloated with oversized nipples from recently giving birth. Her face is very pale with a taint of blood smeared on her cheeks. Her fingerless gloves hold tightly to a few umbrellas. This leads Bo to believe that prostitution is not legally accepted here. For now, though, she is protecting a potential client and will not allow an unruly adolescent to spoil this opportunity.

"Remember," she says, waving her finger. "I know you."

Bowing low at her request, the boy backs away, "No mafficking here, Miss Guinevere."

The youth return to his spot on a porch, acting out in frustration, "The King is on parade, good people! Here! Here! Take pity on the man's greed, for he does not seize the day in any other way!"

"No, mind you, he, Constable. Just another one of them whiffets!" She trots ahead of Bo's bike, waving an umbrella. "I'd be most exultant if I might proffer you some coverage, unless your pleasure is otherwise." She bares her shoulder, "Your secret is with me. A special one for the likes of you!"

Bo dismounts the bike to avoid running into her. He fingers a slit in his jacket and tosses her a coin, "I seek information regarding this flavored ice I am to deliver."

The woman's lip quivers, trying to hold back her emotions regarding the size of the prize offered. "Anything for my services, my Lordship. A servant, I am to you. There's a play pen for the youngsters nearby. No tricks of my own planning and no further treats beyond those you have already offered. I will provide you guidance to King George Street, but beyond that, you must find your own way."

A yellow mist descends upon the rooftops. The air is stifling, and the ice pot is not holding up very well. Bo follows the woman's lead while pushing behind his bike seat. He has arrived in yet another suspicious neighborhood where the windows are shut, and lonely alleyways are connected to less frequented roads.

"The one you seek plays further up the street. Good wishes to your search, my Lord. This is as far as the daylight provides me. Thank you for the fortnight's earnings."

"Yes, thank you."

He hears their laughter as much as he sees their devilish smiles. They are the inhabitants of the streets: guttersnipes, ragamuffins, and scapegraces – all words used to associate them with the poverty and the unseen illness that spreads throughout the city. So hideous their appearance that the words themselves somehow justify their miserable existence. Around every corner and down every alleyway, they are there. Pandering to homeowners, singing below windows, some even stealing from the premises. The dinner bell is off the clock. Hunger has no time, and if ignoring choice words and verbal threats feeds an empty stomach, a day is well served.

The youngest of the children are playing among the dung-encrusted road when Bo arrives. Typical nineteenth-century games of leap frog and hide and seek. Others have more scientific interests, like hanging from horizontal bars and poking at animal carcasses. These children are of no interest to Bo. He is trailing the likes of the little girl – the same one he met at the Auggie Dance. She has appeared from time to time in previous dreams, but never long enough to provide answers to the questions he has. Hopefully, this ice cream is an exchange for that. For now, he must first get through her classmates, who see that he is unattended. They have set a trap, and it starts with the discarded kerchief that he has mistakenly retrieved from the road.

Throwing their little hands on him and scaling his backside, they try their best to bring him to the ground. The attack may have worked if not for a door slam and the call for a different game. Immediately, the children scatter into the buildings, leaving behind a lone girl who casually walks out onto the road. She is between prettiness and disagreeable with her glowing face and tattered clothes. She seems not to care about these sorts of things, instead, crying out: 'Loose to Loose' whenever she finds a dislodged stone. It is a part of the game she plays where winning is always certain and losing is for someone else. She tosses the stone, missing her target intentionally, and then quickly distances herself from Bo.

Thinking he may catch up to her, all is lost when she tramples through a roadside puddle that hides her within a blanket of insects. One can sense that a disease is already in the works here. These are the same puddles left by the night rain that brings the mosquitoes.

On the outskirts of the city, where the late morning dew glistens on the field of yellow stalks, Bo finds a small trail that extends out into the pale, blue horizon. She makes no marks in the dirt; she never does. She does, however, leave a depression in the grass that only her size can make. Bo follows this trail, pushing the bike gently up a slope. He takes notice of two pillars, pale against the backdrop of a dark, unearthed hillside. It first appears to be a large village of unseen residents, but a closer inspection reveals that the homes are actually grave stones. Such people have been sent to this location before without the knowledge they would ever return. Their whereabouts are now known.

Bo carries the bicycle over his shoulder, following a path of toiled soil between sticks and shovels. He arrives before a large gate and leans his bike against a row of imposing bars. Two little girls, well acquainted with poverty, sit on a bowlegged bench, dangling their tattered, buttoned boots and soiled stockings. They are waiting for their custodian of benevolence, who is yet to arrive. Bo lifts a latch and enters into the yard, placing the slushy pot of colored ice on an angled stone. He is suddenly startled by a single clap from the open gate. "Come Berbrie! Come Bermise! Be here!" Upon that call, four little legs leap to the ground and sprint past the bewildered Bo. Their older sister has arrived with a windowsill pie and places it carefully on a tree stump.

"You seem to know the way of things around here, Mr. Fox. You found us with your flavored pot of slush. Oh, do come here, dear sisters! The good sir, has brought you an ice cream pot!"

Both are hesitant with the tall stranger. It is the older Berbrie who takes the first approach. She is most curious to taste the ice because the pies always taste the same. She moves around the rim, introducing her nose to the refreshment. It smells tangy and it feels cool within her nostrils. She takes a palm-size into her mouth, raising her crooked eyes that show a hint of yellow.

"It's the most choice-iest of choices!!" she yells.

The smallest and most defiant Bermise, just slaps at the air and takes the other direction to the pie.

"Let's talk some chat!!" Sprikkits takes several heavy steps forward, pulling on Bo's arm. They sit on a rock, where she pulls out two cups from within her dress.

"Have some tea." Sprikkit's face contorts for a few moments while she transforms into an old-timer. "Have some tea." Sprikkit's face contorts for a few moments while she transforms into an old-timer. "Those steady habits know nuffin' about our car races down here! One of 'dem tells me, whenever they get one of 'dem darn races on the laser screen up north, they have to look out da window to make sure space aliens aren't messin' with 'dem antennas!"

Bo interrupts, "I want to thank you for saving me from all the wee bairns."

"Oh, please. I myself wanted to join in."

"Pardon?"

"Don't be humble, Mr. Fox; you're a childhood's dream. Just look at you; all that height and those long arms. I'm thinking, maybe a quick slide down your legs in the morning; hang around your shoulders in the afternoon. Look'ie up there! Bermise is sitting on top of your hat and eating her lemon pie! Simply splashing!!"

Bo moves his head slightly forward, feeling the extra weight on his head. The little sister appears to be busy picking lemons out of her window-sill pie.

"But you're not here just to bring colored ice, are you?"

"I don't know what I've come for. Just my mind trying to sort out fasheries."

"You're here because there is still doubt in your mind. You thought it would be easy reconnecting with a lady from your past, yet new challenges keep presenting themselves." Sprikkets picks up a handful of stones and tosses them at an open grave. "No one figures to be born with certainty, Mr. Fox, and realizing mistakes comes with time and understanding. Have you made a count of your collective nuisances?" Sprikkits lifts up her fingers and begins counting, "Your roommates, her roommates, her mother, and her father..."

Bo interrupts, "I'm not sure why I have to see her father. My father was always trouble at best."

"Mr. Fox, rewards don't come easy. If you don't put in the effort, you will only find what others like you have already found. That the lessons of life come with misunderstandings. Isn't this why you still rely on gimmicks, fables, and false prophets to get you through your blunders?!"

Bo kicks a stone and watches Sprikkits run to fetch it. "A game of yours?"

"More like a habit." Sprikkits motions for Bo to lean forward and helps Bermise down. "I believe it is important you explain to her that you're not perfect – before she figures this out."

"Beatie?"

"With this one in particular. When she learns a change in you, she'll be quite disappointed." Sprikkits watches Bermise run off to be with her sister. "Your dreams are getting shorter, Mr. Fox, and it is already Saturday. You must stay focused. Do you recall the secret that remembers you?"

"I'm afraid not."

"It always has to do with believing in tomorrow, Mr. Fox."

His surrounding suddenly become very misty. His mum always said there would be a tomorrow, whether you wished to participate in it or not. You only need to attend to be counted. Sprikkits is right; the day will become night again, and shorter each time. He is aware of this now.

There is a presence stirring by a dilapidated army truck. It is a seventy-two-year-old man dressed in tall, black boots and khaki trousers with an orange patch taped to his vest. This is the man who, uncompromisingly, refuses to lose his daughter to someone else's dependence. Ingratiating this man, even with carefully chosen words, will not win his favor either. Unfortunately, avoiding him is no longer an option.

Bo hurries over and extends his hand, "Please to meet you, Mr. Backlebond."

"Don't try me, boy! And what's that on your face?"

"I don't know, I'm smiling?"

"That's smiling? I've seen better smiles on dead people at their viewing. My daughter explained her interest in you. That don't mean you can get cozy with me or her! Not before, not since, not going to happen!"

Bo's smile quickly fades, "Yes, Sir."

"Is that what you wear hunting? You a boozer or something?"

Bo looks over his muddy, nineteenth-century attire, "No, sir, drinking would not make me wear this." Bo lifts his nose to the scent blowing from the truck, "What's that putrid smell?!"

That would either be pig, gator, or buck – or a combination of all three." The old man smacks the side of his truck. "My 1941 Dodge Power Wagon. The first one of its kind to have four-wheel drive. Can't go to war without one." Mr. Backlebond reaches into the back of his truck and unravels a rifle from a burlap sack.

"A muzzleloader?"

"I know what it is!" He holds up the rifle and looks through the sites. "A .50 caliber, thirty-inch barrel; good for up to two hundred and fifty yards."

"Where are you going to have a clear two-hundred yards in a forest?"

"And that's why you get to chase and quarter!" Mr. Backlebond puts his muzzleloader away and grabs his other rifle, dropping a handful of bullets into his pocket.

Bo watches as the old man stands, meditating and breathing in the cold, forest air. He opens his eyes and points to a dark opening in the trees. "On the path before you, Boo, you need a good pair of shoes. Without a good pair of shoes, you experience the path in a completely different way."

It is a narrow, dirt path through a tangled forest of low branches and overgrown foliage. It is this part of a forest where the leaves block out much of the daylight. Each step is like sliding in oversized boots; each breath is like avoiding an oncoming sneeze; and each passing branch is like strapping on a mask of cobwebs. Not once is there a response to his request for his daughter's spirit.

Bo pulls himself up a bank by the stretch of a vine and there he finds the old man standing over a patch of Sego Palms. It must be midday because he can see the light glaring through a narrow slot in the canopy above. He cannot help but feel a deeper attachment to her now more that ever, even though it is just her old man that stands before him. Her effulgent beauty appears in him all the same, being so close of kin. Bo smiles and lets out a deep breath.

And to think the remembrance of you would ever fade.
From the very moment I opened my eyes to find you,

to the final moment when they closed without you,
you will always be there, my luv, as clear as I see you now.

"Get your hands off me, you prurient!! I know how to urinate on my own!!"

Bo gags and covers his face with his hands, "What a foul wheech?!!"

"Don't get surly with me, boy!"

"It's a foost! A real cudgel. Like something just died!!"

Mr. Backlebond stiffens his back and sniffs the air. He flicks the safety nob off and cocks the rifle.

"Do you see any vultures? No, poppy-groper, we got ourselves an Anthro-Amphibious-Being!!"

"A walking snake? That's daft!"

"Like your cocamamy gnomes and woodland creatures?"

"They have been around since the fifteenth century."

Mr. Backlebond takes Bo by the collar, "There aren't enough hours of daylight to see a clear path of understanding between you and me, boy. But if you believe you're on mark for dating my Beatie, you best start understanding everything my way."

"I'm so happy you found it!"

"Right, that's what I thought you would believe."

The old man lets go of Bo and turns his head. A noise in the woods is raising his suspicion. Motioning for Bo to keep his voice down, he flips open his jacket pocket and lifts out a shiny gold bullet. Eyeing the location carefully, he snaps the bullet into the cartridge and clenches his teeth. His eyes now poised along the barrel.

"It's a deer, Mr. Backlebond," Bo whispers.

"It's not a deer. You can't shoot deer on public land in February."

The beast wriggles loose and crashes through the branches, jumping in several small arcs over the brush. The old man scoffs at the buck and swings to his right, forcing Bo to duck beneath the gun barrel. Bo scarcely puts his foot down on a loose stone when his balance is taken away. He slides down through the overgrowth, tossing and turning, until he finally finds himself face down before a pond. Bo lifts his head to the sound of a gun boom, and watches as birds noisily take flight into the forest branches. It is at that moment, Bo sees the vision of the old man across the pond, stumbling back and forth on a large rock.

"It got me, boy!"

Bo gallops and stumbles his way around the pond to reach Mr. Backlebond face down in the muck. "I was mistaken; it was not the Anthro-Amphibious-Being. It was the Florida Yheti."

"It is more the work of gnomes than a steuchy beast, Mr. Backlebond. Let me help you up." Bo extracts him from the mud, noting that his one hand is still gripping the gun.

"I think it's coming back, boy."

Bo follows his eyes toward the bright light gleaming through the open canopy. It is wearing orange coveralls and a horned hat. It also speaks, "Are any of you hurt?"

They both nod their heads.

"Is the renaissance festival in town?"

The man examines the old man's shoulder. "I'm one of the park rangers. Help me get this man to dry ground. It may be dislocated."

Bo moves to the other side of Mr. Backlebond, and they carry him up the slope. The ranger pulls a sling from his bag and threads it underneath the old man's arm. "Are you aware there's a jaguar out here killing dogs at the trailer parks?"

The old man snaps, "I'm after anthropoid amphibians, and he's after woodland folk!!"

"That makes a lot of sense. I'm calling this in. There is an animal in these woods and it's hungry."

"There is no need to call it in, Ranger. I'm not going anywhere!"

The ranger pauses to lift up his communicator, "Ten-four, do you read me? This is Don Carguey; we have an injured older man and his younger partner."

"I'm not his partner. I'm here for his daughter, sir."

"Here that, Carguey, he's after my daughter! He'd be after yours if you brought one!"

"Now, listen, old man, I am here to take you two out of the forest. Ten-four, do you read me?!"

"First, we get the beast who muscled me!!"

"Old man! I'm not risking my life or this boy's life for your fixation on fancy tales!!"

"That's the way I'm having it!"

Bo raises his hand, "Pardon, sir? Do we really have to worry if the beast comes? Will it not go after the weaker prey first?"

They both give Bo a confused look.

A meal is waiting for Bo, prepared with chips in a large bowl and grilled cow meat on a pan. There are also a variety of veggies on the table and tall bottles of flavored fizzies. He sits on the garden steps with a blanket wrapped around his shoulders. His wet clothes are hanging from a line between two trees. A breeze is felt when Beatie passes by with plastic plates in her hands. Her dress has wanted attention; it is light and airy with a large, pink bow affixed to her lower backside. She looks so lovely, particularly when she tosses the bowl of chips to the dirt, along with the pan of cow meat at the fence. Out of the ordinary though, that her hands are having an ongoing argument that he has yet to participate in.

"He took a wee cowp!"

Beatie stops before the opening door and takes a few steps backward. "Excuse me? A fall is what you are trying to say?!"

"Aye."

"And after that, did you actually say you would run from a voracious animal because my father would make a better meal?!"

"That's daft. He didn't die."

Beatie horrified at his response, "Pardon?!!"

"I gave him my coat."

"Why?! So it would slow down the painstaking tearing and ripping of my father's body into little, edible pieces from a carnivorous cat!!"

"Aye, he did not die."

Beatie, in an angry disturbance, shakes her head and scuttles up the steps, letting the door slam behind her. He thought of fetching his amulet; he does have it at his disposal. It is hanging from his pants, but something is not right. No thinking of her own would ever reach such a far-fetched conclusion.

Bo enters the house, holding the blanket around his body. His eyes circuiting the room where he sees a bedroom light, but there is no one there. He quietly strolls to the front room and finds her on the swing in the glare of a porch light. She is chewing on some breaded haggis that appears too large for her mouth.

Beatie's eyes catch a glimpse of Bo looking at her through the window. She pretends not to notice him until he takes a seat next to her.

"Olivia and Nikki asked me about you. They want you dead and buried."

"That has not changed."

"This is curious to me. Their thoughts can never go nice, even when I say good things about you."

Bo does not need to hear their accusations. These are the same poisons told of him before. It was hard to see at the time, but it was apparent to all those who could influence her. He really did believe that parting was the right thing to do. Though, not for a moment, when alone with his thinking, had he not regretted it.

"I have to tell you something, Beatie," Bo lowers his head in shame. "I'm not perfect."

"Oh, I see." Beatie turns her head in dismay. "You could have told me this when we first met."

"Forgive me. I thought you knew."

"So, I guess what Olivia and Nikki have been saying is true?"

"No. Not entirely. I know you better than anyone you know. Even the wee things. You love romance books, you're proud of your ballet, and you're afraid of shadows. You think certain hairstyles attract insects – mostly spiders, because you hate those the most." Bo sets his hand on her knee and gives her a few light squeezes. "Inside your heart, you know this to be true."

"Hmmm," Beatie takes another bite of her haggis and chews for a while. "Odd how you know so much about me."

"I do, because I listen, and mostly because I care."

Beatie's mouth suddenly tires from all the chewing, and she throws the unfinished sheep intestines to the lawn. She is not surprised that her father wouldn't like him. He does not like any drifter who has one foot in one town and the other foot in the next one. It's the life of a backpacker. Something her father warned her about. He even wrote a children's book about it, but no artist would accept the project, feeling the scenes were too gruesome. Beatie shakes her distraught thinking from her face. "I guess my father can be difficult at times."

"You know your father believes in some steuchy, slithering, amphibious fellow with orangutan horns?"

"That's only a start. The Easter Bunny spreads E. coli, and Santa Claus robs homes!"

"Kris Kringle?" Bo then slaps his knee, and both burst out in laughter. "You should have seen him all covered in stench and tree fur! HaHaHa!!!"

"Okay, that's enough."

"Sorry."

Beatie lets out a sigh, "I don't want to share Valentine's Day with just sex, alcohol, or stuffed animals; so, I'll hold your hand to wherever you may want to go, as long as where we go it isn't just about holding hands."

"Your father says so?"

"My momma told my father this before she accepted his marriage proposal."

Bo scrunches his eyes and sits on the couch, still wrapped in the comforter. Once Beatie returns from the lawn, he looks at her with sorrow on his face. "The couch? What happened to fair giveness?"

"The 'couch' is the best place for 'fair giveness.'" She places his folded clothes, still dirty and a little damp, by the table lamp. "I've been meaning to ask you what that rock tied to your pants is all about?"

"It wards off bad dreams."

"Is it expected to work?"

"We'll see." Bo lays on the cushion, shuffling the pillows beneath his head. He reaches for the rock and holds the hole to his eye, carefully following Beatie as she walks toward her room.

Beatie falls forward on the bed and wraps herself in the blankets. She cannot understand her feelings for him, but somewhere inside of her, she doesn't have to. They have this invisible connection that seems to bring them together and it makes her want to purr.

She bundles up under the layers of softness and rubs her face into the pillow. She starts to smile when one eye realizes the closet door is not fully shut. This naturally makes her want to cuss, but she's too tired to deal with it. Then something unnatural catches her attention that forces her to sit up. There appears to be an ink spot drifting out of her closet, and it is making its way toward her bed. "Hah!" Beatie laughs at her overreactive thinking: "It's really just a crepuscular dust ball in a breeze, that's all."

Beatie flips over the other way and yawns several times. She shuts her eyes, but only for a moment. She feels something climbing along the tendrils on the back of her neck and it makes her feel uncomfortable. With her head motionless, she shifts her eyes back and forth to see which way it is headed, and soon finds herself staring cross-eyed at the very same dark spot perched on the side of her nose. It rises up on its hind legs and points toward a darker opening growing in the center of its head. Beatie's voice cracks with a whimpering sound: "Genius Loci. Ohm. Ohm. You are not hungry. Ohm. Ohm. You are just a tired old arachnid. Ohm. Ohm. Ohm." Beatie watches as the dark opening widens further. She clutches onto her bedsheet before a possible scream.

By the middle of the night, the sky has cleared itself of the dreary cloud cover. White holes soon come forth to complement a full moon. Bo feels the warmth of a fire and listens to the sound of voices calling in the far distance. They are calling forth the messenger on quick wings through fast closing doors. Everything slows down and he begins to feel lighter. He no longer feels the strength to hold onto anything anymore and the weight of the amulet falls to the floor.

Beatie slides along the length of the coach and nudges him, "Don't go."

He hears her voice immediately and fights hard to open his eyes. Upon returning, he clears his throat. "Shaddies bothering you?"

"It's very much what I expected."

Beatie plays with his eyebrows and smiles. "Are you, my tomorrow?"

"And for every day af-after-so." He gives Beatie the look of peace and security, and she feels it instantly. Now twined together in the warmth of their arms, she snuggles on his chest and nudges his nose. "Do spiders yawn?"

He truly does know her better than anyone else.

There is a pain that runs through Bo's body, sending his temperature uncomfortably high. He is sweating profusely, as if shaking off some sort of an illness. A sharp crackling sound can be heard, like wet wood being thrown into a fire. He opens his narrow, foggy eyes to find that he is elsewhere. His caregiver's replacement is engaged in preparing some sort of a serum.

Aiden appears with a mysterious urn fizzling with a dark liquid. He sets the tray on the fireplace mantel along with a small clock and turns to see the doctor injecting a needle into his friend's arm. He can't help but wonder why the man would use an object to pierce a man's skin if he were trying to save his life.

"The fireplace needs more wood, Aiden." The doctor waits for a response. He then draws in a long breath and leans back on the chair. "So, Mr. Fox suffers from many unexplained superstitions that require anecdotes, which you locals refer to as treatments?"

"Superstitions? Only familiar peculiarities one must face before dying."

"Familiar peculiarities?"

"Demons, witches, and fairies. What else could they be?"

The doctor gives the caretaker an obscure look, "Are you trying to smooth over what may be the cause to this man's illness?"

"Be it as you may, Sir Cloverly, you won't find a sleek witch among them."

"I am very willing to help this man, but I'm trying to understand the use of fizzling liquids, split varmints, boneset, and other remedies that exist in your books of folklore."

"Do all yourr patients go on to live happy lives, Doctor?"

"Not all, but certainly I make their burdens easier."

"Aye, then I fancy our ratios are the same."

Porta Floyd follows on the man's heels as he crosses the floor, agitating the doctor by swatting his backside with sticks of herbs.

"Will you stop that?!!"

"Don't open the window!"

"I couldn't if I wanted to. They appear to be stuck. All of them with a lock and key!"

"As it should be. The Sloughs, you see, they come from the west."

The Doctor throws up his hands, "We were communicating better when we were wrestling."

Bo watches through slit eyes as Aiden takes the doctor by the collar and drags him to the floor. He closes his eyes and smiles.

FEBRUARY 11: WHY THE DICKENS?

On the bed, Bo rests his arms across his chest, waiting for his mind to make his legs move. He seems to be tired but knows there is no time for a continued rest. Setting his feet down upon the floor, he stands, then quickly sits back down. A heavy sickness fills his stomach, and the feeling of his head whirling in every direction is affecting him too.

After sitting for a moment, he discovers that if he holds his head back and walks gingerly, the dizziness goes away. He sets his hands on the sink, trembling to hold the tap. He splashes the water over his stubbled beard and looks into the mirror. Somehow, he is projecting a more depreciative look – a whiter shade of ailment, if you will. Odd, how he has been feeling the happiest he has ever felt, but this change in his look is coming from somewhere else.

Bo hears the soft tones of varying voices within his head. He looks up at the ceiling, then under the sink. He even looks outside the bathroom door, but he still cannot place the internal source. He returns to the mirror once again, and hears a series of numbers being called out in descending order. It is followed by an urgent voice: "No! Just slap me around a few times; I'll be fine!!"

Bo pulls the twitching shower curtain aside. It is not your typical modern-day spectacle to see an assistant motel manager sitting in a bathtub with his hands tied to a faucet and a gag forced into the stretches of his mouth, but it is even more out of the ordinary to see his roommate grasping the handle of a large swamp root and lifting it as high as the bathwater will allow.

"Sen is possessed, Bo! I saw it happen!"

"Mia, he can possess himself in his own room!" Bo swings the curtain shut and walks out of the bathroom. He is not going to take part in this silliness; he has his own problems.

Mia drags the wet piece of lumber across the linoleum floor, following Bo back to his bed.

"Why do you have to make a big deal of everything I do?"

"Like a wee complaint would have saved this bloke."

"Oh, now you're actually taking interest in someone else's life."

Bo slowly sits back down on the bed, "What's that mean?"

"You have taken no interest in anything I've been doing since we arrived here."

"Ghosts, Mia?"

"Does one have to pretend to hear the spoken words of the past residents?"

"Mia, I have no time to spend on ghosts."

"Well, maybe you should, because I am afraid it's not good." Mia sits beside Bo and leans the large root against the bed. "Much like children, they don't believe in rules, regulations, or any etiquette that should apply to them. Sen opened my eyes to all this."

"Mia, you may want to untie him and take the gaggy out of his geggy."

"Ooh, I forgot!" Mia disappears into the bathroom for a moment and returns, pulling Sen by his arm. His clothes are noticeably wet from the waist down and he is still pulling fabric from the inside of his mouth.

"Tell him, Sen!"

The day manager coughs and swings his arms like a butterfly to stretch out his stiffness. "Okay, have you ever noticed why young people don't like to work anymore?"

"Sen!!!"

"There are many types of ghosts from many different eras, okay? And each of these ghosts expresses their forgotten existence by acting out against harms done to them in the past. Take this motel for instance, Goggy and I have always known its primary use was for a correctional facility. We are talking about well-funded physicians implementing sinister treatments, merely for profit and amusement. As Miss Pearl discovered in the subterranean culture, they used acid tubs for ablution, organ removal tables for discipline, and deep pools for coordination struggles."

Mia shakes Sen's arm, "Sen, I think that's what these experiments were about. Didn't I tell you that's what I thought the experiments were all about?"

"So, now, these sufferers are in some sort of suspended death, acting out their hostilities, until these wrongs are somehow finally corrected. Unfortunately, for most of them, this is an ongoing pursuit."

"Sen rescued me!"

Bo's mouth shifts and doesn't say a word.

"That's when we came across the little girl with the rile seizure. She had the disease that was turning her skin yellow, her vomit into blood, and her body into a waste disposal."

"We simply do not know!" Mia blurts out, then looks at Sen questioningly. "Wait, Sen. Where are you going with this? We are talking about the guests of the motel, not some bratty little girl?"

"I am speaking of a disease that flared up in the summer of 1821 and has left us with a problem we are still dealing with today!"

"Okay, sure, I can go with this. See what he's saying, Bo! Listen to him."

"Mia, you are going along with this?" Bo watches as Mia shrugs her shoulders.

"Others, such as myself, have concluded that the ghosts of the city do not hold the same resentment as those of the motel. It's more about their refusal to leave behind a life they once cherished. All taken away because of some unseen ailment."

Bo stands up and looks out the window. People are drifting about the street and disappearing through the walls of the buildings.

"Do you ever wonder why you have a dream that you cannot explain or a dream you cannot control?"

Bo turns his ear.

"She had fallen ill and was buried a couple hundred years ago. Right outside the city wall. Then, fresh from the womb of the earth, she rose to become this mischievous little girl. We thought this was natural for her age, but then we discovered she had been scouring the town collecting right arms."

"Only right arms, Sen?"

"Something about needing vaccine shots for her relatives. We cannot allow them to get those shots, Mr. Fox. They will be disappointed to find out they don't work."

"Pure dead brilliant! You're a real laughty-dafty, are you not, Mr. Assistant Manager?"

"No Bo, I think he has something there. This could change everything!"

"You are going take a wee bonnie's basket of arms away, so they don't get their shots?"

"To some, it just makes sense."

"Mia, you take her arms away and she'll just find some other body's arms!"

"There is something else we discovered," Sen says to Mia. "Tell your roommate what the sick child said to your mind outside the gymnasium."

"Stick it up your guigui, Coconut Mam!!"

"No, not that."

"Oh, right, she said – the victors will not win this time!"

"She is looking for someone to walk her home, Mr. Fox. We believe she has already found someone, and she is only waiting until he remedies a problem of his own. You must understand that she is a money-maker for this town, Mr. Fox. We cannot allow her to leave."

Bo runs his hands through his scalp, soon looking at the clumps of gray hair in his palm. He quickly places them in his pockets.

Sen reaches out to Mia, "Who is this man?"

"What do you mean, Sen? He's my roommate, Bo."

Sen squints his eyes at Bo, "Look at him. Prove you have never been one!"

"Mar?"

Mia steps forward and pokes her finger into his cheek. "Your color has changed and your skin has lost elasticity. Your hair has a lot of silver flecks in it too." Mia takes a few steps back, "I have caught you chewing on your teeth as well, even pretending to take them out before going to bed."

Bo rubs his face to control a twitch, "Silly jaw, Mia. I'm fine."

Sen puts his hand under his chin, "The condition of a ghost is never truly about its physical health now, is it?"

Bo erupts, "Get out! Mia, you stay!"

Mia walks Sen to the door, exchanging a few words before closing it. She walks across the room and begins rummaging through her backpack for a warmer top.

Bo pushes the heavy root off his bed, "Mia, the wood? What for?"

"I don't know, it just came to mind."

"Like the assistant manager's drowning?"

"Well, why should you have all the fun? You have somebody."

"What happened to you, Mar? You found all this ghost stuff nonsensical. Now you're embracing it?"

"Well, you're never here anymore."

"Can you see how?"

Mia looks at Bo and frowns. "We're going to Saturday service together. You are welcome if you behave." Mia marches into the bathroom and shuts the door.

Bo opens the door to the city and inhales the cool morning air. He is wearing his nineteenth-century garb, all pressed and clean with no lingering odors. It is the best he has to offer on a surprise notice. He falters a few steps or two, reaching out to a light pole for balance. Mia quickly grabs him by the shirt sleeve and pulls him up straight. "Are you sure you are alright? "

Bo is beginning to wonder that himself. He had no idea his physical strength would suddenly give way like that. Bo gingerly sets his feet together and lifts his head. "Nothing is wrong, Mia. I'm a wee stiff from all the walking, that's all."

"Well, you're back to chewing on your teeth again. I don't need to remind you that Sen already thinks you are not quite one with the living. You better try to keep a low profile. He has a lot of influence in this town, you know."

He is wearing a black vestment and a white clerical collar, with a silver cross draped around his neck. Sen can be anything he wants to be; he has that talent Whether it be a contractual painter, a contradicting ghost theorist, or an illusive, mixed-clarity lady-lover, one can be, for sure, treated to a delightful performance without offering a dime. For now, his presentation is that of an overly dressed, clerical advisor, which Mia finds absolutely tantalizing.

Sen approaches and takes her hands, "I am so glad you made it, my children. And you littlest one, who followed the path to hell in the fires of the morgue. Have you not forever been changed?"

"Tell me things I don't know."

"I appear before you as strength and determination, so we may take leave from whatever follows us."

"It was horrible, Sen!"

Sen places his hands on the sides of her head, "I know, particular one. I was there, and a wrong was committed, but I do hope that you did not misinterpret my visit."

"No, Sen! Your visit was greatly welcomed. Seized before me was this bulbous-faced creature in a hazmat suit, only to be rescued by what I found inside. It was horrible, and yet so obvious. I just hope it won't mess with my mind."

"Only if you let them."

"What can be done about it?"

"You must stand strong and be defiant, shortest one. I have taken an oath not to blame those that wish not to work, but in this city, it is hard to understand the difference between the living and the dead when there is a lack of consistency on both sides."

Mia takes Bo by the shirt collar and pulls him toward her. "I love this man!"

Bo tries to smile, hiding the ailment that inflicts his body. He knows Mia wants this, so he steps back, hoping his separation will give them a chance to bond.

"Do you think, maybe, Sen, I can be that consistency? Maybe the difference you can forever understand?"

Sen opens his robe and wheels forth his Penny Farthing, "Let's go forth and see."

Mia claps her hands in joy, "So that bike belongs to you? Should we go church-cycling? There are several services throughout the day!"

"Well, I certainly don't think you should go alone."

"Because of the ghosts?"

"I think it is important. Ride and talk with me." Sen lifts up a very large seat for the two of them to ride on.

Are you alright to meet us there, Bo?"

"Of course, Mar."

Mia spreads her legs across the oversized seat and turns to Bo, winking with a pleased look on her face. Sen waves as they ride off, "Keep your chin up, old boomer! I'm sure a venerable man like yourself will occupy the remainder of your day fruitfully."

Bo continues to watch as they set off together. A bit of a chill is in the air, not uncommon for early February, just not what he has been experiencing up to now. He suddenly realizes a lot of time has passed since his last visit with Beatie. She has long left the couch and is already planning other parts of the day with him in mind. What to bring her? Most of the stores are closed and the ones that are open do not possess a suitable gift. Flowers, however, can be found whenever you need them, and they are sure plentiful in the cracks of the sidewalks.

Feeling he has counted enough, Bo straightens his back and is surprised to see that his aimless wandering has confused his direction. A menacing darkness has replaced the somber blue sky, and more foreshadowing than that – the petals are already wilting from their stems. He must get moving; she will not understand his gesture in this condition. She will not understand their loss of life. She will blame him for their lack of purpose.

Bo feels a poke and turns around to find himself confronted by a sidewalk tree. There is a sensation of fear that not all is well. A shiver comes next that adds a terrible tremble to his hands! His head begins whirling and twirling! Buildings, bridges, and tree-tops – all of them smudging together in one great mess! Bo steps off the curb and feels his head meet the pavement.

Beatie is quite asleep when the chill of the morning creeps through the floorboards. It is trying to strangle the cuddle of warmth she currently possesses beneath the blankets. Sluggish and smiling, she rolls over to feel him again, but he is no longer there. He's not just missing from the couch; he is missing from the entire household. Of course, she understands this. He is probably off on some heroic deed fighting Selkie monsters, stamping out spiders, or shining lights to protect her from the world of confusing.

Left in his place, however, is the turtle-bear. He is wrapped beneath her legs and staring at her for recognition. She tweaks his beak, "Potchfinkle! I see you haven't left me. What do you think we should do?" The turtle-bear responds with blank eyes.

"I know, but he's not here. It's rather rum of you to point that out. Lunch for three? What a fab idea you have there, Potch-kins! Then that's what we will be doing while we wait."

Jettisoning off the couch, Beatie heads into her bedroom with the stuffed animal under her arm. She puts on a warmer shirt, then pulls aside the blinds, letting more warmth into the room. The day is so beautiful, and the sun a forever shine in the sky. The agreement with her boss is to allow her to return the day after Valentine's, and for this, she is indisputably satisfied. But something even better tells her she won't be going back. She has found someone else to occupy her life, and he does not come with orders.

Beatie dances about the room, pulling on the rest of her clothes and spinning about the floor on her back. Just a whole lot of morning silliness. She hugs her stuffed animal again and again, and while tossing him to the air, she sees something that widens her eyes, "What's this? A note stuffed in your waist band?"

Beatie loves surprises; she quickly unravels the paper as fast as her fingers will allow. It's from Bo! It's a Selkie note, and like all Selkie notes, they come with hope and some wet fur. It reads:

'A promise of a world, while ever so pure, and all the kindly thoughts embedded within it, pleasantly unseen.'

"Potch-a-boo, I just love it! And there's so much loneliness to it."

Beatie does not want to forget these words. She definitely wants to preserve them for as long as she can, so she spreads the note tightly over her forearm, then rubs every letter into her throat, forehead and eye socket. For some odd reason, this makes her feel secure and grounded; so unafraid and powerful. In fact, if a bug were to suddenly enter her room right now, she would have no problem squashing it with her bare feet. Or if a shadow were to cross her path, she would 'slap-it-silly' with her very own hand. She can see nothing wrong with this. She would do this without hesitation.

What makes her truly happy, though, is that she has finally found someone that has claimed her heart and all the other organs bound within. Now she wants to share this passion and speak of their devotion, and this starts with the local club, where she can shove it in everyone's face. This was in one of her dreams.

Beatie sits at her vanity and pulls out a pen and paper. She is going to plot out her happiness with a schedule for each dream to come. "I'm rather amused at how simple it can be. What I have been waiting for all my life is someone who really wants me! It rhymes. Hee-hee!"

It is lunchtime, the sandwiches are out on the table, and she is making a special blend of chocolate. It is not the Heilan Coo value, but the value is as good as you get in Boil Town, USA. After a quick sniff, she pulls up a chair for her knee and stirs and stirs, waiting for the marshmallows to slow; then she stirs and stirs and stirs. Licking the powder from her fingers, she decides the cocoa is ready. She pulls out two fine porcelain cups and begins to pour.

"Do I hear someone coming up the walk?" There is an eager look upon her face. Her eyes are wide and unblinking. She then springs to her feet and leaps onto the porch! There is no one there. At least, not yet. It isn't the right moment anyway. All moments should be important, and this just isn't one of them. Besides, she enjoys the wait. It is painfully exciting, cheerfully nauseating, and exultantly demoralizing, but it just seems so right!

Alrighty then, what else can she make? Coasting across the floor into the kitchen, Beatie stands before the burners, rocking from side to side. She tosses a few small roasted potatoes into the air and catches them in her shirt. She is counting on these potatoes, along with the items in her refrigerator, to make up a very tasty meal. Let's see – she has the mosquito livers, crab lungs, pepper hearts, oatmeal larvae, and Panko. However, she does not have the eggs, butter, and chocolate-flavored spam. This means she will not be making a meatloaf haggis.

What else can she make? Inside her shaker cabinet, she has the milk of magnesia, ammonia, lamp oil, and boric acid. The matter is settled; with the potatoes mixed with Panko and a slab of larvae with a mix of magnesia, this should keep the heart and lungs together; add a dab of lamp oil for the savory sauce and – "Voila! a wonderful Beuschel!"

Beatie spins around and around on her heels, sloshing the contents and doubling the portions. Once she feels there is enough for a party of eight, she is ready to serve. Lifting a plate from the kitchen sink, she spreads out the meal across the dish. Oh, what a pleasure it will be to watch him eat a favorite meal of his.

Now she hears another sound. This means she is so desperately prepared to see him! Leaping about and eventually running out onto the porch, this time she is so – not elated! In fact, she is emphatically aghast!! "Shoo-shoo, you mean crow!! Now look what you've done to Potchfinkle's eye ...Why?!"

Beatie settles herself down on the porch swing, rocking with her toes and putting her stuffed animal's eye back together. She sits for the better part of the day indoors, pulling the curtain aside once in a while and poking her head out the window. She even looks into the backyard in case he tries any surprises. The turtle-bear's repaired eye is encouraging, but her joy of waiting is becoming unsustainable. She had hopes that she was the only thought on his mind, but now she is feeling like she is being forgotten.

She makes her way onto the porch, only to be reminded that the noise of the evening traffic means everyone else is having fun. She remains hunched over on the porch chair with her eyes focused down the road. A bug crawls up her arm, but she doesn't take notice. It is almost seven, and the shadows have come and gone. This is not bravery. This is defeat.

He feels a strong chill, as if a warm blanket has been lifted off his body. Bo opens his eyes to a very gray and empty surrounding. He is still in keeping with most of his senses – the smells, the tastes, and the touches from the air, however, his sight is seeing only drab. He appears to be lying in a flowering field that has lost its color. The source that creates this gray is a mystery, considering there are no tall oaks, buildings, or clouds for which a gloom could exist.

"Why the Dicken's (ix)?" Lifting himself from the ground, Bo dawdles dizzily down a beaten path and comes to a sharper descent. Straining his eyes, he sees a small, rural community taking up a very small portion of a large valley. He stumbles the rest of the way down a rocky pathway and into a church door. He is dismayed to find it held in a locked position and won't allow him entry. Leaning awkwardly against the window, he peers in. It is poorly lit with soft candles, but there are two figures occupying the chancel at the Alter. One of the figures stands before a chestnut cabinet, wearing a white surplice over a black cassock. He is emptying a box of its contents onto a table and having a discussion with the other regarding its usage.

"So, what are the chances we will see one tonight? The Illuminator of Foggy Pants recommends some sort of table channeling."

"It is not necessary to conjure up the dead in this town; they all come at free will."

"Where do you get all this stuff anyway? The frock, the collar, bottles of holy water, and papal shoes. You're not a looney, are you?"

"No, my dear, something else of the kind." The man of cloth reaches under the table for a purple stole and places it over his head. "Destiny is before us, child, and we must prepare for the hunt. Before you are a cross, a flashlight, and three bottles of non-metallic elements: oxygen, carbon, and sulfur. Our first encounter will most likely be the image of a little girl. She'll be the one with the rile seizure, often heard moaning."

"A little girl?! Oh, why? I don't even get along with children."

"Everything will be alright, my pernickety one. I have been practicing for this for quite some time."

"I don't know. I have to admit, I really don't feel comfortable with all this impersonation and procedural stuff. I mean, look at you; your dressed as a man of the cloth, and you are not even properly ordained. What if God gets mad at us? Remember what he did to the tribesmen of Moses and the floods of Noah?! How about the way he addressed the Canaanites?!"

The clergyman buttons his sleeves and slips into his red slippers. Grabbing a bag from beneath the podium, he lays it on the table, then quickly places the remaining items in the sack. "There is no need to be nervous, dark one; the Lord too understands the behavior of a child, having once been one."

"The Almighty was once a child? How is that possible?"

"You said it yourself – the short temper, the tantrums – he even played with dinosaurs." The man tosses the lady a light stick and mittens.

"It's cold out there and plenty dark. Generally, at night, their goings and comings are unobserved, but she's a nighttime harasser. If there's any truth to her appearance, we should be able to spot her somewhere between George's and Cordova (x). She's very mischievous and very crafty. She can and will reach into the outposts of your mind to plan her attack."

The lady picks up a psalm sheet and tosses it to the bench, "The very reason I don't like children."

The man grabs a silver cross from his pocket and gives it a light kiss, then loads up a backpack with camera equipment and sound devices.

The lady scratches her head, "It's peculiar how you find this child so fascinating. I would think you would want to spend more time with someone who is more interested in the true you." She rises and does a quick spin. "So, I was thinking it would be more romantic if we hang out in the cemetery tonight, just the two of us; you can bring all this stuff with you."

"Daughter of dark concepts, focus, please."

She sits down and nods her head. "Okay, I am listening."

"There is very little question to what the little girl might do, so you'll need to bring this bible. Particularly focus on the passages between God and Job 28:28. Your line will be: 'And he said on to man, 'Behold the fear of the Lord, that is wisdom, and to turn away from evil is understanding(xi)'. Don't worry about the conversations between God and Satan. I'll take care of that."

Darkness soon blackens the walls of the altar, and Bo's eyes strain further to see. Clutching onto the railing, he stumbles out onto the street, forgetting where he is supposed to be and who he is supposed to be looking for. Squinting at the street lamps ahead, he watches as long shadows encroach along the periphery of his eyes. It only seems natural to take the foot bridge, where he can follow the road beneath the rising moon. It is the only way with a lighted path to see. It is also the only direction where he can find the occasional tree to assist his steps.

Easing up on his legs, Bo stumbles into a small vehicle. He looks up to see a sign above a door that reads: Parfie Der Barbeeb. This name seems to have a place in his memory. Lifting the flower stems, he braces himself for the long walk up the steps. Upon reaching the top, he lurches forward to the window and presses the side of his face onto the glass.

Beatie had planned to stay home and forget her feelings for the day, but a slew of tearful confessions in the morning paper told her that not all is well in the world. She doesn't need an appointment; she never does. Beatie is not a customer buying a product; Beatie is a friend who needs advice. It will be busy; she knows this. She will have to wait; she understands this too. Saturday evenings are like that, with people leaving chairs and others wanting to replace them. She also knows that once the hairnet is tossed to the air, the next one in waiting must be ready for it to land in their lap. Beatie lifts the hairnet to her nose and smiles.

"Come ride with me, Beat'rie; the barn has been cleaned and all the stables have been cared for."

"But you have others waiting," Beatie so graciously replies to the barber.

"Nonsense, Mrs. Ingiago is waiting for her bird droppings to dry; Lady Pluckily is soaking in snail mucus, and I just applied a Mossley Guber Bull Sperm Conditioner to Miss Mufflebee's neck hairs. You are up."

Beatie takes the only seat available, next to the flannel, paneled Mica-thermic-heater on wheels. It can be shared with one another, and that other has a wet towel over her face. This means her time is her own. She shuffles and slides into the chair and sits for a few moments with unblinking eyes, "Genius Genius Loci Ohm. Loci Loci Ohm Ohm. Genius Genius Loci Ohm. Loci Ohm and Loci Ohm. I'm ready."

Beatie knows that when she is talking about relationships, there are listening ears that are adept in cruelty. The thoughts in her head not being what they should be all the time, means the conversation could get 'down-right' freaky. She can't help it; she is feeling like all is lost inside, like maybe he did return to the sea, as Olivia had suggested. Beatie, not being a very strong swimmer, would have trouble keeping up should he swim too far. Then, as Nikki pointed out, maybe he is more interested in witches with sloth-skinned coveralls. Beatie can never wear what Meeshman's does not carry. Beatie's mouth suddenly crinkles and quivers, "Now stop it! Not going to happen! I'm not going to get emotional!"

The barber looks down while talking through the pins in his teeth, "Beat'rie? Are we okay today?"

"Well, you know, *Crazy Super Sundays*."

"Do our ears hear trouble?"

"Oh, it's just the normal situation I'm in." Beatie glances around the room, then speaks softly from the side of her mouth, "So I met this guy..."

And that's all. That is all she had to say. Even though she had but five words to say about her own relationship, each patron quickly joined in to guess her own story – and with very little substance to the truth. In fact, it was no longer about her anymore; it was about their own wretched lives that they thought was more important.

"See Beatie," says Punky Mox, who suddenly appears on a large screen above the door. "The thread of a relationship is so fragile that every day, when it winds tighter and tighter, it only takes one little piece of bad news to create an emotional snap."

"Moxy is right, Beatie!!" they all spoke.

Geezenheat! Why are these strangers interfering with her life anyways? All Beatie knows is that she cannot understand the feelings she has for this man and that maybe her heart is a little frightened. Love is hard to comprehend when afflicted for the first time, so she's thinking they are being a bit too terrifying. She is also thinking that maybe they're being a bit wrong about all this, which is probably what expostulation means to her.

"No, not true that you should say all those things! In actuality, it's been quite foobalicious, with lots and lots of silliness in between. It's hard to remember a time when I felt so super satisfied! I guess I do understand him. There is simplicity in his words. He tells me these things I want to know, and it doesn't even hurt."

Beatie looks around the room to see only denial on their faces. All they see is a naive, young girl with guberstagnation. She can't let them think about her this way, so she pauses and takes several sips of bowl water to wet her tongue.

"And I admit, it scares me too. Sometimes I'm sad, like I don't know what to do or what's going on. Like the mailman hasn't shown up in a while, so

I don't know if I'm still on his mind or if he's mad at me for some reason. So, I'm thinking it's not very fair that he should have this kind of power, especially on holidays when I'm expecting presents."

Mrs. Rocksquirm steps forward, feeling Beatie's emotional plea. "It's just the determination of a forgetful mind. That's all it is, Beatie. My husband has been this way since I've known him."

The barber lays his hand on Beatie's shoulders and lightly squeezes them, "Listen to her, doll baby; you have never faced the biggest fear of your life if you have never loved."

"But Hydragew, it's that very fear of love I don't understand. I can't just turn on a light or throw shoes at it. I know, I've tried, and it keeps coming back at me in my loneliest of times."

"Just the reason you should be saying something to him, Beat'rie. In a way, only he would understand. Not just in the way you would understand."

Beatie's eyes suddenly pop up, like a new revelation had just permeated her skull pipes. "You are so right, Hydragew! I should talk to him in a way a Selkie would wish for."

"A 'what' and a 'who' wishes for 'how'?"

"A Selkie. It's like a Scottish folklore, except it's real. Oh, Hydragew, you should have always been there! At the fair; at the beach; on Talbot! These are the places where the dearest words were ever spoken. It was like the ultimate in sweet *amoebafication*, just to hear his acts of kindness and devotion."

"Hold on, Beat'rie. Amoeba what?"

"Ameobafication! You know – Ameobafied: verb; past tense: Ameobod!"

Beatie leaps up in her seat to recite some of his words:

'If hate aims to deflate us and love aims to inflate us, then where must I find the eternal air that will keep us afloat?'

"When I heard those words, it turned my whole life into a spell! Stories might differ, but what it all means is that if he can remove his skin and change, of course he'll be all nude, but I can help him with that, and then I can put on his skin and change too! I hear it's a lot of fun with bodies joined together in the ocean."

Everyone in the room looks at each other befuddled.

"And I agree; if I were a toad, would he still be happy with me? Touch me kindly. Respond to me softly." Beatie then leaps from the chair, swirling about the patrons with her voice in song:

> *"And if we are forbidden to talk and we all start whistling, is it really that important if we are no longer listening? And what if we speak with our hands and listen with our eyes...?"*

Lady Pluckily interrupts, *"I don't know, but I'd sure like to try,"*
Beatie claps, "Hahaha, my, oh my!

> *Touch me kindly. Respond to me softly. Then what if he gives me a line when he isn't on time?"*

"And he brings you six flowers, when there should have been nine!" calls out Mrs. Ingiago.

Beatie spins twice and latches on to Mrs. Ingiago's arm, "I don't know if he would, but it sounds promising." Rolling her arms and hitchhiking her thumb around the room.

> *"Touch me kindly. Respond to me softly. And if he complains of my Haggis because they were all filled with maggots?"*

Greeting the air about Ms. Scharmeem, who chuckles,

> *"Would he say good riddance if he could not tell the difference?"*

"Of course not; that's silly." Beatie is elated with all the responses. This time, she likes all their ideas; she truly does. "Oh, I've been fooling you all! I have been comfortably happy with all of his faults! Instinctively clever, don't you agree?!"

The barber leans forward, "Beat'rie, your story could possibly be the greatest love story ever told – by man, woman, pronoun..."

"Animals too?!"

"Yes, Beat'rie, animals too."

"Wow!" Beatie sits back in the barber chair, mesmerized by her happiness. It is the nod of peers and the raising of the glasses that made her feel like she is one of them now. All these troubling thoughts she had of Bo were really just mistakes. It is at this very moment she sees a vision where they will be happy together forever. Beatie clasps her hands, "It's like I'm in this dream, Hydragew. I don't know where it goes from here?"

"Well, maybe Ms. Barbie would like to answer that for you."

"Cairn Barbie? Are you kidding? That woman frightens me."

The light suddenly flickers, "Did I hear you say something – the little lost girl who lives down the road?"

With those very words, there comes forth several loud screams, with a shadow ascending along the wall. Beatie throws her shoe at it, then tries to flee, but the front door self-locks. A ghastly, skeletal feature now appears before the flickering light, growing in size.

Beatie retreats to the chair, curling up her legs to protect herself with her knees. She watches as the 'thing that creates the shadow' puts its wet towel down on the chair and retrieves a wig from one of the wall pegs.

"Well, well, well. What an exciting group of attendees we have here. All willing to lend an eager ear to such a drab display of sexual mediocrity. So, tell me all, now that you have had a friendly exchange of ideas with this concubine of displeasures, what have you concluded?"

Ms. Barbie walks before the group while they lower their heads in shame.

"Nothing? Nothing at all. Was I not to be considered in this pertinent discussion of this child's education?"

Mrs. Scharmeem squeezes her hands, "Cairn, you know we hold you to the highest opinion..."

"I don't want to hear any of your puerile excuses, Sheesh. It is my place to point out all the concerns regarding the bourgeois. And to you, my salacious one..."

Beatie's eyes rise slowly to look upon Ms. Barbie's face. A face with a scowl and eyebrows drawn to a dagger. It is the look in every horror movie: always so cold, always so cruel, always bringing her to the edge of her seat for the sake of entertainment.

"It is rather rum of you to seek out pleasantries from such a secondary class of purblind visionary's, all with their jejune opinions of their foregone youth, answering these very questions they know nothing about!"

Beatie averts her eyes, looking for a way to escape from her seat.

"And how enlightening it must have been for you to find an untaken space within this very room and then proceed with a topic that you, yourself, cannot understand." Ms. Barbie leans on the arms of Beatie's chair, trapping her in. "You cannot keep this a secret from me, little one. Dating is no longer a private matter that you can just hide in the pages of a diary. Whether you are rejected or accepted, this town is going to know about it."

Ms. Barbie turns to address the crowd, "So, maybe now we should take time to revisit these questions more closely. I cannot think of another time that would be better served than now."

Beatie shrugs her shoulders and slips forward out of the chair, "Could we schedule another day? I'm pretty sure I can make it then."

"Not so fast, Miss Trollop!" Setting her large hands down onto Beatie's shoulders. "Deceit, my dear, is not your foreplay. It is mine."

Ms. Barbie turns to address the group, "Do you not see this before you ladies? The oldest ritual between a man and a woman, and today it is still being played out by amateurs. Love! HAH! Such a good disease for which there is no pill. Ah, but wait! There is! The casual act of one always departing while the other is so casually being left behind."

Ms. Barbie lifts Beatie's chin with her finger. "Please entreat us. No? That is because love is but a myth, and Valentine's Day without the hanky-panky has always confirmed this."

Beatie looks around the room to see all the demoralized faces. These are her new friends who shared their hearts with her. They also helped create her new song. She has to say something in their defense. "Well, I do love someone and he spoils me to no end! I think love is beautiful, even though you may not think so, Ms. Barbie!"

Ms. Barbie smirks, "I care a little, but not a lot. Certainly not where you are concerned. Besides, there's no need to get upset over a little comment meant to help you, my dear."

Beatie watches in shock as everyone in the room nods with Ms. Barbie in agreement. Suddenly, she is feeling betrayed by the same people she thought she trusted.

"Shall we dislike Mis Trollop, everybody? A show of hands, please!"

The raising of all their hands confirmed their abandonment. These very ones, whom she thought were her newly-found friends, are now turning against her. Beatie acts out, "Did you not hear anything I had to say earlier?! Don't any of you even care about love? Well, then why should I have listened to any of you anyways? You're all just boring, dull, bland, and more boring! You are icky and sticky, and you make your mouths say such things that are wicky! Maybe love is not for any of you, or maybe you are just not good at it!!"

A sound of gasps cries out throughout the room, causing Ms. Barbie to calm the crowd.

"Oh my. Such a bold voice you have there, Darly. You must feel so happy to have said such things."

Beatie stands before the chair and slams her hands down, "I'm not even close to saying enough about such things! You bully everyone into thinking that I'm unacceptable! Well, you are not getting away with it, because you are all nothing but a bunch of overgrown, UNACCEPTABLES!!"

There is another outcry of gasps and a more stern reaction from Ms. Barbie: "Let us be quiet for a moment, shall we? I believe I have exercised quite a bit of restraint now, and I am a little short on patience. These scurrilous attacks from you will not do. There is proof of your wretchedness and it is time that I finally expose you."

Ms. Barbie turns about the room and holds a paper high above her head: "There are things you may all want to know regarding Miss Smutty-Pants." Ms. Barbie turns to Beatie, "I know you don't want to hear this, insignificant one, but there is no boyfriend, and there is no one pursuing you. I just so happen to have the note that was written for you thirty years ago. It was addressed to – and received by – the windshield of your car. It was hardly written in a manner that would be from a 'Lover-To-Be'. This here, everyone, is a visitor's note, crookedly written to make just one point: I am leaving you." Ms. Barbie raises the letter and reads it aloud:

*'I felt it was necessary that we not meet again, and this letter being
the final word on that promise.'*

"This letter was not only written to say goodbye, my dear. It was meant
to say good riddance."

A tear drops from Beatie's eye.

"I believe all of you would agree that this fantasy boyfriend is nothing
more than a dragged-out, beat-up boozer with the name – Iggy, inscribed
into his well-being!"

There comes an uproar of laughter that echoes throughout the room.
Hydragew takes Beatie by the arm, "I would not listen to them, Beat'rie.
The right choice is not always based on the advice of our friends. The true
minority of us still want to believe in love."

Beatie thinks with some uncertainty about this: "What should I think,
Hydragew? You know me best!"

"It would not be fair to comment without talking to him first." replies
the barber.

Hydragew is right! True, she hardly knows him, but that's just how
things are when starting out. She is sure they are very close to that stage in a
relationship where he will be calling her every day, waiting in the cold for her
after work, and silently listening to all her agonizing complaints.

"You should not encourage her, Hydragew. I would not insult her if it
were not common place to do so."

Beatie slaps her hands together at Ms. Barbie, "He did not write that
letter and he's not a boozer! He's not!!"

Ms. Barbie waves off her comment, "Tell her Hydragew. Tell her what
you saw."

"Well," the barber running his hands tightly over his scalp. "I did see him
stumbling about the road and peering into the window of a church earlier."

Beatie's scowl immediately falls apart into quivering tears, "Why are you
all doing this to me?"

"Because, my dear, it is you. You are trash. You are a deplorable. You are a
rightfully neglected, morally reprehensible, unrestrained Puta! I can tell you
for certain that any relationships you become engaged in will eventually, and

predictably, be neglected. You are just a moment in time that will be lost and forgotten in any future to come – accept it!"

Beatie wishes she could take back what she says next, but due to the circumstances, she just felt she had to let Ms. Barbie have it. "Well, haud your wheest! Yer bum's out the windae, Miss Witchity Grub, who hates Selkies!!"

It wasn't just the lights flickering or the crack of thunder echoing throughout the room, which did come with a flash of lightning. It was a face so tense that you could clearly see all the blood running from the pockets of Ms. Barbie's eyes. One cannot put into writing what this lady said next, but it is certain that what was heard in that very room would even cause Lucifer to cringe.

Holding her knees tightly to her chest the, Beatie remained bunched up in the chair the entire time, trying desperately not to listen. There was never an end to Ms. Barbie's words, and there was clearly nothing she could do about it. Her only savior from dissipating into carbonated water was the loudest gasp ever heard from the fourteen elderly ladies in the room.

Beatie raises her head to see the very reason for the delay in her abuse, and there he is – huddled in the most disagreeable position ever seen in a barbershop doorway. His hand is shaking, as if he needs to relieve himself, and his face is plastered against the window demonstrating a misdirected bug hitting a windshield.

"Oh, my, gosh! He is a boozer!" Beatie is absolutely outraged by this revelation. She specifically recalls telling Bo that she has no intentions of dating a man more comfortable with the bottle than her. She does not want to go out there, but she feels she has to. She has to let him know that this is not acceptable.

Bumping into Ms. Barbie and sending her to the floor, Beatie crosses through the room to open the door. She has no words for what she sees. His body is all Jello like, and his face is deathly pale. He appears to be like some gangling, boneless eel creature that thinks it ought to stand. More than once, she has seen him in this manner, the nightclub being the other.

Beatie stumbles down the steps, hoping to avoid him, but soon realizes she had left the door open for him to wander in. The barber beats him with a broom, and Sheesh Scharmeem rolls the thermal heater at him to trip him up, but Bo continues to wobble about the shop, scattering the ladies into disarray. Beatie eventually returns to take Bo by his deathly, cold hand and leads him out the door.

Standing outside with her arms folded and her foot tapping, she waits for Bo to break his silence. He struggles to lift his chin with confidence, so instead, he decides it best to present the flowers he had gathered. Favoring one leg, he squats down and holds his balance with one hand on the ground.

She almost took the wilted stems, but after sniffing the air about him, she decides to shake her head instead. "Street-crack-flowers and fermented sugars?!"

Bo takes notice of her displeasure and responds pleadingly, "I've not been to the doggery."

"Oh, go spare me another tale!" Without another word, Beatie takes off along the sidewalk, swatting all around her as she runs.

Bo sighs and watches her go. He stumbles backward and falls through the open door to the dismay of the shop patrons. He doffs his hat and then hurries back out, but like his head, his legs shake too much to make an effective pursuit. A wet paleness covers his face, and his body can only do what comes naturally. There is a break of bad wind and a final release of trapped air, then comes forth a great swell of water. His legs feel cold at first and then numb. Nothing to be ashamed of. He is incontinent.

FEBRUARY 12: WHERE
THE MEMORIES ARE

Beatie wakes from her drowsiness with her mouth open and panting. Her book is open several pages ahead of where she left off. She drops her hand on the table clock. It is 3:00 p.m., so says the clock. Setting the book aside, she smirks at her cup of cocoa, which is now a cold sludge on the edges of her fine porcelain. All dreary-eyed and mindless, she stands by the window mechanically watching the cars go up and down the street. She understands she is by herself on this one. The evil lady's eyes were frightful, but they were right. She is feeling as if it is a last call to yet another short relationship.

Walking with heavy steps to the kitchen table, Beatie has not forgotten that her mother regularly plans a gathering every Monday afternoon. She picks up her cellular phone and presses the one contact number she has saved to memory. "No, mom. I did not forget. I'll be right over."

She still wonders whether or not she should leave a note. What if he should drop by to apologize?

'Be back around 7:00 p.m.' is all she writes, then stuffs it in the crack of the door. She leaves a sandwich on the porch, spraying it with a little bug repellent should he be hungry.

Beatie lets herself in and closes the door quietly behind her. Her calls do not gather a response, so she thinks it best to inspect the house first. Her mother is very orderly in the disorderly way of things, and as expected, her findings reveal a pattern of misbehaviors in every room. Not just silverware in the shower holders or washcloths in the toilet paper dispensers, but the clothing line is dangling with garden tools, and the undergarments are drying over lampshades. There is another habit Mother has that requires attention, and that is letting the neighborhood children hide throughout the house. So far, everything seems in order.

Beatie returns to the kitchen, where most of the issues are always found, and true to her thinking, she finds the glass pitcher of cranberry juice sweating on a low burner, the China rinsing in an overwatered Teisha green Sansevieria Snake plant, and there is soft produce defrosting in the pantry with empty shopping bags stuffed in the refrigerator.

She puts her hands together and rubs them really hard. "Okay, I can fix this." She turns off the burner, hoses down the China, returns the produce to the refrigerator, and moves the shopping bags into the closet. Of course, she is appalled to have to crush a roach crawling across the floor, but at least there are no spider webs.

Wiping her hands of filth on the towel, she saunters on down the hallway and finds them simply by sound. Mrs. Rocksquirm from Amelia Island is there wearing her 'Plume-de-la-flume' hat. Mrs. Boldastuffin, from the other direction, is there too, wearing her large bracelets and head scarf. The woman still holds a financial license and carries with her a Ouija board intermixed with Monopoly pieces. Beatie's mother finally makes up the trio and she wears her teenage bell-bottom pants with lingerie stockings. The two-tiered hat with plastic antlers makes up her final ensemble.

Beatie brings the plates out to the patio and hurries to retrieve the water pitcher. Both Mrs. Rocksquirm and Mrs. Boldastuffin patiently watch Beatie as she returns to refill their glasses. While unfolding the cold cuts, they nervously signal to her mother that a stranger is in the household, but Mrs. Backlebond just brushes them off.

"Double word, Bayougurgle! That gives me a triple on the Q and double on the rest."

"Bayougurgle? That's not a word! Say it in a sentence!"

"I smacked my back because I couldn't take a crap while listening to the sounds of the Bayougurgle."

"Still not a word. There's not even a Q in it!"

"Sounds like there could be a Q. Oh, for the sake of a gastric-brooding frog, where's the dictionary?"

Beatie watches the three ladies look about the room, soon forgetting what they are looking for, her mother finally raises her head with a smile. "Oh, there's my B, come here and give your mother a kiss."

Beatie gives her mother a kiss, while Mrs. Boldastuffin reaches out a hand. "Psst. Psst. Miss? May I speak with you?"

Beatie quietly steps over and leans down with her ear.

"This tea you are serving tastes funny. Now if you are expecting any kind of tip..."

Beatie lifts the glass and sniffs it. "Oh, Mother. This is the water from the pot that has the dirty cleaning pad in it! How about I get you a fresh glass, Mrs. Boldastuffin?"

From the tray on a standalone table, Beatie unravels the cold cuts and distributes the crackers evenly on three plates. Moving to the other side of Miss Boldastuffin, she replaces her glass with the cold tea, then looks about the lanai to see where she can relax in the declining sun.

"Excuse me all, may I sit with you?"

Her mother sneers, "As long as you can bear the conversation."

Beatie sits in her quiet space behind her mother, in the 'bouncee' chair with a plastic ottoman. She remains half-listening to their conversation, knowing that in moments, she could be called on to handle another food and beverage issue. She does not wish to be alone with her other thoughts, but still thinks it is best not to get them involved. What could she tell them? That each day, she had liked him more and more, then pained by the experience of him failing to appear at her house. Then, when he does appear before the barber shop, he is all sauced, like she should have been expecting this. Beatie's voice suddenly cracks with a slight whimper.

"Beatie, are you okay?"

Beatie straightens up and re-adjusts her mouth, "I'm sorry, Mom, my mind is acting like something is wrong. Would you all like some treats?"

"You're lonely, aren't you?" says Mrs. Boldastuffin.

Beatie smiles at the two ladies and gives them both a salute.

"Shitzsbuckle! Do you need to hear that in a sentence too?"

"Mother, how are you coming up with twelve-letter words when you're only supposed to have seven pieces?"

"It's called home field advantage."

Mrs. Rocksquirm looks at Beatie with empathy, "You have done extremely well, little Backlebond. You found a job, you have a nice place to live, and you don't have to play scrabble with your mother."

Mrs. Boldastuffin leans into her mother, "Loi, how perfect would it be for Beatie to meet the boy down the street?"

Beatie's ears perk up when she overhears the comment, not remembering who lives down the street.

"Is he a good boy?" Mrs. Backlebond asks.

"Ooh, yes. He's a good boy. He's responsible, courteous, and works hard at all his chores."

"Sounds like a good boy. What's his name?" asks Mrs. Rocksquirm.

"Who?"

"The boy down the street for Beatie."

Beatie puts her hands on the seat of the chair and raises herself up to listen. She is curious herself.

"Charlie Bop! That's his name!"

"Stomach-ache, Charlie?!!" Beatie stands abruptly and all three ladies pause with a confused look.

Mrs. Boldastuffin leans forward again, "He's smart too and well respected, and I hear he doesn't drink."

"Not a late-night boozer, is he?" responds Mrs. Rocksquirm.

Beatie slaps her hands together as if scolding them, "He's nine years old!! Did you not all think of that?!" Beatie watches as they all cower with their heads lowered.

"Whose turn is it?" "Mine." "Go ahead."

Beatie sits back down and places her hands over her face.

"Spish, spish." In a low whisper, "I hear he works at the International Snow Burger on Pitt."

"That place is soooo... busy, Loi."

"I bet he manages it."

"I bet he owns it."

Beatie throws her arms up and leaves the room, crossing through the length of the house in a hurry. She just wants to get away from everything. She just wants to put her hands over her face and stuff it with a pillow until she passes out. The door is ajar and her childhood memories still glow with the final minutes of an afternoon light. It is just as she left it. All the old pictures and videos, the mermaids and the ponies, even her dolphin lamp on the bedside table.

Beatie slides along the length of her bed and rolls onto her back. She can still smell the stale perfume and nail polish remover in the carpet; she can still hear the sounds of her old records spinning on the turntable; and she can always envision herself performing a concert before her play toys.

She tilts her head sideways toward the vanity mirror. There are no cosmetics out; only empty perfume bottles of varying sizes. She settles down on the little bench and opens the drawer. There she finds her first watch, given to her by her mother as her first trust with independence. Her father never wanted her to have any independence, so she kept it hidden beneath the scrunchies.

Looking for more memories, she finds a small petri dish amidst the silver cleaner and loose cotton balls. Her eyes begin to blink when she sees a sparkling jewel in hues of red and black. It looks so delicious that she is tempted to bite into it, but she can't. It is her mother's wedding ring, passed down through the generations on her father's side. Its disappearance has always been a mystery because her mother is rarely ever seen wearing it. Not out of disrespect, mind you, but because the metal band somehow gave her a rash.

Beatie holds the ring to the light – such a unique artifact of red beryl. She has no pardon to wear it, but oh, how appropriate it is for her to try on. It fits in a way that makes her feel acceptable and committed.

Closing her eyes, she feels Bo reach around to cover her hands with his. He whispers into her ear, something in Scottish or possibly in Selkish. He bows and lowers his top hat, and in the elation, she lifts onto her toes and follows him across the floor. She feels that powerful emotion run through her when he circles his arms around her waist and spins her ever so lightly before his feet. Gracefully, they side-step across the floor, and she hears the cheers from their admirers. She knows what is coming next. In her mind, there is a growing call for a wild finale, and she is sure she can grant them this. Bo quickly puts her into a fast twirl above his head, while she tosses kisses to the crowd. How lovely it is to feel the lightness of the air, to tuck and roll off the bed, to barely miss the vanity and then slam into the closet door – Ouch!!

Beatie looks around and sadly realizes she is alone again. Or is she? Tilting her head to one side, she hears a faint cough. The closet door, being open when she first entered, is now closed with the light on.

Beatie places the ring back in the dish and shuts the drawer. The sound of shuffling is noteworthy and the falling of boxes raises a suspicion. She turns the knob slowly, and though the light is bright inside, there is quite a bit of darkness where the boxes of dolls are stacked. Retreating a few steps, she considers the possibility of ghosts haunting her dolls. The Illuminator of Foggy Pants does make the argument that there are rules preventing ghosts from traveling beyond city limits. However, who is to deny that one might have slipped into her car on the way home?

"Hello, Heneme?! Miss Malla?! Cinnamon Jefferies?! Ghosts are not allowed outside city limits; you know this!"

At that moment, a murmuring sound can be heard from the largest box. She reaches for an old play rake from the closet corner, and ever so delicately, she lifts the lid. Just as she suspects, a solid shape is found within. Using the end of the rake, she slowly lifts the chin of the stowaway and recognizes the child as belonging to one of the neighborhood families.

"Hi little one. How long have you been in there? I bet you're hungry. Won't you come out?" Beatie crouches down to extract the little one from the box, suddenly startled by a figure standing at the bedroom door.

"Mother, there is a child in my closet!"

Her mother pauses to decipher her daughter's accusation: "The Pequot boy! I found him drinking from the garden's wishing well. He comes into the house, you know. He particularly likes your room."

Beatie looks at the boy, who is still munching on candy pieces from his hand. "Mamma, you leave them a trail of candy?!"

"Chickle Putz! It's their favorite. It requires five of those bags, you know; and with prices doubling these days."

Beatie squeezes past her mother, allowing the little boy to run free out the front door. She then continues on to the kitchen with her mother following, "So I admit, I have some terrible habits, but do raspberry bushes grow oranges?"

"No, Mamma, where are the ladies now?"

"I don't know. For some reason, they always remind me that I need more toilet paper. Anyways, the committee has decided on how to end your loneliness. Now he works late stocking shelves, but I'm sure you'll find the time to ..."

"No, Mom."

"Well, you can't be spending time with that temporary settler."

"I don't know of any temporary settlers, Mother!"

"Well, apparently, this settler seems to have taken advantage of someone's weak heart."

Beatie picks up a sponge and begins wiping down the tables, "My mind is a bit occupied, could we talk about this later?"

"Oh, you know me, I'll probably forget in a few minutes." Her mother gently walks up behind Beatie and lays her hands on her shoulders, "Beatrice Gertrude Backlebond, you are a beautiful, young lady with such promising dreams. I don't want to see you wasting your life on some boozer that thinks a good time waits for him at the bottom of the bottle."

Beatie turns away from her mother, catching a tear rising into her eye, "He's not a boozer; it's just how he was raised to walk."

"That's not what I heard from your father. Oh, Beatie, the boy's a backpacker, foolishly hooking up with any enamored woman for whom he doesn't know – or even cares to know. Marriage to a man like that? Dear me! A deviant sicko to the core."

"Well, Mother, you even said yourself, you have some terrible habits."

"The man dresses like a tatterdemalion! I know that is not an issue you are willing to overlook!"

"Yes, but I can help him with that. Meeshman's regularly has clothes for men, and I can also steal furs that wash up on the beach."

"You are just being silly, Beatie. How would you support him?"

"I thought I might try hand modeling again."

"Honey, you heard your agent. You are much too old for that kind of work. There are younger women every day, coming along with naturally, smoother hands than yours. Now I don't want to hear any more about it. Leaving him is the best thing you can do – for him, for me, for your father, and for anyone else who might be interested. You have known him for less than two weeks, and in less than one more, you'll be done with him."

"No, you're wrong, Mother. I can't explain it, but it's like, I've known him for thirty years. We have this connection that I've never felt with anyone before." Beatie looks down at the dishes. "And you know what?" she grabs a dirty glass and breaks it in the sink.

"Beatrice Backlebond! You stop that this instance!"

"I don't care if he's a boozer, Momma!! He is my boozer! And if we have children, we'll all take up drinking!" Beatie breaks another glass.

"Give me one of those!" squeals her mother in excitement.

"Here, Momma, we only have plastic cups now." She watches her mother throw a plastic cup off the refrigerator and into the sink with a frown.

"Try another, but fill it with Jell-O. Yeh, that's better. I know I'm being silly, but that's what he brings out in me. An ebullience of silliness, and I don't want to lose that. Just the other day, he promised me the world along with the sun and the clouds, and it doesn't stop there; he is even thinking about throwing in the moon and the stars as well."

"Beatrice, your father offered me those same darn things and all I get from him is a backed-up toilet. That boy won't be able to keep those promises. That boy is not from here. That boy is going back to his own country, and by tomorrow, you will be forgotten!"

Beatie pulls loose from her mother, grimacing at the thought of not having another tomorrow with him. Love is supposed to be pleasant, not hurtful.

The sun is well below the tree line, but the light cannot be any brighter than the one shining a pathway to her door. "He left a note!"

Beatie bounds up the steps, does a quick spin, and grabs the note placed in the crack of the door. The paper is still fresh, which means he is probably nearby. Her hands are trembling with eagerness and excitement. She rolls up her sleeves, prepared to absorb every thoughtful word a Selkish man can create, but something is wrong. This is the same paper with the same lettering as before. In fact, there is no writing of his at all. It's just the same dumb, boring 'I will be back around 7:00 p.m.' garbage she came up with several hours ago.

Suddenly, she is feeling this intense insecurity. She wants to swallow, but she can't. All she can do is sit with her legs crossed. It is no easy matter for her to come to her senses, but apparently, he is all of these things the others said he is. Through the many tri-folds of deceptions, she finally sees that Bo is just another naked sea drifter, hanging out at the beach on weekends.

Startled by the music on her phone, Beatie looks down at an unrecognizable number. Should she answer it? She knows that scammers are trained to call when one is most vulnerable. Still, she needs someone to talk to. Beatie bites down on her lower lip, then presses on the answer icon.

"Hello?" There is a long silence. "Please speak up; this is the United States speaking. Oh, sure I remember. We ran into each other at the store. Well, I'm currently seeing someone," a tear drops from her eye. "I think. Yes, well, I have your number on display. No, I know what you may have heard, but he's a great guy and he really is a gentleman. Yes, I know you are too. Thank you for calling. What? No, well, sometimes the disease keeps quiet in the winter months. Yes, I know about all the kissing sores. I remember, then come the little mosquito noises. It gets stiff; that too. I agree, that was a good time at Parageusia's. There was a lot of history, but I learned a lot. Of course, if things don't work out, you'll be the first I call. Very good, Charlie! Say hello to your mother for me. And no more playing in the street!!"

Beatie quietly steps into the house. She can hear her two roommates chattering along in Olivia's room. She looks toward the other direction and hurries off without making a noticeable sound. She does not want to get into it with these two.

She closes the door behind her and falls forward onto the bed. Reaching out to touch the stuffed animal, she stares into its calm eyes. "Whit ye know, laddy boy? Talk to me in Scots?"

She tries to replace her thoughts with 'smil'ier' times. She knows in her own breath that he would like to hear from her again, and there will be melting tears and smiles. That's how it works anyway. She holds his little flippers and raises him to the air, pressing her fingers into its beak. "This could be a long wait, and that's okay. With my full consent, I accept this choice."

She lets out a wide yawn, wondering what the following day will be like. It is a long while before she accepts that he is not coming. Wondering whether her own eyes might see him someday again. She closes her eyes and prays that he will never leave her.

He hears the sound of wood being prodded and feels relieved. A few more logs on the fire would be most welcome if someone could summon that. The room feels cold and there is that feeling of lying in a puddle that he cannot lift his body from. It is making him feel terribly uncomfortable.

The caretaker looks at a small clock on the fireplace mantle and sees that there are thirty minutes remaining before midnight. "Mo Charaid needs more time!"

"For what may I ask?! A few more moments of pain!"

"Is life not worth living for if the mere fact is the alternative is nothing?!"

There is no mistaking the voice of his caretaker, always serving honorably in his behalf. And it is a just request too, since he still wishes to have as many dreams as his mind can produce. It is most unfortunate that the man in charge of opinions is informing his friend to think otherwise. The very reason for his friend exiting the room to the sounds of desperate footsteps.

Bo is now left alone with the man, who not only is in charge of opinions, but also finds his appearance gravely unacceptable. He does not seem to have the doctor's confidence in him when notifying his patients of an unsympathetic death. Aiden should have refused his entry at the door; proof by the man's refusal to have his feet checked for hoofs.

Within a short moment, the caregiver storms back into the room and insists that the doctor attend to his grave friend. He can sense his caretaker does not want to have to plead with this man, but it seems his only choice.

"Don't go, Sir Cloverly. I'm not a lovely man, nor a wealthy one. Mo Charaid is all I have. It is but a simple request for a wee bit more time."

"Based on your behavior and treatments, I don't see the emotional attachment toward this man. Is there a reason?"

"You don't have to love much, doctor, but you do have to love something."

The doctor watches the caretaker cross the room and throw open the windows. He then takes his place at the end of the bed in prayer.

"Now you're making sense."

"The foremost to die always receives the best of honors, true?"

"If his time was spent well served."

At least it is good to hear them talking among each other with civility. To listen to them reach out for a compromise. Bo can feel Aiden's forehead press against his own. He can feel his trembling lips, along with that distinct smell of ethanol on his breath.

"Mo sheann charaid, this man is a general surgeon of devotion, and for most of mankind. At times I question his devotion, but I do have to entrust him with your care now."

"Good luck, Ole Boy!" says the general surgeon, patting him on his leg.

The doctor pulls on the side of his mouth and injects a cold fluid into the pocket of his cheek. It has a sour taste that makes him want to grind his teeth into his tongue. At least the man could have had the decency to reveal what was wrong with him before feeding an acrid toxin. His only description is that he is in pain, and yet, there is no feeling of any pain at all. In fact, he just lost the feeling of his face, and there go his fingers, and now his toes Odd how he wants to swallow, but he can't. His mouth is so dry, as if he had been fed smoldering timber. Bo stretches and yawns for one last time and then feels his body fall limp.

Bo sits wrapped in a discarded blanket hanging from a trash bin. Soaked and cold, he pulls his knees further to his chest to stay warm. The water inside him continues to flow unabated, draining him of his energy. He senses his struggles are coming to an end and decides it is time to make his final reconciliation with life.

To say that I have arrived in this life with all the many wonders before me, filled with many promises that I was so anxious to accept, only to learn later a vastly different interpretation of what life was to be for me and the one I was supposed to expect. Is it maybe that I failed to understand that choices are based on the decisions of others, or am I made to believe that opportunities do exist and I only need to be born propitious and prompt to enjoy the riches? So, why was I not promised I would arrive on time, when instead, I was always perceived as being late?

Bo unlatches the amulet from his belt and hurtles it down the road. "Ye care na by!" Bo yells to the sky. "Had angels come to me before my birth and told me that to accept this life, I would be riddled with faults, found folly in all my words, and worthless in all my pursuit – I would have told those lying carnaptious messengers that they were folly! That they were doolaaly! That they were diddle-geegle-dobber-roaters with only the love they have for false promises!! And I would have told them angels..."

Bo stops when he feels an onslaught of quivering tears overtake his voice. He sinks down against the trash bin and shrouds his head with his arms, oddly hearing another voice.

'Hold your tongue! You have no right to behave this way, and frankly, I take no comfort in these words you so carelessly throw around - like I have mis-wronged you or something! As if I am some sort of an art napper roaming through a vestibule of priceless artifacts!'

Bo smiles and wipes away his wet face with his sleeves. "Aye, Mia. I miss you already."

'And the llama says?'

Bo laughs and coughs, wiping through his remaining tears, "...and you know what I really wish I had told those angels about their life promise? – why not."

FEBRUARY 13: IN
DEATH DO WE PART?

Bo does not regain consciousness. Somehow, he had been expecting this. There are never any compromises in life, nor a representative to speak on one's behalf. He has altogether given up on the idea that the angel meant to look after him ever left his first alehouse. Assuming the angel is Irish or Scottish, the odds are in his favor that the spirit is still there.

Bo hears a voice conjuring up his spirit. He widens his cloudy eyes to see that a thin line has dropped down over his face, followed by a repetitive, nonsensical chant.

"Oogie Boogie. Oogie Boogie."

"Mia. You, what's this all about?" Bo croaks.

"Shh. Me thinks you have an unhealthy spirit."

Mia taps a gutter stick several times on each eyebrow and several times on the center of his forehead. She then places the crooked end of the stick into his right nostril and gently tugs on the hood.

"Mia?"

"Ssshhh!" Turning the stick over, she taps the stick on the tip of his nose, "Beep, Beep, Beep." A slight smile breaks from the corner of her lips. "Sorry, I lost my train of thought."

Mia's head sinks into the pillow next to his, "There must be some answer to this."

"To what?"

"I don't know. I can't put my stick on it. You definitely look different."

Mia tugs down on his lower lip while a sensitive expression takes hold of her face. He looks so small, bundled inside the pillow. So much paler, and there are more wrinkles too. She wants to poke at his ticks, particularly the eye wink that she believes she can rid of with a cheek pull.

"You can't die, MacLeod (xii)."

"What do you suggest?"

"One could amputate your head."

Bo gives her a surprised look.

"Bit extreme? Let me take another look." Mia rises to her elbows and draws up her sleeves. She lifts his head in a slow, almost weightless motion. His hair is so thin. It's like the color of ash left behind in a forest fire. She turns his head to the other side and pokes her fingers into his glands, watching strangely as a round object appears from beneath his pillow.

Mia falls out of bed, scrambling to avoid it from falling into her lap. Scurrying on her backside, she kicks the object beneath the bed. "There was a skull placed under your pillow!!"

Bo nods his head. "It's Henry. He scares off bad dreams."

"It's a real skull!"

"Henry was a real person."

Mia scampers around the room, twisting her hair and slapping her skin as if inflicted with ants. "Bo, have you looked at yourself recently without getting grossed out?"

"What do you mean?"

"Well, how about I show you!" Mia pulls away his sheets. "Lovely! Very much what I expected."

"You think it's bad?"

"Of the eight-thousand zombie movies ever made, you remind me of every one of them." Mia walks over to the window and pulls aside the curtain, ushering light into the room. "Something odd about this city. I have traveled to many places in my life, but I have never seen anything like this before." Mia is bewildered to see the buildings blurred and the streets shrouded in a gray dust.

"It is as if everything is disintegrating."

He would like to tell Mia everything, but she would not understand, particularly when he himself does not understand. It's not the buildings he needs help with anyways; his body is at war with something he cannot see, and it is trying to kill him. "Mia, can you help me up? I feel better." Lifting his legs one by one, Bo rolls forward onto the floor. He feels around for his boots, then crawls toward the place where most of his clothes are.

Mia continues to watch, biting on her fingers as if expecting something on his body to break off. This is not a young man's disease; this is years added to her friend's life. While Bo steadies himself on a chair, Mia takes an inspector's look down at his squishing feet.

"Your shoes are watering."

"I must have been urinating."

Mia has had enough, she goes about the room, locking all the shutters and closing the curtains. She then walks him gently back to his bed. "You're not going anywhere. There is nothing glorifying about a man who fights with death, except that it's been fought before with the same results: Death wins! Who is next?"

"Mia, I'll be fine. Maybe I'll sit for a wee spot, but not much more." When Bo's hand touches the bed, his strength leaves him, and he collapses face down onto the floor.

"Just lovely; have you been practicing that too?" Mia takes his boots off along with his pants and goes into the bathroom to clean them. "Maybe we should enroll you in some potty training!!"

Bo listens to the bathroom door close, and while she tries to silence her whimpers, he works hard to get his legs restless again. He feels terrible about her worries, but for him, there is little time. He knows that his deep, defined thinking about Beatie could recoil away in moments.

He hurries in his effort to put clean pants on by letting them drop to the floor, but while trying to step into the openings, he finds himself sitting on the bed once again. His head soon drops between his shoulders, and he begins to snore.

She is enticed by the warmth of the moon and a path beneath the stars. Across the ocean, he is patient. She will only come as speedily as she will whilst he holds the light above the black waters. He has assured her journey will be more pleasant this time with soft kelp laid before her feet, and a tale from The Fidi Belurdi to listen to on a soft tide. It is the story about the pillow inside the clam, offering an unbothered rest on the ocean's floor. He knows this story and it ends with a smile.

Bo straightens his back, he has some complainable stiffness, but it is not an immediate concern. It is the darkness that creeps across the floorboards that worries him the most. He feels for the amulet in his pocket, realizing he had discarded it in the street.

The rain outside has dissipated into a fine mist. Half the sky is blue and the other half is in shades of gray and black. His direction is simple: follow the beam of light from the parting clouds. By the measurements related to time, he has been too long on absence and too short in attendance. He will need to apologize with flowers again, and there happens to be a unique flower shop on the way. They have a certain smell that can entice the nose of anyone inclined to care, even if the deliverer is not in their favor.

Bo grasps his way up the railing, keeping his hat lowered over his depreciated face. Taking to the knock at the door, the salesperson approaches with caution. What she says to him, he cannot recollect, but her attempt to close the door on his foot is telling. He cannot take offense to this, though, for the shiny petals in the vase are well worth the demoralization. He leaves the money on the counter and departs quickly with an uneasy smile.

Stumbling forward and staggering backwards, Bo throws his shoulders forward with the flowers before his face. He can shield his deterioration with a plant, but his physical well-being presents another challenge. The erratic steps he takes with his right leg requires him to jerk forcefully to keep up with the left one. His only remedy is to find a lamp post where he can rest a moment.

The gleam on her office sign ahead is promising, knowing he has made it this far, but his failing walk still accuses him of being a drunkard.

Every morning, Beatie arrives early to perform her duties of organizing and cleaning the office. Not because it is asked of her, but because of who might be stopping by. In her fanciest of dreams, she imagines it could be a local author or a musician scheduled to play at the local theater. Though it has never really happened, dreams have always been the hallmark to her happiness.

Beatie opens the blinds to the wild streets of tourists, none of whom are paying any attention to the tour displays. The sun is barely out and she questions why a fog would keep the street lights on so late. She returns to the gift on her desk, wondering if it really is hers to open. It is most unexpected, as it is so large. She likes packages left on her desk, but never has one been left behind that is so heavy, and so very close to Valentine's Day. What if it's from Parker Ken? Maybe he is sorry for the way he ignored her at the party. How about Ms. Meeshman? Could she now be entrusting her with a new dress due to her loyalty? Whoever it may be from, the 'gifter' should be arriving soon to express their appreciation for whatever she has done. Oh, how she wishes she had worn the red dress It is so desirable, and she would be more likely to have a better time with it on.

She removes her light blue emblem jacket and sets it on the chair, then takes a seat behind the large box. Her nimble fingers move along the taped seals, where she finds a handwritten note poking from one of the flaps. There is almost never a handwritten note on an unnamed surprise. This one is embroidered with hearts and chocolates. Notes are almost never embroidered with symbols and confectionaries.

"Oh, my, gosh!" She cannot help her face from turning abnormally red. Clutching the corners, she lifts the note to her nose, taking in a faint smell of vanilla.

> *My dearest, Beatie, I feel necessary that we should remain as cohorts, and this letter being that contract for our eternal union. To all the excitement to come, a gift for my 'lumiere brillante'; a fancy way of saying, I can't go on without you.*

"He is so right!! We can't! We can't go on without the other! I believe this is so!" Beatie clasps her hands together, marveling at how romantic all this is. It's from Parker Ken! She just knows it. All that business etiquette writing. She is thinking he needs another chance, feeling this would be the right thing to do. Oh, why didn't she wear the red dress?!

Startled by a cold breeze across her face, Beatie lifts her head to see the front door slightly ajar. She could have left the door open, but what if it's her Valentine's surprise?! Maybe he has softly arrived to clothe her with the intentions of love. Maybe her Valentine surprise is here to whisk her up and lighten her head with a flurry of kisses! Beatie can no longer contain herself with these speculations. She runs to the door and leaps like a gazelle, noiseless and windless, "Come take me, my love!!"

Beatie strikes the opening door with the left side of her face, sending her into an immediate sitting position. Dazed and surprised, she looks up to see Mr. Happiness entering the office. He is cradling an open box of brochures, and behind him is Schmelty Grossbar, the young street messenger, whose mother runs the Improv Theater, south of College and Bean.

"Oh, very good, Beatrice. I see you have received the note and the box."

"The note and the box?"

"Yes, have you not read it?" reiterates her employer.

"It is quite lovely. It talks of unity and companionship, some loneliness and love. All that one could wish for on the days leading up to Valentine's."

"Well, you read it much deeper than I wrote. Will you please open the box?"

With a slight facial frown, Beatie returns to her seat and pulls the tape from the lid. She looks up with disappointment, "Business cards and stationery? This sucks."

"They are your new business cards and new stationary with your very own name in thermography. It's going to be a very busy week here in the old city, so we'll be working late each night. I have asked Schmelty to go ahead and take the old stationary to the library for scrap paper."

Beatie rolls her eyes. Hope coming off her face after realizing the box contains nothing of value. In fact, being required to work during Valentine's is definitely barring her freedom from the most celebrated holiday in her life!

"I want more liberties to do things, Mr. Happiness."

"Excellent choice Beatie, your request is well noted. For your devotion, I give to you these three keys. One for the front door, one for the bathroom, and one for the storage closet. More responsibilities than you could ever wish for."

Beatie holds the keys out, waiting for the lint to drop off.

"Oh, and Beatie...?"

"Yes, Mr. Happiness?" Beatie quickly reaches her hand into the waste basket to retrieve the keys.

"Do try to keep the Free Society Explorers from following you back to the office."

"Huh?" Beatie lifts her head and watches carefully as an elderly man, trying to walk a straight line on an otherwise flat-surfaced road, stumbles into the office window. Not only is his mouth open and his head twitching, but his legs and hands are shaking too.

"Still?! How much can one consume?" It makes her furious to see Bo drunk like this again. So much so, she just wants to spit, but she can't. Oh, this reckless behavior in him! He is probably rejoicing his return to the ocean and stopping by to rub it in her face.

Beatie crawls along the floor and pushes the door to a slam. She then rolls quickly away as his hand drags along the window. Uggh, he's making that horrible scratching noise. Never can she forever forgive him for that. She pokes her head out the door and watches as he staggers down the road, pulling at his hair and slapping his behind.

"And I'm sure I don't like him to do that either."

Although she is horrified by his display, she is somewhat relieved to see him in human form. In a way, he is the Selkie of her dreams and the bearer of meaningful tales that provide her with constant drooling. She should thank him for that.

"Schmelty, before you go, please!" Beatie hands the young boy a note of her own. "I'm not sure why I feel I have to do this, I just do."

"Yes, Mam."

Bo reaches the quiet intersection with the understanding that his eyes have deceived him. He seems to have missed her office, and an urgent voice calling from behind him confirms this. A blur briefly comes into view at such a fast pace that all he recognizes is a strong breeze and a fading whisper. What is left behind is a note in his breast pocket, which he immediately unfolds:

'I don't want to forget. Meet me at the restaurant at six.'

Bo smiles and is immediately reminded of her pleasant surprises. This is her biggest one yet, but it doesn't mention the name of the restaurant. There are so many restaurants to choose from and so little time to find the right one. She likes Indian food, and that being the first thought, must be the right choice. He will need fresh flowers; the ones in his hands have already lost their petals. He recalls that the cemetery at the edge of the city has the best flowers in town. Maybe there is an Indian restaurant in there too.

Bo hobbles around a street corner, a fraction of the size he once was. It was a long walk, longer than expected, and he would have missed the cemetery entirely had he not walked into the iron bars. The landscape of the cemetery has changed since he last saw it. It has a much more menacing appearance with the newly exposed holes in the yard.

He hears a low rumbling sound, and the air turns cold with the flashing of lightning along his peripherals. Bo pulls his hat down snug over his head and passes between the bars. The stones are somewhat scattered, unmarked, and forgotten, and most do not receive flowers, however, there is one gravestone that does. The one the town still remembers. This is the grave site of the little girl, the one with the rile seizure who died quite painfully hundreds of years ago. Bo digs at the ground with his hands and pulls on a long root that holds tight to the stone. With a long heave, he finally lifts up a large bouquet.

It never seems to be a good sign when the leaves block the open spaces of the cemetery bars. There is a loud clap of thunder, the sky rapidly darkens, and the wind decide to howl. Bo hurries with the burden of his legs, swinging his arms for extra momentum. Every flash of light discovers him struggling with his clothes and fighting to stay on his feet. The mad-bomber hat that had provided him with so many years of warmth, no longer fits his shrunken head. His work gloves, which had seen so many years of hard labor, now wobble like oversized mitts on his boney hands. Even his suit, once made to fit a healthy man, now flops about his body like a plastic grocery bag caught on a limb. And still, he holds tightly to the stems of the flowers, fervently denying that his fingers should ever let them go.

Bo kneels before an open door with the heel of his palms resting on the pavement. His lungs are inflamed and his knees are swollen with exertion. There are many people stepping over and around him, and not a single one will offer him assistance. But there is an aroma through the open door that is very reminiscent to pork vandaloo. A favorite dish of Beatie's. One that will assure her arrival.

Bo thinks little of his condition and makes his way into the restaurant. He finds the nearest seat by the door and is happy to see a young maitre'd reach out to him so quickly. She has the most approachable aura about her that brings relief to all of his self-conscious worries. If only she could not be frightened by the series of ticks and left-side quirks that show he is diseased in some way.

In an effort to gain help from the next employee, Bo works up a more pleasant face, applying a few tugs here and a few pushes there. It draws a smile from the young lady who pushes a waste basket and carries a broom.

"Do you have a seat by the window? It's for me and Miss Beatrice Backlebond. She likes windows, you see. She likes the general chit-chat and the candy in the morn..."

"I'm sure I would like those things too, sir, but my job isn't to seat anyone; it's to...."

"But I brought these flowers and she expects them to be happy." Bo places a flower in her hand and watches as a kinder, more gentle expression comes across her face, "I'll do what I can."

Startled by a tap on the shoulder by the lady still holding his flower. "I found a chair the manager will allow you to rest in. It's not by the window, but you will have a view of one." She points to a lonely table by the exit sign. "You will be close to the door, so you will be the first one she sees. I also moved the trash bin a bit closer, should you wish to relieve yourself."

"That would be fine."

She smiles and gives Bo her hand, leading him across the floor to the seat. He bends down into the chair and rests his head against the wall, watching for any movement from his view of the door. He is aware that his appearance is attracting snickers, particularly from the one who mimics his chewing like a cow. It does not bother him; he is not here for them anyways. At any moment, she will appear, and they will waltz once again before a crowd of skeptical onlookers.

Bo lowers his head and closes his eyes for a while. When he opens them, he clears his throat and accents the air with a scribble motion of his hand.

"Miss, I would like to pay for the meal?" He smiles and hands her two crumpled dollar bills. "You haven't ordered anything, sir. You've just been sitting there with your eyes closed."

"I did not order the Pork Vandaloo?"

"Sir, we don't have any Pork Vandaloo. This is a fast-food pizza kitchen. You place and pay for your order at the counter."

"When did Koodas start this?"

The young lady reaches into her pocket for her phone. "Koodas is in Scotland. It closed over thirty years ago."

Letting go of the railing seemed to take all the strength out of him. He has been sitting on the steps for too long now and is starting to mold with his surroundings. The people, the roads, the buildings – none of them appear real anymore. It is as if they have been preserved in some timeless continuum that has slowly withered away their distinct features. He is not going to wait to join them. There are far more distressing matters that now confront him, such as the few, half-open buds that remain on his flower stems.

Picking up a fallen branch for support, Bo stumbles down the steps onto the sidewalk, moving west out of the city, toward the direction where he thought he should be. The streets before him are rarely empty, but this time maybe for good cause. The air smells of cooked timber; the roads are constructed of dirt; and every other building smolders in a bright, fiery ember. Block after block, there is not a living soul, at least not one that is entirely complete. Many can be seen floating between demolished buildings; those with legs seem to hurry, while those without sit in window sills with the expression of indifference. Whatever their purpose, their cold and lifeless presence is starting to feel like his own.

Tying his hat on tighter, Bo finds his way, changing his direction every time he remotely sees something out of the ordinary. He turns north, toward the taprooms and sleepy joints, hoping to reach a more normalized setting of tourists and window shoppers, but what he arrives to is even more unsettling. In a moonlit cul-de-Sac of windowless buildings and dark, immeasurable hollows dug before them, bright white letters of names and dates begin to appear on the building walls.

Bo turns and walks away with great urgency. He is still looking for that uncertain place that he is almost certain still exists, and if not for having to navigate the holes created in his mind, he might just remember who he is supposed to meet. Apparently, his failing memory is gaining on him faster than his remembrance of what once was.

Bo stumbles out onto the road and drags his feet to the next corner. He has always been following the night into the next day, but this time there is no certainty he will ever see light again. Stepping back and forth to preserve his balance, he watches as the remaining lights perish throughout the city. He then smiles, and rests his palms on the ground. He is happy to have been granted this extra time – that even a breath of air could bring him so much life.

"I've lived a good life, and though I cannot prove I was here, I can prove to myself I wanted to be here."

"You're a good fellow, Bo Fox." He hears Connor say. "More than a country is worth."

He only wishes that were true.

It is when the frame of a person can no longer carry itself that the calls for a peaceful rest are justified. With some difficulty, Bo finds his way toward the only spare light made available. A light post shining bright in a small park. He crawls across the lawn and rises slowly onto a bench.

A young lady, seated beside him, glances around a book with a smirk. She thinks she should scream with all those facial tics he conjures up. And does he not know that his suit belongs to someone who is supposed to be healthy? She turns her head back to her book and thinks about this. It's so odd how familiar he looks. Especially when he drops his head in a slumber and snores. It reminds her of this lagoon creature she once shared her bed with. Wait! Could this be the very man she had pretend sex with? She waves her hand several times before his face and notices he doesn't even seem interested. In fact, his whole body is drooping to the point that he might roll off the bench. "Oh, for Iggie's sake," The woman lifts his chin. "Is that you?"

Bo abruptly awakens. A light source behind his eyes suddenly creates an image that he recognizes. He immediately extends his trembling hand toward her direction. "I bought you these flowers."

Beatie fingers the wilted stems, and without further delay, she sets her book in her lap, "We need to talk."

And so, she does. All the time with her forefinger functioning as the ending punctuation to each sentence. She is glad to have known him, and she is certain that love – for a brief moment – can be found anywhere. At least, this is what he believes she had said. She said a great many of other things too, but it all seem so tiring that he just dropped his head between his shoulders and began snoring.

Beatie snaps her fingers twice, "Are we okay?" She looks down at her watch bored with the engagement. He doesn't seem to have that youthfulness and humor she expects from him. Beatie stretches her arm out, "Anyways, how happy I was to know you."

Bo watches his arm rise up and down. He does have words of his own to say, but because his chattering teeth renders him speechless, all he can do is cross his eyes and let his upper lip stiffen.

"Bo! Are you okay? Bo, wake up!"

She shakes his arm and dislodges the flower stems from his hand. He starts to lean forward to retrieve them, only to discover that his body is more comfortable attached to the bench.

"Never mind those!"

He blinks his eyes several times and listens to the sound of pages flipping through a book.

"The fort we keep passing on the way to the city – I read that it is the perfect place to go on Valentine's Day. Apparently, a lot of lives were lost there. Something to do with infidelities between the officers and their lovers."

Bo becomes aware of a gentle tugging on his ear lobe.

"Bo, I am speaking to you about that fort!"

Bo looks with blind eyes at the person his head shares a shoulder with, "I do say, there are two passions of the doting Willoby..."

"Yes, I know," the lady pats Bo on the head. "Let it all out. Most would think you would be use to rejection by now."

Heaviness stands on Bo's eye lids, grows deep inside his ears, and rolls his tongue to silence his breath. A bell tolls and he listens to it echo across an empty room. A pressure is felt on his chest that forces him to take an excruciating puff.

"Hand me my stethoscope!" A blurry face can be heard yelling over his face. Bo takes notice of the anxiety in the voice and wonders the reason for its urgency. He does recognize Aiden on his knee, trying to hide an impenetrable fear that does not provide understanding. Then suddenly, it happens so quickly.

"I'm not getting a pulse!" is for sure what he heard. Anything is possible, and maybe the usual way of saying things; it's just – he has heard those words before, but never thought they'd ever be used on him.

Though both remain silent, while their thoughts are telling. No longer will there be magical words of recovery; no more measuring tools in the doctor's bag to be poked with; or offers of superstitious antidotes to make worse his complexion. He had suffered a grave reaction in the final minutes of despair. To all those the doctor said he could save, be forever at peace.

The doctor moves forward and draws his fingers over Bo's eyes. He then feels the cold sheet placed over his face, and for the first time, it does not feel suffocating.

It should be mentioned that his room was the scene of much to be desired that evening. The eastern windows were thrown open to the incantations of the red-robed curates; the sounds of tossing bells were gyrating on the back lawn; and of course, there was the low drone of bagpipes, marching to the beat of a death sermon throughout the manor halls. A joy to think that others still remember him.

With no lack of companionship, he was well represented at his viewing. Even Bessey made an unannounced showing that brought an end to the evening. The doctor and his wife were there, as were many acquaintances he knew not by name. And, of course, his devoted caretaker. So sad for Aiden and for his services alone. Such hard work for a fearless cause, and now the fear of becoming lonely will be his next challenge.

Bo softly hears his name fade, as if it were a last call to a missing person. There is no immediate thought other than the one he has retained. She will always be a part of the world he remembers, and though their past was brief, it is fair to say, the last few hours made living all the more worth-while, even if it were only for a dream.

FEBRUARY 14:
BAMBOOZLING
APOTHECARIES

He can still imagine them, ever so slight, as he can hear them, ever so soft. And he can still feel the nighttime air and lift his nose to an evening scent. He can hear the hooting and the honking and a taste of salt and timber. The visions of shadows before doorways and the distorted shapes behind crown glass windows. All feels more like a reason than a remembrance. More like a why than a how.

Bo shuffles stiffly past the gatekeeper and ignores his repeated calls for flavored ice. Standing on the hill, he looks upon the wild streets below. Cannon fire is not normally heard with the sounds of flutes and horns, but maybe this is the celebration he is to expect. It is Valentine's Day and his dreams have not faded as one might anticipate. She may have left him on the bench, but she forgot to leave his heart and still carries it with her. This is a possession that a spirit cannot depart without.

Bo checks his coat for his hat and gloves. His journey from here will be his own and neither darkness nor the light, will give him any measurement of time. He will have to find her with prior knowledge from his past.

Bo tumbles backwards down the hill, through the tree branches, and into a ravine of sloppy water. He splashes about aimlessly in the muck, grabbing hold of something putrid but solid. Something is all wrong with his anatomy. He is crooked and wooden-like with collapsible joints; even his arms feel like they are directed by long strings. It is clear that his knowledge of the past has left him with little to be confident about. He will obviously need help; someone a bit more successful and accomplished that he can rely on.

With the support of a cow leg, Bo raises himself before a sign he has seen before with little enthusiasm: *Do Not Enter.* He will heed the warning this time and make his way, not into the city, but westward to where the sounds are heard in the form of amplified crickets. The hope for his condition, conclusion, and continuation is there with a man named Cornelius Bumpkin.

At the four corners of an intersection, he arrives to see an oil lamp glimmering through a dense fog. A shop sign of some fraternal order of wooden horses hangs outside the establishment. He makes his way in his fold-able detachable manner, tossing his long strings onto various objects and pulling himself forward up to the porch. He stumbles over a large barrel, and lying helplessly, he looks up to see two black, leather boots heightened by wooden blocks.

"Would you like a newspaper, Governor?" says the youthful voice.

"What night is it, young folk?"

"Tis the fourteenth of February, sir."

"There's still time. What glow'r is this?"

"Hoyle-Sawyer, sir. It's a kerosene shop. They sell tar too."

"I'm looking for Qui Qua's."

"That also. The two stores double for both."

Bo signals to the boy, "I need help."

The young boy notices that Bo is incapacitated and circles a lamp over his body to see if he has any signs of the disease. The boy then waves his hand toward the door, and soon there are four legs approaching, stepping around Bo and hoisting him into the store.

Bo appears lying on a table, his ears listening to voices around him. Above his face is a bow-shaped mustache with yellow hairs curled about a man's ears. Behind him is a group of six nodding heads holding a chalkboard. Bo surmises that this man is Cornelius Bumpkin. He is a complex but gentle man, educated at the finest schools in the world. Much like Connor, who is sophisticated in the way of bringing sanity to insane issues, this man recognizes the most undefinable ailments, concocts the most egregious ointments, and cures the most cockamamie beliefs that one can assume.

The professor rolls up his sleeves and lifts Bo's head. He carefully looks into his eyes, which are blinking like a light in a faulty socket. "Aghast!" he yells, then turns sharply toward his assistants.

"Write this down! Dilation of pupils with lots of blinking."

He then pulls on Bo's eye lids and tweaks his nose, taking note of each related facial reaction.

"Interesting. I need you to sit up for some questioning."

Bo does not delay upon this request, snapping to an upright position.

"How about any breathing difficulties?"

"Whenever I go under water."

"Do you feel odd when I do this?" The professor tilts Bo's head back and places two rows of bite marks on his chin.

"Wouldn't you?"

"Can you explain the pallid color of your face?"

"I'm from Scotland?"

The professor quickly turns to his assistants, "Scribble this: touch of dyspnea beneath water, negative reaction to prodding of the face, and color is not consistent with those in warmer climates."

"Was your hair always red?"

"Was brown."

"Well, that caps the climax! Seen all kinds of symptoms around here: black vomit, yellow eyes, people covered in tar and feathers. It's no open secret that it's been a horrible summer – the worst in our first year of history. I don't want you to take this the wrong way, but in my professional opinion, there is nothing wrong with you. Sure, you suffered from a recent death, you walk a little stiff, and you survive without the basic necessities of food, shelter, water, and air – but this is quite normal for a man of your condition."

"But professor, I don't understand. I feel like my innards have been ripped from my body."

"Your feelings have nothing to do with your physical being; it is more mental, you see. You have the 'Morbs'. Most likely brought on by the consequences of a woman."

"Is there a cure?"

"Some old orchard might do you good. Otherwise, there is a ship due into port within a few months that should bring other advice. I can send a messenger to you when it arrives."

Bo lowers his body down on a bag of dry goods and lets out a soft sigh, "Professor, I don't have much time. I feel a darkness so thick and heavy upon me, I sense it is trying to erase all thoughts of my bonnie, Beatie."

Professor Bumpkin lays his hands on his knee, "I don't know much about why, when, or even how the end ever comes. I, myself, have always thought it was when you surpassed your quota of squashed bugs. But regarding your own frail will and testament of your loved one, I fear not even the feasts of Lupercalia could help you with this one."

Bo looks at the professor, then leans his arms with heaviness on his knees.

"Then again!" the professor raises his finger. "The mind is able to cure ailments better than any charm, medicine, or gift delivered. To quote William Hazlitt, spoken a year from now: 'Where there is a will, there is a way' (xiii)."

"Can you explain?"

"How about this?" The professor wets his whistle, "Hey Tutti Taitie, How Tutti Taitie, Hey Tutti Taitie, who's fou now? (xiv) Sing it to me, you wretched old man! Hey Tutti Taitie, How Tutti Taitie...!!"

Bo looks up at the crazy professor. He thinks him mad, but he also begins to feel his internals stirring. He has clarity in his mind, and his body no longer feels like a toy. It isn't long before he is dancing across the tables and singing along to this old Scottish song. Outside, the once-yellow glow in the sky is suddenly made clear, and all things that were burned to ash are made whole again. Bo's body now feels a renewed strength. He springs to the floor and pulls his pants back on!

"When did you take your pants off, old man?"

"I don't remember, but I think it best I put them back on."

The door to his motel room is slightly ajar, and Bo has to step over the chipped beef, a broken bag of flour, and a leaking carton of creamed pepper milk to see if all is okay. Mia seems to have left, but she isn't quite gone.

Her belongings are still in the room, and her nightlight is on, but her disappearance troubles Bo, thinking he might be responsible.

He walks into the bathroom to check on his appearance, ecstatic to find that his unkempt meadow of brown hair is back on his head. He draws his lids down and rolls his eyes back and forth. He definitely feels fine; his color has returned, and his face has a smile on it too.

Bo steps from the elevator, and the doors close with a gasp. He approaches the desk of the assistant manager, who is busy eating from a large bag of orange snacks, the very same snacks that can often be traced to Mia.

"Have you seen my roommate?"

The manager knocks over a glass across the desk and quickly mops the water with his sleeve. "I see many people, some leaving, others arriving." Pressing his lips together in thought, "Anything else?"

Bo leans on the counter top, "The button in the lift? The one that reads REHAB?"

"Short for Rehabilitation - takes you to a lower level."

"There are 'doodle-bits' smeared all over this button."

"No, not mine! There is no reason to go down there. The floor was abandoned in the nineteenth century when it was determined the experiments weren't working."

Bo squints his eyes as he watches Sen pull on his collar.

"I mean, seriously. Why would anyone go down there after learning something like that – the Fundoddie family? Hello?!" Sen shoves his hand into the bag. "People from another country?! Haven't seen them since."

Bo watches the manager take a shaking handful of doodles into his mouth, "I am sure I don't want my paying guests to be doing that, am I right? And then what does she go and do?"

"She?"

"What?"

"You said - *She.*"

The manager nervously wipes his forehead, leaving an orange discoloration across his brow. "Sure – she, her, and them – those are the Fundoddie pronouns. I didn't make them up; you did!"

"I did?" Bo holds a stare into the manager's eyes; he knows this man has information.

"Okay, I can't fully blame the Fundoddie's – or you. We tried disconnecting the button to this floor."

"Bit of a problem with '*this*' floor?"

"Something to do with the chains on the lifts. I don't know elevators, but for some reason, when it stops on the lower floors, the bed has this annoying habit of spilling people out into the hallway. Pretty much against their own will, even. We thought about getting it fixed, but no elevator company is willing to go down there."

"Mia might be down there?"

"Hard to say, really. We can't get the lights back on."

Bo shakes his head from side to side, "Didn't you think that maybe it's time to ring the authorities?"

"What are you worried about?!" The assistant manager annoyed by the questioning. "Goggy is taking care of it. Once the generators are cranked up, everything will be fine!"

"What is a 'Goggy'?"

"The one who owns this motel. She's the only one who can go down there without incident."

"No inspections from time to time?"

"Are you hearing yourself? I told you! Who would want that kind of liability? Listen, she's not on that floor. I was down there myself. We were both down there last week! And more recently, Sunday night. I've been watching daily, okay? See the monitors behind my desk? The camera sensors are set up to detect any kind of movement, good or bad.

WOW!! What was that!!? Did you see that?! It was like some Hoojie thing! There it was again!!! It just shot right by the camera. Was that big or what?! But seriously, no way could she be down there."

Bo looks at the camera more closely. "Where does that ramp go?"

"The ramp? Oh, please. It's a million to one she made it that far."

"How do I get there?"

"The M button – it's hidden beneath the console. It's small and very hard to see. No one goes down there, though. Not even Goggy. We are talking about a place where light cannot penetrate the dark. Have you not heard about the bending of light?"

"Einstein's General Theory of Relativity (xv)."

"Except down there, light just does a complete one-eighty."

"It's the motor room?"

"It was the original town morgue. Most of the bodies are out, from what we know, along with the smell, but believe me, nothing exists down there."

A chill runs up Bo's spine. He is reluctant to go alone, but he senses this is where Mia has gone. It's part of her nature to partake in nonsensical ventures like this. Seeing that the manager is unwilling to do anything further, Bo hurries across the lobby toward the elevator. He cannot abandon her at this time in need. This is his friend.

The shutting of the door and slow descent down the elevator shaft leaves Bo a lot to think about. The place where he is going that Sen alluded to has a long history, unimproved by hell. Darkness has been there for an eternity and does not know the existence of light. It will always be dark down there. Dreams do not exist in this kind of darkness. This is where nightmares are found.

When the doors do open, Bo falls forward, just as the manager had suggested. He hears the loud sound of the box going up the shaft and complete darkness quickly closes around him. Already, he detests the morgue's existence. Nothing desirable above ground ever grows down here. Not a single tardigrade, cockroach, or ecoli.

Without direction or aid, he makes his way into the unknown, searching with blind hands and apprehensive ears. There is no reassurance he will ever find Mia, but maybe he can shorten this maniacal search by calling her name. Bo calls three times, and three times again. After the ninth try, he finally hears a response, but it is not from Mia; it is from the morgue he loathes. A heavy, iron door squeaks to a close behind him, and then comes that smell of the cold beneath the boards, like the untouched earth where the bones lie undisturbed. He waves his hand, trying to get a better understanding of what occupies the space around him, when he hears a loud bang above his head and a deafening sound that rings in his ear Next comes a fiery glow of flaming lights that produces an orange cloud. It sears his skin and heats his bones.

He has never believed in apparitions, nor has he any prior belief they should exist, and yet they appear before him as real as a mind can create one. They have bloated heads and empty eye sockets. Their spines flutter beneath them as if trying to keep their bodies afloat. Bo reaches out to touch one, just to make sure what he is experiencing is true, but it withdraws with the other apparitions into the endless, narrow passageways ahead.

Bo walks a few paces to see that a door with bars is emitting a dim light from within. Upon reaching the bars, he sees a small figure seated against the wall with its head tottering back and forth in a quiet slumber. There are soiled trash bags tangled about the feet and a dripping pool pipe turning her hair into a greasy mop.

It's Mia!! It has to be! He found her just like this before, while she was out looking for traces of a Dutch farm in lower Manhattan. Bo feels his way along the wall for any breaches around the bars. He pushes his hands through a fast opening, and with his shoulder, he leans until the wall relents. Bending down on his knees, he raises Mia's face. She is badly soiled and hardly recognizable, but it is her all the same. Using the sleeve of his arm, he cleans a white circle around her face. "What happened to you, Mar?"

Clicking his fingers several times, Mia raises her head from her slumber. She extends her bounded hands toward the light, "The phantom air. It's in the air. Please tell them to go away." Her voice cracks with a whimpering sound, then she burrows her face into Bo's shoulder and blows her nose.

"It's like we're between Heaven and Hell, Mar."

She squeezes Bo's hand tightly, and in drowsy syllables, she explains just how nasty her situation was. It involved a little girl telling her what a bad soul she had and how her calls for help would never be answered. Bo unties the torn hospital gown fixed around her wrists, "Maybe we can loosen these weeds from your feet, what do you think?"

Her hand squeezes tightly onto Bo's arm, and a perfectly round tear runs down her face. "Teuchy, it's you," she says, reaching out to touch his forehead. "You lost all your hair and your face – it's all bone. Is this Henry's idea? It's so smooth, no wrinkles or sagging."

"Mia, we should go. Give me your hand." She holds onto Bo's arm while he helps Mia to her feet.

"We'll take the stairs."

"Stairs?"

Bo points over her shoulder, "Oh."

When the door opens, the thin shadow of a once-healthy man steps forward into the motel room. He slowly shuts the door and sits on his bed, feeling very immobile. The sunlight streaming through the curtains do add some brightness to his soul, but it is his appearance that shows the shell of a man he once was. This will be hard to explain to Beatie.

He lies back on his bed when he touches something solid beneath his pillow. The logbook entries! Flipping through the pages toward the end, he finds that only Mia and Beatie remain on the final pages. The very last page is still left untouched.

The bathroom door flies open, and out steps Mia, wearing a bath towel around her head. She has found a leafy-pattern dress to go with a thick black shawl. She must have found her new self. Before the mirror, she puts a different shade of color onto her eyes and looks up. "I am not the same person I was yesterday."

Bo glances from his logbook to hear her voice.

"I know you very well, Bo Fox, and what you are thinking. That I am incapable of letting go of my prior self to evolve into a new person," Mia gives another look in the mirror. "Lovely, don't you think? What do you think of the eyes?"

"Aye, a lot of blue."

"I admit, I have been feeling a little not worthy of late. So many circumstances to deal with." Mia clasps her hands together with a big smile. "Then came all this talk of dignity and loyalty from you, and it just sounded so promising. I feel like a new person, you know?" Mia looks up at him, expecting a response: "Are you okay?"

"Were you waiting for me?"

Mia does a quick spin and hurries to his bedside; rolling over onto her back, she looks at him with a gentle face. His appearance still worries her, particularly the bare skull with cracks that need filling. She says nothing about it and gives him a kiss instead.

Mia uncrosses her legs, "I want to show you something."

Bo watches her stand and spin, then roll her eyes, "Come on!"

She reaches for a flashlight and a broomstick, then grabs the loose sleeve of Bo's arm and pulls him back to the stairwell. Bo grasps the rail, watching the light shrink around the turns as Mia races ahead. He finds Mia squatting down, swinging her broom back and forth beneath a step.

"There it is, Bo! Did you see it?"

Bo sits on the step, leaning forward, entranced by Mia's broom-prodding, "Mar, this is crazy."

"Isn't it?"

"What's this all about?"

Mia winks her eye at Bo and then slowly extracts a small object: "Happy Valentine's Day!"

Bo lifts up a string with color-coated objects attached to it. He looks at it quizzically, as if forgetting the significance of the gesture.

"You still haven't said anything."

"Of course, I like it. I'd like it more if I only knew what it is."

"It is a necklace with shark teeth made of candy."

"I have aged, Mar. Remind me what it's for?"

Mia takes his hand, "We have come a long way, you and I. We have never shared Valentine's together in the right way. I know that at times it may have been difficult for us to be in the same room together, but there is no room I would rather share, than with you."

"Valentine's, you and me together?"

Mia nods her head, and her eyes go wide with aggression. "Why pray for something you already have when it has always been there before you?" Mia places her hands on Bo's shoulders for leverage. "Something about older men: mature, lean legs, shortness of breath; just knowing that you can't wander too far away or put up a proper fight."

"Mia, what are you doing?"

Mia removes the black shawl and lifts up her shirt, pulling Bo's head underneath. He feels his face engulfed in her bare chest and turns his head to try and breathe. "Well, if you're not going to manhandle me!"

Bo lifts his head out of her shirt, but Mia continues to subdue him by climbing on top of him, "Is this what you're made of stick man?!"

Bo reaches for the stairwell rail and pulls himself out from underneath.

Mia sits back, disappointed, with a mottled look of anger and resentment. She grabs her flashlight and hurries back up the steps, rushing the key into the slot and slamming the door behind her. She fixes the chain and slowly sinks to the floor. She has lived this time and time again, always waiting for what fails to arrive. She does not want to face the future as it currently presents itself: fading into oblivion within the confines of her room, losing her possessions to new tenants, and having to watch from a distance while others share an afternoon tea. This is the life of a ghost.

Bo rattles the door knob, "Mia?"

She wipes her wet eyes with her hand and lifts her head. "You send out the same message every time, and every time your response is the same – retreat. I thought we might be together always. I had that to hope for." Mia pauses to clear her eyes of tears. "Did you expect me to fall to my knees and beg forgiveness? Because I could. Do I need permission to put on a blouse and look all glowing and soft? I think not, but I could. Would it matter?"

Mia lifts her ear. There is no sound from his side of the door, "Bo, are you still there?"

Bo's body sinks to the floor, "You feel betrayed."

"Like you didn't know?" she shakes her head. "Who are you? It's like you are making yourself into something I can no longer see. There is this defiance and arrogance in you that never used to be there before."

She presses against the door and pushes herself up to her feet, finally opening the door with the chain still latched. "How long can you keep up this appearance of being someone else?"

"I think there is a misunderstanding, Mia."

"No, there isn't. You're different. By a whole lot even, and not just your impersonation of a skeleton, but all this certainty and confidence that is so unlike you – and you haven't stuttered once!"

Bo averts his sunken eyes, "Stuttered?"

Mia closes the door and unlatches the chain, blocking his approach with her arm, "Whenever you would get embarrassed or rejected, you would stutter. It was cute, even. Your eyes would blink rapidly, you would get all flustered, and your face would turn all red. Now you just act like some nineteenth-century, 'Wally.' And you still call me Mia!!"

Bo looks at her with an apologetic weakness, "I'm sorry, Mar."

"Not good enough. Do you even see me? Do you ever hear what I am saying? Does that even matter to you?"

"I cannot let her go so she may find her dreams with someone else!"

Mia was afraid to hear those words. She felt she deserved to be the last thought on his mind. Apparently, this is not to be. After a long stare, she lets him in and closes the door. Leaning back against the wall, she watches him walk like a zombie to his bed as if getting ready for his viewing. She is deeply disturbed by the advance of his years. His physique is altogether unfamiliar. His head resembles nothing more than a bare skull; his speech is unrecognizable; and his jaw continues to make those robotic chewing motions.

Bo steps back and forth over his clothes on. He is having trouble bending further than his body will allow him. His shaking is also making it difficult for him to ease into cleaner pants. The grimacing look on his face is about as much as Mia can tolerate. She wants to yell at him some more, but she can't. Every day there has been her friend, Bo. He is not a hurtful man; he is not an oppressive man, nor is he a hateful man. This is her most cherished friend. She has always been there with him, and now she wants to be there for him.

Mia steps forward, "Let me help you with your tie!" She grabs the ends of his bow tie.

"It would make me very happy if you could do that for me, Mar."

She smiles at him and weaves the band into a knot, then buttons the top of his collar, "PTA."

"PTA?"

"Please turn around." Grabbing the end of his collar, she tucks in his tie. "When do you plan on seeing her again?"

"Until I can see her no more."

Looking at his face from ear to ear, she touches the empty spaces around his chin. "Could you please stop chewing for a moment?!"

She wants to make his face more presentable, and that begins with peppering powder into his cracks. At first, his entire skull is hard to color, but the bronzer blends in nicely. She then draws into his skull thicker brows and even paints lips where there were none. He still has a tiring look, but it is not dead tiring. She smirks, realizing it is the best that can be done, then pats the top of his head and smiles, "It can't get much worse, right?"

When Bo pulls his hands before the mirror, he chuckles at how she was able to put a large smile on his face. Despite the impossible attempt, he is happy. He knows he cannot improve on his appearance, but this time there will be no more stuttering words to express his love for Beatie, nor any anticipated rejections to further his delay. Looks will not matter anymore.

Bo creeps over to the chair where his shoes and winter coat lie. Mia places his hat on his head and applauds his appearance. She makes him wear gloves and hurries to bring him another coat. He has a little more weight now, and this makes them both happy.

"There, you look quite sprightly!"

Bo looks at Mia and senses her loneliness from the sadness in her eyes. He senses she had hoped all would have worked out differently. She doesn't want what happens next – having to look for another traveling mate at the next stopping place. Always longing to find that one companion who is ready and able.

"Everything alright between you and Sen, Mar?"

"No. It seems that Sen wants us out of the motel."

"What about the eradication of ghosts?"

"How can one expel what one cannot see? I can always go back to being my stupid self."

"You don't have to do that, Mar."

"Well, I'm not going to! I came here to meet someone," Mia wipes a tear from her eye. "If your whole life is to find a reason not to do anything, you are spending whatever amount of life you have doing exactly that."

"And you spoke with Sam?"

"She was pretty upset."

"And what did you say?"

"Oh, it's not important."

"Come on!"

"I had to tell her that she and I could be more than just friends. I don't know exactly what I meant by that or what that might entail, but she seemed to be overly excited."

"Ah, good on you, Mar."

"Well, the David Attenborough Valentine's special is on tonight. Kind of a tradition, you know."

Bo heaves a sigh of relief. Mia has no wish to go home, even in a dream that does not belong to her; there is more life for her here. This will not be the end of all things for Mia. She has dreams of her own, you know.

Mia finally looks at those hollowed eyes in Bo for some closure, "It's dark out there; are you sure I can't go with you? Make sure you're still not a dunderhead."

Bo chuckles, "No, it's my direction to go alone now."

She is sad to know there is nothing more for her to do, but his quest is his own, and only he can see this through. She gazes at him for the last time, sensing she will never see him again.

"Something tells me that our moment together is at an end. I cannot hate myself for loving you, but the irony is, if I knew that you loved me, I would probably hate you for that too."

Mia suddenly in disbelief about what she just said, hits her noggin several times with her hand.

"It's okay, Mar. What you have to say is not necessary."

"I cannot believe I just said that. None of this can possibly be real, am I correct? My precious time here, a mere invitation of your mind?"

Bo shows a face of sorrow. If he had any glands left, he'd surely let them rain. He gives Mia a big hug and watches her face smile. "You will always be a part of me, Mar. The very reason your still with me now."

Mia pulls down on the ends of his hat and zips up his coat. She decides not to say anything further, but when the door finally clicks shut, she quietly admits to herself that she truly does love Bo Fox.

The bus door closes behind him and he finds himself standing on a dirt road under construction. There is a weather-stained traffic sign that reads: Wrong Way. Beyond that point is black. He turns around to see a single lamp shining brightly over a resting bench. It is the only light trying desperately to push away the advance of darkness. There is one other light, however, and it flickers from a direction he knows.

Buttoning the top slot on his coat, Bo pulls his hat down snug over his head. With the aid of a ground stick, he makes his way toward her house. It is not a graceful walk; reduced to slowness and uncertainty, but the acknowledgement of flowers growing in the grass stimulates his mind, as do the sounds of birds chirping in the trees. Both remind him neither one is to be forgotten.

As in the *Tales of the Fidi Belurdi*:

> *She was feeling a bit forgotten. Nobody would invite her into their home.*
> *Even bugs would not notice her. Is this what it is to be alone?*
> *She had nowhere to go and anywhere to be found.*
> *And only in her dreams would a bird make a sound.*
> *So, she follows their chirps to the nest in the sky.*
> *That's where her spirit now rests in Genius Loci.*

Bo stands before her property, where she is already waiting and waving from the porch. He smiles as quickly as she does while she prances to his best hobble. Bo tries to entreat her by steadying himself on one leg. Not so easy for a depreciated man, but Beatie is quite pleased. She makes a gesture that it is her turn now and lifts up on her toes and twirls about in a circle. Bo is absolutely flabbergasted. and so he responds with a dopey doddle of his own.

He will delay her no longer! Hobbling as fast as she leaps and banging his stick as fast as she stomps, he finally extends his arms, only to watch her curiously pass him by. And chase her, he will, across the lawn where she glissers, and releves and sauters alike; that is until she is received by a well-established man from across the street. A man who had been secretly materializing perennials for her favor.

"Yes, I love these," she replies, holding a large bouquet of flowers before her nose.

The man puts his hands around her waist, and Beatie reciprocates by placing her hand on his shoulder. Then off they waltz, across the lawn, and into her house. It was just that easy. A pleasant farewell was all that seemed necessary at that point.

Bo is still staring at the front door and chewing on his teeth when the porch lights go out. The trumpets of charge calling for a soft retreat. There is no amulet in his pocket to correct this one. No words from his letters to draw a conclusion. The barkeeps, the professors, and the fairy tales no longer provide him with the answers he seeks. All along, it was the same ineffectual dream. He who he is has always been; even if a dream were possible – was never was.

The wind blows low across the lawn and ruffles his clothes. He is shrinking fast, and it becomes necessary to tuck his coat into his pants. He then slowly drags his feet through the shedding of his own flowers, turning briefly to see the light in the corner room go out. Soon her house vanishes behind a growing mist. Already on the road, they are there, reproducing in numbers too frequent to count. The distorted ones. Those same ghastly faces from his past Only now do they mimic his deteriorating image, but they had always been there; he just pretended to never notice.

The bus pulls out just as Bo reaches the corner, his ride disappearing into a cloud of dust. He climbs upon the bench and sits in his oversized coat looking down with a chuckle at his knuckled feet. His shoes no longer filled with his feet. They remain in the road where he can no longer leave behind a print.

Bo lays his hands on his chest and lets his mind drift into a dull resolution of acceptance. She had met another man, he recalls. He is a manager, you know. No one can fault that.

Bo begins to evaporate with the closing of his eyes, and the physical form he had long been associated with begins to fade. A celestial existence appears in a swarm of colorful lights, and soon wings emerge upon the blades of his back. He feels a new birth arriving within him, one with fresh and unburdened thoughts. Of course, mistakes are ahead when following winds too strong to give him a straight path, but let it be known that his preparations from the places he once visited will serve him well when ...

"Give me those!! You're not ready for these yet!"

"Ow!" Bo rubs himself to relieve the pain from the unfastening of his fluffy-feathered wings. He reaches his arm over the bench to see who the culprit of his discomfort could be, and there she is, high upon a wispy cloud – the little girl full of accidental appearances. She is painting a colorful sky with a paint-less brush and an empty bucket. "Shhh! I am almost finished."

She adds several birds and hangs a few daytime stars to the canvas. She then paints herself a ladder down to the bench where he rests. "That makes me feel more at home," looking up at the sky with a smirk. "There are some days when you can judge its height, and still, you really never know how far you have to go."

The little girl removes Bo's hat and looks for signs of any remaining hair. "Let's have some tea!"

"No. No more tea."

"No?"

"No, no thank you, Sprikkit's. Where are your siblings?"

"Berbrie and Bermise? They've both gone ahead. I've been waiting a lot longer than you think."

"Are you my angel or something?"

"Such a delight you are!" the little girl chortles. "Am I your angel or something? I am most definitely a something – a spirit to be precise. But don't expect me to turn my head around for you, those shenanigans are for ghosts."

"I wasn't aware spirits invaded dreams?"

"There was no way you were going to do this on your own! Please, the amulet, the bartender, and the professor – and your friends were not very cordial."

"Mia? I admit, she can be vindictive – along with uncaring, insulting, ornery ..."

"They tried to exercise me, Mr. Fox!" Sprikkits spreads a napkin across the bench. "I do admit, I gave a pretty drastic approach toward settling the matter, but she deserved it."

"I wasn't aware spirits were vengeful either."

"She poisoned me with the most addictive habits! Just look at me! All nervous and shaking. Always having the need to talk about my ongoing distrust toward parental figures. Are you sure you wouldn't like a biscuit or a crumpet? I have Tetley!"

"At the dance, did you...?"

"Sure did. I locked her out, and then in the morgue, I locked her in. That counts two! HAHA!!" The little girl scratches her head. "Why you brought her anyways makes no means to me. It's not like she had to be here."

"I cannot explain it. Maybe to resolve something from before."

"So, did you enjoy your time? You did briefly make a connection."

"I would have gladly slept a thousand more times, had I only known how priceless the dreams were."

"And you do remember when I asked if you could walk me home? I'm not expecting a requital for my time spent waiting, but your company would certainly mean the same."

Bo stands, "I'm ready, Sprikkits. I thank you for all you have done."

"Now wait here!" The little girl makes ripples through the misty clouds and then stops. "Found them!" She pulls on a pair of boots and an aviator cap, then she extends the tips of her wings and skates around in circles, whipping up a flurry of clouds behind her.

"I have lost my wings before going the wrong way in a planetary wind, but we should be alright for now." She ushers Bo to a light shining through the clouds. "Now, let's figure out how we are going to do this."

Bo gives her a surprised look.

"Ready?" The little girl looks to see his face with some reluctance. "Ugghh! Now what?"

"To drift alone for eternity hardly seems a just punishment for a life of stubbornness."

"Oh, here we go again."

"I never meant to hurt her. It's just how it always works out that way."

"Mr. Fox!"

"Dreams have a purpose, you know, they are not just a fleeting thought. Maybe I need more time groveling to her friends."

"Two hundred years later and people are still the same." Sprikkits leads him back to the bench, putting her tiny, little hands on his leg, "It's not what you did that was wrong; it's what you didn't do that they thought was right."

"Pardon?"

"There seems to have been a collective punishment against you, Mr. Fox. There was her mother, her father, her roommates, your roommates, the barbershop – and who can forget being bested by the little boy down the road? Ouch! Everything you did wrong was perfectly right to them! But what I found most cherishable, Mr. Fox, is even though you thought you were charging into the victors to win, you were trying awfully hard to lose again. Seems to be the way with you. Anyways, ready to go?"

"Charge into the Victors? You said that?"

"Gomb-Beezey, Man! No, you said so! I'm not so sure I'll make it home anymore."

"It was just a thought at the time."

"Don't sell me a dog with your happy face, Mr. Fox. The problem isn't with their thinking; it's with yours. It is your own path, not theirs, that you must take." Sprikkits makes a sour face when she sees ice forming on her wings, "Oh, no. Now look what's happening!" She removes the pinions from her shoulders and begins frantically brushing the feathers with her hands.

"Not that you were prepared to do anything about it."

"What do you mean by that?"

"What do I mean by that?!" Sprikkits mimics. "You weren't going to change a thing, Mr. Fox! Blessed it is the light that provides a pathway through your confusion, but the only comforts you seem to rely on are superstitious charms, bar stool conclusions, and bamboozling apothecaries that couldn't cure an ailment even if your caretaker was a brain surgeon!!"

Sprikkits mutters something to herself, then begins warming the wings under her armpits.

"And alcohol, Mr. Fox?! Pray tell, I have never been called the likes of a meater, before but fifteen puzzles later, and your credulity is still relying on suspicious studies of mixology to cope with your sickening sociability!!"

Bo raises a hand in response: "It's not so easy, you know."

"But who knew there were words available and you just had to figure them out?!!"

"That's right!"

She gives Bo a disappointed look. "And what you put that poor girl through! Terrorizing her with nighttime shadows, inflicting her with toxic peers, and then, to top it off in the end, you send her on a date with a nine-year-old boy?! Who invents a mind like yours anyway?!"

Sprikkits frantically throws down her wings when they suddenly burst into flames.

"Oh, but I forgot, you are a man who has taken a great length of self-reflection. Boolah!! She was indignant, not because of her so-called friends, but because of your lack of attention to what she truly thought she deserved!"

Bo looks up at Sprikkits in shame. "I thought I was giving Beatie what she wanted, but I was wrong. I gave her what she did not want."

"A temporary companion; very good, Mr. Fox." Sprikkit drops to her knees and begins smashing the wings to the ground. "She had but one requirement in her quest for happiness. A shower of love is all she ever wanted."

Sprikkits puts her wings back on and turns to the sky. She watches with sadness as the clear path before the heavens quickly closes. "Well, isn't that some pumpkins?

"She is still out there, you know. She has always held you in her heart, even until her own death, which unfortunately happened many years before your own. As I have said, Mr. Fox, it is the secret that remembers you. When every day you thought of her, you always held hope. Isn't that what tomorrow is all about? Because if you cannot believe in tomorrow, then she should have never waited for you." Sprikkits lets her wings drop back into the clouds. "Words I have lived by for two hundred years now, my great, great, great nephew."

She turns around and walks with heavy steps into a growing mist filled with screams and crashing sounds. "Stupid townspeople," he can hear her say.

A charge of energy invigorates Bo's ashen-laid body, and a hole opens within the wispy clouds. With little more than a handful of arm flaps, the heels of his Ghillie Brogues set down upon a sidewalk. His skin color has returned, and his tireless features that once defined hin now disappear behind an acute smile. Bo runs his hand through his disheveled hair and straightens his kilt. He then reaches into his coat pocket for a single, red rose. "Tha mi air mo ghradh a tilleadh."

Bo has been recalled to the streets once again, where a path of light blazes before him. He has heard of the Valentine's festival but has yet to attend one, and already, it seems exciting. The trees are wrapped in cellophane, the plants are covered in candy boxes, people are dressed as confectioneries, and the shop workers are dressed in nineteenth-century garb with their faces painted blue. And never to forget, the glossy, white banner in its final display: the plump, chocolate letters spelling out "Happy Valentine's Day." Such a magnificent display of jubilation.

Bo detaches from the crowd and finds himself before the restaurant where he once had the memorable, rooftop meal. Through the glass window, the noise inside is silent, but there is plenty of chatter to be seen. It does not take long to find her, revolving about the center of the floor at her favorite table. Her scarlet bonnet has finally come out after so many years locked away in a box. She too is wearing the red dress she did not know existed – at least, not until Charlie came into her life. The tall intruder with so many years added to him.

Bo places his hands on the window with the thought of the love they once shared. The warmth in her is there, and he can feel this through the glass. She has found her Valentine, and although it is not with his eyes looking into hers, it is her expression for another that he can feel this love. She looks truly happy, and clearly, the shadows are no longer chasing her.

A haze appears on the glass that obscures his view. Bo attempts to wipe it clean with his sleeve, but his eyes soon struggle to see further. He sets the rose down on the sidewalk and listens to a distant rumble. The banner loosens its hold on the street posts and slides away over the rooftops and down the long, linking roads. The wind next reaches into his pockets to let loose all his undelivered letters, sending them flopping down the street and tossing away into the night sky. A reassurance that they were never meant to be delivered.

He really did imagine he was here – seeing, hearing, and expressing all his desires. He was living a dream as if there would always be another, and he would have been blessed to have spent tomorrow after tomorrow with her, even if it were only a dream.

The thunder claps and lightning blazes throughout the city. Soon there is a chorus of pitter-patter upon the streets, and it is not long before Bo is wallowing up to his knees in rushing water. A scintillating object tumbles into the wide expanse of his kilt, and he quickly wrestles it into his clumsy hands. It is the hogstone, and for some unexplained reason, it wants to shine. Bo chuckles at Sprikkit's comment about superstitious charms and how they falsely decorate what he had wanted to see and not what was truly before him.

Bo lifts the charm to his eye while the rain falls hard upon his face. He recalls the story: "The Dragone Great Eater," the tale about the little child who would eat three meals of aquarium food a day, in the hopes it would turn him into a fish. At the end of the story, there is the sound of munching, slurping, and swallowing, just like in the tale, and it all takes place before one large gulp!

Bo suddenly looks in amazement at all the water vanishing from sight.

"I accept what is true; if I were to say that I knew, the man I would meet, would have to be – do I know you?"

Bo checks his pulse and feels for his heart! There, kneeling beside him in the water, is his beloved! "My lass!" he says in a quivering tongue, "Could we have more time together?"

Her eyelashes bat several times, then she crinkles her mouth, "It won't hurt, will it?"

"You won't be mildly disappointed this time."

She reaches into his hands and lifts the amulet from its chain, "No flowers?"

Bo smirks at the thought of how useless flowers have always been for him. "It wards off bad dreams, but it has no value if it can't bring a smile to your face."

She lets out a big smile and buries her face in his chest, making deflated bowl noises.

"Your inebriated, aren't you?"

She lifts her head out of his clothing with the amulet stuffed in her mouth.

"Superstitious charms and studies of mixology. Still the best I can hope for."

There is a loud crack of thunder that sends shivers through the sky. Bo gives a disappointed frown as he watches the celebrators hurry off the street. Beatie pulls down on her blue bonnet. It is clear she is frightened but fascinated at the same time, just as she had appeared with those ghoulish dancers in the gymnasium.

Bo waits for her to finish a brief mantra, then she reaches out with her hand and pulls him out into the flooded street. She puts her hand on his shoulder, and in a very large, circular sweep, they both make the very same patterns they had made on the dance floor that night, waltzing again before a crowd of confused admirers.

Beatie stops for a moment to remove a piece of wet paper stuck to her face. "What's this?"

"To the pipes it will find its way, discarded in the tainted water of a sidewalk drain, to be erased by the waters of the Matanzas Bay, with the hope that these letters will never be read again."

"Does this come in English?"

A bell-hammer rings out that is familiar to Bo. It is the coming of the Stoorworm, and already, the storm is bringing hard rain with flying debris. Beatie wants to continue her dance, but her inebriation is suggesting something else. In a very long breath, she provides an offer that Bo, in all his born years, had never offered himself. "Maybe we can get to a place where we can remain in peace, away from all of these ill-conceived thoughts that separate us."

Through a pathway between falling debris, created by a strong gust of wind from a spirit's wings, Bo and Beatie quickly scurry into the cover of office buildings. There in the alleyway to the sound of splashing and her humming, they eventually arrive at a small labyrinth of corporate establishments. Bo is hoping to find refuge in any shelter that will allow them entry, but unfortunately, they have arrived at the quietest part of the city, where windowless floors and the occasional lamp post are all that are common.

Drenched, swaying, and laughing, Beatie stumbles with playfulness through a wind that blows her back and forth and onto her back. She slowly stands and clings to Bo, very tired and sleepy. All he can do to reassure her is that they will find a warm, dry place soon if she can just stay awake a little bit longer.

Moving hastily, Bo finds an opening in a construction fence where he finds a block of unfinished affordable housing units. Looking in the windows, he notices the rooms are as empty now as they were when construction began. Beneath his arm, Beatie has gone silent. It is most urgent that he find a resting place soon. There is a dim light at the very end of the alleyway that might provide some hope. He stands before the door and gives it a few gentle, unanswered knocks, but once the handle breaks off in frustration, he pulls Beatie close to his body, and with four long steps, he crashes through the door.

When the door swings firmly shut behind them, Bo is dismayed to discover his refuge is more suitable for the end of one's miserable life. It is empty and it is square; there are no furnishings, save one offbeat grandfather clock; there is a window, but it could easily be mistaken for an air shaft; and if there is any hint of light, it would have to be the dim, yellow tint without the indication of a power source.

"This must be where we wait, Beatie. I'm sorry to report there is nothing natural about it, unless you count our shaddies on the floor."

< SLAP! >

Bo looks at Beatie, who shrugs with a soft giggle. The wet slap reminds him it is something he'll have to get used to. She reaches up to pull his head down with a grin on her face. "This is our room?"

"It is not what I had in mind either, but we can fix it if we like."

Teetering on the tips of her toes, she makes him aware of a mattress lying against the wall. He lifts her into his arms and carries her to the mattress, setting her down and slipping in behind her for warmth. The light in the room goes out, and a bright moon appears through the air shaft in the wall. It casts a glow on her adorable features, which are now scrunched up with tiredness.

He brushes her hair from her face, and she instantly lights up, pressing her fingers firmly into his chin. "Ello Diggy, fancy meeting you here."

She watches as he takes hold of her hand, immediately feeling that everlasting communion between them. "Do you have a last name?"

Bo clears his throat. "It's Fox. Bo Fox."

"Nice to meet you, Bo Fox. Are you, my Valentine?"

"Yes, I am, and each day you need one, you have only to think of me."

She softly mumbles his name over and over again. She is feeling very tired, and only on occasion does she look up to let him know she is still with him.

A long pause follows, and they are both silent. He feels the solid touch beneath the pillow and pulls out the logbook. It is wrinkled with curled pages, and he finds the familiar pen attached to it. Most certainly the same pen that ran dry of ink whenever he tried to express his feelings. The last entry has not been completed.

February 14, Valentine's Day:

These incidents, having taken place thirty years ago, are a reminder of what wrongs I should have wrought and what rights I should have embraced. Waking up every morning to go out into the world, where common sense took the shower and stupidity put on my clothes.

"Is this another Scottish tale?"

Bo startled, raises his eyes to see Beatie making a question mark with her fingers. "I like tales, you know." He smiles and watches her hand drift aimlessly back to his chest.

Details over an uncaring incident thirty years ago are already forgotten. Our worlds are not so flat after all; we have come full circle to start our conversations over again. And all those beautiful thoughts we will have.

Thoughts about where we are going and what we will say, what we will see, and what we will do. Our days will no longer have dates or times attached to them, and our hours will be stretched beyond those of the coming night.

Never again will there be a need to worry about the past, because the prior days will always be shorter than the tomorrow we wait for.

Bo sets his head against the wall, "My only wish is that I should have discovered these thoughts thirty years ago."

"Are you leaving me already? What did I ever do to you?" Bo looks down at Beatie's brooding face with little creases forming on her forehead.

"Nothing, blossom, you answered a dream of a dying man and brought him to a place we now call home. And on this very Valentines Day, and each one going forward, we will be dreaming the same happy dreams where we are never apart."

Beatie makes a faint gesture by nodding her head and squeezing his hand. There is a slight rise and fall of her chest, then her head tilts sideways and she goes silent. Bo rubs his nose after a tear drops from his eye. "Some of the sky's brightest days are before us now, my love."

> Sprikkits was right about not giving up on tomorrow. It will always be a day filled with laughter and lunacy and jubilation and joy from those very putzy people you imagined as they imagined you. Such as the Manly Bunyan Critter Boots that came into your store? Or how about the dry sneezing Pappa Canoe Kock that was in there the day before? And who can forget the Popple Piddle Peesh Poodles howling in your home? Friends that would never abandon you or make you feel alone.

> They have always been your yesterday, and they will always be your today, and you won't ever forget them for the things that they say. And the most important friend will forever be there too, for if you could ever call anyone by the name of Tomorrow, they would always be there waiting for you.

Bo leans his head down to see she is not moving. His soft voice speaking to her, but she can no longer hear him. Stroking her hair, she can no longer feel him. She is far away, having a dream that her search is over and that she has found her eternal Valentine.

"Coorie doon my sweet luv, I am sorry I ever left you." Bo chokes up and wipes his eyes with his sleeve. "I just want you to know that I always missed you madly. You were always my Valentine."

The clock strikes the midnight hour and will do so three hundred sixty-five more times. There will be no account of his visit here. No footprints in the sand. No features held in any photos. The streets where he once walked, the benches where he once rested, and the buildings where he once slept. No longer will he be surveying the fields for which he once called home, but instead taking to the skies for which he is yet to measure. In life, he was the color of the earth, and in death, the color of the sky, forever surrounded by the warmth for which we search.

Somewhere beyond the earth's glimmering rim, a new day is approaching, and a young man will once again emerge from a dream, arrive in a small town, and leave with the love he intends to spend eternity with.

Bo runs his fingers through her hair and away from her eyes. He sets down the logbook and sets down the pen. He gives her one of those awkward smiles, and then reads to her the *Tales of the Fidi Belurdi* ... for as long as he can remember tomorrow.

Happy Valentine's to all and to all the many morrows to come, Bauregard Heathan Fox

NOTES AND REFERENCES

Authors, Film, and Song Citations

(i) Wanger, Walter (Producer) Lang, Fritz (Producer, Director). 1945 Scarlet Street {Motion Picture} United States, Universal Pictures.

(ii) Sullivan, K.E Scottish Myths & Legends, "MacCondrum's Seal Wife", Brockhampton Press, 1998, Pg 49

(iii) Theodor Geisel, The Sneetches and other stories by Doctor Suess, "The Zax" Random House,1961 Pg 57

(iv) Theodor Geisel, How the Grinch Stole Christmas by Doctor Suess, Random House, 1957 Pg 46

(v) (Parody) Oscar Hammerstein II Lyricist/ Richard Rodgers Composer, "The Sound of Music" *Prelude/ The Sound of Music*, RCA Victor March 2, 1965 Track 1 Initial release Mercury Records Published 1959

(vi) (Parody) Simon & Garfunkel, Scarborough Fair/ Canticle *Parsley, Sage,Rosemary and Thyme* Columbia Records, 1966 Track 3

(vii) John Keats, "Ode on a Grecian Urn", Annals of the Fine Arts for 1819, Published Anonymously.

(viii) Alland, William (Producer), Arnold, Jack (Director). 1954 Creature from the Black Lagoon [Motion Picture] United States, Universal International

(ix) Charles Dicken's, "A Christmas Carol. In Prose. Being a Ghost Story of Christmas." December 19, 1843. Chapman and Hall.

(x) Zanuck D R and Brown, D, (Producer), & Spielberg, S (Director). 1975 *Jaws* [Motion Picture]. USA:

Zanuck Brown Company and Universal Pictures. "If he is a rogue and there's any truth to territoriality at all, we got a good chance of spotting him between Cape Scott and South Beach."

(xi) The Holy Bible English Standard Version, God and Job 28:28. "And he said on to man, 'Behold the fear of the lord, that is wisdom, and to turn away from evil is understanding.' "

(xii) Davis S, P and Panzer N, William (Producer) & Mulcahy, R (Director).1986. *Highlander* [Motion Picture] UK Canon Films, United States 20th Century Fox "You Can't Die MacLeod. Accept it."

(xiii) William Hazlit, "Where there is a will, there is a way." 1822 The Fight

(xiv) Unknown, "Hey Tuttie Tatie", Nils Brown *Hey Tutti Taiti, Scots musical museum*. Jan 19, 2014 , youtube.com/watch?v=xqy.

(xv) Albert Einstein, Regarding deflection of light. Theory of General Relativity Published 1915

Internet References for History and Terms
*Alan, stooryduster.co.uk/scottish-words-glossary/words-s.htm
*Citystaug.com/693/our-history
*Ghostcitytours,com

*History of St. Augustine, Florida en.wikepedia.org/wiki/history_of_st._Augustine._Florida Page last edited 15, September 2022

*Nineteenth Century Slang: Compiled and edited by Craig Hadley, Copley-Fairlawn City Schools https://www.copley-fairlawn.org[1]

*Scotland Welcomes You – scotlandwelcomesyou.com/scottish-sayings/ Updated September 13, 2021

*Victorian slang terms: Compiled by Erin McCarthy updated Jan 3 2022 https://www.mentalfloss.com/article

---

1.   https://www.copley-fairlawn.org/

www.ingramcontent.com/pod-product-compliance
Lightning Source LLC
Chambersburg PA
CBHW032024240626
47154CB00003B/774